THE KISSING GATE

www.transworldbooks.co.uk

THE KISSING GATE

Susan Sallis

BANTAM PRESS

LONDON · TORONTO · SYDNEY · AUCKLAND · JOHANNESBURG

TRANSWORLD PUBLISHERS
61–63 Uxbridge Road, London W5 5SA
A Random House Group Company
www.transworldbooks.co.uk

First published in Great Britain
in 2012 by Bantam Press
an imprint of Transworld Publishers

A CIP catalogue record for this book
is available from the British Library.

ISBN 9780593069516

Addresses for Random House Group Ltd companies outside the UK
can be found at: www.randomhouse.co.uk
4009

The Rand   st Stewardship
Council (FSC   tion organization.
Our books   -certified paper.
FSC is th   by the leading
    er   peace.
                                                      nd

CPI Group (UK) Ltd, Croydon, CR0 4YY.

2 4 6 8 10 9 7 5 3 1

MIX
Paper from
responsible sources
FSC® C016897

For my family and friends with love

One

Gussie was reclining, enjoyably self-conscious, on the sofa, the end dropped down to accommodate her long legs. Book, notepaper, envelopes and two pens, in case one wouldn't work, were on the stool within reach if she felt like making an effort. She closed her eyes; she had after all managed to get up and shower, which was enough for now.

Gussie had had one of her summer colds and had burned, then shivered, through the previous day, then sweated it out profusely during the night. Now she felt weak but whole again. She had wanted the house to herself; to make tea the way she liked it, cut thin bread and butter and savour each bite. It was a precious time, this coming to life again.

Ned, of course, had not wanted to leave her; Jannie had said nothing, which meant she was desperate to go. Laura Ashley in Truro was having its end-of-summer sale and the dress in the window might still be there. Besides which, and somehow far more selfishly, she occasionally caught Gussie's summer colds and bore them less stoically than her older sister. Ten years older: it was quite a lot of time in which she might become more like her talented sister and less like her – very ordinary – mother. So she bit her lip and said nothing, and Gussie's sheer common sense naturally won the day with Ned.

So Gussie put her head back on the sofa cushions and smiled and thought of the two of them, probably at this minute walking from Truro railway station down the long hill into the town. They would both be doing giant strides, just as she had taught them when Jannie at last learned to walk. It was Ned who had always made the difficult return trip interesting, organizing the three of them into a train. 'Coupled up now?' he would yell, and Jannie would forget about wanting to be picked up and grab on to Gussie, and they would all make chugging noises and arrive laughing at the booking office.

Yes, Truro railway station had featured often in their shared lives: a grand start to a theatre trip or a shopping spree, but a muscle-shattering haul back up.

Gussie's smile deepened, and she closed her eyes and thought how marvellous it was to be part of such a mixed family: Ned, tall and still gangly, with red hair, snub nose and pale, almost colourless eyes – presumably like his father; Jannie like Ned's mother, small, blonde, somehow Nordic. And herself . . . who did she take after, with her father's dark hair in its single plait and his dark eyes but not his strangely inward look? Was it her mother, the wild Zannah Scaife? Or was it her grandmother, conventional but also loving and kind?

It was so simple really. Mark Briscoe, the painter-in-a-wheelchair, divorced with a nine-year-old daughter, had married Kate Gould, also divorced and with a seven-year-old son. And then they had had a baby of their own.

Gussie smiled again. She had realized for years now that Kate had made the family into a strong unit. She was a proper home-maker, so happy and content with her life and her children. 'The Beautiful Briscoes', she called them.

Gussie's smile widened. In spite of all these wonderful thoughts, how lovely it was to have time without her step-brother and half-sister. A few hours to come back to life. Just to lie here; not to read or write postcards or plan her next project. Just to be.

Idly she began to work out how long they would be . . . an hour to get there, if the connection at St Erth was on time; an hour's intensive shopping; an unhealthy fast-food lunch, perhaps by the river, and then – the door crashed open, slammed shut, a scurry in the passage, the living-room door flung wide, and there they were!

They all spoke at once.

Gussie said, 'What's happened? Why are you back?'

Jannie said, 'We actually got there! We got off the train, and the down train was waiting on the other side and we ran over the bridge and just made it—'

Ned spoke and moved at the same time. 'You haven't got the telly on – we thought you'd have – dammit, it's not even plugged in.' He reached down, scrabbling for the plug and its socket.

Jannie said, 'I bet it's not true! They were talking about it on the train, that's all, and Ned overreacted as usual!'

'What? What's happened, for goodness' sake? You both look so wild!'

Ned panted, 'New York. A plane has crashed into the Twin Towers. It's bound to be on the telly.'

Gussie swung her legs to the floor and knocked over the stool. Envelopes scattered. She ignored them and said, 'What? Don't be ridiculous. It couldn't happen—' But she stopped speaking because both Jannie and Ned were talking all at once. She looked from one to the other; the babble began to make sense. She focused on Ned, who had at last got the plug into its socket and was fiddling with the remote. She said, 'Darling. Ned. Don't look like that. It won't affect Mum and Dad. The meeting wasn't arranged until . . .' Her voice died as the picture materialized on the screen. It was obviously a disaster movie beloved of daytime television programmers. A skyscraper toppling . . . toppling . . . 'Try the other side.'

He punched buttons. It was the same movie.

He said slowly, 'This is it. This is happening. Now.'

They watched, aghast, incredulous. At some point Jannie began to cry and Gussie held her as she had held the five-year-old after her first day at school. 'Darling, it will be all right. They won't be there.'

But they *could* be there. Even when Gussie went into the kitchen and made coffee and cut cheese sandwiches for lunch, they knew. Because if they weren't there they would be telephoning to reassure 'the kids'. And the phone did not ring.

The awful thing was, 'the kids' could not ring through to New York. The huge impersonal hotel on the margins of the East and West Sides where the Briscoes stayed on their annual visits was pretty hopeless at taking messages anyway, but all lines to America were jammed. The three continued to watch the television avidly, unsparingly, praying for some kind of personal message to come through: 'Mark and Kate Briscoe reported slightly injured . . .' 'An English couple wishing to get a message to their family back home . . .' It was a lifeline between Cornwall and New York. Or maybe not a lifeline at all.

It was mid-afternoon when Ned said slowly, 'I think we

have to phone one of these emergency numbers they're giving out.'

Gussie flashed him a look. 'We don't even know they're there, Ned! If Dad was having a bad day, Mummy will make him stay in bed . . . It's the bloody hotel we want. We've just got to be patient and keep trying.'

Ned cleared his throat. 'Trouble is, Sis, we don't need to know, do we? That couple we saw. Jumping out. Holding hands.'

'Shut up!' Jannie screamed. 'Don't say it!'

Ned held Gussie's gaze. 'The bloke. Didn't you notice?'

She forced herself to breathe normally. 'It was too far off, Ned. You couldn't possibly see.'

Jannie screamed again, something incomprehensible, then flung herself on to Gussie and grabbed her shoulders, pushing them as if she was trying to hold them together. She squeezed her eyes tightly shut; Gussie could see the muscles in the upturned face contracting fiercely. When Jannie spoke it did not sound like her. There was no more panic or protest; she grated each word harshly.

'I saw it, Gus. You've always said what amazing vision I've got. And I saw it. The man had no legs.'

Gussie could almost hear her father's dear, familiar voice saying to his wife, 'I'm not facing my Maker with these bloody things, Kate!' and would even . . . perhaps . . . laugh as he unstrapped his tin legs and let them fall.

As if in confirmation, the telephone rang at last.

Gussie and Ned had so often joked – actually joked – about being 'half orphans', though in fact neither of them was. Gussie's mother, the famous Zannah Scaife, lived in France in a house called Glorious Isolation, not far from Nice. Ned's father, Victor Gould, had left Ned and his mother having a 'nice little holiday' in St Ives and gone to live in California with another war painter. He could have returned at any time, yet when Kate Gould accepted Mark Briscoe's proposal of marriage and had gone to a solicitor about a divorce, he made no objection. He had become an American citizen by then, which made the whole thing very easy indeed.

So neither Ned nor Gussie was short of parents, but liked to dramatize the situation occasionally, backed up by Kate, who often went out on to the veranda at suppertime and yelled down the harbour beach, 'Sustenance for all orphans of the storm!' None of the neighbours even raised an eyebrow because the Briscoes were artists and artists were like that.

Once, when Jannie was seven and Ned a precocious fifteen-year-old, he made a ponderous attempt to make matters clearer. Seated at the table after the usual summons he said, 'Absolutely the opposite, Mother dear. Gussie and I have a plethora of parents!'

'How do you mean?' Jannie asked with infant bewilderment.

'Work it out, Titch. I have two dads and one mum. Gussie has two mums and one dad.'

Naturally Jannie had wept and Gussie had comforted. 'You did things properly, Jannie darling. One mum and one dad.'

But that wasn't what worried Jannie at all. 'Don't like my bruvver calling me Titch!' she had wailed.

Gussie comforted her, and Kate paused with knife poised above the cheese flan, which Dad always called a quiche lorraine, and said thoughtfully, 'Actually, you two are quite lucky. Having a spare parent is a kind of insurance policy. It means you won't lose any of us!' She grinned. 'You poor things. Always someone to look after!'

Ned, still showing off, said, 'There's always euthanasia, of course.'

Gussie was genuinely shocked. 'That's not funny, Ned!'

'Not meant to be!' he came back defiantly.

And then Mark had appeared, stumping along the passage, leaning his shoulder on the doorframe as he twisted himself round, the house fitting his body like a glove. Kate eyed him quickly, then began cutting the quiche. He was grinning from ear to ear. She spoke without anxiety.

'Busy day?'

'Yes. But – oh, my dears – it's happening! Inside the womb of that lump of marble, there's a madonna! She's curved with the shape of the lump. She's protecting a child. It's amazing.'

'Sounds like those Russian dolls, one inside the other again and again.' Gussie smiled congratulations at her father.

Kate said, 'Sit down, take the weight off those legs. This might be the right time to bring in some assistants. Who was that student you used last year?'

Still grinning enormously, Mark lowered himself gingerly between Ned and Jannie. 'I know, I know . . . not just yet, though. Might unstrap the legs and work from a stool.'

That meant he couldn't bear to hand over any of the arduous chipping away of the marble. Kate made a face.

He said quickly, 'A bit longer, Katie love. Let me be there for the moment of birth.' He grinned down into his younger daughter's face. 'Like I was with Jannie.'

Kate made another face, this time of astonishment. 'I think I might have been around at that particular moment!' she protested, and he laughed and said, 'You were God's marble, my darling. The beginning of all things!'

Gussie and Ned rolled their eyes at each other and then laughed, trying to pretend they weren't embarrassed.

Jannie looked at each of them in turn and then said, 'What's a woom?'

And Ned, quick as a flash, had said, 'It's what we're sitting in right now, Titch!'

Jannie had turned pink with indignation and shouted, 'That's a room, you bloody idiot! And don't call me Titch!'

Kate exploded a protest and glared at Ned and – of course – Jannie cried and Gussie cuddled her.

People started to call later that evening. They were proud of the fact that Mark Briscoe had lived among them, learning to walk on tin legs so that he could manage the many steps of Downalong. They hadn't been so pleased when he married Zannah Scaife, a wild child, daughter of a wild man, and when the babe had come along six months later – in August – they had shaken their heads and wondered what sort of child she would be, named for her birth month, with a shock of black hair and a yell that cut through the peace of the row of terraced cottages like a knife.

But Gussie had grown into such a conventional child. 'Takes after her grandmother,' people said. Which had been useful when Zannah had left St Ives and gone to live in France because she needed 'space'. Gussie had been eight years old and, with the help of ancient Mrs Beck, had kept house perfectly well, exactly as her grandmother would have done. Until her father had remarried.

Gussie had thought the rows might have started again. Rows about money, mostly because – according to Zannah – they had been living on the Scaife legacy and Mark refused to pander to the tourist trade and paint pretty pictures, or make replica Cornish Crosses.

There were, however, no rows. Life suddenly seemed in

tune with the tides and the boats bobbing below them in the harbour. They no longer had a diet of fish and potatoes alone. Fish was for Fridays and came in wonderful sauces with creamed potatoes fashioned into fancy shapes. There was always a roast on Sundays, and in between there were salads and cheese flans and boiled gammon. When Kate had a few days in bed producing Jannie like a conjuror, Ned did the cooking for one day and fashioned the mashed potatoes into a cot; Gussie managed the second day with a pasty the size of a dustbin lid, which lasted two more days; then Kate took over again and – as she had said – handed Jannie over to Gussie.

Life was so easy, none of them could quite believe in it. The new school in Truro came up to expectations for Gussie, but to come home was even better. Ned adored his new sister *and* his old one, as he hastened to say to Gussie. He got a place at Penzance Grammar School when the time came, played with Jannie and went out in the boats with Old Beck. He made two attempts to make contact with his father, but there was never any response and eventually, after inviting him to his graduation, he gave up.

Gussie saw her mother three times but never enjoyed her visits. Zannah had made unpredictability a way of life, and Gussie was always frightened she might turn up and wreck what they had got. She adored her father and after a very short time she loved Kate deeply. She had made a token attempt to dislike her by saying, 'What can I call you? You're not my mother, so it can't be Mummy.'

Kate had frowned, thinking about it, and Gussie had chipped in quickly before she could say something nice, 'What about Kath?'

The frown deepened. 'I don't really mind. It's just that the way you say it makes it sound like phlegm.' She opened her eyes wide. 'Oh, gosh, did you mean it to sound like that?'

Gussie found she could not hurt this woman with such a huge stomach, who made lovely food and was always smiling.

'Of course not! I didn't think . . . and I don't want to call you Kate either, because Zannah always wanted to be called Zannah.' She bit her lip, realizing for the first time that she had rarely called her mother anything but Zannah. She stumbled on helplessly. 'Ned calls you Mum. Sometimes Ma. Can I call you that too? It seems a cheek, so if you don't like it . . .'

'I love it. Honestly, Gussie. I just love it. And are you all right with Gussie?'

'Yes.' Gussie responded vigorously to the smile. 'I like Gussie. But not Gus because it sounds like a man. And not August because that sounds solemn.'

'Gussie it shall be then.' Kate hesitated and then said, 'And . . . Mum. OK?'

'Yes. Because Ned always says Dad. And it's nice.' Gussie primmed her ten-year-old lips. 'And it's proper too.'

It might have been that day or the next when Daddy got the commission from the States to make a stainless-steel icon for St Patrick's Cathedral in New York. And now, in 2001, he worked regularly for a trust called The Spirit of America. He was famous. They became . . . perhaps not rich, but well off. With his hands he earned enough money to look after his family. In his wheelchair and on his tin legs he got around St Ives, boarded planes and went to America, swam in the sea as he always had done. And he was happy.

But now he was also dead. And so was his dear friend and wife. And that meant that after all the joking and laughing about it, Ned and Gussie really were half orphans. And Jannie was totally orphaned.

They walked along the tide-line that night. There was a big moon showing behind Westcott Pier.

Jannie whispered, 'What are we going to do?'

'We'll go over. See where it happened. Talk to the chairman.' Gussie breathed in the September air and thought of the dust and now the bodies.

Ned said, 'I think I might apply for a sabbatical. Give some time to thinking about it.'

Gussie nodded doubtfully. 'I suppose I could make some adjustments in the diary too.'

Jannie wailed; a thread of sound in the moonlit dark. 'That leaves me with finishing at college. My God. I *lived* with them. They came to Exeter often to see me. They've gone and you two are planning to go off together . . .'

Gussie and Ned circled her with their arms. They closed their eyes and held on tightly. Jannie's sobs reduced and she whispered, 'Sorry.'

'No . . . no . . .' Gussie breathed.

Ned said, 'We've lost our mum and dad. We're in the same boat, Jan. Never feel alone.'

They could feel Jannie nodding beneath their heads. She gave a tiny laugh and said in a trembling voice, 'The same boat. Three of us. Yes.'

Tentatively, Jannie did what she had so often done in the past. She reached up and took the end of Gussie's plait in one hand and Ned's quiff of orange hair in the other and quavered, 'You both belong to me, OK?'

'OK,' Gussie and Ned replied in unison.

Then Gussie said, as Kate would have done, 'The Beautiful Briscoes!'

And they walked on.

Two

'Mummy, this is my friend. His name is Ned—'

'How many times do I have to tell you *not* to call me Mummy?'

'Sorry. This is Ned and he's two years younger than me and I am looking after him while his . . . mother . . . is at work.'

'Great. And to whom are you talking at this moment?'

'You. Zannah.'

'At last. Thank you, Gussie. See how it works? You are Gussie Briscoe. I am Zannah Scaife. You are my daughter but you are a person in your own right and I respect that. I do not call you "daughter".' A big sigh, then a wonderful smile. 'How do you do, Ned? I am delighted to meet you. I have come to take Gussie home for an early tea because we have to go to Newlyn this evening to see some paintings.'

Ned looked at her warily, then held out his hand. 'Is it an opening? My father is a painter and Mum and me go to openings with him. Sometimes.'

'Does he have a name?'

'Yes. It's Victor Gould.'

Zannah was suddenly all attention. 'Victor Gould? The Gloucestershire artist? My God. Is he here? In St Ives?

18

'No. He left us here when I was six. I think he lives in America.'

Zannah lifted one bare foot free of the sand on Porthmeor beach where they were standing in the afternoon sun, and shook it. Her three ankle chains jingled. She did the same with the other foot and the same happened. She always said you couldn't have too many ankle chains if you had ankles like hers.

Then she said, 'D'you want to have tea with us? Mark has made some scones and I've got cream.'

Ned looked longing but shook his head. 'Better not. I'll help Jem take the donkeys up to the field. Mum will be home by then.' He turned, then remembered his manners. 'Thank you,' he said.

Zannah and Gussie watched him tramp through the loose sand to where Jem Maddern was leading two donkeys back towards the row of beach huts.

'He looks a nice boy,' Zannah said.

'He's very nice.' Gussie took her hand.

'And what is his mother like?'

'I don't know. She works, and he helps Jem with the donkeys and Jem asked me to take him off for a bit. He doesn't smile much and Jem thinks he puts the customers off.'

'Jem would, of course.'

They both laughed. Gussie swung her mother's hand as they passed a group who were gathering up picnic things and sounding tired and cross. She loved being seen with Zannah, who was much too beautiful to be anyone's mother, especially hers.

'Is Daddy home yet?' she asked.

Zannah said with laboured patience, 'Mark. His name is

Mark. And no, he is not home yet so we will call into the studio and dig him out.'

They tramped over the rough neck of the Island and came upon the tangle of sheds and converted garages owned or rented by working artists. The Scaife studio was large and gaunt. Gerald Scaife had specialized in enormous paintings the production of which involved stepladders and long-handled brooms. Zannah had grown up here, physically attached to her father by a long cord, happily dabbling with paints, and later – though not much later – whittling balsa wood with sharp knives. The smell of paint and turpentine was as necessary to her as oxygen. She flung open the door and stood there breathing it in with eyes half closed.

The studio was empty of life.

Gussie, anticipating trouble, said quickly, 'Listen, Zannah. If Mark is ill, I'll stay behind and look after him.'

'He had no intention of coming with me. I wanted us to go as a family. No one believes I am old enough to have had a child, and here you are, almost nine years old, and every time something special happens you have to stay and look after him because he's too damned embarrassed to show himself!'

'Mummy, you know it's not like that! He can't help getting tired—'

'I'll wager a fiver that he's swimming!' She stabbed a furious finger at what looked like a pile of stair rods in the corner. 'Look, there are his bloody legs! Someone called – one of the other painters, no doubt – and he's gone in his chair!' She threw back her head. 'Someone is coming from the Whitehorn Gallery tonight – to see the show, of course, but to suss out the talent generally. And we make such a good group! Oh God, we're never going to make it if Mark won't show himself! The painter is as important as his bloody work. Gerald taught me that and I've tried to pass it on to Mark.' She lowered her head and unclenched her fists. 'And please don't call me Mummy – it sounds ghastly!'

'OK. But really and truly, it doesn't matter about Daddy – Mark – and me. It's *you* people notice. And you could show some of your things, you know you could. Your carvings are just great. And your pots.'

'Darling girl. You wouldn't understand. I could sell my stuff like hot cakes. And where d'you think that would leave our dearest Mark?' She looked down at Gussie's face, so like her father's. 'No. You're too young. Let me just tell you, briefly. If you're beautiful and have got a personality, it doesn't matter that you're no genius. If your sister dropped you off a railway bridge when you were a baby and left you without any legs, then you do have to be a genius.' She stared into the peculiar tea-brown eyes of her daughter and saw bewilderment. 'Don't worry about it, Gus. Daddy is happy being Daddy; he doesn't particularly care about being Mark.'

They closed the big doors carefully because some of Gerald Scaife's work was still stored there and was what Zannah called their insurance policies. Then they climbed the steps to Wheal Dream and walked along the wharf to Mount Zion. There was no sign of Mark but two of the towels were missing from the clothesline in the yard, and the wheelchair, neatly folded inside the door, was gone.

Zannah went into a real rage. Gussie hated it when words flew like bullets at him even when he wasn't there. 'Selfish swine' and 'bloody hopeless' made her cringe, and she was glad that Mrs Cledra heard them and came round to say that Mark had only gone for a swim off the old pier and would be back in five minutes. Just time to get his tea on the table. She looked significantly at the mess that had to be cleared away first and Zannah made a sound like a spitting cat.

Gussie began stacking newspapers, emptying ashtrays and putting her mother's makeup into its little bag. Zannah watched her silently and then said, as she so often did lately, 'I can't take much more, Gus. I mean it this time. You could look after things here for a bit, couldn't you?'

'Course I could.' Gussie shook a cloth over the table. She put a cruet into the exact centre of the cloth. 'Shall I make boiled eggs and put out the heavy cake?'

'Oh, darling, you understand me so well. That would be great.'

She ran upstairs and came down minutes later with her old hippie bag on her shoulder. She grabbed her makeup case and stuffed it on top of a lacy nightdress. 'I love you. And I love Mark. But sometimes it's a question of personal survival.'

Gussie said, 'OK. And I do understand about calling you Zannah, 'cos I don't like it when you call me Gus instead of Gussie.'

'I'll never do it again, honey.' Zannah embraced her in a suffocating hug. She was laughing with tears streaming down her face. 'But do call Mark, Daddy. He would prefer it. And try to get him to do some sculpting. His hands are so sensitive. He should be a sculptor.'

'OK,' Gussie said again.

She did not even wave goodbye to her mother. When her father came bowling along the wharf in his wheelchair, tin legs in their holder at the back, hair still dripping on to his shirt collar, he was not surprised to find they were having tea without Zannah.

'Don't say anything, sweetie, but I hoped she might go on

without me. Those openings make my back ache.' He took the top off his egg with one strike of his knife, then did the same for hers. She told him about Ned and he told her that he had carved a dozen 'Joanies' that day for the new shop in Fore Street. Joanies were the traditional Cornish doll, scorned by modern children but still beloved of tourists. Mark allowed himself to carve them occasionally, especially when the bills came in.

'Funny, Zannah was saying you should be a sculptor.'

He roared with laughter. 'I don't think she would consider a Joanie to be sculpture, sweetie, do you? But she will be pleased I've earned some money! And making Joanies is carrying on a tradition rather than pandering to the tourists!'

Zannah didn't come home that night. The next time they saw her was in Plymouth at the office of their solicitor. She went to live in France in the Lower Corniche a few miles inland from Nice. She had her father's money and she left his studio for Mark, on condition 'you get away from the little stuff and do something big'. He made no promises. By that time he had started on a work that would eventually become the symbolic *High Hope* outside St Patrick's Cathedral in New York. And it was Kate who assisted him, encouraged him, made him believe in himself.

'I won't be coming back, Mark. Not keen on seeing you with someone else. But you will always be welcome at Glorious Isolation.'

'I feel as you do, Zannah,' Mark said steadily. She nodded.

'Gussie, you'll visit, won't you?'

Gussie nodded. But it was difficult. Baby January arrived and was instantly adored by both the other children. Then there was Cirencester Agricultural College and a dissertation titled *Planting with Nature,* and a follow-up book called *Putting Back What You Take Out,* which proved unexpectedly popular.

She had seen her mother three times in twenty years. Each time there were different men in attendance. Zannah seemed younger and happier but she made very little work in those years. Instead she planted vines. And then some more. When Gussie was commissioned to work on the new project in one of the gentle inlets of the peninsula, Zannah sent instructions on how to start a vineyard on the south-facing banks of the creek. She wrote, 'This is something I can give you, sweetie, nothing to do with the Briscoes . . . The land is in our blood.'

Gussie knew somewhere deep inside herself that her mother was right, but she fought the connection. After all, she had chosen to study at Cirencester long before Zannah planted those first vines. However, she followed the instructions that arrived so regularly and the grapes from the Cornish Creek vineyards became not only well known for their wine but were a joy to behold. From the north-facing side of the creek the opposite bank appeared to be clothed in velvet, which subtly changed colour through the seasons.

An article about Gussie's work appeared in the *English Garden.* A small photograph stared out from the page; she really did look like her father, that wide open face, dark hair and eyes, snub nose and determined chin. She still wore her hair in a single plait down her back and had coiled it into a fat bun on her neck that day. Ned had stared at it, surprised. 'My God. I didn't realize you were . . . well . . . actually, beautiful!'

She had been embarrassed and told him to shut up. But

like a fool she had sent a cutting of the article to her mother and Zannah had been similarly struck by the photograph.

'Come over for the summer, darling,' she wrote. 'I can do things for you. And you need me. You are so vulnerable. Obviously that Kate woman is not helping one bit. We can go down to Monte Carlo – I know the right people – good connections for you and great fun. OK, I can hear you reminding me of the fun we had with the boat. Not that kind of fun, darling. But just as interesting and even more exciting.'

She had never gone. She had met Andrew Bellamy by then, a corporate lawyer and a businessman. He had started Albion UK back in the eighties; Gussie Briscoe became his protégée.

Three

The first farewell was on the Thursday two days after the
Twin Towers fell. It took place in the chapel dedicated to
St Nicholas, built on the top of the headland. The headland
was called the Island, and could well have been one once, but
was now joined to the mainland by a narrow strip of land on
which huddled most of the old fishing cottages.

The tiny chapel could hold twelve people and that
Thursday morning there were fifteen and a dog. The dog
lay outside the open door where below, the milky blue sea
turned lazily on to the small beach. The congregation
stood shoulder against shoulder inside the cell-like granite
building with its bench altar and clay chalice.

Before the liturgy began, the priest pronounced the special
prayers for those who had died in the terrorist attack in New
York City. Gussie bowed her head, holding Ned's hand on
one side and Jannie's the other.

'In the midst of life we are in death . . .' She swivelled her
eyes in their sockets and looked at the dog. He was a mixture
of collie and Labrador, a retired sheep dog belonging to
Thaddeus Stevens, who was a retired shepherd. Thaddeus
pulled himself up from his walking stick and touched the
dog with the ferrule, very gently. The dog turned his head

and looked up, and Gussie witnessed a moment of complete understanding between man and animal. It gave her a jolt. The dog knew. He came every Thursday, whichever denomination took the service; she had seen him often. She had not seen this moment of intimacy before.

'We have lost two of our fellows in this terrible disaster . . . people we see every day in the town . . .' Gussie felt Jannie's hand tremble within hers. She squeezed it tightly. On her other side Ned squeezed her hand and she wondered whether she had been trembling too.

'. . . a welcome for them that is beyond our comprehension. The gates of glory will open wide and the trumpets will sound . . .' Ned cleared his throat; the sound covered Jannie's first sob and Gussie released her hand and wrapped it around the slim young shoulders. Not twenty-one years old until next January, and both parents dead. Gussie held her close and felt the tears trickle down her own neck. She had accepted Kate as a mother such a long time ago she could barely remember Zannah. Had her father really loved Kate Gould as he had loved Zannah Scaife, the wild child of St Ives? Or had he felt bound to marry her when she became pregnant? Gussie thought how little it mattered; all she knew for sure was that they had been happily comfortable, all of them, together. They had been a proper family.

'We extend our heartfelt sympathy to their children, who are with us today.' For a terrible moment Gussie thought the priest was about to mention Zannah Scaife and Victor Gould – 'divorced and almost forgotten', as Ned had once said – but he finished there and went to the ragged niche chiselled from the granite.

The congregation watched as he blessed the sacraments. A murmur went through the tiny church: 'Blessed be God for ever.' The priest presented the clay platter with its small pile of wafers to the woman on his right and she took it, lifted a wafer between long, purple fingernails and passed it on. Gussie straightened ready to take her turn and saw that Ned was looking at his watch. Was he anxious to get back home to the constant callers? The neighbours came with pasties and heavy cake – 'useful for visitors from away' – and the artists' fraternity were only too glad to eat them as they told the children what a wonderful sculptor Mark had been and, more than that, what a wonderful human being. Ably supported by Kate, of course. As if Kate were a sort of superior female servant.

The platter arrived and departed. Thaddeus appeared to savour his wafer with epicurean panache before selecting another one and dropping it on the floor for the dog. The priest took the platter back hurriedly, and though his expression did not change Gussie could tell he did not approve of the dog sharing the body of Christ. She caught Ned's eye but he hadn't noticed.

The chalice began the rounds. Jannie's tears had already dried in the September sun and her face had the blank dried-out look of someone barely awake and completely unaware of what was happening. She took the chalice automatically and put it to her lips. She never drank the wine. 'It looks like blood,' she had said as a newly confirmed fifteen-year-old. Kate had tried to explain. Mark had enlarged by using his sculptures: 'They're not real, honeybun – you know that. They are symbols of something else.' But Jannie had stuck to her guns. 'I know all that – I'm not as dumb a blonde as I look, thank you very much – I just cannot drink what it symbolizes and that is flipping well that!'

'Well, yes. I suppose it flipping well is!' Mark had said.

Now, as Jannie passed the symbolic wine to Thaddeus, Gussie noticed a tiny fleck of clay on her upper lip. The chalice had obviously not been flipping well properly fired. She almost grinned, then stopped, holding her breath as Thaddeus swigged vigorously and looked down at his dog. The priest reached out and grabbed the chalice and took it to the altar to finish off the dregs. The service resumed.

Afterwards, they were like the Royal Family, standing by Father Martin in the sunshine, shaking hands and thanking people for their 'thoughts and prayers'.

Thaddeus Stevens took his dog a little way off and then waited politely while the animal lifted a leg. Father Martin said, 'A difficult situation . . . yes, we find ourselves in a difficult situation. We can arrange a very nice memorial service, if that would be acceptable to you?' He did not wait for a response. 'It need not be too soon. Some people in similar circumstances wait a whole year, you know!' He gave a sort of guffaw at this. 'There will be a great deal for you to do. Of course there will. You will probably wish to see the actual place—'

Ned interrupted fiercely, 'A memorial service is being arranged. On the site. By the ambassador, I believe. We are in touch with friends over there.'

'Wonderful. Of course. But your friends here will want to have the opportunity to remember them. As I said in my short homily this morning, they were our pride and joy and we cannot let them go without some kind of formal – well, actually fairly informal – farewell.'

Ned said something incomprehensible, Gussie said, 'Thank you, Father.' Jannie said tearfully, 'That is just lovely. They were so modest, you know. They would love to hear that they are a pride and a joy. Of course, they will always be a pride and a joy to us . . .' the tears were overflowing. '. . . when you said about Daddy being a wonderful sculptor and Mummy a wonderful human being I knew you had understood them. Everyone thought Daddy was a wonderful human being because of having no legs, and of course he was, but he was always a slave to his stones. That's how he put it, didn't he, Gussie? Didn't he, Ned? A slave to his stones!' She choked on a laugh then pressed on fiercely, 'But Mummy put her heart and soul into being a human being. And she was.'

Gussie said fervently, 'She was the best human being I know.' And Ned was suddenly overcome and turned away.

Father Martin stopped being an Anglican priest for a moment and gathered them all to him with unexpectedly long arms.

'My dears,' he said, 'we are all victims of the human plight, you know. We're in it together. Remember that. We're all in the same boat!'

He was not to know that he was using such a very apt metaphor, and when Jannie made a little owl-hoot of pleasure at the coincidence, he thought she was about to weep again. He had another more conventional service in Carbis Bay in half an hour, so he said quickly, 'God bless you all.'

As he peeled away, leaving them with Thaddeus and his dog, Ned said quietly, 'And the boat we sail in.'

Thaddeus looked at Jannie and nodded. 'Well may you laugh, child. 'E means well, 'owever. I do assure you of that. Difficult for 'im 'cos 'e's supposed to love us all an' 'e offen dun't find us very lovable.'

He poked at the dog, who had lifted his tail and squatted. 'Cain't do your business 'ere, me 'ansome. Come on 'ome now.' He started down the slippery grass towards the thin neck of land joining the Island to the town. 'Got 'is own latrine in the yard,' he called back. 'Saves me getting down to pick up you-know-wot.'

They watched him till he got to the gate where he called something back.

'What was that?' Gussie asked.

Ned had not heard either but Jannie, sharp of eye and ear, said flatly, 'What everyone says. Take it day by day.' She shook her head despairingly. 'As if it might get better.'

'It will.' Gussie and Ned spoke automatically and together, and because it was spontaneous they looked at each other and laughed.

'It's all right for you two!' Jannie screamed at them like a fishwife. 'You've still got a father and you've got a mother!' She stabbed an angry finger at each in turn. 'I haven't got anyone!' And she was gone, hurtling uncaringly towards the gate, skidding and recovering and going on.

Ned said, 'Oh God. She hasn't got a key to get into the house. Come on.'

Four

They held the second farewell service in the parish church at the end of the month.

None of them felt able to go on with their lives; the television news showed repeats of the disaster day after day and the body count went up and up. As Jannie said, 'We need closure. Father Martin might be able to give us that.'

The other two looked doubtful but agreed. When she went shopping Gussie was usually accosted by friends, and complete strangers, for 'the date of the funeral'. She said to Jannie, 'It's not only the three of us who need closure. The artists . . . they're putting flowers all around the sculpture shed.'

Ned said gloomily, 'The new chairman of the Trust – what's-his-name – Harry McKinnon – he telephoned. He wants to take over the shed. Didn't mention money but the implication was there.'

'We don't need money,' Gussie said. 'And anyway, I thought he was in hospital when it happened. Appendix?'

Ned shrugged. Jannie said, 'It's not only the artists who are keen, is it? Jem Maddern's father used to play with Dad when they were kids . . . those people in the Tregenna shop who ordered the special sweets he chewed when he was working . . . the Fishermen's Lodge. It's no good you two holding back, we've got to do something.'

So they talked to Father Martin and the service was arranged for 29 September, which was a Saturday. That very morning a letter came from a Reverend Eric Selway in Sussex. He had been sent their address by the chairman of The Spirit of America as being 'victims of the recent terrorism', and as he and his wife were arranging to take a group to New York as soon as it was possible to get near the site, he was extending an invitation to the three of them to join various family groups from all over the British Isles in a short service of remembrance.

Even Jannie looked startled at this. But when the other two shook their heads decidedly she had second thoughts.

'Actually,' she frowned prodigiously to stop her usual tears, 'don't you think, perhaps, we need to see . . . where it happened? Father Martin seemed to think we would.'

'I don't,' Ned said definitely.

Gussie was less certain. 'Will it help? Perhaps after this service today, we'll have had enough.' She touched Jannie's arm reassuringly. 'Even good things can be overdone. Remember Dad with the clotted cream?'

Jannie spluttered a laugh and then mopped her eyes. 'It was so *not* like Dad to take that last spoonful. But, actually, he never had clotted cream again, did he?' She frowned once more. 'Listen. I should be in Exeter right now starting my third year. Gussie, you should be doing the Musgrove Estate—'

'I gave the project to Heritage Gardens. They'll do a good job. I can't work, not yet.'

'That's what I mean. Ned should be in Bristol and he's not. We have to get to a point where we can go on again.'

'And you think a trip to New York will do it?' Ned snorted a laugh.

Gussie said, 'Be fair, Ned. It might be the right thing. Shall we talk about it after this service?'

He looked at her and then nodded briefly.

The congregation overflowed across the road and into the Garden of Remembrance. The atmosphere was warm, a mellow warmth that melted any resistance the Briscoes might have felt. It wrapped around them. This service had been intended for other people, people who needed to remember Mark and Kate Briscoe before they went on with their own lives. The siblings had seen it as a duty. Now they saw it as a comfort.

But a week later they were still in the cottage; Gussie said she was cleaning every inch of the house, Jannie said she was planning her dissertation, Ned began on the repairs he should have started in August when he'd first arrived.

The second letter from the Reverend Eric Selway said they had been offered an hour as near to the site of the Twin Towers as was safe. He had not heard from the Briscoes so was unable to reserve them seats on the chartered flight or rooms at the hotel, but if they wished to join the others for the service they would be very welcome.

They passed the letter from hand to hand. 'We're like old-fashioned invalids,' Gussie said. 'Have you noticed how slowly we do things now?'

'I can't get started on my diss,' Jannie told her miserably. 'I've got notes galore on approaches to teaching children with physical difficulties and I keep reading them and not being keen . . . I *was* keen, you know I was.'

Ned looked at the letter. 'I wonder whether we should give

this a try. I wish Mitch was still holding the reins. We'd go like a shot then.'

'I could telephone the new chairman, McKinnon – Harry McKinnon; ask his advice,' Gussie suggested doubtfully. 'He might tell us to wait for a while until the general climate cools down.'

'In other words, he won't want us cluttering up his place.' Ned made a face.

'We wouldn't stop with them, Ned! We'd go to the old Palace Hotel on Times Square. We could walk in Central Park. Do you remember the carousel, Jan?'

Jannie looked at her, then Ned. 'No. And I need to. Ring Mr McKinnon, Gussie. Please.'

Gussie worked out the best time to ring and did it the next day. The others sat either side of her at the table in the kitchen, which had been Mark's flat when Etta, whose house this had once been, was alive.

Gussie cleared her throat. 'Am I speaking to Mr McKinnon?' A long pause, then she said, 'Oh . . . sorry. Is he there? Yes? OK. Thank you.' She covered the mouthpiece. 'It was the butler, I think. He's going to connect us.'

'Butler?' Jannie looked at Ned. 'Mitch didn't have a butler, did he?'

'No. I think this chap has serious money.'

Gussie waved a hand. 'Yes, Mr McKinnon. Gussie Briscoe here. We have been contacted by the organizer of a re-ligious service for British relatives to be held at the site of the Twin Towers. We don't know whether or not to join his group.'

There was another pause, much longer, while she listened, nodding now and then and making little noises into the receiver.

'Well, yes. We are able to come. But not if it is going to be . . . you know . . .' She waited again and said, 'Can you explain? I'm sorry I didn't quite catch . . . yes, I do under-stand that you have to get back into harness. Of course. We don't expect you to put off the trip. But you think this sort of thing is worthwhile? Lots of these services? Carefully managed? Well, we would like to meet you and your wife too, but we have no idea what the itinerary might entail.' She frowned with concentration as his voice took over again. Then she said, 'Listen, we'll try and get you on the phone from the Palace Hotel. It's where we stayed with Mum and Dad; we know it well. Yes. It's a Friday – yes, the twenty-sixth of October. Yes. Perhaps. Yes.'

She waited, then put down the phone. 'Looks like we're going. Couldn't hear very well but I don't think we'll see him because they're off to California soon. He's quite keen about something – didn't get it.'

Jannie said, 'Neither did I, and I can usually pick up the main points of someone else's conversation.' She grinned. 'So be warned! But he sounded . . . bossy.'

'Yes.' Gussie spoke slowly. 'But he was all for it. He kept saying we could make it. He said it several times.' She looked at Ned. 'Let's go,' she said suddenly.

Ned booked a flight from Heathrow to JFK. They would arrive the day before the service and spend two days afterwards revisiting places that held special memories for them. Jannie started a list with more enthusiasm than she had felt for her college work. Gussie rang Eric Selway to ask whether they could join his party for the actual service. He said he would send them the itinerary and they could fit in when and where they wished.

'He sounds all right,' Gussie reported uncertainly. 'Very sort of middle-of-the-road. But all right.'

Ned was reassuring. 'We don't need him to be inspirational. In fact, if he starts anything inspirational it will interfere with what we need . . . We just need to be where Mum and Dad were. So that we can *see* it. Maybe understand it. A bit.'

'They are all going back the day after the service – overnight flight. They will have been there a week. He suggests we meet for dinner the day we arrive. He'll book three extra places. At the Florabunda. Just off Fifth. We can get a cab.'

Ned nodded. 'Sounds a bit formal. Never mind, we'll show our faces.'

Jannie spoke without thinking. 'If I'd got that dress from Truro I could have worn it.' Then she looked aghast as her own words hit her and said, 'Oh my God!'

They reached for each other as they did so often. And then Ned released the girls and stood up. 'Time for a cup of tea. We're going to New York where it happened. We obviously need to.'

Five

Before they left, Uncle Rory came to see them. He had married Daddy's sister, then discarded her and gone to live abroad for years. At the time of this marital disaster, Ned had wondered aloud whether divorce could be genetic. But Aunty Rosemary had lived at home and had been indispensable when it came to looking after her parents. Now she lived quietly in Bristol. She never visited her brother but entertained the whole family in the big old house whenever they needed to 'do business', as she put it. Ned maintained that Rory had broken her heart and was thankful they never saw the man, even when he was home and living in Trewyn Place, which was oftener after his father died. Gussie might have met him half a dozen times in her life; he had come to Jannie's christening. He ignored Ned; Ned was irrelevant.

It was Ned who opened the door that dismal October morning. He recognized 'Uncle Rory' but did not stand aside to let him in.

'How may I help you?'

Rory stood there, saturnine, somehow aggressive. 'I am Rory Trewyn. I suppose I'm a sort of uncle to the three of you. Great-uncle. In-law. Twice removed. Something like that.'

'Do you want to see Jannie?'

'I'm assuming she is back at Exeter. Her final year, I believe. I came to see August, actually.'

Gussie spoke from the yard below him. She had a basket of laundry ready to peg out on the crisscross of lines.

'I'm down here . . .' She saw who it was and for the life of her couldn't remember his name. 'Do go into the parlour. I won't be long.'

Rory, who must be well over seventy, grunted and swung himself over the railing and into the yard. Gussie gasped; Ned said, 'Christ!' but the railing held and Uncle Rory looked mightily pleased with himself.

'Used to do that when I was a kid and went out in the *Forty-Niner* with Philip Nolla. I could always find him down here, mending his bloody nets.'

Gussie was angry. 'You could have killed yourself! Damaged the cottage too!'

She dumped the basket and looked at him. He was crouched over his knees, breathing audibly. 'Are you all right? Can you get into the kitchen?'

'You mean the cellar?' He straightened. 'God, you sound like Etta Nolla.'

He walked carefully through the door, cast an eye around the converted pilchard cellar, still hung about with nets and floats, and sat himself at the table.

Gussie glanced up at Ned and made a face. 'Thank you,' she said drily to her uncle's back. She had not known the Nollas but her father had shared his memories. He had always remembered them with love and gratitude as his benefactors, but there were others who had called Etta lesser names. Shrew. Even witch. Ned made a face back and Gussie grinned as she went into the half-light of the kitchen.

She said briskly, 'You've only just caught us, actually. Jannie is joining us tomorrow and we are taking the sleeper to London.'

'I heard.' He looked at her. 'You're a woman.'

'True. Do you want some coffee?'

He shook his head and produced a hip flask. 'How old are you, August? Thirty? Thirty-five?'

'Thirty, and please do not call me August.'

'I almost called you Zannah. You're very like her, you know.'

'Everyone says I look like my father.'

'Well, they're wrong. You've got legs, for a start. Good ones.'

She flushed with anger. 'No prizes for good taste, Uncle. But then, no prizes for much really.'

He swigged energetically. 'Come on, woman. You didn't expect me to call the next day, surely? I didn't even know they were in New York until someone told me poor old Martin was praying for them in church!'

Gussie looked at him with disgust. 'I didn't expect anything at all. Not from you, of all people. Anyway, your rather strange condolences are accepted and as we are going away tomorrow, we can say goodbye.'

'Hey! Hang on, woman! I came to tell you something.' He swigged again. 'Zannah telephoned. I knew by then. She's pretty cut up. You haven't been in touch.'

'I wrote to her, Rory. I've heard nothing.' She sat down heavily.

'Oh, she'd had that letter, yes. But she expected you to go and see her. You know your father was everything to her.'

'That's why she buzzed off when I was eight years old, was it?'

'You were a difficult child.'

'What?' But even as she exploded with incredulity she was thinking, Was I? Was that why Zannah needed space? Did I make her claustrophobic?

She said, 'You can't know anything about us – you were never around. You and Dad never got on.'

'Zannah talked to me. I knew her father, Gerald Scaife. He talked too.'

'Why would either of them talk to you?'

'It was my bucolic period. People talk to drunks because they'll forget.'

Gussie looked at him, saw the shift in his eyes. She said slowly, 'You slept with her, didn't you? She was one of your many so-called conquests.'

'Ro had left me. Sauce for the goose . . . you know the old saying.'

'I heard you threw Aunty Rosemary's stuff out of the house.'

He gave an impatient gesture, sweeping her words into the past. 'The thing is, you should go and see your mother. You're not the only one grieving, you know. Take Jannie with you. I hear she's taking it badly. You've still got a mother, after all – go and see her.'

'I think you should leave. Now. If Ned comes down he won't stand for—'

He was laughing. She knew now that he had been goading her all along; his laughter was even more galling. She snapped, 'Oh, shut up! No wonder Daddy couldn't stand you!'

Unexpectedly that did shut him up. He lumbered to his feet, put his hands on the table and leaned on them.

'I wonder whether Mark knew about my doubtful origins. There was certainly something that put him off. He liked

41

everybody.' Rory pushed himself upright and sighed a single irritable puff. 'Doesn't matter now, of course. Too late.' He crossed the yard to the steps, then turned and looked back. 'You're not as beautiful as Zannah, but you're very like her. Please go and see her, Gussie Briscoe. She was as mad as me and slept with everyone . . . but Mark was always number one. You must know that.'

Gussie pulled a shirt from the clothes basket and began to peg it on the line. 'Goodbye, Uncle Rory,' she said firmly.

'Goodbye . . . August.' He emphasized the last syllable, making the month into a pompous adjective. It was childish but he enjoyed it. She could hear him chuckling as he walked down Mount Zion and on to the wharf.

So they were in New York, staying at the hotel just off Times Square where they had always stayed, though when Ned took the trouble to count how many times, there were very few. 'Actually only four: that first time, when they unveiled the St Patrick icon, then the next three unveilings. Then you were at Cardiff, Gus, Jannie was getting over chickenpox and went to stay with Grannie, and I wasn't really interested.'

As they got out of the yellow cab and wheeled their luggage through the plate-glass doors into the foyer, which was milling with people like the concourse of a railway station, they captured instantly the familiar feeling of sheer energy that rose like the steam jets from the pavements.

They had booked a family room; for three instead of five. It had seemed the natural thing to do but as they each signed the register it suddenly felt . . . odd. However, nothing was said by the desk clerk and there were very few porters; the clientele wore backpacks and needed help with map reading rather than portering.

Gussie took the keys and the three of them made for the elevators. They were whisked up to the twentieth floor and emerged almost opposite the door to their room. It was, of course, smaller than their old rooms had been: a king-size bed and two double ones, but the bathroom still sported two showers, two basins and two lavatories. Unexpectedly, on the low table opposite the beds was an exquisite flower arrangement: roses of all colours in a mist of gypsophila.

Jannie exclaimed delightedly and rushed to read the card aloud. '"With love and sympathy shared. From the Friends in Bereavement."' She looked up at the others. 'Isn't that wonderful? Look, there's a phone number in case we need help. Will the others get this sort of thing?'

'I should think so. We'll soon find out.'

Gussie was unaccountably weary. She sat on the enormous bed and stared at the blank television. She wished wholeheartedly they were not meeting a load of strangers in six hours' time. She had been able to contain her grief and horror at home. Going through her father's things, informally with Jannie and then formally with the solicitors, she had kept walls around her emotions. They had been hers. She had shared them with Ned and Jannie, but others who had called, and who nearly all told her that they 'understood' or 'could imagine', had been outside; they were nothing to do with the horror, or the grey sadness that would go on for always. *These* people, these strangers, however, they knew. They could not be pushed away.

Ned said, 'All right, Gus?'

'Yes. I'd forgotten the bleakness of this place.'

Jannie claimed the bed directly opposite the television. 'How can you call New York bleak? All those people – going places – doing things. Made me realize that I might be able to take a gap year next year.' She discovered a fat pot of snowdrops on her night table. 'Look at this! Snowdrops – my flower!' She picked up another card and read again. '"To January Briscoe. With love from all the Trustees of The Spirit of America."' She looked from Gussie to Ned. 'I didn't think I was going to cry so soon but . . .' Then suddenly she lifted her chin. 'Dammit! I am not going to cry! I feel . . . I don't know . . . proud.'

'Attagirl!' Ned took the last bed in the row and discovered a pot of cyclamen. 'My God, they've done it for me too!' He skirted the beds and picked up a pot of sturdy hyacinths. 'And for you, Gus.' He showed her. 'Jannie's right, we should be proud – and all that energy – that's what I remember from before: the sheer energy. We're going to survive this, Gus. Stop looking so woebegone! We're here. With a shedload of other people all in the same boat. Go with the current – that's what we have to do. Go with the flow!'

She managed a wan smile.

They met at the Florabunda as arranged and were introduced to their fellow mourners. The meal was long and elaborate, but at least each course was manageable. As children they remembered using one of the Howard Johnson outlets round the corner from the hotel where the food was over-abundant.

Sheila and May Smith were on their table: single sisters mourning a third, the adventurous one, Rose. They seemed timid at first. 'Rose was the outgoing one,' they explained apologetically. They had always been together, first with their parents and then on their own. 'A threesome. As you seem to be. Perhaps you feel frightened. All the time. As we do.' Sheila had introduced both of them, obviously forcing herself to overcome her shyness. Ned and Gussie smiled ruefully but Jannie responded unexpectedly.

'Oh, yes. I did. And having to get on with life seemed . . . wrong. Cruel. I wanted to be unhappy. Always.' She leaned across the table almost eagerly. 'It's so much better since we arrived here. Everyone is grieving. It's the right thing to do.'

Sheila Smith raised her brows. 'I hadn't thought of it like that. Had you, May?'

'No. But I am so glad you spoke . . . Jannie, did you say? Yes. It makes one feel less . . . isolated. Perhaps.'

Sheila nodded emphatically. 'It does. And less angry, too. We always took our holidays together. Devon. The Lakes. Even Scotland. Rose was determined on this trip to New York. Five days all inclusive. Broadway show. Radio City. The Empire State Building and the Twin Towers.' She stopped speaking and swallowed convulsively. 'If we'd agreed to it we would all have gone together. But we stuck our toes in. Stubborn. We have been angry with Rose, angry with ourselves.'

May said in a low voice, 'Sheila dear, don't be upset. These young people . . . long lives ahead of them, we hope . . .'

But Jannie leaned forward further and actually touched the back of Sheila's hand. 'Thank you for being so honest. I was angry too because I had lost both parents. But now – at least they went together.' She looked round at the other two. 'We hadn't thought of that, had we? Daddy couldn't have managed without Mummy. They had to be together.'

Before they could respond, the Reverend Eric Selway leaned between them and started to 'firm up' the following day's arrangements. An area had been allocated for such occasions, anyone could join them – friends, relatives, general well-wishers. The service sheets, which were in their pack with street maps and other information, would be handed around. His wife and two other members of the group had brought their violins so that the hymns could be accompanied. He smiled at Jannie. 'As you see from the programme, we are meeting at the hotel at nine tomorrow. Two hours before the coach is due to take us to . . . the site. You do not have to join us for a run-through but you will be most welcome if you'd like to.'

They had made up their minds not to attend the rehearsal but Gussie looked doubtfully at Jannie. Ned said quickly, 'I would prefer to walk down. So count me out.'

Gussie waited. Jannie sat back in her chair. She smiled at Ned. 'We already decided to walk down – the three of us.' She looked up. 'It's all right, Vicar, we've gone through the Order of Service lots of times.' Gussie added her reassurances that they knew the area and would meet the others at the coach park.

Sheila said, 'We would walk with you. But I'm not too good on my feet these days.'

'We'll look for you.' Jannie gave the Smith sisters each a smile, then looked at the menu. 'Is it time for puddings?'

Ned suddenly grinned at her. He said in his mother's voice, 'A sorbet first to clear the mouth. Then your Alaskan pie.'

'Voice no good but ten out of ten for the effort,' Jannie acknowledged.

They all announced what they were having and, under cover of the babble, Ned said, 'Well done, Jannie. You were right. We needed to come here for something like this.'

The next day was heavily overcast but, blessedly, not raining. Ned called the chairman of the Trustees while the girls showered and dressed. He sat hunched on the side of his bed, head down. None of them had met Harry McKinnon. He had joined the board since they had given up on the New York visits and they had been unable to become as close over the phone as they had with the first chairman. Mitchell Liebermann – 'call me Mitch' – had visited them several times and had guided them all through that first amazing white-water ride of success. They still quoted from the nuggets of wisdom he had handed out: 'You're the same people you were before, right?' 'This is a separate thing – you're lucky it's far away – of course you don't have to leave your cottage. In fact, it would be the worst thing you could do.' And to Ned he had said, 'Watch your mother – she knows how to handle this.' He had come out with them in *Forty-Niner Two* and eaten pickled mackerel with relish. He had been at the Annual General Meeting on 11 September and died with his friends. Harry McKinnon had been in hospital having his appendix removed and was still alive.

Ned bent low over the telephone, his forehead almost touching his knees.

'It's very kind of you. We sort of booked the trip with a group and . . . no, we're on a regular flight . . . no, not exactly committed.' He listened, his head now supported by his free hand.

Gussie, dressed in what she called her office suit, put her hairbrush carefully on to the glass-topped dressing table and went to sit by Ned. He flicked her a glance and she saw with a shock that he was close to breaking down.

The buzz of the telephone voice stopped and they both registered Jannie singing from the shower, a jazzed up version of 'Show Me the Way to Go Home'.

Ned said, 'Well . . . there are three of us here, sir. I need to . . . sorry – Mack – I need to see how they feel. May we phone you this afternoon?' He waited again and then put down the phone and looked at Gussie. 'Something unexpected,' he said hoarsely, and covered his face with his hands.

Jannie emerged from the bathroom looking as fresh as a daisy and rushed to him, her face wide with questions. Ned dropped his hands then held them up helplessly. He said hoarsely, 'There's a tape. Mum and Dad – they phoned. There's a tape.'

He told them about it as they walked along Fifth Avenue.

'Sorry, girls. When he said that Mum and Dad actually phoned him that day . . . God, I didn't know what to do. I should've let you talk to him. I suppose I thought it would come better from me.' He made a ghastly face. 'Anyway . . . then . . . at the time, you can imagine what it was like to be here, actually seeing and hearing it all. The phone rang. His wife was there. He was in hospital, of course. When she realized who it was and why. It was coming through on the answer machine. I don't know why they didn't tell us before now, Jan. Sorry. I was so . . . oh God, I don't know. He didn't give me much time for questions. If only it had been Mitch.'

Jannie was bouncing like a rubber ball. 'But we're going to hear them, we're going to *hear* them!'

Gussie held her arm. Ned's voice became stronger. 'I'm not sure whether it will be a good thing. We're on some sort of even keel now, but this might capsize us. I don't know whether I want to hear Mum's voice like this – from the grave. And he wants us to go there after the service. Listen to the tape together. He's had copies made for us to take home. To keep them alive, he said!'

Jannie held his arm. 'I know what you're thinking, Ned. He's a businessman first and foremost. He wants to keep the *sales* alive. Perhaps. Probably. But that's part of his job. It was part of Mum and Dad's job too. Never mind that. This is beyond that – beyond the world, even! Don't you understand? We're going to hear them. When we listened to those messages on television – I mean, awful but wonderful too. None of them was panicky; they were messages of love – all of them! How wonderful for us to have one, because that's what it will be. A message of love. For us.'

He looked down at her face. Her eyes were shining brilliantly and this time not with tears. He managed a wry smile. 'You're a strange mixture, Jan,' he said.

Gussie squeezed her arm. 'A very special mixture.' She forced a smile. 'We didn't expect this, did we? We'll have to go.' She frowned slightly. 'More than that, we *want* to go. Desperately. But, right after this service? Perhaps we'll be expected to have lunch together? Then there's dinner again tonight at the Florabunda. Couldn't we make it tomorrow for the McKinnons?'

'That's the other thing. He – Mack – and his wife are off to California early tomorrow. They're behind schedule – that's what he said – because of the appendix and Nine Eleven. This was how he talked – sorry. So it's today or in a month's time.'

'We can't wait that long,' Jannie stated.

Gussie capitulated. 'No.'

'I told him we'd ring him this afternoon. After the service.'

Jannie said, 'I wish this had happened the other way around so that we could hear their voices before we see where it had all happened.'

'Tell you what,' Gussie said. 'We'll listen to it often, of course, but when we get home, let's listen to it while we're standing on the Island by the chapel and let's face out to sea.

D'you remember what Dad said every blessed time we did that walk?'

'Of course,' Jannie replied. 'He told us that the next land-fall from the Island was the United States of America!'

They tried to laugh. And then Jannie said, 'That's Sheila, waving her umbrella at us.'

Ned tried to sound like his mother. 'Best foot forward, troops!'

Six

The dust had settled over everything, disturbed in wide swathes by machinery still searching . . . for something . . . anything. The perimeter was fenced and the exclusion zone beyond it was wide, but there were designated spaces for mourners, and in several of these groups were gathered, obviously praying together. The British group was being led by a man in uniform towards an area canopied with canvas and identified with a wooden cross. Beneath the cross was a table and in front of that, bench seating.

They settled themselves, a few self-consciously but mostly wide-eyed and rigid with the horror at this macabre reality. The depth of the pit in front of them was shocking, the area of devastation was vast, the smells, which had gathered power as they left the bus, were familiar as coming from any building site, yet underneath that familiarity was something else. Perhaps it was different for each person there, but for ever in each memory was the smell of death and total destruction.

Gussie shrank in her seat, head bowed as if in prayer but actually in an effort at self-control. Ned sat next to her. Jannie was next to Sheila and May Smith and was reaching over to hold both their hands. The low cloud seemed to seal them off from the sounds of the city so that, as they all became still and able to look around them, they could hear the chanting of a group of monks in saffron-yellow robes, and see them, oddly misty, in the distance.

The Reverend Mr Selway was standing, leaning on the bench that would become the altar, sharing the shock they were all feeling. His wife touched his arm and he turned and smiled briefly at her, then lifted a case on to the bench and opened it. Between them they prepared the table with a cloth, then the traditional bell, book and candle; the chalice and plate. It was blessedly familiar to most of the people there. They breathed the polluted air and opened their service sheets, which told them that an appropriate silence would be kept for private prayer. They bowed their heads and waited for the first greeting, 'The Lord be with you.' To which they would respond, 'And also with you.' Their personal silence mingled with the chanting and for the first time the outside world could be heard as a police siren screamed its way alongside the barriers. Another bus disgorged its passengers: skull caps, dark suits, an all-male group. They filed towards the monks. Far below them an enormous digger roared into life. The small pocket of near silence began to crumble. May blew her nose.

Suddenly, when Gussie could feel her nerves stretching physically, Eric Selway flung his arms wide and lifted his head towards the solid lid of cloud. The group stared, caught unawares; this was not the normal Anglican procedure at all. Gussie and Ned exchanged glances. Jannie appeared to lengthen her arms so that she was almost holding Sheila and May Smith together.

Selway's voice was loud, inappropriately so.

'Open wide the gates of glory!'

The words boomed over the pit, circled it and came back to them like a boomerang. Gussie gasped and clutched at Ned, Jannie looked round at them both wide-eyed. It was as if Father Martin's words came to them, magnified into a command rather than a plea. And they were everywhere, fragmented, then coming together. Open . . . gates . . . glory. As the final 'glory' hammered back at them they all, as one, rose to their feet.

The clergyman turned to face them and smiled. 'The Lord be with you,' he said. His voice was normal, friendly; it did not reverberate, it was just for them, the living. They all looked at him. 'And also with you,' they said in perfect unison. And the service continued conventionally except that the chalice and plate were passed from hand to hand just as they had been in the chapel on the Island back home.

The violins were produced. 'Abide With Me' was sung shakily, 'Morning Has Broken' with certainty. As they all filed back to the bus, praise was almost fervent. It was as if the sheer horror of the occasion had melted away. No one mentioned the dramatic deviation from the service sheet.

'Vicar, we want to thank you . . . comfort . . . consolation . . . we are so glad we came. Your organization of this whole trip has been wonderful.'

As they identified their bus and made their way towards it, the reason for this visit seemed to be tidied away and talk turned towards the evening's meal.

Gussie said quietly, 'Did it strike you that Selway's opening words were almost the same as Father Martin's?'

'Open wide the gates of glory,' Ned said pensively. 'A triumph instead of a terrible defeat.'

'I wish he'd done the whole thing – the trumpets sounding. I just loved that.' Jannie grinned. 'And if a dog had wandered in too . . . Can you see now why it doesn't matter how often we do this sort of thing? The words can be said a hundred thousand times and still be comforting!'

She sighed and turned to another subject. 'What I don't understand is why they didn't get in touch with us immediately. The McKinnons. About the message from Mum and Dad.'

Ned nodded. 'Don't know. He was probably too ill after the operation. Then he'd have all the business of the board to sort out.'

'Yes, it must have been a nightmare. There were so many of them,' Jannie said. 'And they were more than fellow Trustees. They were friends! Mitch and that nice man from the Bronx, and the representative from the City Museum . . . Sorry. It's just that sometimes it hits home.'

'The West Coast members weren't there, apparently,' Ned said.

'How do you know that?' Gussie asked.

'He told me. Mack. On the phone.'

Gussie might have followed this up but as they approached the bus, a man in a chauffeur's uniform touched her arm.

'Excuse me, miss. Are you the Briscoe family?'

Gussie said, surprised, 'Yes.'

'Mr McKinnon has sent the car for you. He hopes you will join him for lunch.'

For a moment Gussie was tempted to see this as a cavalier act, but Jannie chipped in eagerly, 'Well. What could be better? Let me just tell Sheila and May.'

She looked at Ned with raised brows and after a moment's hesitation he nodded. He did not enjoy being bulldozed like this but he could see it was the most practical arrangement. It was going to be a difficult meeting however it was arranged, but this way it would be quickly over. They were going home the day after tomorrow. He remembered Selway's voice echoing around the wasteland where formerly had stood a miracle of design and engineering; he tried to picture the gates of glory and could see only one of the many kissing gates on a footpath near Zennor. He smiled at Gussie. That would do. That would do wonderfully for Mark and Kate Briscoe.

Seven

So the third farewell took place that afternoon.

The McKinnons lived in an apartment overlooking Central Park. The chauffeur would have dropped them at the wide canopied entrance where a suitably grand porter awaited, but they opted to stay in the car and let him take them into the underground car park and then up in the service elevator.

Perhaps it was his pristine uniform and his expertise with New York traffic, but they did not find him as friendly as most New Yorkers until they were actually in the elevator. Then he said, not looking at them, 'I – we – are so sorry for your loss.'

The formal phrase sounded completely sincere and was too much for Jannie. She said, 'That is so kind,' then put her hands to her face. The chauffeur cleared his throat. Gussie held her sister as usual.

Ned said, 'Yes. Most kind. Everyone . . . most kind.' He too cleared his throat. 'The service . . . it was quite a wonderful experience. Surprisingly.' Everyone nodded, even the chauffeur. The elevator slowed and stopped smoothly. Ned said, 'We're Gussie, Jannie and Ned.' He indicated the others in turn. 'What is your name?'

'Michael.' The man met Ned's eyes. 'My wife looks after the domestic side of things and I see to transport. She's Emily.' The doors slid open on to a wide foyer and there was Mack, leaning on a stick, his free hand held out in a gesture of welcome. They all recognized him and realized they had met him when he had come to England after he had joined the board. They saw, too, that he had aged shockingly.

Ned went forward to take the outstretched hand and was immediately drawn into an embrace. Gussie followed and then Jannie. Mack held her away and looked at her carefully.

'You have a Scandinavian look, Jannie. That comes from your mother, of course. But there is something . . . Gussie has it too. The Briscoe eyes? I don't know.' He sighed sharply and turned towards the solid door flanked by flowers. He nodded at one of the enormous arrangements. 'These keep coming, you know. People are kind.' Michael moved ahead of him and held the door open. 'Michael found you, then? We were worried you would be caught up in some kind of tour of the site. Marion suggested Michael ought to come and try to rescue you.' He glanced at Gussie. 'Marion is my wife. She is the one who actually heard the telephone message.' He cleared his throat. 'At the time.'

Gussie began to feel ashamed that they had thought the McKinnons high-handed and even insensitive. She said quickly, 'It must have been terrible, you in hospital and – and – everything.'

They were ushered into an enormous space, rather like one of the galleries in St Ives where the main reason for the walls was that they provided hanging space for art. The whole area was lit by a semicircle of windows providing breathtaking views of Manhattan.

Before they could respond to these surroundings, a

wheelchair bowled around one of the walls. It contained a tiny woman, Dresden-delicate, almost frail until she was near enough for them all to see her face.

She went into free wheel and held out her hands. 'Welcome, welcome. I'm Marion. I couldn't manage the trip to England when Mack came over to meet all of you so this is a treat for me. Thank you for changing your plans and coming here like this. It could be a sad occasion but . . . it's not going to be. Is it?'

She looked round at them challengingly and they all found they could smile back at her. She led them round one of the many corners of the room to where a table was laden with crockery and another small – though not frail – woman was already loading a plate with seafood. Michael stood by her, took the plate, smiled at the others as they came to the table.

'This is my wife, Emily. She and Kate – Mrs Briscoe – were buddies.'

Marion smiled up at Gussie. 'They were Mark and Kate to everyone here, as you know. We really only knew them after Mitch retired from the chair but – ' she paused and then said strongly – 'we loved them.'

Gussie cleared her throat. 'Dad always wants to talk about local things and Mum talks about . . . us.' She heard her own words and corrected herself. 'I mean, they did.' She glanced at Jannie, who was nodding, her face still blotched with tears.

Mack too cleared his throat. 'Let's keep them in the present tense, Gussie. They're still with us. That's a fact.'

Jannie beamed at him. 'That's lovely. Thank you. And it's great that you all knew them. We didn't realize that. We sort of grew up with Mitch.' She transferred her beaming smile to Emily. 'I bet Mum loved talking food with you, didn't she?'

'Sure she did.' Emily beamed back. 'She'd come into the

kitchen to see what was cooking. Said she had to get the appropriate juices ready.'

Jannie was surprised. 'We always had water. She said juice spoiled the taste of the food.'

Emily laughed unrestrainedly. 'She meant her digestive juices, honey! Gee, no wonder she loves you three. You're something else!'

They all laughed and then crowded round the table with their plates. Quite suddenly, for the first time since their arrival in New York, the siblings were at ease. Even Ned, who had been against this meeting, relaxed enough to admire the room and its amazing contents. When the girls took their plates to the window and tried to identify various landmarks, he wandered off around the apparently random walls and stopped, grinning, in front of a Jackson Pollock hanging next to a small, early Picasso. Mack's voice came from behind him.

'Does it offend you? Mixing the two? We keep changing the hanging spaces so that they can be friendly together. But these two . . . it tickled Marion. Michael thinks it's sacrilege.'

Ned grinned at him. 'Surely it's not that random? There's a link – they were both innovators.'

'Sure, that's true.'

They moved on to a Constable. Then a Hockney. They talked of Lowry and the Newlyn School. Ned felt more comfortable than he had since his parents died.

Mack said suddenly, 'I'm off to California tomorrow. Did I mention it on the phone?'

'Yes. To do with the Trust?'

'The West Coast board members could not attend the annual meeting. They wanted to postpone until I was out of hospital but your parents were already here and Mitch knew how to handle the whole thing – better than I did, in fact.'

There was a silence. Ned swallowed. 'Perhaps the point is
. . . similar to your choice of picture positioning.' He gave
Mack a wry down-turned smile. 'Sometimes the mismatch
turns out to be just right.'

Mack was silent, thinking about it. Then he sighed and
shook his head. 'I can't see it at the moment, Ned. All I can
do is to try to put us back on track. We were meeting, as you
know, to discuss your father's latest contribution to the Trust.'

Ned nodded. He had not thought of an agenda; but it was
true that Mark Briscoe was dominating the work owned by
the Trust.

Mack cleared his throat. 'That's why I'm going to
California, Ned. To see your father.' He moved along to
another Hockney; one of the swimming pool scenes. 'Mark
had offered to talk to him personally. I don't know whether it
would have worked. Anyway, he didn't turn up. He likes the
warmth of the West Coast. Well, you know all this.'

Ned was stunned. 'No. I did not. Mum and Dad didn't talk
a lot about what was happening commercially. They talked
about what Dad was actually working on. But then, they
wanted to know about Gussie's latest project and how Jannie
was doing at Exeter. And Dad was always interested in my research work. Always . . .' He heard his own voice breaking up.

'Yes. Sure. I was forgetting. Mark Briscoe was your dad. I
guess Victor Gould gave up that role a long time ago.'

Ned managed to change another cough into a snort.
'When I was six years old, actually.'

'Yes. Sure.' Mack nodded. 'It was just that . . . Victor offered
us a set of paintings for a song. Then made a huge fuss about
some small contractual thing and withdrew the offer.' He
glanced sideways. 'He can be awkward.'

'Yes.' Ned recalled his mother's heartbreak all those years ago. 'Yes, you could say that.'

Mack said, 'Let's go and get another drink.' He moved back, then said suddenly, 'Any chance of you coming with me tomorrow, Ned? You might be able to swing the whole deal.'

Ned stopped in his tracks. He could remember his mother saying when the Trust first approached them about the sculpture for the cathedral, 'We have to be careful, Mark. They are businessmen first, art collectors second.'

'Is this what it is all about?' he asked.

Mack did not pretend. 'Getting you on our side?' He gave a small smile. 'I guess we didn't want to lose our Briscoe contacts. And the fact that you are Victor's son—'

'I never want to see him again,' Ned interrupted. 'He dumped my mother and me, and if it hadn't been for Mark Briscoe . . . No. I can't come with you to the West Coast to kowtow to my father. We're going back to England the day after tomorrow, anyway. Flight is booked.'

He walked over to where Jannie and Gussie were laughing with Marion.

'We must go, girls. These people need to pack.'

Marion looked up from her wheelchair. Mack started to speak and she said quietly, 'Leave it, darling. It wasn't that good an idea.' She reached for Ned's hand. 'It was mine. My idea. I thought you might want a chance to take over from Mark and Kate. Forgive me.' She shook the hand gently. 'Don't go off in a huff, Ned.'

Ned forced himself to return the pressure of her hand. 'Sorry. It's all so surprising.' He managed a smile. 'Listen, would you mind very much if we took the tape with us?'

'We assumed you would. It's such a private thing.' She looked round at them. 'I heard it . . . the first time. But

I was sobbing and yelling. I haven't listened again. *We* haven't listened to it. Let us know when we may. We have our copy.'

There was a silence, then Gussie said hoarsely, 'Thank you. We had the wrong idea. We thought you might want to – to – use it in some way. For the work of the Trust. We're sorry. Really sorry.'

Jannie said earnestly, 'It is a private thing, you're right. Yet how can it be private when the whole world saw it happening? People we've never seen have called on us back home and talked to us as if it has happened to them – and in a way it has.'

Ned said nothing. He too was ashamed of his knee-jerk reaction to the McKinnons. But the girls did not yet know that Mack had wanted him to see Victor. Ned stood between them and watched Michael and Emily wheel away the table of food. It was all so smooth, so engineered.

It was also the signal for their departure. Gussie accepted the neatly wrapped package containing the last words from their parents. It was so ordinary yet its significance was beyond extraordinary. Technology had given them a symbol that might well prove impossible to bear.

They parted on good terms. The lift dropped to the basement in about six seconds and Michael held the car door open for them. They got into a current of yellow cabs and ground their way to Times Square and then past the familiar Howard Johnson restaurant to the hotel.

Michael's parting words were, 'They're good people.' And then, 'They loved your parents.'

In the elevator Jannie said suddenly, 'They had no flipping right to love our parents!'

Ned and Gussie both smiled at her childish indignation, but they nodded.

Gussie said, 'If only it had been Mitch.'

'Yes, but we would have cried a lot. And Mum used to say that crying just gives you a headache,' Ned reminded her.

'It would have been worth a headache.'

The lift doors opened, they slid the key-card into the lock, trooped inside, sat on the first bed and held hands and waited. Nothing happened.

Jannie groaned. 'Just when we could do with it there's not a tear between us!'

Then they began to laugh. Gussie fished in her bag and put the square gift-wrapped tape on the bedside table. They stared at it.

Jannie whispered, 'Oh God . . . oh God . . .'

They bowed their heads. Then Ned fed the disc into the player and clicked switches. When the dear familiar voice of Mark Briscoe came into the anonymous, flower-filled room, they lifted their heads, shocked at its normal, conversational tone. The girls gasped, drawing in air as if they had been under water for too long. Ned stared wide-eyed at the bank of technology, waiting for a picture to appear on the black screen of the television. He blinked hard to disperse the absurd expectation, then took Jannie's outstretched hand, put it on his knee and sandwiched Gussie's hand with his own.

Mark said, 'Hope you get this, loves. You'll understand why, so no need to explain. Mum thought it would be a good idea to send you a message.'

Kate's voice overrode her husband's. 'It was his idea. I'm worried it might make the future worse instead of better!'

'It won't. You need to know that. You need to know that

we're not taking all the fun with us. We're leaving it for you. That's a promise.' A pause. 'Strange, I can't think of anything to say. It's as if just by holding the phone we are linked. I'll hand you to Mum for a moment.'

Kate's voice was louder than Mark's. She sounded very strong. 'It's been wonderful knowing the three of you. Sorry I kept asking you about your life before me, Gussie. I wanted to get the complete picture. I wasn't lucky with girl friends until you came along. Thank you for loving me, for loving Jan, for loving Ned, for loving your father . . . for all your loving. Keep it up, it's a great gift. You shared it with me.' Her voice stopped abruptly and Mark's took over.

'We love you – you know that. Jannie is going to be something wonderful. Ned and Gus, you might need to look at other options. Not sure. You'll know the right ones when they come along.' They heard him draw a breath, and as background noise crescendoed, he said quickly, 'We've decided to chuck my legs out first and follow straight after, darlings. Don't want to wait for the final curtain. Better to leave while we're ahead!' There was a gasping sort of laugh and then their voices in unison: 'Bye! Just for a little while! Bye!' And they replaced the receiver.

Their children stared, waiting for more. It was too brief.

Jannie broke the silence. 'There was nothing else to say.' She was not weeping.

Ned nodded, then shook his head and actually smiled. 'So typical. So bloody typical.'

Gussie retrieved her hand and patted the other two. 'That's what makes it wonderful. It's so typical, so normal. I bet Mum put down the telephone and then said, "Let's get on with it!"'

Jannie stopped staring at the player and looked at Gussie.

'You're right. I can almost hear her saying it!' She asked, 'Is this what an anticlimax is? Did we expect them to come up with some gem of wisdom? Or offer to appear at midnight when it's a full moon?'

Gussie gave a little smile. 'It wasn't the time for joking. So, no, that's not what we expected. We got them, just as they were. Our parents. That's good enough for us. Yes?'

After that, everything seemed easier. Dinner at the Florabunda had its moments. Several of the party were in obvious distress; one man did not speak or eat and Mrs Selway sat by him talking in a low voice now and then. Sheila and May seemed happy with the service and their shared lunch afterwards.

'It did help,' Sheila said, and May nodded agreement. 'We don't know how or why but it made us feel . . . better. We think.'

'Was it because of the gates of glory?' Jannie asked.

It was the first time anyone had mentioned the triumphal opening of the service and even now no one in their vicinity picked up on it. But May said, 'It was a bit like Dunkirk. When we thought we'd been beaten and then Mr Churchill made it into a victory.'

The next day most of the group went on a tour around the shops before their flight home. The Briscoes took Sheila and May to the Cloisters, where they could look down on the Hudson far below and sit in the autumn sun. They exchanged addresses. 'If it's only a card at Christmas . . .' Sheila said.

'After Christmas things might be better. Two thousand and two. It sounds hopeful,' Ned replied.

'I can't imagine . . . anything. We can't go back and we don't know how to start again,' Sheila confided.

65

Gussie looked out at the length of Manhattan. She loved her work but, like Sheila, she could not imagine going back to it.

Jannie said sturdily, 'My last year at Exeter. I'll just get on with it and hope there's a job at the end. English graduates are two a penny. I might travel.'

Ned and Gussie could not imagine Jannie with a back-pack far from home. As Ned glanced at Gussie, he felt her uncertainty echo in his own head. Neither of them had done any work for almost two months. He loved his research work in Bristol; it was important, it might matter to thousands of people. But it would go on without him. He could under-stand how Jannie felt only too well. Yes, she should travel . . .

He took a deep breath. He knew what he was going to do. He would wait until the new year and then, long after the McKinnons had done – or not done – their deal, he would see his father. The man who had left him and his mother twenty years ago and who was now in his eighties. Victor Gould, the artist. And Gussie, dear Gussie, who would, so obviously, fit into his mother's shoes and look after the cottage and her father's work and always be there for Jannie and himself, Gussie should go and see her mother.

Eight

Jannie was the first to leave.

In spite of the precious message from their parents, Gussie and Ned were still in a strange no man's land, a grey directionless place of half-decisions; but they both noticed that Jannie had changed. She still wept copiously but then, suddenly, when Gussie offered the usual shoulder, she held out one arm and gasped, 'I'm OK. Honestly. Just . . . all those people and that smell . . . and then Mack . . . and the message from Mum and Dad, like the messages in bottles we used to launch at Christmas . . . and everything.'

When they were on the plane coming home she leaned forward to look across at the other two, smiled gratefully and said, 'Thank you for taking me to see John Lennon's Memorial in Central Park.'

The main reason for the long ramble through the park on their last day had been to see the famous carousel where a three-year-old Jannie had ridden so joyously with applause from her family. But twenty-year-old Jannie had no recollection of that innocent time and had spent nearly an hour standing next to the Lennon stone. She joined the other two where they were sitting gazing back the way they had come towards the building where the McKinnons had their apartment. She had smiled reassuringly at them.

'Isn't this marvellous? All these people coming to think about a man who seemed so wild and yet sang such common-sense songs!' She stared at the groups of pilgrims around the simple memorial and raised her hand slightly in what could have been a salute or a farewell. Then she said briskly, 'We must come to the meetings as often as we can. We'll be invited because of Dad, and we need to show that we belong – like he and Mum did – to all the people. You know, like in John Lennon's song.'

Finally, after the sleeper deposited them in Penzance station and the taxi had taken them along the A30 back to St Ives, she surprised them again. It was bitterly cold in Zion Cottage, and though they had been away less than a week, the house looked neglected and the grey morning light was unwelcoming. Gussie started to make tea and Ned fiddled with the boiler and then switched on the heating.

Jannie put her big shoulder bag on the kitchen table and scrabbled through it, emerging triumphantly with a piece of paper. She waved it in the air. 'Phone number. Sheila and May. Must check that they got home safely and let them know that we did too!'

'You're not going to ring them now?' Ned said. 'It's seven thirty in the morning; they won't be up.'

But Jannie was already punching numbers into the kitchen phone and then announcing their arrival to a surprised Sheila.

'We're home, Sheila. And you too. Everything all right?' She listened intently, a whole range of expressions crossing her face. Gussie made the tea and put mugs on the table next to Jannie's bag. Ned looked for his toothbrush and made signs that he was heading for the bathroom. Jannie was making small sympathetic sounds into the receiver by this time. Then she said, 'Well, why don't you come here? As you say, Sheila, all of us will be disorientated this Christmas. Come to us for a week! It's a great idea. Completely different.'

Ned and Gussie halted in their tracks, staring at her. She turned her mouth down. 'Are you sure? If you change your minds . . . yes. Of course. We understand completely. We'll be in touch again – must tell you about Central Park. Better go. We're a bit jet-lagged, I think!' Then she replaced the receiver.

'Poor Sheila. May was ill on the plane coming home and Sheila is wondering how they're going to get through Christmas. So I asked them to come to us. I knew they wouldn't, but it was worth a try.'

Gussie was wide-eyed. 'Where on earth would they have stayed?'

'With Mrs Beck, of course. They could have come to us for all their meals and we could've taken them to Land's End and Cape Cornwall. Everywhere is so lovely and empty, it would have done all of us a lot of good.'

Gussie looked at Ned, who seemed to have given up on the bathroom and was using the water in the kettle to fill hot-water bottles.

She said, 'I have to admit I am relieved, Jan. I think we should close ranks for a bit longer.'

Jannie hugged her sister. 'We'll always be in the same boat, darling. But we need to do things. Open up. For the sake of Mum and Dad, really.' She choked a little, swallowed, then went on, 'I'm going back to college, and I think you and Ned should start working again. You're sort of lost at sea.'

Gussie leaned away and stared into those Nordic-blue eyes

with some surprise. 'My God, you're right, of course. But . . . aren't you with us any longer?'

'Where? Oh, lost at sea?' She frowned, thinking about it. 'Well, yes. But I am plotting a course. It might change. But I'm going to get down all my notes for the dissertation by the beginning of the spring term – stop laughing! Then I'll spend that term writing it up. Really working on it. Before all this business – ' she waved her hand – 'I booked to do some observations at a special school in North Devon. I want to do that before I actually start on my final draft.'

'I wasn't laughing. But you didn't tell us about this placement.'

'Not a placement, a week of observation, that's all. I wasn't keen at first, and we were having such a gorgeous time with Mum and Dad before they went to the AGM. I wanted to forget all about college for the whole of the summer! And then, well, you know . . .' Her voice trailed off and Gussie waited for the tears and the hug. Neither happened. Jannie added, 'After I've handed it in, I'm going to apply for a job.'

'I thought you were going to travel.' Gussie spoke teasingly, but Jannie did not grin or shrug her shoulders.

'I am,' she said. 'I'll be eligible this summer to teach English in India. There are lists in the Junior Common Room – schools that can accommodate graduands – mostly in the south. Food and accommodation only, so not many people can afford to apply.' She made a wry face. 'I can, of course. I gathered from something Mack said we're probably going to be fairly rich.'

There was a silence.

She said in a small voice, 'I'm sorry, Gussie. Please don't cry. I didn't mean to be so horribly insensitive. It's just that

I sort of learned something from going to New York. There were so many people who were grieving in so many different ways. Some wished they had been killed too. Others were like us, not knowing how to go on . . . Sheila and May were the most like us, weren't they? And after we left the Cloisters on their last day they both said they felt better for coming and for meeting us. And I said I felt better for meeting them. I wasn't just being polite, Gussie. I *did* feel better. I could see them – I mean, *see* them. They . . . they're flipping well *disabled* by what has happened. The randomness of it all. And then I started to think about disablement. We've been disabled. Like Dad without any legs, except that he never had any. There's no special school for us so we have to learn somehow to cope by ourselves. I'll find out more when I do my observation week.' She paused, looking suddenly uncertain and added, 'Won't I?'

Gussie swallowed hard. 'Yes. You will. You will, Jannie. You're right, of course, you will have to open up to find out!' She smiled wryly, then went on determinedly, 'And don't worry about Ned or me. We'll have to find our own ways, but we'll get there in the end.' She flung her arms around her sister. 'Darling, I'll have to shed a few tears but I'm not unhappy – honestly. I'm really proud of you!'

Jannie reached round and tugged gently on Gussie's plait. 'Listen, pour the tea. No milk, I suppose? Let's see whether it's gone off . . .'

Gussie freed herself and scrubbed at her face with a tissue. She watched Jannie sniff at a bottle of milk and said in a small voice, 'Jannie, you will come home for Christmas, won't you?'

'Of course. A swim at high tide and a drunken orgy with the Becks!'

Ned did not join in the laughter. He was by the stairs again, holding three hot-water bottles and his toothbrush. He said, 'I'll skip tea, if you don't mind. I need to sleep.' He started to clump up the stairs.

Gussie called out, 'Ned! You're all right? You do understand that Jannie has to do this?'

He stopped and looked down at them. Their faces, looking back at him, were so blessedly familiar. For some reason he felt heavy with dread. He faced the unpalatable fact that he did not want to move forward, open up, get on with life. Whatever they called it, he didn't want it. He wanted to stay here and try to go backwards. Maintain Zion Cottage and the Scaife studio. Go fishing with the small remaining fleet of boats. Let Gussie take his mother's place and Jannie be the baby of the family.

He said, 'Of course I understand. I'm just . . . whacked.'

He went on up the stairs and as he tucked the hot-water bottles into the girls' beds he knew there was something else. He hated the thought of it and refused to 'plot a course', but at some point he really did have to go back in time to before he belonged to the Briscoes. They had become his anchor and he had to – somehow – cut himself free and go back to another time; the terrible time; the lost time. He had to see his father.

He reached his room in the attic, put his hot-water bottle into his bed and stood in the dormer gazing out at the harbour and the fishing boats. The tide was in and they were bobbing beneath the pier unloading their catch. And somewhere way out across the seas was Victor Gould, who lived in California and was an old man now. Born on Armistice Day in 1918 and named Victor. With an estranged son who must look like him because Kate was blonde and blue-eyed and so was Jannie.

He shivered; if he looked like Victor Gould might he actually be like Victor Gould?

Ned took a deep breath and let it go against the window-pane, where it flowered immediately into a mist. He had to confront this man. He had to leave Gussie here on her own and go back to the States and find out why Victor had left his wife and son all those years ago. He felt sick.

Having slept all morning, they went for a walk late that afternoon. None of them wanted to but Gussie rallied them.

'We've got to separate day and night somehow. Get some Cornish air into our lungs too – help us back into our proper sleep patterns.'

They headed automatically for the cliff path beyond Porthmeor, where a sharp wind failed to move the lid of cloud out to sea. In the ten days since they had walked this way, winter had come. Gussie buttoned her jacket up to her chin and Ned stuck his hands in his pockets. Jannie took their arms and drew them towards Old Man's Head into the lee of the rocks.

'You're not enjoying this,' Jannie accused the others. 'We've got to make a conscious effort – come on now! I know you're not happy about me going back to Exeter before Christmas, but just listen . . .' She reiterated her intention of returning to college. She wanted her tutor to register that she was 'still alive' and very much part of the course.

'There's only four weeks left of the term, Ned. I wish you wouldn't look as if I'd stabbed you or something. Did you think I'd given up?'

'Yes.' He stared at her wryly. 'I didn't want you to, of course. I was all prepared with about five very cogent arguments as to why you should finish your three years! You've whipped the carpet from beneath your wise older brother's feet!'

Jannie leaned her back against the base of the rock tower. She looked less certain. 'You don't think I can do it, do you? You see me as a dumb blonde!'

Gussie cut through the following gabble from both of them. 'Listen, you two, this time yesterday we were in New York. We cannot make decisions today. Let's turn back – I'm absolutely frozen – have fish and chips and a proper night's sleep.'

Jannie agreed. 'We need to play our message again.'

Ned said, 'Actually, this time yesterday we weren't in New York. We were in mid-air. And for ages before that we were hanging about in the airport.'

'For Pete's sake, let's get going!' Gussie said.

'This is like old times,' Jannie giggled. 'Proper old times.'

So they walked back, talking of those old times. Remembering without the agony of regret.

That evening Aunt Rosemary telephoned from Bristol to see how they had fared in America. They took turns at the telephone. Gussie was last and hung on to it a long time. The other two were not surprised. Rosemary said often and without tact, 'You are the first-born, my dear. Besides which, you take after my mother and she had a head on her shoulders. You are the one who will need to do the bizz.'

Now she said briskly, 'There are some documents here I'd like you to see – and to sign if you agree with what they propose. All three of you. Any chance of you driving up so that I can explain it properly? I've talked about it with the solicitors and, briefly, Mark, Kate and I were joint owners of this house. You might already know this. Anyway, I would like you to take on their shares. And the sooner the better. Inheritance tax and so forth.'

Gussie glanced at Ned and Jannie, half asleep already. She took the bull by the horns. 'We'll come in a few days, Aunty Ro. Then on the way back we can drop Jannie at Exeter. Does that sound all right?'

The other two looked surprised.

'I shall look forward to that. I am delighted that Jannie is going to finish her course. I was afraid that would all go by the board.'

They said goodbye and Gussie replaced the receiver and smiled across the table.

'We're probably going to be joint owners of the Briscoe house in Bristol.'

Jannie said, 'Never mind that. Did you mean it? Will you take me back, see me settled in that awful student flat?' Her recently found confidence sounded shaky.

Gussie nodded slowly. 'The fact that we are needed to sign documents and so forth – it's rather pointing the way, don't you think?'

So only five days later, after a few hours in the tall Georgian house in Clifton, they left Jannie in Exeter and came back to St Ives. The weather was unseasonally warm, and Somerset, Devon and Cornwall shone in the November sunshine. Ned carried Jannie's bag up three flights of stairs and they all crowded into the tiny bedsit.

'I've changed my mind,' Jannie said suddenly. 'I don't want to do this. We can't break our threesome – not yet, anyway.'

Gussie said, 'Darling, do what you think best. Talk to Ned. I remember where the kitchen is – I'll make some tea.'

But as she looked around at the kitchen, shared by the three other students in the house, she said aloud to herself,

'She can't stay here. Not after what has happened.' And yet Jannie had returned at the beginning of October and managed somehow. But that was before they had gone to New York. Gussie felt her mind whirl into uncertainty again. Automatically she found mugs and washed them, boiled water in a saucepan because the electric kettle was nowhere to be seen, made the tea and poured it, milkless into the mugs. She trudged up the stairs again and felt a pang of real fear for their future. Financially they could afford to live together in Zion Cottage and try to resurrect the past. Perhaps that was not a good thing at all.

Ned opened the door and looked out. 'Let me take that . . . It's OK, it was just a sudden fright. She's fine. Doesn't want us to hang about too long.'

They drank the tea and Jannie told them three times not to worry. They left.

Ned and Gussie had lived by themselves in the cottage for almost the whole of October and should have been used to it. Now, arriving back without Jannie, it seemed odd. Just five days ago they had arrived home from New York, bonded by their experiences there. Their threesome had been reinvented somehow; Jannie had changed it in some way. And now she was not there. They sat in the parlour drinking their way through yet another pot of tea while the light slowly faded outside the window and the gulls finished wheeling and screaming around the incoming fishing boats. Ned, who had done most of the driving, announced he needed to have an early night. Gussie nodded abstractedly and stirred her tea. She wondered what on earth she could do with the rest of the evening.

Suddenly from Smeaton's Pier came a burst of colour. They

both stiffened, thinking it was a distress rocket. Colours poured from it; red at first, then enormous green droplets settling into golden rain.

'My God.' Ned looked at Gussie across the darkening room. 'It's the third of November, the Saturday before November the Fifth! It was in the paper – they're doing the firework display early this year so that the children can stay up late!' He laughed suddenly. 'Can't go to bed early now!'

Another rocket shot into the sky, closely followed by spurts from smaller ones. He stood up and peered sideways through the parlour window.

'Everyone's out there . . .' His voice petered out as a cheer went up, and then applause. 'I haven't been home for Bonfire Night for, well, ages!'

Gussie put down her mug and went to the window. Another rocket soared up and they both laughed as they heard children screaming with mock terror.

'It's as good as the Millennium display!' Gussie said.

'Won't last as long, though.'

They had all been together for the Millennium and it had been a night to remember.

'Grab your coat, Gussie. Let's get out there before it's over!'

'Are you up to it?'

'No. Are you?'

'No.'

They hunted for hats and scarves, and went down the steps on to the wharf. People greeted them warmly as if welcoming them back from the awfulness of their grief. When the show was over – as it soon was – they declined invitations for drinks at the Sloop and went back into the house, certain that everything was going to be 'all right' now.

'It's a bit early but let's hibernate as from tonight, shall we?' Gussie suggested.

Kate had decided years ago that they would 'hibernate' in the cellar from January to March. It had been converted into a flat for Mark and was warmer than 'the rest of the house put together', besides being completely accessible for the wheelchair.

Gussie hung up her woollen hat. 'We can watch the little television and I can start on the angels.' She always decorated the whole house with paper angels every Christmas; but never as early as this.

Ned said contentedly, 'Sounds good. In that case I'll get the supper. Are there sausages in the freezer?'

'There are.'

They grinned at each other comfortably and went downstairs to the kitchen. Then the phone bleeped in the hall to tell them someone had called them and left a message, and they both did an about-turn and went to see what it was. Gussie got there first, by which time, for some silly reason, they were both laughing.

Jannie's voice came into the tiny hall loud and clear. 'Where are you? Ring me back. As soon as you get home.'

Gussie picked up the receiver and keyed in one, four, seven, one then three. It rang twice then Jannie's voice said, 'Thank goodness. The traffic must have been awful – have you only just got in?'

'No. It was nearly five o'clock by the time we'd got the car on to the Island and unloaded—'

'Five o'clock? Why didn't you phone me? I've been worried sick! Where have you been?'

Gussie looked at Ned. 'She's been worried about us.' Then to Jannie she said, 'We didn't think. We saw you into the house so we knew you were safe . . . we were having a cup of tea and we realized they were doing the fireworks early this year for Guy Fawkes' Night and we went down on the wharf to watch them.'

'Oh, are they doing the same here? Let me just look.' There was a pause then she said, 'I can see stuff somewhere by the cathedral. Nothing here. I'm too far from the campus really. Oh, I don't mind; I never liked the noisy ones. And it's always so cold just standing about.' She sounded wan.

Gussie said, 'Darling, are you OK? We should have phoned to check on you but—'

'You didn't need to check on me, as you just said yourself. But you should have phoned to let me know you had got home safely. I really was worried.'

'Sorry. Really sorry, Jan. We're missing you and didn't want that to come across the phone, perhaps.'

'I'm missing you. Terribly. But I've got to get used to it. And I've already phoned Hartley School and confirmed my visit. It's the week term ends so I can come straight home from there.'

They talked for a while longer, then Gussie gave the receiver to Ned and went on downstairs to get the sausages from the freezer and then find paper and scissors.

Soon, Ned came into the kitchen and feigned astonishment. 'Jannie was worried about *us*! Is that a first?'

'Probably not,' Gussie said peaceably. 'But we often don't mention things that matter. We must phone her every day. We have to keep in touch.'

She was still convinced that all would now be well.

Ned was in the cavernous Scaife studio engaged in the apparently endless task of sorting out Mark's earlier work, separating some of the Scaife paintings for storage, generally tidying up. He and Gussie had been at the cottage, just the two of them, for over a month, and he had needed to get away from Gussie and think through his plans before he broached the subject of his visit to California. It was only when he came upon one of Mark's paintings that he realized the sheer impossibility of the whole scheme. How on earth could he have considered for one moment leaving Gussie alone in Zion Cottage? Had he thought that she would go back to her flat in Plymouth and start up again? She had handed over her latest project so that she could stay with Jannie and himself and, as far as he knew, had no more enquiries waiting.

He propped the canvas against the wall and stood away from it. Then he took another step back and folded his arms. The painting was very much in the style of the Newlyn School: a small girl, perhaps six or seven years old, wearing a red gingham dress, a single plait already halfway down her back, ankle-deep in the sea; her back was towards the painter as she stared at the horizon. He knew it was Gussie. The plait identified her but also her stance, weight on her left leg, hands entwined and beneath her chin as she gave serious consideration to what was before her. If she had been older and he had been with her, he could well imagine his own voice asking what was taking her so long to look at the sea and sky. And she would probably have said – as indeed she often did say – 'Daddy told me. You have to look at things and let them soak into your head. Proper, like. It takes a long time.'

Ned said aloud, 'How can I leave her?' He clenched his hands, put them to his chin and went on staring almost in imitation of the painting. Then he added, 'Ever.' His hands dropped automatically and his eyes widened, startled and then horrified. He whispered, 'Gussie . . . oh my God. Gussie. She's my *sister*, for God's sake!' And then he picked up the painting, put it behind a pile of others and returned to Gerald Scaife's rendering of the Island as a giant penis thrusting into the sea. He went on talking aloud as if to Scaife himself. 'Can't say I like this one, Gerald, but some of your big works are pretty wonderful. I have to admit.'

A voice behind him said, 'Yes. They are, aren't they? He was before his time, of course, but now . . . things have changed.'

Ned turned quickly and cricked his neck. He held on to it, screwing up his eyes. 'My God! You gave me a fright!' His heart was pounding; had this knowledgeable stranger heard everything?

'No knocker on the door, I'm afraid.'

'But the damned thing screeches like an owl when you open it and I didn't hear a thing.'

'I eased it open gently. I came to St Ives to see Gerald Scaife's stuff and can't find a soul who knows a thing about it. Then someone pointed out the studios and said there might be someone doing some cataloguing – I think he said cataloguing.'

'Old Beck. I told him I was going rat catching.' Ned looked at the stranger. 'Joke. Sorry. I'm a sort of relative of Scaife's. What can I do for you?'

'You can allow me to take photographs. I represent a collector. My name is Bellamy. Andrew Bellamy.' Ned took the proffered hand and the man said, 'I won't be in your way. The *Cape Cornwall* painting is up for auction with others from the Trewyn collection and if I could get *The Island* to go with them, my client would be happy. Very happy indeed.'

Ned felt himself withdraw. This man wanted to buy

Gerald's painting? He had never quite understood about the ownership of Gerald's work. It had belonged to Zannah, Gussie's renegade mother, but had she let her ex-husband have the remaining pictures when she gave him the studio?

Ned said, 'Actually, I don't think the Scaife paintings that are still here are for sale. I'm not certain, of course. If the Trewyn collection is being sold off, perhaps . . . I really can't help you.' He felt an urgent need to get back to Gussie.

'I'm on my way to see Zannah Scaife. Scaife's daughter, you know. She is still alive, of course.'

'She lives abroad, I'm afraid. She moved years ago.'

Andrew Bellamy was already adjusting the lens in an expensive-looking camera and nodded at this information. 'France. Somewhere in Provence,' he said absently.

Ned turned back to the stack of paintings and adjusted them so that he had another glimpse of the small girl with the plait who was staring at the view that had so inspired her grandfather. He tucked it in safely and said, 'I have to be going now, Mr Bellamy. And I need to lock up.'

The man laughed and fitted the leather cover over his camera. 'You certainly do! I like to think my property is safely protected!' It was a joke, of course. Then he added, 'Shall I be seeing you at the Trewyn sale, Mr . . . ?' Ned said nothing and the man went on smoothly, 'It's scheduled for the end of January. That's two thousand and two, of course!' He laughed again. Ned had no idea what he was talking about; he did not laugh.

'Afraid not,' he said. 'I'm scheduled to be in California early next year.'

He heard his own words and wondered if they were true.

Bellamy stepped outside on to the sandy path that led directly down to Porthgwidden Cove. He looked around him.

'Bit bleak. Time of year, of course.'

Ned rarely disliked people so instantly. 'You're not look-ing at it properly. It needs to soak in,' he said.

Bellamy laughed again; what was so funny this time? 'I think we'll both be soaking it in tonight, old man. This is known as a sea fret, I believe?'

Ned fiddled with the padlock on the corrugated iron door and ignored the man who, thank God, was already moving off, but still called over his shoulder, 'See you in the Sloop later?' And when there was no reply he stopped and said unexpectedly, 'I think a friend of mine came from St Ives. August Briscoe. Do you know her?'

Luckily in that instant the sea fret decided to change into a downpour so the man could not have seen Ned's face.

'No.'

Ned passed him and started up the hill instead of making for the wharf. The man immediately disappeared into the rain but still Ned pressed on and came to Zion Cottage by way of the maze of backstreets.

No lights were on and the rain drove into the yard from the sea. Further up the terrace of cottages three children were singing 'Hark! the herald angels sing' beneath a streetlamp. One of them held an umbrella, which, as Ned unlocked the kitchen door, turned explosively inside out and blew into the darkness of the harbour. He closed the door behind him and clicked on the light, smiling at last. The big kitchen was warm and Etta's old range glowed reassuringly. There was a note on the table.

Ned, mackerel in the side oven. Have yours when you're hungry. I might be a bit late. Rory called again. Reckons he's going to auction off the house and all its contents and go to live with Zannah! Ring me at Trewyn if you need to. See you later. From Big Sis!

He pulled one of the kitchen chairs close to the range and sat down to read the note again. He had not realized that the condescending Andrew Bellamy had meant that the whole of Trewyn House was to be sold. Surely Uncle Rory should have consulted Aunt Rosemary first? Why had he told Gussie? Why had Gussie gone back with him? How did Andrew Bellamy know Gussie?

Ned was suddenly anxious. Rory was unpredictable and reckless too. Had he taken Gussie over in his boat or his car? Either was potentially dangerous. Ned looked at the note again, the rounded letters . . . He thought of the girl with the plait and remembered her vulnerability. His eyes were stinging. He threw the note into the fire basket, scraped back his chair and went upstairs to the telephone.

Thank God Gussie picked up the phone the other end; he couldn't have faced Rory.

'Listen, Sis. I'm going to the Island car park to get the car. I'll be with you in half an hour.'

'Oh, Ned, would you mind? Rory's trying to tell me that he's only selling up so that he can go and live in France with my flipping mother!' She imitated Jannie's voice and tried to laugh but he could tell she was near tears.

'Is he drunk? Why did you go with him?'

'I don't think he's drunk. He wanted to show me something. Rosemary's clothes. The story was that he chucked all her stuff out and locked the door against her. But he's kept her clothes – her wedding dress, everything. He wants me to have them.'

She was crying properly now and Ned felt his own eyes fill

with anger at bloody Uncle Rory. And at Andrew Bellamy, who was a snake in the grass and knew his sister.

'I'm on my way, Sis. Hang on. Oh,' he swallowed, 'before I forget, do you know someone called Bellamy? Andrew Bellamy?'

A pause, then explosively, 'What are you talking about? Didn't you hear what I just said? Rory did not throw out Rosemary's stuff. He wants me to have it.'

'Sorry. Sorry, Gussie. Put your coat on. I'll be there in half an hour.'

'Haven't taken it off.' She sounded cross, but not upset any more. Just annoyed at his irrelevance. 'It's like a tomb in this place. The sooner he gets rid of it and leaves Cornwall the better.'

'Yes, Sis.' Ned pretended to be meek. He put the phone down and left for the car park. He was relieved. She did not know Andrew Bellamy. And Rory was leaving Cornwall. Ned told himself that just in case Rory did go to live with Zannah Scaife, Gussie must be persuaded to visit her mother soon. Dear Gussie . . . darling Gussie. She had always looked after her younger brother and now it was his turn to look after her. He smiled into the sea fret as he unlocked the car. Nothing unnatural about that. They would go their separate ways for a while and then be together again.

85

Nine

At the other end of the line, Gussie held the telephone receiver in its cradle as if she expected it to fall to the floor. In the December twilight the reflected colours striping the hall from the stained-window glass were muted. Ever since Rory had shoved open the massive door and ushered her inside Trewyn House she had felt this sense of imminent decay. The curtains and upholstery and the squares of carpet were all faded and dusty; she had thought suddenly that probably nothing had been done since Rosemary left. Intentionally or not, Rory had let the house preserve her memory. Like Miss Havisham.

She had said things like, 'You don't sell a house because it needs care and attention, Rory. Anywhere you go will need that. You can't escape house maintenance – not ever!'

He ignored her shock and surprise at his decision to 'get out once and for all' and just pointed out various evidence of decay. Then he took her upstairs and said, 'Never mind all that. I brought you over to look at Ro's things. She said she never wanted to see them again and I could chuck them into the sea. But when I saw you, when I dropped in – ' he guffawed loudly, remembering his leap over the handrail and into the yard – 'I knew they'd look good on you. You've got a look of all the bloody Briscoes. Plus a dash of Zannah. A hint of her craziness. Ro could be crazy, but Zannah was kind. And Ro was not.'

Gussie knew then that he was drunk. She shouldn't have come with him, especially in his speedboat. But there had been something pathetic about him. She sighed sharply.

'You need me to walk down memory lane with you, that's it, isn't it? Or do you want me to tell you about New York and the awfulness of it all?'

'I heard you'd got some kind of a tape recording. A father's last message to his daughter. Something like that.'

She looked at him with disgust. By this time they were standing in Aunt Rosemary's room, which presumably had been his as well at one time. The other rooms smelled musty but this one was different. She noticed sprigs of rosemary tucked into the mirror surround.

'It was for all of us, and it was from them both – Mum and Dad.'

He erupted. 'Why do you call her Mum? Her name was Kate and she was not your mother.'

'Oh, Rory, she was my mother. Zannah insisted on me calling her by her name. Kate gave me the choice and I chose to call her Mum. And I loved her far more than I loved Zannah. So be careful what you say.'

He looked wild at that. Gussie remembered her father once describing Rory as 'uncontrollable, like a pirate', and at that moment he did look like a character from *Treasure Island*.

'You loved that – that – *Hausfrau* better than Zannah Scaife? For God's sake go over to France and see Zannah! You've forgotten your own mother, wrapped in domestic cotton wool all these years: the difference between a nice cup of tea and a glass of champagne!'

'Shut up!' Gussie held up a hand and heard the phone ringing in the hall. 'That will be Ned. I left a note. Excuse me.' She leaped down the stairs two at a time and could have wept when she heard Ned's blessedly familiar voice. She wanted to say, 'Come and take me back to Zion Cottage and let us stay there for ever,' but then he said something that knocked everything else out of her head. Andrew. Andrew Bellamy. Andrew was in St Ives and looking for her. She stared down the dark hall; the coloured stripes had gone. Ned made a sound on the other end of the line and she'd snapped at him before she could stop herself. Then Ned said, 'Get your coat on, I'll be with you in half an hour.' And she told him she hadn't taken it off because it was so cold. She put the phone down and stood very still.

Rory came down the stairs a step at a time, leaning heavily on the banister. She registered this and remembered again his vaulting over the handrail at Zion Cottage just before the three of them had left for New York. He was such an old fraud.

She said, 'Ned is coming for me.'

'I'd have taken you back.'

'You've been drinking.'

'That's why I brought the boat.'

'Same applies.'

'Not really. Think about it.'

'Death by drowning rather than in a car crash?'

'Well, depends on your preference, of course.'

He sounded as if he might be giving up and she was sorry. At least their repartee kept any thoughts of Andrew well in the background. She shivered.

'Actually, we could die of hypothermia right here.'

He reached the floor and stood where he was, hanging on to the newel post.

'Couldn't pay the bills so they cut me off. Bastards.'

'The old Rory would have had a store of driftwood for the kitchen stove. Probably mackerel in a frying pan.'

'You never knew the old Rory. Who told you that?'

'Dad. Aunt Rosemary. Gran. Old Beck.'

'OK. This Rory is far more practical. He's selling up and going to live in the sun somewhere.' He was silent for a while and so was she. She thought that she would have to leave Cornwall too. She would go after Christmas. She could not risk Andrew finding her.

'Rosemary talks about me sometimes, does she?' Rory asked.

'Yes. Not often. How you met at Knill's Monument.'

'But she still hates me?'

Gussie forced herself to think about it. 'I don't know,' she admitted. 'Dad thought she did. And Ned said that when married couples split up they always hate each other. But actually, I don't think Kate hated her first husband. She never talked about him, though.'

'And Ro talks about me?'

'Yes. Sometimes.'

There was the sound of a car turning off the A30 to Redruth and starting down the drive.

'Listen, Gus,' Rory said urgently, 'I thought of going to see Zannah myself. As soon as I've got rid of this bloody albatross.' He waved a hand around the dark hall. She could feel his eyes turn on her; they gleamed blackly. He even had pirate's eyes. 'Come with me. Come on, let's do it together.'

She was astonished out of her immediate fears. 'You must be joking! And please do not call me Gus!'

'You sound just like your mother!' The car drew up outside the front door; gravel splattered. He said, 'That's Ned. Think about it.'

She didn't answer; she was pulling at the heavy door. And there was Ned. She ran down the steps and into his arms. Rory stood at the top and called, 'I'll bring those frocks and things over. Better check with Ro about the jewellery. I gave it to her so she probably hates it.' He started to turn away and she could only just hear his words. 'Unless she doesn't.' And he gave his most piratical laugh.

Ned helped Gussie into the car. She seemed to be weak at the knees and clung to him. In spite of the December fog, he was sweating.

'You all right?' He tucked in her coat and shut the passenger door, came round and got in beside her. 'It's warm tonight.' He unzipped his jacket and wound down the window.

'It was freezing in that house. Everything was . . . awful.' She fastened her seat belt and huddled down. 'But, oh, Ned, I think as soon as Christmas is over, I will have to go and see Zannah. Uncle Rory is planning to descend on her as soon as he's got the money from the sale of the house and its contents. He'll be rich for a time, and he's a drinker and a gambler and needs looking after. She'll end up as a skivvy. Also, it's going to be difficult for Aunt Rosemary . . . I'm not sure, but I think he might get in touch with her again. They are chalk and cheese! How on earth they ever got it together . . .' She rambled on for a while; it was better than letting herself think about other things. Eventually she stopped and waited for him to tell her she must stay in St Ives.

He said, 'Actually, Gussie, I think that's a good idea. I've more or less decided I will have to go and visit Victor Gould. He's pretty ancient so it will have to be soon. Mack put me off by asking for my help – talking Victor into signing a contract donating some of his work to The Spirit of America. It made me livid at first. Now I can see it wasn't intended as a ghastly commercial thing. In fact, I feel it might be good to take a hand in the business of the Trust.'

She was astounded. 'You're planning to go off after Christmas to – to California? You were the one who did not want to go to the States for the memorial thing!'

'I know. But, frankly, Sis, I don't want to be a research chemist any more. There are plenty of others to take my place. I never came near to being indispensable.'

'But you are doing something that could make a difference!'

'Me and fifty others. Yes. It will go on, love. Without me.' He started the car and crunched back to the main road. He had called her 'love'. He often did and she hadn't noticed. 'It's so different from what you do,' he went on. 'Nobody will create the same sort of landscape you will. Dad was a sculptor and so are you, but you use the land itself. That's wrong – you don't *use* the land, you work *with* the land. You emphasize a beauty that is already there so that the most obtuse of us can see it, feel it. Oh, Gus, you have to go on with your work.'

She watched the Christmas lights of Lelant flick past her window. She said slowly, 'That's the second time I've been called Gus this evening.' Ned said nothing and she continued, 'I never thought of it so concisely. Grandfather Scaife used to talk about seeing the land through its relationship to the sea, and of course Dad was always looking for what his lump of granite or marble might be hiding.' She glanced round at him; his dear face was visible in the flash of a brightly lit

Santa Claus. She said, 'Perhaps you should see Victor. He is a painter and perhaps – nothing to do with getting him to sign contracts with The Spirit of America – seeing him could show you what you should do next.'

Ned shook his head. 'I don't want any of his genes, Sis. When I think how it must have been for Mum all those years ago, it still makes me cry. I was six when he popped us into that boarding house and left. No, I'm going to confront my personal devil. Get to grips with life.'

She said in a low voice, 'Thanks for staying this long.'

He was silent again. The car began the long descent past Porthminster beach. A line of creamy surf swept up the shore as if it would eat every grain of sand. They both saw how erotic it must have looked to Gerald Scaife.

She said slowly, 'We'll always be the same three in the same boat. Won't we, Ned?'

'Of course, Gus.' He flashed her a grin and she managed a wan smile.

Nothing more was heard of Andrew Bellamy. He had bought Old Beck a pint of bitter in the Sloop and enquired about August Briscoe. Like Ned, Old Beck had mistrusted him immediately and declared he'd never heard of a woman with such a name, and was she a lawyer or a preacher or summat like that.

'Went on and on about the Scaife paintings. Reckon he's after that stuff in the studio. Sniffing around like a dog, he were.'

'Glad you didn't mention Gussie. I did wonder whether he was one of her clients but she didn't remember him.'

'He were staying at the Sloop for the night an' leaving today. Taxi picked 'im up just as I were going to chapel.' Old

Beck was a preacher of the hellfire variety. He never entered a public house unless he was preaching the next day. 'I need to know about hell and redemption on a personal level,' he would say, tapping the side of his nose.

Ned was startled. 'So you might have mentioned something during your session?'

Old Beck was affronted. 'He were under the table before I'd finished my fifth pint. Thought he was safe with Cornish cider.'

'Ah,' said Ned.

'Ah,' agreed Old Beck, nodding wisely. 'Them what lives by the sword will die by the sword. That cider were brewed out Leven way. I did warn him.'

'You can't do more than that.' Ned thought of Bellamy's condescension and smiled.

Jannie came home fresh from the special school at Hartley. She was so full of emotions she almost fizzed. She had had her hair cut in spikes but it curled close to her head and would stay spiky only if she smothered it in gell.

'It looks so pretty in those close curls, Jan,' Gussie told her as the gell lost its staying power and the curls reappeared. They were decorating the parlour window with a sleigh scene and Jannie had just caught sight of herself in the glass. She shook her head impatiently.

'Remember that old film we watched – just a year ago? What was the name of the little girl in it?'

'Shirley Temple.'

'She could get away with little curls because she was about five years old! I am twenty-one next month, Gus! Wasn't that the age of consent in your day? So why would I want to look like a five-year-old movie star?'

Gussie said weakly, 'She was dark and you are blonde.'

'It was a black-and-white film. I'm going to have to grow it long and scrape it into a ponytail. I just wanted to be a bit different from every other student in the whole world!'

'You'll always be different,' Gussie said peaceably. 'Incidentally, why is everyone calling me Gus lately?'

'Are they?'

'You just did.'

'Did I? I didn't notice. Perhaps it's because you're the head of the family now and Gus sounds more serious? That's why these bubble curls are hopeless for me. I need to be taken seriously. Oh, darling, I want to work at Hartley School so much! It's just so marvellous, Gus. I can't tell you, you'd have to go there to know what I mean. It – the whole place and everyone there – is absolutely inspirational!' She moved back from the window, a cardboard silver bell hanging from her little finger. She looked up at Gussie, who was standing on a chair arranging a line of her paper angels along the pelmet. 'As soon as I get my Certificate I'm going to do a crash course in engineering and then Geoff says he'll take me on.' She saw Gussie's expression. 'Geoff is the headmaster and he's married to the matron. Each of the house staff are qualified teachers, obviously, but have other skills too. One is an experienced physiotherapist and another was a ballerina in her day. And another is just great at BSL – that's British Sign Language. They call him Dr Spock. He's deaf himself and a wheelchair user. There are six deaf students.'

'It does sound inspirational, Jan. But . . .' Gussie affixed another paper angel and turned to look into Jannie's face. She looked different. She had always been beautiful in a pale, Nordic way. Now she was fired up; incandescent. 'But why on earth do you need to be an engineer?'

'I need the basics. They've got a chap – Robert Hanniford – he services all the equipment. But better than that, he invents new stuff. He's working on an electronic hand. Just rods of metal at the moment, but as soon as he's got the movements right, I can measure the full lengths and stitch a soft leather glove.'

Gussie watched the blue eyes darken with enthusiasm. Yes. Incandescent was the right word for Jannie. Gussie realized her little sister was in love. She felt a pang of fear.

She asked cautiously, 'What does your tutor think about this? Is it a reputable school?'

'He got me the placement. I was going just to observe, but you have to pitch in as soon as you arrive!' Jannie laughed as she hung her bell from an angel's wing. 'I'd just arrived, shaken Geoff's hand – there was a girl waiting to see him – wheelchair – and he asked me whether I would take her to the loo. When she had directed me to the cloakroom, told me where to park the chair, how to lock the wheels, how to wriggle her jeans and pants . . .' Jannie stopped laughing and reached for another bell. 'She's marvellous, this girl. Her name is Evie. She's fifteen and she wants to be an actress.' She hung the bell and went to sit on the table. 'She'll do it, too. I know it already.' She smiled up at Gussie. 'She told me that Geoff would find all sorts of things for me to do. One of them was to mend one of the wheelchairs. That was when I met Robert.'

Gussie climbed down and sat on a chair. She had been almost twenty-six when she had been in love with Andrew; Jannie was now almost twenty-one. It had been hot in June 1997, Mum and Dad had been alive . . . actually living and breathing and providing total protection; now it was cold and grey, the Millennium had come and gone, Mum and Dad had gone. Everything was different. And this was the first time that Jannie had fallen in love; her big sister must not spoil it – must not spoil anything. Besides, Robert Hanniford was not an entrepreneur with an eye to business.

She said, 'Tell me about Robert.'

Jannie needed no encouragement. As Ned said when they waved her goodbye on 4 January, 'I bet we know more about this Robert chap than he knows himself!'

Meanwhile, Christmas was a mixture of pain and pleasure. The three of them had difficulty in believing that last year Kate had presided over the kitchen and Mark had led the carol singers along Fore Street to the ancient parish church. They kept everything very low key, locking themselves away on New Year's Eve and emerging cautiously to welcome the New Year in with a dip long before the traditional swimmers arrived.

In the afternoon, when Jannie was supposed to be packing her case for the new term, Rory arrived with two large dust-bin liners full of Rosemary's clothes. Jannie was intrigued and spread them out on the big kitchen table. Rory was morose, sitting by the range, denouncing the New Year 'and all who live through her'.

'It won't be me,' he told Ned, who stood over him disapprovingly. 'You don't have to guard your womenfolk any longer, young man. I've had it. Up to here.' He put a hand on his head. 'Bloody house. Bloody pictures. Whoever would have thought Gerry Scaife would be . . . what do they call it . . . collectable? There's a stupid word if ever there was one.' He looked at Ned. 'I could do with a drink, lad. Rum, if you've got it. Whisky will do.'

'I'll make you a cup of tea.' Gussie looked warningly at Ned. 'Hot sweet tea, that's what you need.'

Rory stared up at her; she thought he looked like a blood-hound.

He said, 'I can't get away for a few weeks, Gus. But then . . . the world is my oyster! Let's have a couple of weeks with Zannah and then come with me to the Caribbean. It's another world. Speightstown first thing in the morning. The monkeys waking up, the mahogany trees looming out of the heat mist—'

'I've already booked a sleeper on the Riviera Express from Paris to Nice, Uncle. I'm staying with Aunt Rosemary over-night going and coming back. So I can take the clothes with me.'

His hangdog expression hardened. 'I told you she told me to chuck them into the sea. They're for you and . . .' He gestured towards Jannie, who was running a silk shawl through her fingers with some reverence.

'Jannie,' Gussie supplied in a dry voice. 'Now drink your tea and get along to the Sloop. I imagine that was the real reason for coming into St Ives.'

He was suddenly angry. 'You know very well I was bringing Ro's things across, miss! Christ-a-mighty, you sound and act just like her! Rosemary Briscoe and August Briscoe. Conde-scending bitches, both of you!'

Jannie looked up, startled.

Ned said steadily, 'That's enough. Don't say another word. Just leave.'

Rory switched his gaze, looking surprised, as if noticing Ned for the first time. There was a long moment of silence while the two men stared at each other. Rory was solidly massive compared with Ned; but he was in his seventies and Ned was twenty-eight.

Gussie held out a mug of tea. Rory blinked and looked

at it, took it from her and drank it down, though it must have been scaldingly hot. Then he lumbered to his feet and made for the door. Ned followed him, watched him cross the yard and go through the gate. It was late afternoon, almost dark. The lights from the Sloop were like a beacon and Rory walked towards them. Ned closed the gate and went back inside.

Jannie was twittering, 'Gorgeous clothes and high drama! What more could anyone ask for the close of Christmas!'

Ned grinned, glad they saw Rory as 'a character'. He said, 'A little less drama and a lot less of the mothball smell!'

Jannie laughed, holding yet another frock to her and prancing around the kitchen. Ned was thankful to hear Gussie's reluctant laugh. She went to the sink and swilled Rory's mug, then assembled more mugs and poured tea for the three of them. They sobered and sipped carefully, wondering how Rory had been able to drink his in one go.

'Dead from the neck up, if his diplomacy skills are anything to go by,' Ned said.

'Yes.' Gussie sighed deeply. 'But d'you know, I rather think our uncle Rory is still in love with our aunt Rosemary.'

'Hard Cheddar,' Ned scoffed. 'Rosemary is well out of that marriage. I take it she had a schoolgirl crush on him that died a very quick death.'

Gussie shook her head. 'I don't know. There were so many stories going around at the time, and Dad hated people gossiping about his sister so we never heard what really happened.' She sighed. 'I suppose I'll have to take the clothes but Ro is not going to be happy about it.'

Jannie started to fold them slowly and with appreciation.

'She was quite a dresser in her time, wasn't she?' Ned said.

'Still is,' Jannie replied. 'She goes for fabrics. Cashmere. Linen. Silk. Expensive stuff.'

'Clothes say a lot about their owners.' Ned held up a fox fur. 'Perhaps that's what it was all about – Rosemary was a big spender.'

'Rory was too. And now he has to sell up.' Gussie stood up, putting a decisive end to the conversation. 'Listen, I'm going to get down another suitcase and pack those things properly. Tomorrow we can load everything into the car ready for the off the next day.' She looked at Ned with raised brows. 'It's going to be rather odd for you, the two of us abandoning ship like this and leaving you on your own.'

Jannie turned and put her arms around her brother. 'Oh, Ned, will you be all right?'

'Idiots, the pair of you. Can't wait to have the place to myself. I'll tidy up so that we won't be able to find a thing when we reassemble at Easter. Then I'll batten down the hatches, switch everything off and take the Heathrow train with narry a worry in my haid!' He slid into an execrable Scottish accent and the girls laughed obediently. The urgency that had goaded each one of them into action was not so obvious now as it had been, but they all knew that it was still there.

They were still searching for something.

Ten

Gussie had forgotten so much about southern France, and the overnight train from Paris did nothing to reawaken any memories. Nice station on a January morning – barely eight o'clock – could have been anywhere in Western Europe; the sea that bordered the famous Cote d'Azur was far from blue; gunmetal grey suited it well. She changed trains here for a single coach 'stopper', storing her case on its wheels beneath a shelf holding a wicker basket of furious-looking hens and hoisting her backpack to the front before settling herself on a double seat away from the sea. The changeover after a long sleepless night had made her feel cold and slightly sick. She sat very still, eyes closed, until the train jolted into life. Then she opened them wide and fixed her gaze on the outside world while she stretched her whole face. It was a lesson taught by her mother when she suffered from car sickness on the long journey to see Grandma Briscoe in Bristol. How odd that she should recall it now when she was on her way to see Zannah.

She shivered and tried to concentrate on what was outside. Off-white hotels, palm trees. The resort was coming to life at eight o'clock on this grey January morning; there were even joggers. She cupped her hand to the window and peered ahead and then behind, and thought glumly that the quickly shifting glimpses of the town could have been of any tourist resort – Bournemouth, Brighton, Torquay . . . She hadn't slept, her head ached, and the coffee and croissant on the express train from Paris seemed a long time ago. She wished she had not come. Andrew Bellamy had long gone from St Ives and Ned was not leaving for California for another two weeks and intended to stay on a day-to-day basis only. But according to Uncle Rory, Andrew was returning for the sale of Trewyn House. She sat back and clutched her backpack to her. She felt as if she might be disintegrating.

A woman came swaying down the open carriage carrying a bulging shopping bag. She collapsed next to Gussie and turned smilingly to apologize for the bag, which was encroaching on to both their laps. Gussie caught a phrase here and there and gathered that the woman was visiting her daughter in Monaco and had brought her some provisions from their grocery shop. Somehow Gussie managed to smile back and said she was English. The woman immediately translated her own words.

'We run an old-fashioned – um – how you say *épicerie* . . . ?'

'Grocery shop?' Gussie supplied.

'Grocery shop. Solange will tell me she can get everything within a few metres of her apartment. But this is not so.' Gussie then heard about Solange and her ineffectual husband, who could not keep a job and seemed incapable of cooking a meal for his wife so that when she came in from work she had to bring provisions and cook them or, worse still, buy ready-cooked food. Gussie was reminded of her eight-year-old self when Zannah first left. She had thought she was looking after her father very well. How 'ineffectual' she must have been. And how marvellous when Kate and Ned had moved in. How absolutely marvellous.

The woman said, 'You have come from Paris on the express and you are tired. I will be silent.'

Gussie smiled her thanks. 'If I sleep will you wake me at Eze-sur-Mer?'

'*Ah, oui*. Certainly. Now close your eyes.'

Gussie never knew whether she slept or not. She was conscious of the train slowing down and the woman's voice in her ear, then she was gathering up her things and making for the end of the carriage. The woman was hanging out of the window to wave to her and Gussie stood still, waving back, breathing in proper memories at last as the little train swayed on to Monaco.

It was the scent. To smell oranges in midwinter was absurd, yet that was what she was smelling as she half closed her eyes and took a long breath. Oranges and something else. Lavender? Roses?

Behind her the sea – still not azure but no longer gunmetal grey – was already picking up sparks from the pale sunshine. She opened her eyes wide to take in the perception of colour. She remembered doing this as a child, unconsciously burning impressions into her head. Then when she was fifteen she had learned how to do it consciously. A friend of Zannah's had collected her from St Ives and taken the Plymouth ferry to Brittany, then driven down. It had been summer and the colours were vibrant. She had stored each one and was able to see them whenever she wished. They were not so vibrant now but there were flowers – here, there – everywhere. Cornwall prided itself on its early flowers but this was different. Enormous poppies were appearing, waving from a sheltering bush. Daffodils and tulips were blooming together, side by side. The glossy green and white of a camellia guarded the station gate. She noticed the bus was waiting for passengers; she was the only one. She trundled her case towards it.

Zannah had suggested coming to meet her in the car but Gussie had turned down the offer. She said she wanted to be able to take in the countryside from the local bus, and Zannah had agreed after very little persuasion. It was a long drive and would have meant her leaving 'GI', as she referred to her house at six in the morning. 'I know what you mean about absorbing the local atmosphere, darling.' Her voice had the same lilt it had had when she had complained about her husband's complete lack of interest in social occasions. 'And I want us to be able to talk properly when we get together. I'm such a hopeless driver I can't talk and drive at the same time!'

Gussie clambered on to the bus with help from the driver, found a seat and settled into it thankfully. They waited another half an hour for the next 'stopper' to arrive but there were still no other passengers and at last the bus roared into noisy life and they pulled away. Gussie did not mind the delay. It gave her time to gather up the pieces of herself that had seemed to be discarded on the long train journey here. She half closed her eyes and tried to absorb the shapes around the colours as if it were the next landscape project. Soak it up. Understand it.

When the bus jolted into life, she closed her eyes completely. It was two hours along the Middle Corniche until they reached the ancient farmhouse Zannah had called 'Glorious Isolation' – or latterly, GI. There was time to sleep again.

She dreamed of Jannie, beautiful Jannie, volatile Jannie. Jannie in love and suddenly centred. There she was as a very small girl, trudging up the hill to the railway station at Truro. And there she was again, walking down Fifth Avenue, suddenly sure of herself. *Centred.* Not quite the right word somehow . . . Gussie deliberately surfaced, still searching for a word that would describe the change in her sister. As she opened her eyes it came to her. Anchored. Jannie was anchored. It had started to happen in New York and continued at her school practice. Gussie frowned slightly; she hoped it was not too much to do with falling so blindly in love. She forced herself to smile at her trite thought and closed her eyes again, determined not to transfer her own ghastly experience to Jannie.

Andrew Bellamy would be at Trewyn House soon, bidding for the Scaife drawings that Rory had bought because conventional Rosemary hated them so much. What a strange relationship that marriage must have been. Gussie moved her head on to her backpack and settled more comfortably. Rory and Rosemary. She remembered a playground rhyme from twenty-five years ago. 'Change the name and not the letter, change for the worse and not the better.'

She woke when the bus jolted to a stop.

'*Nous arrivons.*' The driver shuffled out of his seat and took the handle of her case. She was still his only passenger. They were opposite what looked like lich-gates, very solid, a roofed archway above, but no coffin rest that she could see.

She joined the driver. 'Is this the local church?'

He did not understand but saw her total confusion. He said laboriously, 'The gates. The gates . . . glorious.'

Her eyes widened incredulously. 'The . . . the gates of glory?'

He shook his head, losing patience. 'You ask for Glorious Isolation.'

Gussie let her breath go in a puff of realization. 'Of course! I am so sorry.' She remembered it now; for goodness' sake, she had swung on those gates even though she'd been fifteen! She scrabbled in her backpack and tipped the driver far too generously, and he opened one of the gates wide and held it while she trundled her case past him. She smiled and said in farewell, 'Merci . . . you have opened wide the gates of glory!' She laughed, then stopped abruptly and wondered whether she was going mad. Was that what trauma really meant? Disintegration?

The wide path going upward in a gentle curve to the left was finished in loose gravel, which made wheeling her case hard work. It was sunk between banks starred with primroses and topped with a variety of trees. Silver birch already sprouting young green leaves vied with aspens quivering spasmodically in a slight breeze. Between the banks and the trees the driveway was like a tunnel and there was no view at all. Almost immediately she managed to get a stone in her shoe and with some relief she sat on the left bank, which gave her a sight of the road and the sound of the bus roaring onwards. No. She wasn't going to go mad; not yet, anyway. She took off her shoe and shook it vigorously and told herself the fresh air would soon rejuvenate her. She felt nauseous. And she still wanted to weep. She could almost hear Kate's voice saying, 'Come on, best foot forward. Sooner you get this next bit over, the better.' That's what she needed: Kate's sheer practicality. If she was going to stay at Zion Cottage and keep her father's reputation going, that's what she must do. Become Kate.

She got up, pulled the case towards her and discovered that the rickety wheels slotted into the small drainage gutter between gravel and bank so that it moved far more easily. And so did she. The gentle bend became steeper and she plodded around it and then stopped again. Perhaps a quarter of a mile ahead the trees stopped and the drive opened out into what looked like a car park. Beyond that was a very green apron of lawn and there was the farmhouse, apparently growing out of the ground, crowning the hill.

She stopped, delighted. The sun was shining directly on to it, lighting each small window brilliantly. It was immediately familiar, though much tidier than she remembered. The outhouses had been made into separate cottages, the field leading down to the woods was transformed into manicured lawn, the car park was home to a tractor, a four-wheel drive and several mopeds.

Gussie stopped again and leaned on her case to admire what Mark had always called her mother's 'retreat'. Both this and Glorious Isolation were absurd names because Zannah attracted visitors like flies. No doubt the cottages were full of them at this moment. She had seen its potential immediately the agent drove her up the muddy drive because although she loved having people with her she was certainly no hostess. The outhouses were her first project; the drive was her second – after her first visitor's car had to be extracted from the mud by a crane.

Remembering, Gussie suddenly felt she understood her mother at last. It was so easy to see; staring her in the face. Zannah had wanted to get away from her daughter. Twenty-four-hour responsibility for a child was too much for her. It had been ridiculous to think that she might be inveigled into becoming some kind of carer for Uncle Rory. Zannah was not – definitely not – a carer. Gussie joggled her backpack into position and started walking again. She wondered which of the cottages would be hers.

As she emerged from the trees and on to the enormous parking space, there came a scream from the house, a door was flung wide and an unmistakable voice yelled, 'Gus! My darling girl! You're here and I'm still making your bed and choosing what books you're going to read.' Zannah's equally unmistakable figure shot from the doorway like a bullet and hurtled down the long apron of manicured grass.

Gussie had wondered how she would greet her mother after a nine-year gap. She had agreed to visit for her twenty-first birthday and when she arrived, there had been a full-scale party taking place that evening; in fact it had already begun and Gussie could not even take a nap before changing into the skin-tight dress her mother had bought for her. 'You've got a good figure, Gussie. Show it!'

Now there was no time to plan a conventional peck on both cheeks, or even decide whether to stall her with an outstretched hand and a good shake. Zannah hurled herself over the gravel and almost took the two of them to the ground as she flung her arms around Gussie, gripped the backpack and rocked them all together while she sobbed, 'My God. I thought you wouldn't come. Rory said – you can't take any notice of that old idiot – but he said you'd come, and then he said you were in America! I wanted to see you so much, darling! So very much! I didn't know what to do. Mark gone – dreadful – dreadful. I thought I would fall to bits.'

She withdrew slightly. Her face was already streaked with tears, her dark eyes tragically enormous. Gussie had to believe she was sincere. Hadn't she herself thought she was disintegrating?

'Darling, I loved him – he was such a little bugger – I wanted him to get longer legs but apparently it all depends on the centre of gravity and he'd have had to put on about three stone. But he couldn't dance, you see, and that was when I started . . . Oh, never mind all that, Gus. You know

I loved him. I've never stopped loving him. It didn't matter to me that he was so bloody short and couldn't dance. He was the sexiest man I've ever met. We danced in the sea, you know. We loved doing that. Oh, Gussie . . .'

By this time she was clutching Gussie's arms and gradually slipping down towards the grass. Gussie held her up somehow.

'Come on, Zannah. Let's go into the house. People will wonder what on earth is the matter.'

'People? Oh, you mean the *gîtes*. Darling, I cancelled all the bookings when you said you were coming over. I don't want other people coming between you and me – that's what's happened all these years. We have to bond now, sweetie.'

She stopped speaking and drew a long shuddering breath. Then said, 'Rory said I had to be positive and I know he meant I had to remember all the good old times. But those times make me cry so I am trying to think that Mark and Kate have just stepped aside so that there is no one between you and me. I want you to stay with me always, Gus. I need you and you need me.'

Gussie drew back, disengaged one side of her backpack and bent down to remove another piece of gravel from her shoe. She had forgotten her mother's intensity and was shocked by it. She wanted to run. Run back to the family her father had made. She remembered him saying, 'Zannah pours a cup of tea as if it were the last act she will do on this earth and must be made into something splendid.' He had spoken with mock despair because he loved her for it.

Gussie felt a tug at her shoulder. Her mother pulled the backpack free and hoisted it around her own neck. She said in a perfectly normal voice, 'Come on, sweetie. You must be absolutely whacked. I've got tea and orange juice and the toaster awaits!' She held out her free arm and cried, '*Marchons, marchons!*' She was laughing. Gussie felt her trembling spirits rise. She stood up and took the handle of the case in one hand, Zannah's arm in the other and they trudged up the apron of greensward and into the house.

Much later she deliberately reminded herself of how marvellous the following weeks had been. She extracted it and looked at it carefully and saw the gradual renewal of their relationship as it had been when she was an eight-year-old and her mother had been beautiful and funny as well as unreliable and outrageous. She was still all those things, but the last two did not matter any longer, probably because Gussie herself was almost thirty-one and understood why her father had loved Zannah though he did not trust her; but, more importantly, why he had loved and trusted Kate.

The first two days they spent in the house. Icy winds blew from the top of the Alps and froze most of the early flowers. It froze Gussie, too. She must have got a bug from the lovely woman with the provisions from the *épicerie* because she started to shiver on her first night and by the next morning her temperature was high and her bones ached horribly. Zannah leaped to the occasion, kept her in bed, made a fire in the little grate in her room and brought up dainty meals. When she had taken away the tea things, she reappeared in some kind of medical uniform holding a copy of *What Katy Did*.

'Story time, darling! This is what mummies do and this one didn't do!' She laughed as she put more wood on the fire and then came to the bed to plump up Gussie's pillows. 'That's right, sweetie, rest your head on this lavender pillow. Just sip this. It's my favourite – sleeping pills dissolved in vodka. I want you to go to sleep halfway through a chapter. And wake up – better!'

Gussie was full of doubt. Sleeping pills in vodka? Zannah in a nurse's uniform – why had she got that so near to hand? But the sheer luxury of being looked after was too much, and Gus sipped and felt her aching muscles relax. She let Zannah brush her hair and replait it loosely, comfortably. And then she listened to the story of the little American girl who had lost her mother and tried to take her place for the rest of the family. She remembered now that on the few occasions when Zannah had decided to become a caring mother, she had always read extracts from *What Katy Did*.

The next afternoon Zannah let her come downstairs and sit by the enormous open grate. The chaise longue was pulled sideways on to it so that Gussie had a view over the trees to the sloping vineyards beyond. Zannah told her about renting them to a neighbouring farmer so that she could concentrate on her work.

'Actually, darling, I was terribly lucky there. I don't know how good I am really. I just get into my darling daddy's shoes and do what he would do. Big canvases – you must see my studio some time – plenty of scaffolding. I can still run the length of the staging with a paste brush in one hand and a bucket of paint in the other.' She chuckled. 'I am not an artist with a palette, Gus! Nor a smock!'

Gussie asked idly, 'What do you wear? Jeans and a T-shirt?'

'You must be joking, honey! I work in the nude. Hasn't that got into British mag land yet?'

'Mag land?'

'The society magazines, as they used to be called. I have goals. The society magazines are one. Dealers are another.' She cupped Gussie's face. 'Don't look shocked, darling. Of course I still sleep around. It doesn't mean a lot. Not really.' She looked suddenly sad. 'I live in the modern world, Gus. Self-promotion is everything. I started making enquiries about my father's work a long time ago using a fake name. I posed as a collector. I actually bought several of Daddy's paintings – as they were mine anyway it was no skin off my nose. But I reinvented his reputation. His work would have died by now. I have made him a "must-have" for corporations, municipal buildings. And people who live in mansions and palaces and have a lot of wall space!' She laughed again, patted Gussie's cheek and went to the fire. 'And then Grace Elphinstone died. What do you think of that for a pseudonym? Grace Elphinstone.' She rolled it around her tongue. 'It was a pity she had to go, but she served her purpose well. How could she have been a serious art collector with any other name? Anyway, she disappeared. And suddenly Zannah Scaife, who painted after her father, surfaced in France, of all places. And people came to see her. Some of them just stayed to watch her painting!' She looked over her shoulder mischievously. 'I wonder why that was, Gus Briscoe? Well may you look disapproving now!'

It was no good, Gussie had to laugh. Zannah was delighted.

'At last! You have always had a solemn streak, my darling, but I was starting to wonder whether that dreadful business in New York had eliminated any trace of Scaife!' And then she too threw back her head and laughed helplessly. 'That was an almost-poem, Gus! A trace of Scaife!'

When they had sobered, Gussie said, 'You succeeded in relaunching Grampa's work. I think Uncle Rory will do well out of his collection.'

'Oh, Rory. He came over here in such a state.'

'He said the same about you, actually.' Gus glanced down

at her mother, who was sprawled elegantly on the hearth rug. The roots of her hair were grey. Unexpectedly Gussie felt a clutch at her heart.

'Well, he was right there. I couldn't really believe in a world that did not contain Mark. I needed to see you, Gus. You are living confirmation that he was here.' She rolled round so that she could see her daughter. 'Thank you for coming over. I couldn't face St Ives again, darling. That's where it all happened. When my mother died having me, I became immediately an almost-daughter. Then I saw Mark and loved him and became an almost-wife. I had you and I was an almost-mother.' She saw Gussie's expression and made a dismissive gesture. 'It's better than nothing, my darling. Don't worry about it. I have had such fun – Mark was such fun. When we danced underwater it was . . . perfect. Nothing "almost" about that.' She reached up and took Gussie's hand. 'Since then I've been an almost-wine grower and now an almost-painter! That's the best of all because it's working so well.' She started to laugh as she shook Gussie's hand gently. 'You see, I am the complete and perfect confidence trickster! That's why I can do all these things – almost – so bloody well!' She waited until Gussie managed a laugh, then she released her and scrambled to her feet to put another log on the fire. 'I created a market, Gus. And then filled it.' She turned, glinting a smile. 'Nothing "almost" about that, is there?'

'Oh, Zannah . . .' Gussie felt helpless. 'I remember . . . I remember . . .'

'Go on. Say it. Just say it, darling. It might hurt but I need you to be honest.'

'I remember when you were around, it was like the sun coming out.'

Zannah was holding the high mantelpiece and looking

into the fire. She was silent. When she turned she was smiling much too brightly.

'That is the best, most wonderful thing anyone has ever said to me, darling.'

Her mascara was only slightly smudged. Gussie was certain – almost certain – that her mother was completely sincere.

Another day, and Gussie knew she was back to full health. It was just as well because Zannah was bored with being a nurse. She brought up croissants and coffee as usual and then hovered uncertainly by the door.

'Is it worth lighting a fire in here, sweetie? You can come down to the kitchen and sit by the range, can't you? Don't be too long because the bloody thing goes out if you don't keep feeding it with wood.'

'I feel fine. I'll be down when I've finished this.'

'Take it easy. I'll see you at lunchtime. I've got about a hundred tins of wonderful game soup in the larder. We could have some of it. What d'you think?'

'Sounds great. Where will you be?'

'Studio. I'm painting the ravine. Very like Daddy – your grandfather. The water splitting the land. Terribly sexual.' She was already letting the door close behind her. 'I've already got a buyer – he wants to see how it's going.'

Gussie stared at the door. This was how it was, of course. Zannah's attention span was less than an eight-year-old's.

The coffee was delicious, the croissants just warm enough and there was honey too. Gussie relished it all, smiling slightly. What a blessing in disguise her cold had been. Somehow or other mother and daughter had bridged an enormous gap. Zannah had not changed, so Gussie knew she must have done. Well, obviously she had, fifteen years old and still swinging on the lich-gate . . . was it really all that time ago – half her life ago? Her father would have pressed for another visit during her agricultural course, surely? And she had been very much in touch with Zannah during the 'vineyard days' – didn't she visit then? She frowned, licking her finger and gathering up the flaky crumbs from her plate. Of course. It was then that she had met Andrew. Andrew had changed her. Andrew had changed everything. She had retreated into herself, gone back to smaller projects. Run to Zion Cottage whenever she could.

She squeezed her eyes shut, physically refusing to let those memories run on. She had always intended to tell Mark and Kate; make it sound absurd and melodramatic. And now she couldn't.

She cleaned the plate one last time, licked her finger and got up.

She had no idea where Zannah's studio was – in fact, she knew very little about the layout of the farmhouse. Certainly the kitchen, next to the big living room where she had stayed most of yesterday, was the warmest spot at the moment. The range was very like the traditional Cornish variety, and she stoked it generously then explored some of the cupboards and the walk-in larder next to the window. Zannah had exaggerated about the soups, of course, but there were at least two dozen tins there; Gussie was amused to see they were all from a well-known British firm. She could imagine her mother entertaining a few carefully chosen guests with a big tureen of 'local game' soup, 'home-made' bread and a truckle of help-yourself cheese. And why not? It was good food, after all, made special by Zannah's sense of the romantic. Gussie found the utility area, a besom broom behind the door. She began to sweep the enormous flagstones in the kitchen, wash the surfaces, put some fruit in a bowl and place it in the centre of the table . . . She was enjoying herself. The sun came through the small windows and lit the room. There were copper pans hanging from one of the beams and they glowed orange. It was beautiful.

An hour later she had laid the table with thick pottery soup bowls and enormous heavy plates, fed the stove again, discovered the percolator and was sniffing suspiciously at a pitcher of milk in the larder. Satisfied, she went in search of her mother.

There was a big porch over the outside door full of boots, raincoats, fishermen's gear, cricket bats, hats of all descriptions and other various muddles. She stood outside and gazed around her. The apron of grass and the parked cars and mopeds were to her left. In front, the land dropped quickly into woods and beyond that must be the sea. Or the vineyards? There was a barn on her right. That had to be the studio; it was high enough to accommodate the enormous work Zannah was trying to do; besides which, a tinny sound was coming from it. Edith Piaf telling someone that she had no regrets. It could have been written for Zannah.

Smiling wryly, Gus walked across to the postern set in the enormous double doors at the front of the barn. She opened a crack and called, 'It's me. Gussie.' Then went in.

The scaffolding was set up along the left-hand side of the building, which appeared to be almost as big as the nave of Truro Cathedral. A narrow walkway of planks was laid near the top, and at various intervals Zannah had hooked a paint pot over the uprights, each with its own brush protruding. She was standing in the middle of the construction, her arm fully extended as she brought a swathe of black paint from the top edge of the canvas to her feet.

'Can't stop in mid-flow, sweetie!' she called. 'Give me a sec.'

The brush swept upwards and then down again. She straightened and put a hand in the small of her back. 'Wow! That's the seaward edge of the ravine. A sheer drop. I had to go with it.' She leaned on one of the uprights and looked down. 'What are you grinning at? It's meant to be a work of art and works of art must not provoke a grin!'

'I'm grinning because you're fully clothed! Daddy would have known instantly that you were fibbing when you told me you painted in the nude!'

'Gus! It's winter, for God's sake! And I paint like that for others who need to be impressed, and there are no others around! Thank the Lord I don't have to impress you with my obvious genius.' She was laughing, hanging on to the scaffolding pole, putting the paintbrush back in the pot, wiping her hands. She was neat-fingered, methodical. She wore an old shirt over her jeans and sweater, and Gussie could not see one spot of paint on it.

'I've made coffee – d'you want some?'

'I always have a break at this time – how did you know?' She was clambering down now. She could have been sixteen rather than sixty.

Gussie looked innocent. 'What time is that?'

Zannah looked up, caught her eye and laughed. 'Obviously it's coffee time! You are definitely better, aren't you?'

'I often have these sort of colds. Twenty-four hours at the most.' Zannah hooked her hand through Gussie's arm and they went through the postern sideways. 'Matter of fact, I was just getting over one of them when the Twin Towers went down. Lying on the sofa – you know – in the parlour. Ned and Jannie had gone to Truro for the autumn sales and heard people talking about it on the train and came straight back.' She held her mother's hand tightly into her side. 'I thought it might be something to do with my cold – delirium or even a terrible dream. Then they switched on the television and there it was.'

Zannah made a sound but said nothing. She brought her other hand round and held on Gussie's arm with both hands.

'It was like a nightmare. Did I tell you that Jannie actually saw them jump?'

Zannah cleared her throat. 'No.'

'Sorry. Of course not. This is the first time we've spoken . . .' she tried to laugh, '. . . and I have to get one of my colds!'

'Perhaps . . . it might have been good – then – to have a cold. Helped you to talk it through. You are always so buttoned up, Gus. This is the first time you have mentioned the – the disaster.'

'Nine Eleven. They're calling it Nine Eleven over there.'

'I know, darling. I know.' They went into the kitchen and the warmth wrapped them like a comfort blanket. Zannah put Gussie into a chair and hooked another to her with her foot then sat in it, still entwined into Gussie's arm.

'Did Jannie really see Mark?'

'She saw them both. They jumped together. She identified Dad because he had already thrown out his legs.'

'Oh dear God . . .'

'I know. We couldn't believe it – we refused to believe it – until then. And then we knew. We might have pretended once or twice but really, we knew.'

Zannah put her forehead on Gussie's shoulder and pressed hard. Gussie waited for what seemed like ages, then she said, 'Come on, Zannah. Let me pour the coffee. I can hear it perking away like mad.'

Zannah lifted her head. She looked every bit her sixty years now; her face was ravaged. She whispered, 'I know this sounds horribly dramatic, but, darling, I would have given everything to be by his side then. Kate was . . . lucky.'

Gussie took the shoulders in her hands, registering how thin they were. She said, 'We know. All of us know that. Dad and Mum knew. They didn't sound panicky, just sort of regretful, but that was for us, not for themselves.'

Zannah dropped her gaze, and the tears continued to flow. She whispered, 'They phoned you? You should have told me that, Gus. You really should have told me that.'

'We didn't know ourselves until we got over there. Mack – Mr McKinnon, who is the new chairman of the Trustees – he was in hospital at the time, but his wife was at home when the phone went. She let it run so that the message was recorded. They had copies made and gave us one when we were there.'

Zannah's head went down between Gussie's hands. She sobbed. Gussie took her in her arms and held her close. She rocked gently.

'I've brought a copy with me, darling. You can listen if you like. It's not really personal. It might help you. It's helped us because it's so . . . ordinary. We wondered if we should hear screaming – explosions, perhaps. Nothing like that. As Ned said, he half expected his mother to tell us that there's a casserole in the freezer for our supper.'

Very gradually Zannah's sobs hiccuped into long trembling breaths. At last she was still. She whispered into Gussie's sweater. Gussie only just heard it.

'You really loved her, Gus. Didn't you?'

'Yes.' Gussie's voice was firm; there must never be any doubt about that. 'You'll understand why when you listen to the tape.'

'That . . . that would be . . . nice.'

Gussie lifted her mother and smiled. 'Yes. It would be nice.

Now dry your eyes and let's drink coffee and discuss what I can get for tonight's meal. You can go on with your painting for the important client. And I can cook dinner.'

She propped Zannah into the back of the chair and stood up, and Zannah watched her wonderingly as she poured coffee into the pottery mugs and put them on the table. Gussie caught her eye and smiled.

'You know, I feel better for talking about it. Didn't think I'd ever say that!'

Zannah got up slowly and pushed the two chairs forward. She nodded and sat down again. She said, 'Oh, Gus . . .'

'I know. It's because of the cold. And yes, we did talk about it before – the night after it happened, actually. After that cold.' She handed a mug to her mother and picked up her own. 'And since we're being so frank, why are you calling me Gus? You know I'm always Gussie.'

Zannah sighed deeply, recognizing the need to be 'ordinary'. 'You're not Gussie any longer, darling. Gussie was a little girl. One of three children. Gus is the head of that family now. Suits you better.'

'That makes me sound out there on my own. And I'm not. There's three in our particular boat.' She grinned at Zannah. 'There's room for a fourth if you want to join us.'

It was too much to expect of Zannah. She bumped her coffee mug down so that half the contents bounced out. Then she lifted her head to the ancient beamed ceiling and howled like a dog.

Gus sighed. 'Oh, Ma . . . for goodness' sake.' At which point Zannah redoubled her efforts and Gussie enfolded her just as she had always enfolded Jannie.

119

Eleven

Some time during the following two weeks, it became obvious to both women that their roles had reversed. Gussie was now the mother, Zannah the child. Gussie simply could not imagine calling her mother anything but Zannah and she accepted that she herself was no longer 'Gussie'. Jannie had been right: Gus had a more authoritative ring to it. Zannah had used it from the moment she arrived, as if she, too, recognized the changeover.

So it was Gus who prepared meals and Zannah who played with her paint pots in the barn, yet was careful not to bring any mess into the pristine house. And when Zannah got excited about her 'dealer-man', Gus smiled indulgently and told her not to count her chickens until they were well and truly hatched.

They were easy roles for both of them; Zannah, in spite of wanting her glorious isolation, had never been really alone at the farmhouse. There were the paying guests in the *gîtes*, of course, and often there were 'boyfriends' who stayed in the house and advised her about her work and wanted to see the paintings her father had left her. Gus was under no illusion about them. Zannah confessed to what she called 'occasional flings'.

'Keeps me on my toes, sweetie,' she said as she swirled her hair into a ridiculous minaret.

Gus shook her head resignedly. Zannah was so like a schoolgirl; no wonder people came again and again to stay in the small converted cottages and help her out with chores. She rewarded them by sharing her vivacity, her sheer *joie de vivre*.

In the evenings they would talk. Gussie lit the fire in the living room during the afternoon and laid a kitchen trolley with tea things. Zannah would lie on the rug in front of the flames and talk about the nineteen sixties when she had come home from boarding school for good and 'discovered' Mark. She spoke often of their swimming escapades. 'We were in the water oftener than on dry land.'

She tilted her head so that she could look at her daughter upside down. 'I was the one who pushed the wheelchair off the end of Smeaton's Pier at high tide. Grandma Briscoe never forgave me. I told her that he had asked me to do it. You've heard all about it, I expect.'

Gussie had, and still could not repress the shudder of sheer terror each time she heard it.

'Sweetie pie! It wasn't like that – I knew he'd be all right but I dived in anyway and we swam into the harbour together and then went under the arches and laughed our heads off!' She sighed, remembering things she could not tell her daughter. Then she added, 'The bloody chair was all right too. Just sat in the sand until low tide, then Grandma Briscoe came and pulled it out.'

It was no good, Gus had to put aside her very personal nightmare and chuckle. She could imagine her grandmother's pregnant silence during all this hullabaloo. And Zannah, encouraged by the chuckle, went on to tell of other things and other men. Men who could dance.

Suddenly she was still, staring into the fire, eyes dark and enormous. For some reason, Gussie put her hand on the thin shoulder by her knees and squeezed gently. Still, Zannah was silent and the slice of profile that was visible to Gussie was outlined by a tear.

'Can you tell me?' Gussie asked.

'I just remembered what he said once. He said . . . he said . . . oh God, he said to me, "I can die for you, Zannah, but I cannot dance." He'd had his tin legs only five minutes. He always said if he'd had flesh-and-blood legs he still wouldn't be able to dance because he had no sense of rhythm – and that was bloody true, Gus! So why did he say that? Because he wanted me never ever to forget him! He wanted me to feel guilty for the rest of my bloody life!' She wrenched herself into a sitting position and put both hands to her face and wailed the last words.

Gussie slid off the chair and sat cross-legged next to her mother. She waited for the storm to pass and then said in her most sensible voice, 'But he didn't want you to be unhappy, darling, did he?'

'Didn't he? Are you sure of that?'

'I am indeed.'

'He found Kate bloody Gould soon enough, didn't he? *He* was all right, Jack! And so was she. I might have . . . looked for consolation. But I didn't get myself pregnant within a year of our split!'

'Zannah, why are you saying these things when they – Mark and Kate – aren't able to put their side?'

She was silent for a while and then said sullenly, 'Well, you're going to do it for them, I assume.'

'I think that's a presumption rather than an assumption. I can't speak for them either. But I do know one thing: we are sitting here warm and well fed, talking like real friends, and I can't speak for you, but I am happy. I never thought I would say that so soon after losing them, but I can say it.'

Zannah twisted forward and grabbed Gussie into her arms. 'Oh, my darling girl! I am too. And I never thought that either of us would say that.' She hugged her daughter and then sat back and crossed her legs too.

'And another thing.' Zannah was trying to sound like Gussie, trying *not* to sound like a drama queen. 'I'm not insanely jealous of Kate. OK, she got Mark, but I got my daughter back. Not a bad deal.'

Gussie looked round at her with a resigned grin. 'You really are a hopeless case, Zannah Scaife. You always manage either to say the wrong thing or to say the right thing in the wrong way.'

But Zannah was looking out of the window, her attention span exhausted. 'Guess what. It's snowing.'

By suppertime there was a millimetre of snow on the grass apron. Gussie tugged the heavy table in front of the range and set the chairs so that they both had the heat at their backs. She put the Lancashire hotpot into the side oven and tore a loaf into pieces. A peculiar muffled tapping came at the window and there was Zannah in ice-caked mittens and Scandinavian hat, beckoning frantically. Gussie ran to the porch.

'Come on, quickly!' Zannah was already running towards the apron where the snow was transparent and the grass pushing through it very obviously. 'This isn't going to last and we have to make a snowman!'

'Supper's ready—'

'It will wait half an hour, for Pete's sake! Get some wellies on – gloves in the box with the cricket bats – quick!' She had made a football-sized snowball and started to roll it into something torso-big. Gussie watched her for all of three seconds and then turned and grabbed her coat. 'Go with the flow . . .' she muttered as she searched among the cricket bats without success, then found gloves in a drawer neatly arranged with scarves and hats.

By the time she had rolled enough snow into a suitable head shape and placed it on top of the melting torso she was hot enough to discard the hat and scarf. Zannah disappeared into the porch and emerged holding a Tyrolean trilby, feather and all. She put it on the bald snow-head, panting with helpless laughter as she did so. And then they skipped around 'our very own sculpture' and trailed back in, dripping melted snow in every corner of the porch, leaving sopping wet gloves on the radiator and padding into the kitchen and as close to the range as they could get without burning themselves.

Gussie sneezed and Zannah was on instant alert.

'I shouldn't have let you . . . just after that wretched cold.'

'You "let me", did you? I could have sworn you *ordered* me out into that freezing weather just so that you could succumb to your intense desire for an instant sculpture!'

Zannah pretended to be beaten. 'You should've been a lawyer.'

'I thought of it, but I read up about the College of Agriculture and that was that.'

'Did you have lots of boyfriends and go to dances?'

'I suppose I did, but nothing serious until . . . later.' She avoided her mother's avid look and went on, 'Zannah, play some music while I get out the plates and the hotpot.'

She was surprised when Zannah went obediently to the

stack of CDs in the corner and fiddled with switches. An Ivor Novello song surged poignantly across the farmhouse kitchen. Gussie wrapped the cast-iron pot in a tea towel and put it on the table. Why on earth had she asked for music – to stop her mother asking more questions? She might have guessed that all her CDs would be about moonlight and music and romance.

Zannah waltzed slowly back and held out her arms. 'Will you have this dance with me? Just while the plates cool off a little.'

Gussie put down the tea towel and stared at her mother. She was still beautiful, still vibrant. Her daughter was still proud of her.

'It is my pleasure.' She enfolded the thin shoulders into a long arm and they pirouetted slowly around the table. Zannah tilted her head to the ceiling and closed her eyes. Gussie saw the lines; they were deep enough to throw their own shadows. Above them, following the hairline, was another line: a scar. She felt suddenly awkward.

She said, 'I cannot believe this is happening.'

Her mother smiled but did not open her eyes. 'Give in to it, Gus.'

'Well . . . that's what I'm doing. That's what I mean. How did we get to this place, this time? We've been strangers since I was eight years old and after two weeks together, we're dancing in the snow.'

Zannah opened her eyes at that. 'Not quite, darling.' She chuckled. 'That's the sort of thing I say. You see? We're not strangers at all. We share the same genes. Go with the flow.'

They were the words Gussie had used to herself in the porch; she could have smiled and gone with it. But she said, 'You've had a face-lift, haven't you?'

Zannah kept her eyes closed. '*Naturellement,*' she said with a Birmingham accent, then shook her head slightly. 'All these questions! Just live for this moment, darling! How are you feeling – at this precise moment?'

'Embarrassed.'

The eyes flew open. 'What rubbish! Embarrassed for-sooth!' But she stopped dancing and went to the table. 'Come on, let's eat. I'm surprised you're not worrying about the food getting cold.' Her particular moment had gone. Gussie felt as if she had slapped her mother – or child – and spoiled things for ever. But that was ridiculous.

She said weakly, 'I should have left it in the side oven.' She unwrapped the hotpot and took off the lid. It was, of course, red hot. She ladled out two plates of the lamb and vegetables and sat down with a bump.

Zannah said, 'I'm not really hungry. Think I'll have an early night.'

'Sit down. Eat.' She looked across at the stubborn, set face. 'Please, Zannah. I can't help being how I am. At least I was honest.'

Zannah stayed where she was and after a few moments picked up her fork and started to eat. Gussie did the same, then took a torn piece of bread and pushed the basket side-ways to her mother. Zannah smiled wryly and helped herself.

She said, 'Everyone has them here, darling. Face-lifts, I mean. And the sort of people I need to impress don't need to see an aged woman.' She let the smile dissolve into a giggle and looked at her daughter for a response.

Gussie obliged briefly. Then she said, 'Usually face-lifts tend to lift the face.'

Zannah frowned. 'What do you mean?'

'Your face has not been lifted, darling. You have a tiny line of a scar, yes. But your face is . . . your face. Beautiful because of that.'

'Well, I did not want to look sort of set in stone. You know how some people do not dare smile – probably cannot smile!' Another laugh. 'I told them to go easy on the lift!'

Gussie nodded slowly, wanting to be reassured. She replenished their plates. 'Eat up. You are much too thin. And don't tell me that you have to be thin for your impressionable contacts. It's not how you have to be for your anxious daughter!'

Zannah was back to herself; she looked at the full plate with dismay. 'I can't afford to be overweight, Gus! How would I get up on that scaffolding?'

Gussie actually fed her mother as her mother had once fed her. She loaded a spoon and pretended it was a train. 'Into the tunnel, choo-choo.' She was definitely embarrassed then but Zannah laughed inordinately even as she swung her head away.

The snow had gone by the morning and throughout the week the weather gathered itself together for an early heat-wave. Gussie swept and polished and hung out the laundry, shopped in the village and cooked meals. Zannah worked all the daylight hours and on the Sunday announced that 'the end is nigh'.

'I'm going to finish it tomorrow, which means we'll have a whole week together before the money-man arrives. If this weather holds, sweetie, we'll take a picnic to the ravine and you can see for yourself why I wanted to do a Scaife job on it. Quite spectacular, not unlike bits of Cornwall. Actually, I think I've got it, too. Daddy's work was always somehow sad. The sea gradually, insidiously invading the land. This makes you angry. It's a slash, a rape, a statement of dominance.'

Gussie had seen the painting every day since her cold had passed and did not recognize its dominance. Her chief reaction had been bewilderment.

She said, 'It will be good to see you at ground level for my last week.'

'Darling, d'you have to go? I know you will be embarrassed – oh that word! – at my antics with Broomfield.' She rolled her eyes. 'Louis Broomfield. Can you imagine that being a real name? But he'll only be here two or three days. Then we could have another lovely week before the *gîtes* begin.'

'I've reserved a seat, Zannah. You know that. And I'll be back in the summer. I'll fly to Nice and hire a car.'

'I'll meet you, darling. We can have a couple of nights in Nice, if you like.'

'That would be marvellous.'

That evening when she took a mug of tea to the studio, her mother was cleaning brushes. She was naked, her body covered in daubs of black and purple paint. She laughed and passed Gussie a hammer.

'Make sure the lids are hammered on, would you, sweetie? And don't look so shocked. I wanted you to see what the visitors see!'

She was so thin yet not emaciated. She looked like a child.

They took a picnic to the ravine. Gussie carried it in her backpack: bread, cheese, olives and a slab of Cadbury's dark chocolate she had brought with her because one of her childhood memories was of Zannah eating it avidly for 'instant energy'.

Gussie's last week had seen the weather rocket into spring.

She knew it was the same at home because she had spoken to Rory the night before. His sale had gone through and he was staying at the Sloop and revelling in the sunshine. 'If this is climate change, then bring it on!' he'd roared down the phone. Unexpectedly, she had felt depressed. The four weeks with her mother had established a routine that suited her very well. She had expected a hectic round of social 'occasions', but because of Zannah's work this had not happened. And now, as they started up a steep track apparently carved through a meadow of flowers, she wondered whether she was returning to the seesaw of grief that seemed now to be a way of life at Zion Cottage. And she would be on her own for two weeks at least because Ned was in California and had an open ticket back home, and Jannie was . . . in love.

'We'll stop here for five minutes. Have a breather,' Zannah called over her shoulder. She pulled herself up and around a large boulder and leaned on her arm. 'You can see Nice from here.' She held out a hand for Gussie and hauled her alongside. 'I meant to take you shopping there, sweetie. Buy you some designer clothes. All the maternal things I've never done!'

'I don't need any more clothes, Zannah.' Gussie was panting, marvelling that her mother was not. 'Do need a drink, and we haven't got anything.'

'Yes we have. There are springs popping out of the ground everywhere. And I've got a couple of beakers . . . hang on.' She fished a plastic mug from her pocket and scrambled to the other side of the rock. Gussie was suddenly conscious of the sound of water. She thought of all that melting snow on the Alps above them and glanced upwards nervously. Then Zannah was back with two full mugs of spring water.

Gussie lowered herself to the ground, leaned against her backpack and drank. The water was ice cold and tingled deliciously.

'Better than wine?' Zannah asked. Gussie nodded. Zannah went on, 'Can you hear the water? That's the Brussac carving its way through the living rock. It starts – is born – in the High Corniche and by the time it reaches the Rhône it has calmed down, but it has put its heart and soul into getting there. And we're going to watch all that effort and energy and we're going to take some of it with us.' Zannah was aglow with enthusiasm. She stood up, helped Gussie to scramble to her feet and rebalance the backpack, and forged on, bent almost double on the slope, which became steeper with each step.

Gussie began to feel strange, as if her head were whirling with doubts and unidentifiable fears. She wasn't afraid of heights – she had dived and jumped from promontories all over Cornwall – yet the sudden realization that she was about to see the original of her mother's huge painting in the converted barn was terrifying. Her breathing became laboured and by the time Zannah stopped again, she was almost sobbing.

They were on a plateau that led on the left to another meadow, and on the right to what must be the lip of the gorge. For some reason the noise was less here. Zannah helped Gussie off with the backpack, unwound a small groundsheet from beneath her jacket and spread it out, weighting it down with the pack.

'This is where we'll eat,' she announced. 'But first we must sit and have another drink and then we'll go to the edge and look over.' She was already moving into the meadow, crouching by a runnel, filling the beakers again. Gussie collapsed on to the groundsheet and put her elbows on to crooked knees to rest her head. She told herself that she must be all right because her mother had noticed nothing. She straightened her back and took the overflowing beaker, sipped and felt instantly better. What a fuss she was making; there was nothing wrong. The climb had tired her, that was all. Perhaps they were high enough for the air to be thinner . . .

'I know how you're feeling, sweetie,' Zannah said. 'It's a bit like having one drink too many, isn't it? An exhilaration that exceeds all exhilarations!' She lifted her beaker. 'The consummation of water and land. The ultimate celebration. Here's to Nature's very own wedding, Gus!'

Gussie sipped again and felt strength returning to her legs; she had not realized that she was trembling inside until it stilled. She smiled at her mother and lifted her beaker high.

After a while they scrambled up and went towards the sound of the water. The land folded into a lip making a natural barrier, which masked the sheer drop and offered the perfect viewing point. Zannah pulled Gussie towards it, grinning in the face of the sudden explosion of sound. She gestured, then put her own arms on the lip and looked over. Hesitantly Gussie did the same. For a second she understood completely how her mother felt about this place; understood the beauty and the power of it. The torrent was almost a waterfall; the land reared up to their right in cliffs; the cleft made in the cliff over thousands of years spouted the water outwards so that it appeared to leap with sheer exuberance before it found the land again and rushed beneath them and then out of sight.

Gussie registered it, looked down and saw the drop,

remembered the sea beyond Clodgy, felt the air as she rushed downwards; a terrible nausea rose inside as she slid down the bank and into semi-consciousness. She felt her mother's arms around her, tipping her forwards. She was violently, horribly sick.

Zannah said matter-of-factly, 'I think you had better tell me all about it, hadn't you?'

They were somehow back at their picnic spot, the roar of water was reduced to bearable levels and Gussie was chewing a piece of bread and feeling stronger by the minute. She had tried to apologize, told her mother she felt a perfect fool, but she had been only too happy to lie back, breathe the air, drink the water and now eat some food.

'I wondered whether it was something to do with being so high up—'

'Come on, Gus. You know very well you've got to be three times as high as this before it becomes serious. Are you sure you're not sickening for something?'

'Quite sure.' Gussie took some cheese from the large plastic box. 'This is good. Plain. Wholesome.'

'Why are you so sure? Do you often faint like that? I mean, you live by the sea, for goodness' sake. You were brought up as a rock climber. Don't you remember how we used to jump off that rock just west of Five Points?'

Gussie continued to savour the cheese. Then, in the face of her mother's waiting silence, she said, 'As a matter of fact, that early training you gave me probably saved my life. I'd forgotten about it. We had a lot of fun, didn't we?'

Zannah smiled delightedly. 'I wasn't all bad then?'

'No.' Gussie had no answering smile. 'That's what made it so . . . peculiar . . . when you left. Mind you, for ages I thought you'd come back. And I was not sure that would be a good thing.'

Why was she talking like this? She wanted to eat her cheese, close her eyes, block everything inside her head.

Zannah's smile went too. 'Why? You were happier without me?'

'Daddy was. He didn't enjoy the rows like you did.'

'Didn't they ever have rows? Him and Kate?'

'No. Sorry, but they were perfect together.' She should not say that; it was hurtful, deliberately hurtful. Her mother was silent for a long time. When she spoke at last her voice was different. Bitter?

'This is the truth game, is it? So might I point out that they felt bound to get married because she was pregnant?'

Gussie had to go on. 'If it's the truth game, then you know Daddy would not have allowed that to happen. They were in love, Zannah. You have to believe it.'

Zannah was silent for so long, Gussie began to regret the whole thing. She said tentatively, 'I was very cautious about Kate at first but as time went on – especially when Jannie arrived – I grew to love her. I really loved her, Zannah. I still loved you but I loved her too. Can you get your head round that?'

Zannah almost barked a laugh. 'Not really, I suppose. I've always thought it was a marriage of convenience – he needed a live-in carer and she needed a family background for the boy—'

'Edward. We call him Ned.'

'That's it. Ned. I remember him. You looked after him now and then.'

'I taught him what you had taught me. Rock climbing, pool fishing, mussel picking.'

'Jumping off cliffs into the sea?'

'Nothing dangerous.' Gussie spoke quickly and Zannah looked up, suddenly aware.

'A-a-agh.' She stared at her daughter with narrowed eyes. 'Ned jumped. Hurt himself? Kate was furious; Mark, too, after losing his own legs. There was a row. What happened? Did you run away?'

'I just told you. I did not show Ned that special jump. He hasn't got a head for heights. I'd never have done that.'

'Something to do with that jump. And you're not going to tell me about it.'

'I've forgotten all about it and—'

'No, you haven't forgotten. It would help you, Gus. It's something to do with our jump. Something to do with me.'

'Oh, for goodness' sake. You had been gone nearly twenty years!'

'So. You were . . . twenty-six? Twenty-five? Your father told me you were engaged then and the man was a rotter; that you were back home for a while getting over it. Only you didn't. Obviously, you didn't.'

'I *did*! That was the point! I *had* forgotten and then your painting reminded me of some of Grampa's stuff in the Scaife studio . . . and now—' She gestured behind her. There were tears pricking her eyes. 'This!'

'He disapproved. He was a tight-arse, for God's sake, not worth tuppence if he couldn't appreciate my father's work! Couldn't you see that?'

Gussie was openly crying now. 'It wasn't like that!' She was nearly shouting. 'I was pregnant and he wanted me to have an abortion and I didn't, and he was so angry and said I was ruining his life, and I told him he could walk away and never see me again and no one would know who the father was, and he pushed me off the cliff. He tried to kill me, Zannah! And I thought he had, but of course, in spite of the twenty years I remembered the overhang was concealing that cave and I swam into it and clambered up and away from the waves, and when the tide went out I climbed back up.' She looked at her mother piteously. 'But I lost the baby, Zannah. I lost it there. In the cave. No one knows about it. He killed my baby.'

Zannah stared, shocked. It was the kind of melodrama that appealed to her. But not when it concerned her daughter.

She gathered Gussie to herself and rocked her for a long time. Then she whispered, 'Let's go back, darling. Don't button yourself up any more. I need to understand this and you have to talk about it for both our sakes.' She stroked the damp face. 'Is that all right?'

And after a few seconds, Gussie nodded.

Twelve

The cold was beginning to seep up through the rocks. It seemed to Gussie that her mother was unnecessarily anxious to get back down to the farmhouse and 'talk'. Typical Zannah: avid curiosity but small attention span. And then, as she stood up, Gussie realized that her muscles had stiffened, the inner trembling was still there and, in spite of the sunshine, the short day had lost its sparkle.

She watched numbly as Zannah humped herself into the harness of the backpack and urged them both into the meadowland. Her blunt statement – accusation – whatever it had been – hung in the air. Truthful? If it was truthful then Andrew Bellamy was evil. And he wasn't evil. Or was he?

She knew she could no longer tuck away that terrible time and pretend it had never happened. She had said those words to her mother and they had released a torrent of memory as strong as the torrent of the River Brussac. Even as they had climbed towards it she had felt her body responding to the landscape and had known at some level of consciousness that this would happen.

In a way it was a relief. Kate and Mark had been away when she introduced Andrew to her birthplace. They had never met him. When she eventually crawled back up the cliff and reached Zion Cottage, he had long gone. He had not even called the rescue services. No one had known she was missing. It was a blessing. She told herself that it was a blessing over and over again. Yet, when it became obvious that she was not dead, he did not get in touch. She could not believe it for months: he could have had a daughter or a son. He never tried to find out. How he must have hated her. When she heard he was in St Ives and had actually asked about her, she was terrified. Was it possible – it could not be, yet it might be – that after more than four long years he was going to try to kill her again?

By the time they got into the kitchen her skin was hot, yet inside she was still shivering. She seemed unable to do the simplest things. Zannah pulled off her boots and pushed her into a chair next to the range, made tea and held the cup to her mouth until she sipped it. Then she took the cup into her own hands and watched as Zannah started to make toast. She made an effort to pull herself together.

'There's soup in the fridge . . . I'll get it . . .'

'I know, darling. I've put it on the hob – d'you see? Smells lovely. We'll have it with hot buttered toast – instant nourishment – and then you are going to talk. Are you warm now? Here are your slippers.'

Gussie realized that her feet were propped almost inside the open side oven, the slippers right inside it. She managed a quivering smile as she bent down to put them on. She thought of the poor bedraggled creature who had let herself back into Zion Cottage that night in June. She could have done with her mother then, and yet had wanted no one to see her utter degradation.

She managed a square of toast and a mug of soup, and did indeed feel instantly better.

'I shouldn't have told you,' she said. 'Now you're going to get all het up. It's over, Zannah. And it made me what I am, I suppose. I grew up that night. I thought I was doing so well, moderately successful, wonderfully in love. I discovered . . .' She choked and then went on tritely, 'I was wrong.'

There was a silence. Zannah was watching her, probably getting all the wrong messages.

Gussie said desperately, 'Listen, I probably *was* wrong. Quite wrong. He lurched – it was a shock, after all – he obviously hated the thought of being a father and I had imagined he would be pleased!' She forced a laugh. 'What an idiot! He probably almost fell over with the shock and knocked me over the edge! Imagine hearing that sort of news on a headland!'

Zannah closed her eyes. 'If the tide hadn't been in, Gus, you would have been killed instantly.'

'I suppose so. But it must have looked pretty hopeless any-way. You know how it boils around those rocks. And if, by the time he looked over the edge, I had dived into the cave, he must have thought . . .' She dropped her head. 'The tide had ebbed by midnight. As I climbed back up, I put two and two together. He hadn't raised any sort of alarm. No one knew he was there. I wasn't surprised to get back home and find he had gone. It was for the best, of course. I went to bed with three hot-water bottles and just waited until I felt better. Mrs Beck was the only one who asked about him and all she said was that she thought I was bringing my young man down for the week. I told her that we had broken up and she said there were plenty more fish in the sea.' She managed a smile at her mother and Zannah grinned back.

Gussie said, 'D'you know, I feel better! I should have told you ages ago instead of letting it fester away inside me.'

'It's like a boil. And you've popped it. So there is a relief, but there's poison too. Come on, Gus. Drink your tea and talk.'

'I've said it all. That's it. I have never had anything more to do with Albion UK since then. I took on a project for Tregannon House, funded by Natural Earth – Daddy made a little sculpture garden there. Kept to the budget with his help, of course. I knew it was good. It led to something for another of the big Penwith houses. I began to see how important it was to keep what had been laid down a hundred years ago and work from there. I learned about growing pineapples next to compost, for the heat. And you had already got me interested in grapes. There's a very sheltered valley on the south of the peninsula where I've got a tiny bananerie going. I thought everything was pretty good until that day last September when Dad and Mum were killed. And even then I did not realize that the enormity of it made it less . . . personal. And there were the three of us – always the three of us. We have been in a limbo – self-induced. And we know we can't stay there, which is terrifying in itself. Jannie is moving on already. She has fallen in love and that is a great healer as well as a great destroyer.' She stopped at her mother's cry of distress and shook her head. 'Yes, you're right. I must not generalize, of course.' She focused on her mother and said, 'I think it is the very randomness of everything that makes me tired.'

'Meaning?'

'We were going on fine and then Nine Eleven happened. Random. Then I thought I might be able to work from Zion Cottage and keep the place going for all three of us – like Kate did. And then Ned wanted to see his father – his birth father – and Jannie somehow became strong and then met this teacher chap . . . all random.'

'Maybe not so random. We're never going to understand it, Gus. And we're allowed our own way – isn't that what free will means? I'm having fun with my free will – I'm not looking for meanings any more. Waste of time. Now and then you get to a place when you can look back and see a meaning. That's a treat. Other times, not a lot makes sense unless you make it so.'

'Oh, Ma,' Gus smiled without so much as a tremor, 'you always had such energy and drive, and it's still there!'

'And you've got it too. Don't close it off, sweetie. Just because of one bad experience – two bad experiences.' She looked suspicious. 'More than two?'

'No. Two will do.' She thought of the time when Zannah had left. But that had not been such a bad experience. Zannah had somehow laid a foundation for the random. Even at eight years old Gussie had known that.

She said suddenly, 'It wasn't as if I hadn't been warned. There was a mature student at college. I slept with him twice, then he took up with my best friend. I felt an idiot then but after he'd done the rounds – only five women in our year group, but all five fell for him – I didn't feel so bad. We laughed about it. About him. It was wounded pride then.'

'Probably the same with this Bellamy chap.'

'No. We were colleagues, then friends. We became lovers much later when he said he wanted to be my life mentor.' She thought her mother groaned. She went on quickly, 'He was good for me, my career rocketed. We had so much in common. We did everything together. It sounds so silly, but he washed my hair, did my nails . . .'

'He took you over? Body and soul?'

'I suppose so.' Gussie sipped yet another cup of hot tea. 'But I encouraged it – I wanted it. I thought it worked both ways. It *did* work both ways. I shopped for him. He was hopeless with clothes, terribly formal. He loved it that my background was what he called "arty-farty"! He wanted to be an art collector and I could tell him who to look out for . . . you know.' It all sounded so weak now. But Zannah nodded. She knew only too well.

Gussie said, 'I didn't tell him about the baby at first. I wanted to be sure. We were sharing everything and this was the ultimate. When Kate rang to say she and Daddy were taking Jannie away for the spring bank holiday week and the week after, I asked them if I could bring a friend down to the cottage for a few days. It was the perfect place to tell him. I thought – I thought . . . Anyway, he was angry. So angry. As if it was my fault. He wanted – demanded – I had an abortion. When I said no he asked me what right I had to keep a child that was unwanted. He said I was a schemer. Irresponsible. He brought up private things . . . oh God!' She put her cup down with a clatter and covered her face with her hands.

Zannah got up and held her close.

After a while Zannah said matter-of-factly, 'And then he pushed you off a cliff into the Atlantic Ocean and left you for dead. Must have been a nasty shock when he discovered otherwise. Expected the arm of the law on his shoulder at any moment, I would think.' She crouched and moved her daughter's hands so that she could look her in the eye. 'Oh, Gus, you should have reported him immediately. He is not fit to roam this earth unscathed.'

Gussie started to cry and, once started, she could not stop.

Once again Gussie felt she was convalescing from one of her feverish colds. Zannah refused to take on her nurse role again and insisted on a daily walk. They visited friends.

'Not the kind who come to the *gîtes* and think I'm a bit of a genius!' Zannah said to Gussie. 'My real friends here are French, very practical. Mostly growers. Others, mixed farming. Traditional. You'll love them. We won't see them all – of course not, darling – just the ones who are within walking distance. The Rivières – they rent my vineyard. And Madame Monsoon – she was a poet and now she grows herbs and posts them off all over the world.'

So they paid their calls and Gussie found herself enjoying the company of her mother's neighbours, grateful they were near at hand for her. She knew that her mother would have liked to continue their 'talks'. Occasionally she exploded unexpectedly with a vitriolic, 'If I could get my hands on that man, I would kill him!' but Gussie never took the bait. She told herself she had got it all out of her system. It would not worry her again.

Then, suddenly, Zannah was saying, 'I can't believe it's your last day! We've done nothing, absolutely nothing. That bloody painting took up too much time!'

Gussie reminded her of their walks and the way her mother had 'nursed' her.

Zannah waved a dismissive hand. 'Yes, that was the mother thing, I suppose.' She looked pleased. 'But in the middle you had to take over, poor darling.'

'I got to know the house that way. I can picture you here now.'

'What? Naked on my scaffolding?'

Gussie primmed her mouth. 'Yes. And making a snow-man.'

Zannah nodded. 'And dancing. Thank you for that, Gus.'

'My pleasure.' Not strictly true, but it was what her mother wanted to hear.

Zannah sighed. 'Listen, what shall we do today? Would you like to go into Nice? Yes, let's do that. I'll buy you something memorable. A designer outfit. Or a watch. Yes, jewellery. And we'll have lunch.'

Gussie would have much preferred to walk to the village for some fresh bread from the *boulangerie*, pick watercress from the brook beyond the barn and make soup, but she smiled agreement. 'Back before dark, Zannah. I have to pack and I'm going to have another try to ring Ned.'

Zannah frowned. 'I don't like you going back to an empty house. Zion Cottage is such a dump.'

'Zannah! At least admit you had some happy times there!'

'Sorry, sweetie. But I was never there on my own. Not like you will be.'

'I'm staying with Rosemary just to break the journey.'

Zannah made a face. 'Oh, well, even Zion Cottage in mid-winter will be bliss after that, I suppose!'

Gussie eyed her humorously and after a while they both laughed.

Zannah took the four-wheel drive to Nice. It was hair-raising.

'You're an even worse driver than Rory Trewyn!' Gussie gasped as they scraped past a tractor on the very edge of the Middle Corniche.

Zannah beamed. 'Thank you, darling. Be sure to tell him that; it will infuriate him!' But she admitted to being tired. 'I don't drive far these days. You can have a go on the way back.'

They eventually ended up in the diamond boutique just behind the Promenade des Anglais. Zannah had set her heart on giving Gussie a traditional watch. 'You missed out on your twenty-first watch. I've still got mine from my father.'

She pushed up her sleeve and revealed an exquisite cocktail watch. 'I won't influence you – I'll look around the front of the display area.'

She drifted off and Gussie was left with an assiduous assistant and an array of watches that meant nothing to her. She allowed herself to be taken over, admiring the various models, knowing that she would never wear any of them because the watch she already had was the last present Grandma Briscoe had given her. It was practical, unobtrusive yet easily read.

The assistant suddenly understood this and suggested in her charming English that Gussie might like their silver locket watches as a piece of jewellery. She presented one of them on a black velvet stand and Gussie was struck by its slightly old-fashioned look. Might there be any future occasions when this could be worn? And would Zannah approve?

She looked round, then crouched slightly to peer through a display framework. She heard her mother before she saw her. Zannah had seen someone she knew and was greeting him or her enthusiastically with arms outspread.

'Louis! Darling!'

Gussie's heart sank. She remembered the name, Louis Broomfield. The dealer-man. And he was a day early. Typically Gussie ran a list of the contents of the fridge through her head, wondering what sort of meal she could concoct. And then she forgot all that as Zannah clasped someone to her and a head appeared above hers. Gussie stiffened as a man's face came into focus. Blond as a Viking; predatory like a Viking. It was unmistakably Andrew Bellamy's head.

She reached behind her with one hand, feeling for the counter. She intended to run. To disappear. Find the car, perhaps. Mingle with the crowds along the Promenade. Anything.

And then those intensely blue eyes widened as they met hers between the display shelves. He saw her and recognized her immediately, as she had him. Just for an instant she thought he was going to give his delighted smile and lift a hand from Zannah's shoulder to hail her, and then something absolutely unexpected happened. His face changed. It was as if it slackened, became pliable, jelly-like. He seemed to cling to Zannah instead of to embrace her. His whole body changed with his face. She stood there, transfixed, holding the counter behind her but no longer wanting to run, watching him disintegrate. The Viking no longer victorious. The Viking, abject.

Andrew Bellamy was frightened. How foolish of her not to have realized that he ran from Bamaluz Point because he was frightened – terrified, in fact. And he had hidden from her until his greed for money had forced him back to St Ives where he had skirted around the place making sure that he did not bump into her.

She moved back until the counter supported her waist, then she turned quite naturally and said, 'Yes, I love the locket. I will take it. Can you gift-wrap it? It's a very special present from my mother.' She smiled at the girl and the girl smiled back. She felt a little surge of triumph and did not know why . . . had she won something? The eye contact with Andrew? Yes, she had definitely won that, but more than that: she had won something within herself. It was almost physical; a sense of her body settling into itself, reordering itself. She hid a grin from the young assistant because she had a ridiculous, cartoon-like flash of lungs nudging heart a millimetre, digestive system glugging freely, the aftermath of her inner shaking settling, relaxing. Just as she had watched Andrew Bellamy's collapse, so now she watched her own body flow comfortably into itself. Comfortable. She had lost her baby; part of herself. Now, standing in this place sparkling with faceted light, she was whole again. It was wonderful.

She took the silver-wrapped package from the girl, smiled, thanked her and walked to the door and out into the winter sunshine. Her mother did not call after her; perhaps Andrew – or Louis – was still clinging to her and she was wondering what on earth to do with him. Gussie let her smile grow and grow at the thought. Her mother was more than a match for Andrew Bellamy, just as she had been a match for Louis Broomfield. Two confidence tricksters head to head. Gussie knew already who would win.

The car, big and black, was waiting in the car park and Gussie had the keys. She got into the driver's seat and began to sort through her bag, putting her new watch in its shiny wrapping into the glove compartment, checking on her passport and train tickets. She glanced at the watch her grandmother had given her almost ten years ago. Her mother would arrive at any moment, wondering why Gus had left the shop so abruptly. She would be alone, of course, because Andrew was terrified of meeting Gussie. It would be interesting to discover what he had told her – if anything. And what she had told him. Gussie was willing to bet that Zannah had got in first and urged him to meet her daughter, who was leaving for England very early tomorrow morning. In which case he would say nothing. He would turn up at the farmhouse exactly as planned because he wanted this deal to go through.

At that precise moment in her thoughts, there was a tap on the driver's window and Zannah was there.

'Darling, where on earth did you get to? Are you all right? I got held up by Louis Broomfield, of all people – didn't you see us? I thought for a horrid moment he wanted to come back with us, but no, he's staying with someone from the Guggenheim. Of course.'

She came round the car and got into the passenger seat. 'Are you happy to drive, sweetie? Well, I know you drive one of these things over the countryside when you're working.'

Gussie started up and manoeuvred carefully into the flow of traffic. She told her mother about the locket and its inner watch. 'It took so long to wrap I thought you'd already left. And then I saw you with your dealer-man.'

Zannah chortled. 'I bet you thought I'd bring him home! He's staying with some American and arriving at the farm tomorrow as arranged. So you could have joined us and been introduced.' She chortled again. 'He wanted to know if he was my only guest. He thinks it will be easier to bring the price down if he has me to himself.'

'We'll phone the Rivières when we get back. And perhaps Madame Monsoon would stay overnight?'

'To chaperone me? You must be joking, Gus!'

'Zannah. His real name is Andrew Bellamy.' She took a hand off the wheel and held her mother's knee. 'It's all right. Really. He's not a murderer. He saw me, recognized me. He was terrified. He's a man with a plan of action that I could smash instantly. He now thinks I ran away, out of that shop, and I expect he discovered from you that I have been convalescing after the shock of losing my family. So he's going to go ahead with the deal he has made with you.' She squeezed her mother's knee hard. 'I think he is a weak man. But just in case . . . you cannot stay in the house with him on your own. You really can't do that, Zannah. For my sake, if not yours.'

Zannah ceased trying to interrupt with gasps of furious outrage. There was a silence in the car while Gussie crossed the interchange and started on the country roads. Then Zannah said with a catch in her voice, 'I'll kill him.'

Gussie glanced sideways; her mother's face was running with tears. She drew into a gateway and stopped the car; enfolded Zannah in her long arms and held her tightly.

'Not before you've upped the price and got a cheque in your hands!' she whispered.

Zannah choked on a laugh but then sobered. 'Darling, I am so thankful that you can take it like this. Have you laid that particular spectre, d'you think?'

'Of course. I should have realized . . . He worked as legal adviser for Albion UK, very reputable landscape designers. When I became his – his – project, he left them and promoted me like mad. And then, well, I suppose he became an independent dealer and worked for whoever was interested. He likes walking a tightrope in the commercial world. I wouldn't have done for him at all. Too conventional. I'll never know whether that shove was simply disgust, or an attempt to do away with me. It obviously frightened him more than me!'

Zannah made a little moan. 'He conned me, didn't he? I thought I was on to a good thing. The conner conned!'

'But then, he can't be certain that we're not having this conversation. He'll either disappear – not turn up tomorrow – or he'll gamble. And just in case he does, I'm going to ring Madame Monsoon.'

Gus started the car again and they drove several miles before Zannah burst out again, 'I'll kill him!'

Gussie gave a wry smile. 'He won't turn up. Too scared.'

'Too scared to settle down with you and lead a quiet life. Not too scared to risk everything on a dodgy deal.'

'We don't know that his deals are dodgy.'

'I'm willing to put money on it! He'll turn up tomorrow. And I'll kill him!'

Gussie's smile exploded into a laugh. 'I've danced with you, remember! And watched you painting in the buff! You probably weigh under eight stone.'

'I have a gun, Gus. And I know how to use it.'

'Oh, well then. That's settled.'

'You don't think I'm serious. I've got nothing to lose. I've been a lousy mother. Here's a decent chance to put things right. No one else can do it.'

Again Gussie glanced sideways. Her mother's face was set.

Gussie took a deep breath. 'That scar. Along your hairline. It is recent. And it's nothing to do with a face-lift. Is it the reason you wanted me to come over and see you?'

'I have always wanted you to come over and see me. You must know that.'

'There was an urgency. Rory kept banging on about it.'

'Losing Mark. Properly losing him. Knowing we would never jump into the sea from the pier and swim to the arches . . .'

Gussie knew Zannah was crying again. She said, 'I'll do it for both of you. I promise.' She waited and then said. 'Was it a tumour? Has it been removed?'

'Yes.' The voice was suddenly strong. 'It'll be all right. Of course. There was radio therapy after.' She laughed brightly. 'I had to wear a mask. Like the phantom of the bloody opera! I looked quite good, actually.'

Gussie gripped the wheel hard. Rory must have known all this.

Zannah said, 'Don't worry about the dealer-man, darling. If he turns up, he won't be staying. Our local gendarme will be coming to discuss a complaint I received – loud music at my last party. He told me off on the phone and thought that would do but I must ring him and ask him to pop up. He looks rather grand in his uniform.'

Gussie said, 'We should talk. About the tumour. How will you manage?'

'No. Sorry, darling, but that is something we will not talk about. We have had our lovely time together. Just as I hoped. We lived together as mother and daughter for four weeks.' She leaned round so that Gussie could see her face; it was alive with laughter. 'That is as much as I can manage, Gus!'

Gussie laughed too. They slowed for the first of the bridges in Deux Ponts, and on their left and above them appeared the tall roof of the barn where Zannah's paint pots still hung from the scaffolding.

'You know I will come if you need me.'

'I did need you. And you came.'

Gussie was about to call her mother the ultimate drama queen. And then she did not.

The journey home was long and gave her too much time to worry about Andrew Bellamy's visit to Glorious Isolation. Gussie told herself that basically he was a coward and would back out of it. But he was also a gambler, and she could not be sure of anything.

At Marseilles the train was held up for an hour and the dining car ran out of supplies. She missed her connection in Paris but the night ferry had waited for the next train and the passengers filed on at midnight, looking like refugees.

By the time she had changed trains at London and arrived in Bristol it was mid-afternoon of the next day. Andrew Bellamy had come and gone; or perhaps not come at all. Gussie crawled into one of the taxis outside Temple Meads and arrived at the tall old Briscoe house in Clifton just as darkness crept along the Avon Gorge.

Aunt Rosemary was pathetically pleased to see her. 'I've been phoning Zannah and there's been no answer. When I switched on the news at lunchtime I thought you would not be coming home at all. Were you still there when it happened?'

Gussie stared at her blearily. She felt unreal. Rosemary drew her into the sitting room where a tea trolley was drawn close to the fire. Outside, the street lights snapped on and highlighted the rain.

'It's raining,' Gussie said.

Rosemary said, 'It's been raining all day. You must have seen it from the train.' She pushed one of the armchairs closer to the fire. 'Come on. Feet in fender, tea in tummy. D'you remember Mummy saying that? No, you wouldn't. It was always summer when you spent any length of time with her.'

But Kate had said it. Gussie held out appreciative hands to the fire. 'I'm all out of kilter, half of me still on that dratted train stuck in Marseilles. The other half back in Deux Ponts with Zannah.'

Rosemary put a mug of tea in the outstretched hands and started around the room, switching on table lamps. Mark had told her once she was not a restful person and she had asked him tartly whether he could have been restful if he'd lived with Rory Trewyn. He had said nothing. He had, after all, lived with Zannah Scaife for twelve years. Gussie smiled at the memory and Rosemary said briskly, 'That's better. I take it you've had a dreadful time. And now this. Zannah is quite the most selfish woman I have ever met.'

'I've had a good time. A really good time in all ways. And I shall soon orientate myself again, don't worry.'

Rosemary came and sat down, her knees almost touching Gussie's. 'You don't know, of course. I thought it might have made the papers this morning. It happened yesterday. In the afternoon. You'd have left by then.' She put out a hand. 'It's all right, she's fine. And loving the limelight, of course. We'll watch the news at six, it's sure to be on again. She's managed to convince everyone that she's a heroine. The man she rescued looks like a terrified rabbit. I wouldn't be surprised if she deliberately pushed him into that river before she dashed along the bank and hauled him out.'

Rosemary was laughing inordinately by this time and went on to recount similar incidents from Zannah's time in St Ives when she had jumped from Bamaluz Point and dived off the end of Smeaton's Pier without a stitch on. 'Of course, it was still just about the sixties then and people used to do those sorts of things. We're a little bit more careful now.'

Gussie stopped staring at her aunt and gazed into the fire, seeing the River Brussac from above, wondering how on earth Zannah had inveigled Andrew to go with her; remembering her adamant intention to kill him.

She said slowly, 'She's got a brain tumour. She's not selfish, Aunt Ro. Not now. I don't think she cares about herself any more.'

'Oh my God. Are you sure?' She looked at Gussie's face and shook her head from side to side, slowly. 'Of course. She'll want to go out with a bang, won't she?'

152

'Yes.'

Gussie continued to stare into the heart of the fire and after a while Rosemary pushed the mug of tea towards her mouth. She drank and at last smiled properly. 'She's incorrigible. And indefatigable.' She made a face at her aunt. 'She worked most of the time I was with her – one of those huge canvases Grampy Gerald used to love. And if she had planned this . . . incident . . . it could not have worked out better. Who knows, she might beat the bloody cancer too.'

Rosemary lifted her own mug. 'Here's to Zannah.' Carefully they touched mugs.

Gussie said, 'I'm glad to be home.'

Thirteen

Ned leaned on the wall, looked out at the harbour and told himself that nothing had changed. It seemed an age since he had leaned here, noted the boats moored alongside Smeaton's Pier, checked that the lifeboat was still housed, wondered about the weather, then gone into the kitchen to feed the range and make tea. He would do all that now. But when he sat at the big table and drank the tea and ate the toast, he would be on his own. Alone. Every day confirmed it and every day it became less bearable.

The table would look enormous spread before him with nothing on it except a stack of newspapers, mostly unopened. There was no precious list containing cryptic messages like 'Flowers for C' or 'Ring Ro re bed'. He had kept that particular list and left it on the table for two or three days after Gussie's departure, then told himself he was a sentimental idiot and thrown it on the range. There was no way he could fool himself that anyone else was living in Zion Cottage. Gussie would not be clanking the gate in the yard as she came in from her morning walk and Jannie was most definitely otherwise engaged.

Jannie was working like stink at Exeter to produce the best dissertation anyone had done in the history of the University, and Gussie's last letter had said she would now wait to hear from him with his American address. She had been in France for two weeks. And when she came home there would be no one here for her either. She would not be arriving at any moment from her morning walk to regale anyone with all the news.

He almost gave in and let himself cry, then forced a tight grin. It was still murkily dark this grey February day and there would be no 'news' unless the lifeboat had been called out – and nobody wanted news like that. As a teenager he had complained about the lack of 'news' during the winter and Gussie had said instantly, 'Don't worry, little brother. I'll make up some news for you.' For a while, until the joke ran out of steam, the Briscoe Morning News had often been the highlight of winter weekends. 'I do 'ear,' Gussie always slipped into a broad Cornish accent, 'as the cauliflowers down Nanceledra way be turning pink when they're cut. Buyers upcountry are going crazy for 'em. Jem Tregothen is putting that-there cochineal in the rain butts and 'and-watering his lower field. An' when 'is missis did rinse 'er 'air in the rainwater, she ended up a red'ead!'

Ned stopped grinning because he also remembered that until the rest of the family had exploded with laughter, he had actually believed in the pink cauliflowers. He had always believed what Gussie told him. From the moment she arrived into his life – on Porthmeor beach when he was five years old – he had believed every word she said. When he realized that the story of the pink cauliflowers was a joke he had found it the funniest joke he had ever heard and had been surprised to find that none of his classmates gave it more than a passing smile. 'That sister of yours – sounds as mad as a hatter!' That had come from Maurice Hain, who had then met Gussie just before she went to Cirencester and had fallen in love with her instantly. Everyone did, of course, and she never seemed to see it. Nearly all his friends went on about her dark eyes and her long legs. Maurice had even gone mad about her plait and told Ned he wanted to unplait it and comb it through and through with his fingers. Ned had wanted to smash him in the face.

And now she was gone to that crazy mother of hers, who would parade her around France and marry her off to someone with pots of money and charm, and who would obviously be the man Gussie had waited for all her life. She would be thirty-one in August. How did someone like Gussie Briscoe get to thirty-one without getting . . . trapped? Yes, that was the word. Trapped. She needed to be free. To plan her marvellous land sculptures; to stand facing the sea and using all five senses to soak up every bit of what was around her. Nobody could understand that. Nobody could understand that except another Briscoe. Except a Briscoe who had lived with other Briscoes in a very small house where, in the middle of family turmoil, there had always been that huge sense of eternity just outside the tiny windows.

Ned levered himself upright. A sleek white boat had emerged from the murk that hid Hayle Towans. He recognized it even in these conditions. Its powerful engine was turned down to a chug as it made its way between the buoys and moored at Westcott Pier, opposite Smeaton's. That meant it would take Rory Trewyn at least ten minutes to walk to the harbour and right the way around it, past the Sloop to Zion Cottage.

This was the sort of news Ned did not want. He was tempted to grab his coat and clear out. Rory had already called three times in two weeks and talked endlessly about 'the good old days' when, apparently, men were definitely men and women were – most definitely – women. Ned found it distasteful somehow. He knew about the sixties, of course, but they had happened forty years ago. Almost half a century, for Pete's sake. And what went on then was close to Gussie's 'news'. Fabricated.

He looked wildly around the kitchen. His supper things from last night were still much in evidence. And he had wanted to go through his travel plans this morning. But, but, but . . . Gussie had seemed to have some kind of sympathy towards her poor decrepit old uncle. He was no blood relative, yet, yet . . .

Ned gave a huge sigh and went to replenish the wood stove. Dammit, he could offer Rory breakfast and an hour's chat, surely? Poor old devil knew all about living alone. Perhaps Ned could pick up a few tips. He grinned – naturally, this time – and switched on the electric kettle, then gathered his supper things into a washing-up bowl. It could be that Rory Trewyn's company would help him to forget the huge empty space that belonged to Gussie.

Rory grappled inside his oilskin jacket, wrestled out a flat bottle and tipped it over his mug of tea.

'Shouda done it years ago, of course. Thought she'd come back – she always fancied herself as lady of the bloody manor. Now it's gone. And all the trappings with it. Gave her clothes to Gus. Well, you know that, of course. Did she take 'em down to Bristol?'

Ned buttered toast and pushed the plate over to Rory. He felt as Gussie must feel about this wreck of a man: resigned.

'Not sure. There was a lot of luggage in the car.'

'You shoulda gone with her. Seen her to the airport. Looked after her.'

Ned just stared at him and Rory waved his hands blusteringly and said, 'Well . . . you coulda driven the bloody car back here, anyway. How you going to get to where you're going?'

'Sleeper, Penzance to London. Shuttle to Heathrow. Plane to New York. Next day internal flight to LA . . .' He droned it out and would have gone on except that Rory made a dismissive sound that caused him almost to choke on his brandy-laced tea.

'All right, all right. I get the message. You know what you're doing a bloody sight better than I do!' He swigged again and grinned. 'Both ended up with a bit of money and the world in front of us, haven't we?'

For a moment Ned almost exploded; he was on the point of ordering the awful old man to leave and not to come back this time. And then something happened. A terrible sense of emptiness seemed to fill the kitchen. It was dark and it was cold. It came from the ceiling, the walls, the floor; it dimmed the brightness of the range; it was a physical thing; clammy. It smelled of despair and hopelessness. It had happened before but not quite like this.

He took a deep breath and felt a chill in his lungs. Then he tried to imagine them all here. Mark and Kate, Jannie and Gussie. Around the table. Here. It had worked before and he had ended up with his head pillowed in his arms, sobbing helplessly.

This time it did not work. He could still see Rory, still hear his words. His chest was freezing and he could not take another breath. Nobody died of grief. Unless they did.

Rory's voice was much too loud, it pushed back some of the

cold; the darkness that was dimming the fire stayed where it was at the edges of the kitchen.

'Stop it, my boy! Mark was on his own here when Etta died and he thought he was going crazy. Then Zannah came and saved him. An' you got Zannah's daughter. You'll be all right, d'you hear me? You'll be all right!'

Ned discovered he was sitting down and a brandy bottle was against his chin. He took it and swigged once. The darkness receded further. He could breathe.

He bowed his head. Rory was pushing wood into the range now, then spreading marmalade thickly on to toast. Ned ate it obediently.

'At least you've got a father and you're going to see him. That little January girl – how do you think she must feel?'

Ned swallowed; the toast was delicious. He gulped his tea and spoke in a low voice. 'She's in love. Everything she does now is towards . . . dammit, I've forgotten his name.'

Rory gave a laugh like a cannon shot. 'Now that's what I call normal! Mind you, she'll soon pound it into your head so that you'll never forget it again. But in the meantime his name doesn't matter. Being in love is totally time-consuming. But there are other things that can be just as absorbing. Finding out about your father is one. I don't know a thing about your father. Looked him up here and there and discovered he's a bit of a genius, so you should be in for quite an experience. But I do know something about Gussie's mother so I know for sure that Gussie is having a very full time of it.'

Ned ate more toast and listened as Rory rambled on about facing reality and making the most of what they had. 'If the money can make life better then don't act as if it's poison, my boy. They left it to you to help you, not to make everything even more bloody awful!'

Ned finished eating and pushed away his plate. He looked at the rugged features of the old man opposite him.

'How did you know . . . what was happening just then?'

'That's how it was at Trewyn. All the rooms and the passages and the – the – stuff. I was adopted, y'see. None of it was mine, not really. Ro was mine. And then she wasn't. And I went away and worked. Why? Keep the old place going for the sake of my father who wasn't my father at all? Came back and it closed in on me. The walls fell in and suffocated me. Couldn't breathe. Went to see Zannah – like a shot in the arm. Wonderful woman. And she said sell the bloody place.' He upended his bottle and set it down on the table with a bang. 'I know all about the grief that takes your breath and squashes your body into a pulp.'

Ned leaned back in his chair and let his arms hang. So this was grief. They had thought they were grieving and talked naïvely about the three of them together. They had made plans: put down anchors, plotted courses . . . It seemed suddenly absurd. There was no escaping the damp dark tide of grief. And Gussie was coming back to it. He would be gone and Jannie's term-end still to come.

As if he was plugged into Ned's thoughts Rory suddenly said, 'Came to tell you I am off to see Zannah in a couple of weeks. But I can put it off. I'll move in here for a few weeks. Be here when Gus gets back.'

Ned stared at him then barked a laugh. 'Sorry, Nunc. That would be Gussie's worst possible nightmare. She'll be staying with Aunt Ro for a while anyway, then calling at Jannie's.'

'Nunc? I'm not your uncle, my lad! Gus understands me – you don't.'

For some reason Ned was furious. 'You're no blood relation to Gussie, either, so don't pretend there's family feeling!'

It sounded childish but it found its target. Rory actually bristled.

'Look here, you oaf! Everyone – anyone local – will tell you that my mother was Rose Carne from Zennor. Only the Briscoes know about my father. He was Madge Briscoe's brother, Neville Bridges. I reckon that makes me Gus Briscoe's great-uncle twice over, don't you?'

Ned stared, speechless, his mind twisting with the effort at working this out.

Rory nodded. 'Yes. That makes Ro and me cousins. We couldn't live without each other. And we couldn't live with each other either! What a bloody mess!'

Ned said numbly, 'Does Gussie know this?'

'I would have thought Daddy might have told her, don't you?'

'Possibly.'

'Probably, more like.'

But if Mark had told her she would have told Ned. She would have made a joke about cupboards and skeletons.

Again Rory tuned into his thoughts. 'She doesn't tell you everything, you know. That bloody awful chap who came to get a look at the Scaife paintings before the house sale, he told me he was engaged to Gus for a short time back in the summer of ninety-seven. Did you know that?'

'Yes, yes – I knew! Now go, for God's sake go and leave me in peace! You are certainly not my uncle and I don't have to put up with this . . . this . . . poisonous gossip! Get out – now!'

Rory looked down at the wide face staring up at him. Then he upended his bottle for the last time, walked to the bin in the corner, deposited it gently inside, and then let himself out into the courtyard. His dignity was damaged when he skidded slightly on the wet cobbles and swore lustily. Ned heard it and relaxed. Stupid old man, that's all he was. But perhaps he had saved Ned from the total madness of grief and given him back . . . what? Something from the past? And why had Ned's reaction been so dismissive to the reminder that once, a long time ago, Gus Briscoe had been engaged to a man he had never met until a few weeks ago, in the Scaife studio?

Ned tilted his chair towards the range and felt the warmth creep up his back. He had genuinely forgotten that time when Gussie had been engaged. It was over before he saw her, so he had never taken it seriously. But that summer when they had all gone on a cruise to Scandinavia to celebrate Gussie's twenty-sixth birthday, he had thought she was thinner, less . . . less lively. Somehow. He was very involved with his new job and he did not associate anything with a broken engagement. After all, what that meant was that Gussie had escaped the trap for a while longer.

But could Rory be right? Could that pushy 'dealer-chap', who had been fishing for information about the Scaife paintings so recently – could he have been the man Gussie had considered spending her life caring for, loving, sharing with him all the intimacies of marriage? Ned remembered his name. Andrew Bellamy. He couldn't remember the name of Jannie's chap. But he could remember Andrew Bellamy. A creep of the worst kind.

Ned sighed and stared up at the black beams above him. Too much information. He did not want to know about Neville Bridges, who had died a hero of the Spanish Civil War and left a legacy back in Cornwall called Rory Trewyn. He did not want to think about Rory and Rosemary, who were first cousins and bound together in so many ways. And he certainly did not want to think of Gus giving up her precious freedom to an out-and-out rotter like Andrew Bellamy.

He said aloud in a firm voice, 'Check tomorrow's itinerary. And get your case down the attic stairs. For God's sake, *do* something!'

He stood up and made for the door.

He went into automatic for the journey. Before he left there was a telephone call from Sheila wishing him good luck and mentioning that she had left her umbrella in the hotel booked by Eric Selway – did he remember the name of it? He said he would find out and what did the umbrella look like. She had bought it at Macy's and it had their name on every panel. He said to leave it with him. He got a yellow cab at Kennedy and asked for Mack's Central Park address but via Macy's, where he bought an umbrella and asked for it to be mailed to Sheila's address. He tried to imagine this sort of thing in Penzance and smiled.

He was dropped at the front of the building this time and was amused by the porter, who chatted amiably about the flight and then told him that the 'McKinnon family' were doing fine. Apparently Michael had his usual winter troubles. 'His thumbs don't work. Arthritis. Makes holding a steering wheel kinda tricky.' But Mrs McKinnon was doing fine. 'And if she's OK, then they're all OK!'

They arrived at the penthouse and as the elevator doors sighed open there was Mack, hands held out in welcome. And behind him came Michael to take over the luggage and re-assure the porter that his thumbs were 'doing fine'. Ned was ushered into the apartment where another welcome awaited from Marion and Emily.

He thought of Zion Cottage, empty, deserted.

Marion said, 'I think you might be like me about travelling,

Ned. Come and sit down and have an old-fashioned sherry before lunch. I guess you left home over twenty-four hours ago and you're completely disorientated.' She bowled her wheelchair around one of the open-ended walls to where the big table was laid at one end only and Emily was already pouring drinks, but left them to hug Ned enthusiastically.

Marion went on seamlessly, 'I always rest after lunch and perhaps you would like to do the same? We're so pleased you've come to us this time. We want you to feel completely free. If you plan to visit friends just go ahead – anything.'

He smiled at her. 'I don't want to see the site again.' She smiled back, obviously reassured somehow. He sipped his sherry feeling ridiculously formal, then added, 'How did you react to the recording? We found it more reassuring than, well, anything.'

She smiled back at him widely and looked up at her husband. 'Oh, Ned, we're so glad! We did wonder if it might not be – I'm not sure – satisfactory to you. Yes, that's the word. It was just lovely and ordinary . . . you know, the next thing they planned to do. Together.' She was stammering untypically. 'We wondered whether you might expect some – some special words.'

Mack joined in. Emily said something too. Ned nodded at them all. The apartment was full of sheer goodwill. He hoped it was a good omen. In the plane there had been a moment when he almost blanked out the whole idea of seeing his father. He could do it again, here and now. He could make this visit to the McKinnons – to Macy's, even – the entire object of his trip. His father had not responded to his letter asking if they could meet.

He said abruptly, 'Did you see Victor Gould? Is he still alive?'

Mack glanced at his wife then said, 'No, we didn't see him. I saw him alone. I would have liked Marion to meet him. She would have won him over, I'm sure. Anyway, obviously he is still alive. We would have let you know if anything had happened to him.' He looked rueful. 'Or, in fact, if we'd had any news at all. He'd already offered us his land- and seascapes. He added the skyscapes to that. But he's got family portraits there – paintings of his home town. We'd love them but he's never going to let them go.'

Ned was surprised by his mixed reactions. If his father had been ill, his silence would have been understandable. As it was, Ned still did not know what to do about the visit.

He said, 'I haven't heard a dickybird. I really don't know whether to get on that plane tomorrow or not.'

Then he had to explain about rhyming slang and there was much laughter, then Mack tried to reassure him.

'Apparently he never writes letters. People turn up some-times and he just rushes out into the desert and hides until they've gone. He's got a very efficient manservant – protects him. He lives the life of a hermit.'

Ned tried to grin. They had a good share of nutcases back home but not many hermits. He faced Marion and returned to the subject of the precious recording.

'Actually, getting back to Mum and Dad, we didn't know what to expect from the tape, but we were . . . yes, as you say . . . satisfied. Totally satisfied. We keep playing it. It's like having them in the room with us. Gussie says we won't need to for ever because we'll just know they're always there!' He thought of that empty kitchen; the sheer emptiness being a separate physical entity. 'It hasn't happened yet,' he finished lamely.

Marion said quietly, 'It will.' She took a deep breath, sipped at her sherry glass and looked up again. 'How is Gussie? We had an airmail. She'd had a cold and her mother nursed her splendidly for twenty-four hours, then got bored!' Marion laughed. 'Gussie was not a bit surprised. And as her mother then disappeared into her studio, Gussie could get better in her own time and find out about the farmhouse. She loves it. She has somehow made her own space there.' She added quickly, 'That's how it sounded to me.'

Ned nodded. 'We've spoken on the phone and I picked that up too. She was dreading going in the end, but something must have happened because quite suddenly she couldn't wait to get away!' As he spoke he thought back and knew he hadn't imagined the change in her attitude. He frowned slightly, thinking harder, wondering whether Rory had exploded his little bomb. But Gussie would have been intrigued, not scared off. And she would most certainly have shared it with him. Yet she had almost panicked. And she had not shared that with him.

Mack interrupted his thoughts. 'You're all trying to make sense of the past, aren't you? You don't have to worry, you know. Your personal pasts – all three of you – are to do with Mark and Kate. And they made sense of everything.'

Ned looked at him, surprised at his sentience. 'You hardly knew us as a family, yet you're so right!'

Mack looked surprised too. 'That's what the message says, Ned. We sort of knew already. Mitch told us about your lives and most of us envied you. You seemed to have the whole thing worked out. But it was that message that confirmed it for most of the people over here who knew Mark and Kate and who had certainly heard about the three of you.'

With a shock Ned saw that the older man's eyes were filling with tears.

Marion said reassuringly, 'Don't worry. Mack is very emotional, as you know. We all need to cry. Grief can't be stoppered up for too long. Of course we support you and Gussie in wanting to reconnect with your biological parents. But if it doesn't happen – for whatever reason – then your real family history is already wonderfully in place.' She gave him a small smile. 'No strings attached.'

He remembered his prickly reaction to a proposed visit last time they were here. He smiled too. 'Sorry about that. Anyway, I think the arrival of his unwanted son might have a very adverse reaction to anything commercial.'

Mack put a hand on his shoulder to indicate that his emotional moment was over. 'Just think like your sister, Ned. She wants to console her mother for the loss of Mark, perhaps tidy up things for herself. Your father has lost his ex-wife – perhaps he needs consolation too. And if you can tidy things up for yourself at the same time . . . there's a definite point to this visit. We wish you well.' He grinned suddenly. 'Don't worry, I've given up hope of including any more of the Gould pieces in the Trust's collection. We're looking for new painters and sculptors.'

Ned picked up the conversational ball. 'I wish some of Gussie's work was transferable to canvas.'

'We include site-specific work, you know, Ned. We've got photographic stuff from all over the world. Are you any good with a camera?'

'It's part of my work, of course.' Ned spoke slowly, already wondering whether it would be possible to record some of the things Gussie did with earth, water, stones . . .

Marion laughed. 'Look, lunch is late already and Emily has been making some miniature Cornish pasties. Please have one, Ned.'

Michael passed a plate and they all tried the tiny pasties, which were delicious but not at all like the Cornish variety. Ned munched and thought how wrong he had been about the McKinnons. They were not the hard-nosed business-people he had imagined. He went into the guest room for a long afternoon's sleep and emerged feeling better than he had since Gussie left for France.

Before he left for his plane the next day he tried again to phone Gussie. He got through all right, but the line was bad and their shouted exchange simply confirmed that Gussie was doing fine and he had arrived in New York safely. On the other hand, Jannie phoned him and sounded as if she were just next door.

'I'm almost there, Ned!' She sounded tired and ecstatic at the same time. 'I need a couple more case examples. I hate thinking of any of them as "cases" but that's a bloody dissertation for you. Not that mine is anything like a dissertation, and my cases are completely anecdotal anyway.'

She listened to his news and he could almost see her nodding. 'You sound good. Better. You needed to do this, didn't you? I didn't actually realize . . . Ned, would you mind terribly if I spent some of the Easter vac at my school? Well, you know, not exactly mine. Hartley. Where I did that practice.'

As if he could forget Hartley and its assembled cast. Robert. That was the name of Jannie's chap, Robert . . . Hanniford. He felt absurdly pleased to have remembered the name.

Jannie was still talking. 'Well, I could pick up some more anecdotes, of course, but mainly it's because four of the kids can't go home for the hols and they're staying at school, and of course they need help. I won't use up the whole holiday but—'

'Jannie, shut up a minute. Of course we won't mind. It's important. And if you can make it home for a few days before the summer term, just to tell us what is happening with you—'

'Ned, I absolutely love you to bits. I'll be sending good vibes all the time you're in Pasadena or wherever it is. And I want you to tell your dad about Gus and me and how much we love you. OK?'

'Oh, Jan. It's more than OK. Now, I want you to take care of yourself—'

'*Naturellement* – oh, no, that's for Gussie. Sure thing, kiddo. You too. Got to go, Ned. Good luck!'

He held the receiver after she had gone, staring at it. Her sheer ebullience was still emanating from it. When he replaced it – gently – he wondered aloud whether she was the one who would hold them together. Her disintegration had been instant and she had lost her temper with them because they had not understood her need to proclaim their loss and share it with the whole world. Now she was getting herself together – had been doing so since their arrival in the States last October – and it seemed he was the one who was disintegrating. He wasn't sure about Gussie. She was, after all, the strong one. But there was this business about Andrew Bellamy. And somehow Rory might upset her particular apple cart too. As for himself, what the hell was he doing here? What did he hope to achieve, for Pete's sake! He was still staring at the phone. It occurred to him suddenly that this was the way Mark and Kate had sent their last message. He swallowed fiercely, his whole being consumed with the desire to see them again. He pictured his mother's face; her voice telling him to 'calm down'. . . to 'do something constructive' . . . to 'get on with life'. And he whispered furiously, 'What can

I do except wait for Gussie to get back and try to reconstruct what you two managed to do so effortlessly?'

There was a sound from the door and he looked up to see Michael waiting for him. His face showed that he had heard Ned's angry question.

Ned said, 'Sorry, Michael. Sometimes . . . you know . . .'

Michael nodded, cleared his throat, said, 'Comes over you now and then. All those people . . .' He cleared his throat again and in a stronger voice he said, 'None of my business, of course, but there is something you could do. Might help you. Or not. I don't know. You could try to talk Victor Gould into letting the Trust exhibit some of his stuff.'

Ned stared at him. He said slowly, 'Did Mack ask you to have a word?'

Michael grinned. 'He'd kill me – worse still, he might fire me – if he knew what I just said. But it was what Mark and Kate would have done.' He shook his head. 'Take no notice of me. I didn't know them like you knew them.' He began to close the door. 'Mack's taken Marion for her therapy. He didn't want to make too much of saying goodbye, hoping you will stay again on your way home. I'll take your bags down to the car and wait there. Can you say something to Emily? She would like that. She thought a lot of Kate.'

He was gone. Ned stood up stiffly and went to one of the windows to stare across the treetops to where the carousel must be. He was frowning prodigiously as he tried to work things out. His mother had warned him against commercialism yet had accepted that first offer years ago from Mitch, who had been chairman of the Trust then; indeed, he remembered her 'negotiating' very successfully, not for money perhaps but certainly regarding the site. And Mack was a good man; as good as Mitch.

He walked through the enormous apartment to the kitchen and hugged Emily to him. Her hands were floury; she held them wide, laughing up at him.

'I wish you well, honey. Your ma would want you to be happy. Remember that.'

'I will. And I'll see you soon.'

'Promise?'

'Promise!'

'You know what you're doing?' She stood there, hands now held over her mixing bowl. 'Mack showed you the village, right on the edge of the ocean, the house a way up from it. Just get a taxi and—'

Ned laughed. He suddenly felt in charge of himself.

'I know what I'm doing. Just this once I actually know what I'm doing!'

He pecked her cheek and made for the lobby.

Fourteen

It did not work out as planned. Nothing did any more; looking back over the past six months he saw life as a series of shocks. This time he had imagined it would be he who would deliver the next shock. Plain old Ned Briscoe, who never did anything exciting, would turn up practically unannounced and say to the ancient man in the wheelchair, 'I did write. Several times. No replies.' Slight pause, then the knock-out: 'I'm your son.'

He had to smile at his own absurdity, but somehow it had helped him to get on the plane and make a real effort to invent another scenario, much more targeted and hard-nosed. This one was more difficult because he was so far off being either targeted or hard-nosed. In fact, what the hell was he doing, sitting on a plane bound for Los Angeles, intending to meet a stranger who had accidentally become his father?

He almost struggled out of his seat but the woman next to him suddenly said, 'Please don't worry if I grab you when we take off. I think I'm old enough to be your grandmother so you won't get the wrong idea.'

He glanced at her, surprised. This was America and she was American. And she – and her daughter – would have had to be about fourteen to make her his grandmother. Then he met her eyes and saw sheer terror there.

He put his arm on the rest between them and turned it, opening his hand as he did so. 'Grab it when you need it,' he said, and smiled.

She put her hand on his immediately; her grip was like iron. 'Thank you. You're English too. You're supposed to be scared of flying.'

'Am I? Oh, you mean the English in general.' He smiled ruefully. 'I didn't know that. Actually, I'm scared of a lot of things. Strangely, flying is not one of them. But I know about being scared.'

The stewardess came round to tell them to fasten their seat belts. The engines appeared to be racing. The woman's grip tightened.

Ned said quickly, 'I don't like those rides where they take you up very high. We've got one in London called the Eye. Apparently there are wonderful views from the top. I couldn't do that.'

The woman was breathing quickly and audibly. He said quietly, 'We're airborne now. Does that make it better?'

She said on an outward breath, 'Yes.'

'Good.' Ned moved his hand slightly and she released it.

'I'm real sorry. Did I hurt you?'

He grinned. 'Not seriously. But what happens if you sit next to a frail elderly lady?'

'I don't know. I sat by a man going to New York and I'm sitting next to you going home!'

'Your first flight! So you know very well you'll be all right from now on.' He spoke with more assurance than he felt and she looked doubtful. He said, 'You've done it twice successfully.'

'It's worse when we land.'

He had encountered this stubborn pessimism from a young Jannie. He said, 'You need a mantra. Let's see . . . "If you give me your hand, we'll float down to land." Will that do?'

'Oh, gee. You make it sound like this flying tank is some kind of thistledown!' But she was laughing anyway. He sensed that now he would get her life story; but at least it meant he couldn't think about Victor Gould or why he was here in the first place.

The amazing thing was, as they came in to land, she said thoughtfully, 'Seems a good thing to do. Before he dies. I mean, if he was born in 1918 he must be pretty old. And it might not mean much to you but I guess you'll always regret it if you don't make the effort.' There was a silence, surprised, on his side, as he wondered what he had said to put her so thoroughly into the picture. Then she said, 'Oh, for goodness' sake! We've landed and I didn't grab your hand!' He hoped very much that he had deliberately told his story to divert her terror. He laughed and so did she. 'Did you make all that stuff up? About famous painters and all?'

Ned shook his head. 'I don't know. Can't remember what I said now!'

She leaned over and pecked his cheek. 'Well, I think you're just the sweetest man I've ever – ever – sat by in a plane!'

He had to wait for his luggage and she had just a shoulder bag, so they parted, and when he went down the moving walkway to the concourse he was still smiling. He found a sheltering pillar and paused to feel through his pockets for his father's address. Then he stopped. That first scenario of his was tempting, but ridiculous. Supposing the old man had a heart attack? The second – hard-nosed, etc., – probably would evoke the heart attack. He would go to a hotel, have a meal, make a phone call. Behave like Ned Briscoe.

Then a voice below him said, 'Hey. You must be Edward Gould. I can see the likeness.'

Ned looked down. The man wasn't all that short; he wasn't exactly overweight either. He was stocky. He was very stocky. Bald too. Eyebrows showed up too much, nose might have been broken at some point.

'Conrad Porter. Ex-wrestler. Victor's home help.' He held out a hand like a ham and Ned shook it. It seemed to be his day for hands. 'Professionally I was Con the Terrible. But Victor has always called me Conrad, and I kinda like it. I tried to call him Vic a coupla times, but it didn't work.'

'Well . . . I'm pleased to meet you, Conrad.' Ned's varied scenarios weren't working either. He said, 'Is, er, Victor not well? I mean . . . is he expecting me?'

'Sure. There was a message on the phone just yesterday with your arrival time. I'll take that.' He swung Ned's backpack on to one shoulder, which effectively put him out of Ned's vision. 'I got your room ready after your letter, anyway.'

They were suddenly striding very fast along an automated walkway. Ned was out of his depth again. He concentrated on his legs, which seemed insubstantial next to this Conrad chap's short and very workmanlike stumps. He registered that they were covered only to the knee; Conrad was wearing shorts. Ned swallowed a laugh. He must remember all these moments to share with Jannie and Gussie.

They emerged into brilliant sunshine. The heat was intense. Conrad swung the backpack to his other shoulder and Ned could see his face. Ned was reminded of the oven glove that hung next to the range in the basement kitchen of Zion Cottage, big and battered, protective.

'It's good of you to meet me like this,' he said. 'I can manage New York fairly well. But this – this is the New World, all right.'

Now they were in a car park. It was lined with palm trees. Palm trees in a car park? Conrad lifted his heavy brows towards their waving tops. 'They shade the cars. Save on the aircon.' He went unerringly to a grey Ford, almost invisible among the enormous limousines surrounding it. He flicked a remote and the car clicked a greeting. Ned went to the left-hand seat forgetting it was the driver's side. Conrad said, 'You can drive if you like, Edward.' He held out a key.

Ned laughed. 'Sorry. Never driven on the right. Forgetting where I was for a moment.'

Conrad grinned back and waited till Ned was seated in the passenger side before getting behind the wheel. 'Victor never drives. Something to do with getting on a horse. Seems like in England you get on a horse from the right-hand side, so you have to drive on the left. Right?'

Ned laughed again and put on a ghastly accent. 'I guess so.' He was pleased when Conrad gave that melon-like grin again. He realized that he liked him. 'And by the way, Conrad, everyone calls me Ned.' He dimly recalled something Kate had said back in their other life. 'Your father had an uncle – died before he was born – called Edward. He was always known as Teddy. And you have the same name but will be Ned.' Sitting there, toes searching for a non-existent brake as they surged into traffic outside the airport, Ned wondered whether he might be able to ask Victor about the unknown Teddy.

Conrad eased the Ford into the fast lane – which Ned had

to remind himself was the slow lane here – and said, 'OK. Ned it is.'

The drive took almost four hours. Mack had said it was a long trip but somehow the fact that he recommended a taxi had made Ned think it was no longer than an hour. They came off the carriageway as the last of the city disappeared into hills.

Conrad said briefly, 'Pacific Highway. Going down through the hills now, then cut across the headland. Oldfield Village is in the corner. One of the first fields to be mined. We're about a hundred miles along the bay.'

Ned said, 'I thought the house was in Oldfield Village.'

'It's the postal address, and there's nothing else in between or much beyond, so we're Oldfield Village.' Conrad flashed the grin sideways. 'Dennis brought Victor out here – he had this cabin on the beach. But then Dennis met this Irish girl and they got married and went to Ireland, and Victor stayed on. He was probably happier on his own.' He grinned again. 'He didn't have to work hard at being a recluse. He was a natural.'

'And you applied for the job of – of – house manager?'

'Not really. It sort of happened. He'll tell you. But he's serious about being alone. He never makes a phone call; let's me phone for groceries and once for a doctor. Otherwise, whatever happens, happens.' He wasn't grinning any more. 'If you hadn't turned up, he wouldn't have done a damned thing about it. He works all the time – goes into himself when people do find him. He was invited to the last meeting of the Trust. Didn't go, of course, else he'd be dead now. But Harry McKinnon came to see him just last fall. After coupla hours – got some lunch for him took him round the studio – Victor excused himself and left the house. Didn't come back for two days. I thought he was dead. Found him in the hills – neat little camp he'd set up. Took no notice when I yelled at him. Came home as meek as a lamb.' He frowned. 'I've got to tell you this. You've got to know . . . certain things.'

There was silence. They were going through an orange grove. At the edge of the road appeared a stall, a woman was sitting in a low chair by several baskets of oranges. She had her feet on one of them and was reading a book. Ned continued to digest Conrad's basic information and wondered what he was getting himself into.

'He's over eighty.' He watched Conrad's face as he negotiated the stall carefully and followed the road as it wound between the trees. The smell was overpowering. 'Is it dementia?'

'You crazy? He's the sanest man on the planet, for God's sake!' The face was angry and the words slowed right down. 'He – does – not – want – to see – people.' He puffed exasperation. 'Listen, if he doesn't want to see you when you get there, then he won't tell you to get lost, he'll just disappear.'

'But . . . for two days? He's eighty-two!'

'Eighty-three actually. Birthday last November.' He lifted a hand from the steering wheel. 'That's how it is, Ned. That's why we've got this car – Mister Anonymous, he calls it – that's why we live in a cabin on a beach without a proper address.' He turned his mouth down. 'You have to know. He said, "Tell him nothing", but you have to know.'

Another long silence at the end of which Ned said, 'Thank you, Conrad. And thank you for staying with him – riding it out in some way.'

'He can't do much about me. Dragged me out of the sea ten years ago. Stuck with me, wasn't he?'

Ned asked no more questions. He said simply, 'Lucky man.' Conrad smiled again. In a curious way he looked beautiful.

The beach house was stuck between two dunes; Ned wondered fleetingly what would happen if there was some kind of sandstorm. It looked like a very large version of the chalets that sprouted from the towans across the Hayle estuary at home. It was surrounded by a wide wooden veranda, and the central house was rectangular with windows on the two sides he could see as they drove close to some steps and parked the car. A squat chimney emerged from the apex.

Conrad was following Ned's gaze. 'We can burn wood. But Victor has found a seaweed that burns very slowly – ideal for keeping the stove going overnight. But it smokes badly so we have to save it until it's dark.' He got out of the car and reached for Ned's backpack. 'He'll be watching you from inside the house. He'll want me to take the bag but he'll approve if you take it from me.'

Ned did as he was bid and suddenly laughed. 'Sorry, Conrad. It reminds me of someone back home who is always trying to make an impression – it never comes off. Is all this worth it?'

Conrad shot him a fierce look. 'Let's just get you face to face. This could be good for him.'

The sand was firm up to the veranda steps; Ned was able to shoulder his bag and look across at the sea and take some comfort from its obvious familiarity. It seemed likely this was the closest he was going to get to Victor Gould. He began to wonder whether he was acting like Rory bloody Trewyn and making an enormous drama out of a situation that should be tackled quite differently. Grief could not be assuaged by trying to put the past to rights. Grief had to be accepted; had to be endured. Wasn't that how his mother would deal with it?

The weather was still, the sea calm, a few waves creaming in; he longed for a swim. After the early February chill of New York, California was too warm.

'Watch the step,' Conrad said. 'I raked out the wrack yesterday and the first step is steeper than it looks.'

Ned switched his gaze and saw that the cabin was built on short stilts. Beneath it a canoe and two surfboards were stored. He followed Conrad, hoisting himself on to the first of the steps by grabbing the handrail with his free hand. His father could be behind one of those windows, watching him, assessing his potential, ready to make one of the disappearances Conrad clearly dreaded. Then, beneath the shadowed veranda, a screen door was pushed open and a figure stood there, holding back the door, peering across to where Conrad was standing. A voice – a voice that struck some chord for Ned – said, 'Didn't you bring him? Wasn't he there?'

Conrad stood to one side, revealing Ned, half obscured by the pack on his shoulder.

Conrad said, 'He was there, boss. He's here now.'

Ned hoisted himself on to the sandy boards of the veranda and stood still. The man did not move; he still held the open screen door as if needing support. The silence, the stillness, were not easy, and Ned was just summoning the courage to say something and wondering what to call his father and whether he might even turn and run – though could an eighty-three-year-old actually run? – when Victor spoke.

'So you're Edward. My son and not my son. I'm your father and not your father. You'd better call me Victor.' He left the door; came forward holding out his hand.

180

Ned took it. They shook once, then dropped hands.

'Actually, I'm called Ned. But Edward is fine.'

'Ned! Of course! Your mother suggested Ned. I wanted Teddy, after an uncle I never knew but learned to idolize anyway! And she said she rather liked Ned, so you became Ned.'

Conrad appeared from the open doorway with a stick and Victor took it and leaned on it. 'Thanks, Conrad. Shall we go in? Strange how tiring it can be sitting in a car. I expect you need a drink and some food. Lead the way, Conrad. Let's show Ned the layout. Bedroom first – dump your stuff – then bathroom probably. And back here for a picnic. You used to like picnicking, Ned.'

Ned swallowed. He hadn't been prepared for the charm, for the total welcome. God, was he going to do what he had been doing at home and start to cry? He swallowed again, hard, then said, 'Yes. Victor. Thank you.'

Victor made his way further up the veranda; Ned saw a table, dishes covered with old-fashioned umbrellas of fly netting, a tall jug. Then he followed Conrad through the door and into the comparative dusk of what seemed like a very ordinary living room: armchairs, a big, squashy-looking sofa, books everywhere, on shelves but also in piles on the floor.

Conrad was chortling. 'He's made that meal and laid it up . . . he was so damned nervous I didn't think he'd be here even! This is going to work, Ned!'

'Might he go? Now?' Ned did not want him to go. Not now.

'Can't be a hundred per cent. Don't think so.'

They were in a very dark square hallway. Conrad flicked lights on, opened a door, indicated a bed. 'Drop your stuff, man. Bathroom's next door. I'm going to sort out the food.'

He saw Ned's hesitation and said, 'He ain't gonna leave home today. He's . . . he's . . . dammit, he's happy!' The low-energy lights picked out Conrad's melon-grin and Ned grinned back. This wasn't how he'd imagined anything – anything at all. It was good.

It was a strange and delicious meal. There was a plate of thin – oh, so thin – bread and butter and a jar of apricot jam next to a plate of ham – thick cut – and hard-boiled eggs. The eggs were still in their shells and Victor was peeling one when Ned arrived on the veranda again.

'Wasn't at all sure you'd turn up, old man,' he explained.

Ned smiled and sat down gingerly on an ancient folding chair. It was amazingly comfortable; he adjusted a cushion into the small of his back and looked out to sea. It wasn't really like home but the sand and sea were common denominators and the way the dunes ran down to the flat beach could be a large version of Hayle Towans. But not really. It was the space; the enormity of it. And this was the Pacific and not the Atlantic.

Victor replaced the denuded egg. 'There's a farm, six, seven miles inland. Fruit farm, of course, but they keep hens. Conrad makes bread now and then. Otherwise it's a monthly forage at the local supermarket and a heavy reliance on our deep freeze.' He glanced at Ned. 'Guess it's different where you live.'

'It is.' Ned wondered how far he should go with the reminiscences and decided to jump in at the deep end. 'There are supermarkets everywhere, but car access in the old town is difficult. And Mum believed in shopping locally anyway. So we pop out and get things when we need them. We've got a fridge-freezer but we couldn't stock up far ahead.

The shops are all within easy walking distance.' He hesitated looking at the table. 'Mum used to like making her own jam. We used to pick blackberries in the autumn.' He stopped.

Victor pushed the jam pot towards him. 'I remembered. The other night, in bed, I remembered she had jam on everything. Apricot was the best I could do.' He paused and when Ned still did not speak he said, 'The bread and butter – cut very thin – is from my own childhood. My mother kept up her standards even when she – they – were scraping the barrel. Thin bread and butter was economical as well as keeping up standards!' He laughed and Ned tried to join him.

Conrad appeared with a bowl of tomatoes in one hand and a cucumber under his arm. 'Victor doesn't care for pre-pared salads but I can cut this stuff up in mayonnaise.'

Ned shook his head. 'Fresh tomatoes. I can eat them like strawberries. Love them.'

Victor nodded happily. 'She brought you up well. I knew she would.'

Ned looked up, appalled, and saw that Victor had no idea of how his casual words sounded: totally condescending and dismissive. He dropped his eyes quickly and held on to the rough wooden arms of his chair as if he might fall off at any moment. He wanted to react violently; wanted to hit his own father, tip the table up. But more than that, he wanted to lift his head to the roof of the veranda and cry for his mother. He closed his eyes against the tears. Conrad was saying something about pouring the tea. Ned shut it all out and visualized his thoughts in written words across his own knees . . . she was valued. So much. Adored by Mark Briscoe and her three children, respected by everyone who knew her. Loved. Loved. Loved.

Victor's voice came through at last, 'Ned, do you take sugar?'

He shook his head.

'Are you all right, old man?'

So this selfish old man hadn't realized; he really had not realized. He was worse than bloody Uncle Rory. It was up to Ned to finish the visit here and now or to go on with it. He stayed where he was; he couldn't throw in the towel yet.

He said quietly, 'She was so wonderful. Sorry. I can't get used to them . . . not being here any more.' He was conscious of Conrad pushing a cup and saucer across the rough grain of the table. He said, 'They were always *there*.'

Victor helped himself to sugar. Conrad said, 'Boss, you don't take sugar.' But Victor picked up his cup, sat back in his chair, and stared up at the dusty roof of the veranda. There was a long silence. Conrad took a large slice of the ham and an egg. 'Hungry,' he said through his first mouthful. 'Been out all day.'

Victor lowered his gaze. 'So you have. And so have you, Ned. Eat something.' He sipped his tea and made a face. 'Conrad, this is disgusting.'

Conrad nodded, Victor laughed and drank the tea. It gave Ned time to drink his own tea and swallow some of the agony of grief. He took a slice of the thin bread and butter, folded it over and bit into it. Somehow it clogged up his nose. The other two continued to wrangle in an amiable sort of way while he found a tissue by which time his plate had been filled with ham, eggs and tomatoes. He began to eat dutifully, tiny forkfuls and then larger ones. Conrad poured more tea and he drank. They were talking now about someone called Frank who had gone off for a walk before Ned's arrival and not returned.

Victor said, 'He'll be fine. You know what he's like. Now and then he needs time to himself.'

'But he knew we wanted him here today of all days.'

'Oh, come on, old man! How could he possibly know that? Less of the drama!'

Conrad visibly simmered and Victor turned to Ned. 'As you doubtless know, Ned, I am not a religious man. But I think – I am certain, in fact – that if they were always there for you in life, then they are still there. Can't go into it, but . . . maybe some time I can explain a bit more.'

It had been at least fifteen minutes since Ned's protest and he had to realign his thoughts and conclude that the arguments – about the sugared tea and the man called Frank – had been to give him recovery time.

All he could manage by way of a response was, 'Yes.'

It seemed enough. Victor asked him how the McKinnons were. And then if Central Park was still there.

Ned nodded, unsmiling. 'The McKinnon apartment overlooks it, so I can safely say, yes.'

Victor nodded too and returned to his meal. Conrad got up and carried plates away, returning with ice cream.

'Try it with some of the apricot jelly,' he advised. 'I'll make coffee – give me half an hour. Then you should go to bed.' He stared at Victor. 'Ned's gonna be on his knees at this rate.'

He rounded the corner of the veranda to where the kitchen must be. They heard him bellow, 'Frank! Time for bed!'

Victor said, 'He hates it when Frank goes off like this. Frank keeps an eye on me. Doesn't let me walk in my sleep.' Was that what Victor called his escapes into the mass of dunes? And Frank was some kind of bodyguard?

Victor stretched out in his chair, obviously easing cramped muscles.

'Frank is a German shepherd. Black, ugly-looking dog. But his eyes . . . they tell a story. I've done a couple of paintings

185

of him. Haven't got the eyes. Not yet.' He turned and smiled. 'I've looked out two paintings of your mother, old man. You might like one of them.'

Ned said, 'I didn't know . . . I was six . . . I never saw her sitting for you.'

'I did them later. Afterwards. I couldn't see her properly when we were together. She just reminded me of Davie all the time.' He shook his head, his voice wry and very tired. 'I knew Davie was dependent on me and probably didn't realize that I was more dependent on her – that she was my life. Tried to join her . . . all that sort of thing . . . Kate rescued me. I hope she understood, Ned.'

He looked, waiting for an answer. Ned had no idea what he was talking about. He stared through the sudden twilight and saw that the old man was leaning towards him, almost falling out of his chair, waiting for an answer as if his life depended on it. Ned gazed back, helpless.

And then, thankfully, there was a scrabble at the base of the wooden steps and the unmistakable sound of a dog's claws coming towards them along the veranda. Victor, forgetting his plea, twisted round and said, 'Thank goodness you're home! You've worried Conrad to death!'

Frank approached them in a crouched position as if about to leap. His tail waved and lashed frantically and took all his hind quarters with it. He put his chin on Victor's knee and looked at him.

Victor said, 'Oh, those eyes . . . all right, old chap. I'm still here. And this is the man I was telling you about. This is Ned. Say hello.'

The dog turned his eyes without moving his head and registered the figure in the other chair. His tail slowed, he no longer crouched, but he went to Ned and put his chin lightly on one of his hands and then sat down and surveyed the table. 'Give him the rest of the ham on your plate, Ned,' Victor said. 'You'll have a friend for life.'

Ned did so. The dog accepted the offering and then favoured Ned with a long, deep look. He had golden eyes; they appeared to understand just about everything.

Victor said, 'You go off now. Conrad will feed him properly, brush some of that sand out of his coat. Frank might station himself on the veranda outside your door. Don't mind him.'

'I don't mind him one bit.'

Ned stood up; he was exhausted. He thought he should say something but could think of nothing. He managed a brief goodnight and then walked into the central hallway, still lit but dimly. He went briefly into the bathroom and then straight to his room.

He woke as usual in the small hours and knew with sinking heart he would sleep no more. He dragged the top blanket around his shoulders and opened his door to the veranda. The night sky was full of stars. Underneath them lay Frank, very still but wide-eyed. Ned went to him and kneeled down. He put his head on the dog's powerful shoulder, felt the rough tongue by his ear lobe, began to cry.

Frank did not move. Now and then his tongue would tell Ned that he was still there, still understanding. At last, drained completely, Ned lay still. The dog's tongue was still. They slept on the hard, sandy floor, Ned's blanket over both of them.

When they woke it was getting light. Ned was cold and sore, and stumbled back to his bed but could not sleep again. He thought of Gussie and Jannie. The only ones who understood.

Except Frank, of course.

Fifteen

Victor did not appear the next day.

'Too much excitement yesterday,' Conrad said, as if Victor were a child.

'Excitement?'

'Tension, I guess. Stress. But he doesn't like those kinda words.' Conrad looked up from a toaster. 'He's been building up to this meeting with you for a long time.'

'Yes. So have I.'

'How old are you?'

'Twenty-eight.'

'He's eighty-three. And he's still grieving.' Conrad looked down at the toaster and said, 'Some things you don't get over, man.'

He opened a lid and Ned realized the chrome machine was not a toaster but some sort of grill. Conrad removed two plates, each containing bacon and hash browns. Ned was suddenly hungry.

They ate in the kitchen. It was not the shining laboratory most American kitchens seemed to be. There was a range and a gas cooker and a deep sink, all united by a long bar holding other 'toasters'. Conrad pulled out two stools and produced cutlery from a drawer. 'OK?' he asked. Ned nodded enthusiastically. Victor's absence was a relief, in a way. They both ate ravenously. The dog appeared, black and ferocious-looking, very polite. He sat between them and waited. Conrad left two rashers of bacon so Ned did the same. They disappeared with one swish of Frank's tongue. Conrad said apologetically, 'We only feed him from our plates at breakfast.'

Ned looked into the dog's amazing eyes and nodded.

'Victor told him to watch you through the night – did you see him on the veranda?' Conrad asked.

Ned nodded again, remembering the comfort the dog had given him.

'He's generally outside Victor's room. Sometimes inside too.'

'Did you get him as a guard dog?' Ned put out a hand and Frank came and touched it with his velvet nose, then loped through the door into the hall.

'He'll stay with Victor now.' Conrad sighed sharply. 'We didn't get him. We think he was running away from something, someone. Came out of the sea one morning, caked in sand, bones showing. Victor brought him back to life.' He poured black coffee and pushed it across to Ned. 'Victor makes a habit of pulling things out of the sea. Beach-combing. He's got bottles and bits of boats . . . keeps it all in his shed. Where he paints. I don't go in there.'

'He is still working?'

'Not so much. But last October, after Mack McKinnon came over, he started on something. Don't know what it is but it's still in progress.'

Ned frowned uneasily. 'Mack McKinnon is chairman of the Trustees. The Spirit of America. He would like to have some of Victor's work.'

'He won't get it.'

'You don't think he is actually working on something for them? It's strange that he started work straight after Mack's visit.'

'Could be. But I doubt it.'

Conrad stood up and Ned said, 'That was a great breakfast, thanks. Listen, let me clear up, get to know where everything is. Then I'll swim, walk along the beach. Don't want to get in your hair.'

Conrad was uncertain. Then he went to a drawer. 'Here. This is his cellphone. I'll call you if he surfaces.'

As Ned washed the plates and opened and closed cupboards and drawers, he wondered what Conrad did when his 'boss' slept or worked. What sort of life did the two of them have in this peculiarly old-fashioned house on the deserted beach? At first their relationship seemed simply man and master. But then Conrad's concern would rear up protectively and become very much more than a servant's would be. Although he was obviously keenly pro-Ned at the moment Ned had no illusions about his own position. If Victor was going to be ill because Ned had turned up then Ned would have to go.

The clearing-up finished more or less successfully, Ned went back to his room and picked up a towel and his swimming trunks. The cellphone was a boon. He intended to swim, then sunbathe and ring Gussie in France. Maybe Frank would appear and they could swim together.

He walked until the dunes hid the beach house from his view, therefore presumably, hid him from Conrad and Victor. Then he sat down and put his head on his crooked knees and closed his eyes. He felt truly alone for the first time in days. Since Rory had left that murky morning . . . which was actually less than a week ago. It was incredible.

He forced himself to recall the utter loneliness of Zion Cottage without Gussie. Old Beck came in with news from the Fishermen's Lodge: a sighting of a tunny fish by the Coastal Watch people, weather upcountry coming down fast, plans passed for making Trewyn House into flats . . . Rory hadn't mentioned that. Visitors were few since Gussie had gone to France. Ned could have got company in the Sloop, or just walking along the harbour and back through Fore Street. But his loneliness had little to do with company. It had lifted slightly when he had been with the McKinnons; it had descended again and wrapped him around when he'd arrived in California. He frowned, remembering the woman on the plane who had asked for his hand. That had been a chink. Just a chink in the coldness.

He had never thought of himself as a depressive; in fact, he realized now that he had never thought much about himself before. He was Ned Briscoe, member of the Briscoe family with tentacles here and there, none of which mattered much.

His work had mattered at first. The proposition he had put before the interviewing panel had been simple. At that time, a great deal of work and money was being spent in the medical research field endeavouring to 'tag' cancer cells within the body so that the chemicals attacked the damaged cells only. He suggested that alongside that work, they should look for ways of screening good cells, leaving damaged or suspect cells isolated and vulnerable to the deadly drug.

It had taken him a full-blown thesis to get that simple message across but that was it in a nutshell. And he had believed in his own hypothesis and worked hard to get his team organized and as committed as he was himself. It was called the Isolation Project. It had been running for two years, and the only people who still believed in it were Gussie and himself.

He lifted his head slightly and looked at the sea. He loved the sea, but not like Gussie loved it. Sometimes it terrified him. It was like watching evolution in progress. Evolution, in fact, going backwards. What was happening exactly? Was the sea some kind of monster designed to grind rock into sand so that it could be swallowed up? Was old man Gerald Scaife right after all and the sea was intent on gobbling up the land?

Ned squeezed his eyes tightly shut – God, he really was depressive. And this place wasn't helping. But at least he knew he had done the right thing in resigning from the international drug company whether they believed in him or not. He had been back to the laboratory twice since Nine Eleven and recognized the sheer drudgery of most research work. He had resigned just before Christmas and told no one, not even Gussie.

He pulled out the rather large mobile phone from his pocket and stabbed out the series of numbers that would connect him to Gussie. The ring tone took ages to start, and when it did it was slightly fractured. He knew that meant he wasn't going to be able to hear her. He rang off and immediately stood up and threw off his clothes. After visualizing the sea as a voracious entity he had to hurl himself into it, and then, quite suddenly, it was all right. The sun shone, the cold was more intense because of it, the free movement of arms and legs was a joy as always. He could be at home on one of the beaches. People long ago had named seas and oceans and made them sound separate and different, but the mass of water that covered the earth was all one. He floated on his back and narrowed his eyes against the intense blue of the

sky. The unbroken waves lifted him, then lowered him carefully. He let them woo him away from his depression. Dad
had been a great believer in hydrotherapy; he was always
throwing himself into the water and glorying in stretching
his stunted torso.

There was that word again. Glory. The gates of glory.

Ned grinned ruefully. And from the shoreline there came
a bark. It was Frank. They swam to meet each other. Then
Frank licked Ned's face and Ned actually laughed. They
swam back to the beach and Ned towelled them both and
then they left the pile of clothes and ran until they were
dry. He had just shrugged into his jacket when the phone
rang. He whipped it out; if it was Gussie he would know that
everything was all right and the world was settling about him
again.

It was Conrad.

'Tried to get you, man. You've been gone eight hours. I
sent Frank to find you.'

'He found me.' Ned grinned down at the dog, whose
tongue was lolling from between those efficient-looking jaws.
Why on earth didn't dogs sometimes bite off their tongues?
'We had a swim, then a run. Sorry, Conrad, must have been
away from the phone longer than I thought.'

'Victor is up. Walking to meet you. He'll need an arm on
the way back. You OK, man?'

'Yes. Yes, I am. Thanks.'

'See you. Lobster for supper.'

The phone went dead. Ned grinned down at Frank. 'This
must be man talk – no frills attached. I'm used to babble,
Frank. Dad sitting there, grinning appreciatively too. But
this is OK. Conrad is OK. And Victor . . . an elderly has-
been?' Unexpectedly, Frank growled deep in his throat.

'Sorry, old chap. I forgot he rescued you. Come on, he's on his way to meet us and it's hard going on this sand.'

Victor had a home-made walking pole and looked like someone from the Old Testament. He did not spurn Ned's offer of an arm, and with the double support they made good headway along the beach. Frank walked ahead of them as if testing out the ground.

'Conrad can't get used to living with the sea, sky and sand,' Victor commented, stopping to stare out at the horizon. 'He was a professional boxer, you know. Did some wrestling, too. But there was some hanky-panky with the organizers and he tried to make a run for it.'

'Hanky-panky?' Ned laughed; the old-fashioned slang did not suit Conrad in any way at all.

'Dirty dealings? Yes, very much dirty dealings. But I've played it down for years – don't want to make too much of it. He used to get nightmares and scream the place down.' He sighed and coughed slightly. 'He didn't lose a fight he was meant to lose and they dropped him off a boat out there.' Victor nodded at the sea. 'Can't swim, of course, but he had a friend aboard who threw him a life belt. He hung on to it and was washed up a couple of miles along the beach. He wasn't conscious. I had to put him back in and float him down to the cabin. He acts like I rescued him. He would have been spotted anyway. Helicopters do a regular sweep along the coast.'

'Even so . . . time was of the essence.'

'He's learned to live with it. But some day he'll have to go and find the guy who gave him that life belt. He can sell the house and set up in the village.' Victor resumed walking and glanced at Ned. 'You don't mind, do you, old man?'

'Mind?'

'Me leaving the house to Conrad. I knew you'd be well provided for.'

Ned said gloomily, 'Jointly, I think we're millionaires.'

'Don't scorn it, Ned. You can do a lot with it. Have they got you on the board of Trustees yet?'

'What – The Spirit of America? No. But if they ask . . . Gussie will want to do it.'

'Quite a girl. Not surprising, with Mark Briscoe for a father and Gerry Scaife's daughter for a mother.' He smiled at Ned's face. 'I did some research twenty years ago when Kate and Mark hooked up and I've done a lot more since Nine Eleven, Ned. Should have done it before. Should have done it for Kate's sake and for yours. Grief makes you selfish, Ned. You look in instead of out.'

Ned thought about it and said huskily, 'Yes.'

They walked up a steep dune and the house appeared below them. They stood, getting breath into their lungs. Frank lolloped down to the veranda steps and crouched, waiting.

Victor said, 'Is there anything I can do, Ned? Did you have anything in mind when you contacted me – anything at all?'

'No. Not then. It was a desperate move, in a way. I could see that Gussie had to contact her mother. And in that case, I thought . . .' His voice petered out and he could think of nothing more to say.

Victor rattled a sigh. 'You probably realized that you still had a father. It was one of those "stages of grief" they're always on about.'

Still Ned said nothing, and they stood on the dunes in the sunshine watching the dog, who had now put his head on his paws.

'You would not be looking for consolation,' Victor said. Ned made a sound and Victor added quickly, 'That was not a question, Ned. When you sent me that first letter via McKinnon, I knew how angry you were. And why wouldn't you be angry? I have never done anything about being a father, and I am old and a recluse, and I am still alive. The man who was your true father, who was probably your best friend, was young, disabled and never grumbled – am I right?' He glanced round into Ned's face and nodded. 'I am right. He was a good father. And he is dead. I wondered – especially after we got the phone message announcing your arrival – I wondered then if your sheer tenacity meant that you intended to kill me.'

Ned made a sound then. An astonished shout. He raised his hands in protest and Victor stumbled a little as the support on his left disappeared. He steadied himself with his pole. Below them the dog barked and Conrad appeared on the veranda and looked up.

Ned opened his eyes wide and then turned and looked his father full in the face. 'I might have had a job on my hands,' he said, inclining his head towards man and dog below them.

They both laughed. When they looked again, Conrad was wheeling a trolley of food from the kitchen and the dog was up and wagging his tail. Victor put a hand in the crook of Ned's elbow and they long-strode down through the sand.

The lobster was delicious. Ned surveyed the wreckage of shells on the plates and insisted on clearing up. When he emerged from the kitchen the other two had retreated into the living room and were listening to a news programme on the radio. Frank was dozing in front of an ancient two-bar electric fire that smelled of burning dust. Ned watched them for a moment, recognizing their unlikely companionship. He knew so little about either of them. How long had it been since Victor had towed Conrad through the shallows? And what about Dennis Wakefield, who had fled to America with Victor back in the eighties? Had they been one of the first legal gay couples? Had Dennis been an Aids victim?

Frank got up and prowled to the screen door, and Ned went inside and the small domestic scene broke up. Conrad announced he was going to the village tomorrow and would check the deep freeze before going to bed. Victor asked him to go to the hardware store and get some torch batteries.

'Oh, and the drug store, too. Soap. Lavatory paper.'

Ned grinned at that. It dated Victor inexorably. Even Old Beck asked for a toilet roll.

'Come and sit with me for a bit, old man.' Victor indicated a chair. 'I'll switch off this rubbish and we can hear the sea. High tide tonight. I feel stronger at high tide.'

Ned nodded as he settled into a deep leather armchair. 'Strange to think we both live by the tides. Dad always said his stumps stopped hurting at high tide.' There was a pause and he said quickly, 'I didn't mean anything by that. It was just that he had these small . . . beliefs. They made him very human. In a way.'

It was almost dark now but he saw Victor smile. 'For me, too. I like to hear that sort of thing. I want evidence that Kate was happy. I left suddenly. I never knew your father personally and he hadn't made his reputation by then.'

Ned felt the old revulsion in the pit of his stomach and tackled it at source.

'Why did you go? Was it me? Mum was always telling me to be quiet because you were working but I never ever saw you work. So . . . maybe I wasn't quiet?'

Victor turned in his chair and stared through the dusk. 'Christ. Of course it wasn't you. God, Ned. When you were born I thought it might work. You were so great. Sturdy. Real. Practical – like your mother. And then . . . it didn't work. I poisoned everything I touched. That was the trouble. I couldn't paint. Dammit, I couldn't see what was around me. I had lost my gift of seeing *through* things – they made no impression on my mind.' Ned vividly recalled Gussie standing on the edge of the sea, absorbing what was before her.

There was a pause then Victor spoke slowly, very clearly. 'And I had been unfaithful. That's why I went. Infidelity. It's a terrible thing, Ned. Believe me, it's the worst thing.'

Ned stared back, astounded. Infidelity had never been mentioned. And then he remembered Dennis Wakefield. Dennis Wakefield the artist from America who had . . . taken Victor away?

He cleared his throat. He was determined to continue to tackle this head-on. 'Were you always gay, then? I didn't know. Mum never said . . .'

He could no longer see Victor's face but the sudden explosion of laughter told him he was wrong.

'Dear Ned. You are very much like your mother, you know. She was impulsive in her way. She saw a problem, identified it, did something about it. As quickly as that, almost.' Victor got to his feet with some difficulty; Frank did too and led the way to various light switches. The living room glowed around them, shabby, comfortable. Victor settled himself again, slightly askew so that he could look at his son. He said, 'I was not gay, Ned. Dennis wanted to help me back to some kind of artistic life. I knew it was the right way to go. Better than walking into the sea and giving Kate a few more burdens to shoulder.' He dropped one arm and fondled Frank's ears.

'He owned this place – sold it to me three years later when he went to Ireland. He's married now but he keeps in touch – checks that I'm still working at least two hours a day. Swim every other day. Food . . . sleep. He – he *dragooned* me back to life, Ned. It was the only way.'

Ned found he could no longer meet his father's eyes. They saw too much. He too put down a hand and touched Frank's sable coat. 'Mum did not speak about it. Neither of us did. I – I labelled you as a deserter.'

'Well, you were right about that. I could see only the infidelity.' As Ned's gaze swept up with surprise, he caught a slight grin on Victor's face as he carried on. 'Though if I hadn't been unfaithful, you would not have been born, Ned. And I would have missed out on something. I'm not sure yet, but I suspect I would have missed something glorious.'

That word again. Ned felt sudden exasperation. He said flatly, 'Sorry. I don't get it. This infidelity thing. Are you talking about your work – your talent?'

There was a silence in the room; it was tangible, like soup. Thick with . . . something.

Victor said at last, 'Do you not know about Davie? Didn't Kate tell you?'

'Sorry. Never heard of him.'

'Not him. Her. My wife. Davina.'

Ned put his hand back on to the arm of the chair; it was heavy as if the thickness of the silence held it down. Ned knew now that the silence had gathered itself into a soup of memory. He thought suddenly: This is why I came, this is the reason for my existence . . .

He spoke through the same thickness now in his throat. 'You must understand that I know nothing about my mother's life before me. She wanted everything to begin with her marriage into the Briscoe family. I see now that she saw it as giving me an instant family. Normality. Happiness.'

'Then I will stop talking, Ned,' Victor said. 'She saw that there would be a problem for you, she identified it and she did something about it.' His smile was wide. 'Dear, dear Kate. I'm not about to ruin your wonderful solution.' He tipped his head to the ceiling as if he could see his ex-wife on the lime-washed rafters. 'It worked. And now I have met our son it is still working.'

He began to heave himself up again and Ned almost did the same. Frank stayed exactly where he was between the two armchairs, and Ned sat down again. He said loudly, 'This is why I came, Victor. I didn't know – now I do. I have to under-stand this. You have to tell me. I can't leave Mum and Dad in the wreckage of Ground Zero until I know. Perhaps they can't even go through the gates of glory until I know.'

Victor collapsed back into his chair. He sounded mildly surprised. 'Gates of glory?'

Ned explained quickly. 'We thought – the three of us – that we could bring them down to our level again by imagining the kissing gate along the cliff. It was always such a performance to get Dad through. The wheelchair wouldn't go along the footpath so he had to be on his legs. So he went first – he didn't like doing that – and closed the gate and leaned on it and she sort of squatted down and kissed him through the bars. The legs made him too short to reach to the top.'

Victor said, 'Did he mind?'

'I don't know. But Mum made sure he knew that she didn't mind. They were quite embarrassing at times.' Ned smiled. 'The guys I brought home from school and college and work – they didn't know who to fall for first: Mum, Dad or Gussie. I suppose I can add Jannie to that list now.'

Victor smiled back. 'Thank God you were so happy. I was never sure. Even when you arrived here, I wasn't sure.' He leaned over and put a hand on Ned's arm. 'Stay true to all of it. It's so important, Ned. That's what I am trying to say. Don't do what I did. Be faithful.'

'I still don't get it,' Ned said. 'You haven't told me exactly how you were unfaithful.'

Victor was surprised. 'I lost my wife and was ill with grief. Your mother had nursed her through the last months. She nursed me, too. And I thought I could forget Davie by loving Kate. She was so lovable, Ned. You know that.' He dropped his head into his hands. 'When she told me she was pregnant, I knew I would have to marry her. It was only right. Give the baby my name, protect them both . . . it was how I was brought up, Ned. You can understand that.' He looked over his hands and Ned nodded.

Victor's voice dropped. 'It didn't work. When you were born, it came to me that it was never going to work. Davie couldn't have children. I had been unfaithful to her twice over. Kate and I – we got right away from Gloucestershire. Went to St Ives and tried to live in the artists' colony. That didn't work either. Davie would have loved the place: the Newlyn School, the feeling of being back in the twenties.' He put both hands in his lap and looked at Ned. 'Can you begin to understand?'

Ned swallowed and dropped his eyes from the pleading face. All he knew was that his mother had been rejected. Not even second best.

Victor said, 'I think – I am almost certain – that she was relieved. She knew Dennis better than I did at first. He was a bit of an outsider like me, and she had him to meals, that kind of thing. I'm surprised you don't remember him, old man. He tried to teach you how to play baseball. He used to arrive on the beach and say, "Howdy, folks," and you took him off.'

Ned frowned, concentrating on a fleeting glimpse of a thin gangle of a man and then realized it was Jem who looked after the beach donkeys. He said, 'I don't remember anything much before I was five.' He had started school then, and identified the girl in Standard Three who looked at things so intensely.

Victor said, 'I've tried to block things. I've managed to do it with the war. I couldn't live with that.'

'But what about your war paintings? They made you famous.'

'A-a-agh.' The sigh had become a groan. Frank was up with his chin on Victor's knee. The long tongue came out and tried to lick sideways at the hand that was clutched into a fist. Victor immediately relaxed and fondled the dog's ears. 'It's all right, old chap. No pain. No pain.' Frank subsided slightly.

Victor said, 'The price we pay for true empathy, Ned. We see the cost of it when we see how our feelings affect animals.'

Ned felt tears behind his eyes. He had always understood that his mother could not show him any more love than she showed to Gussie; now he could hear her words when she placed new-born Jannie in his arms. 'Two sisters, Ned. Bit much, I suppose. Good job you can take it.'

Victor said, 'I didn't want to do those paintings, Ned. But I knew they'd sell. And then I could paint what I wanted to paint. And I could marry Davie. And everyone – everyone in the family – would be happy.' He leaned down and looked into Frank's eyes. 'And that's how it was. I must never forget that. Never. We had over twenty years, precious years.' He looked up. 'I wish you could have known Davie. What a stupid thing to say – if Davie was alive, you wouldn't be here, would you? But she would have loved you.' He squeezed his eyes shut as if to clear them and then went on, 'Ned, I'm sorry, I realize that every word I say is hurting you. Forgive me. I'm going to bed now and we'll start again tomorrow. Fresh slate. No more memory lane, eh?' He patted the dog. 'Listen, you can have Frank again tonight. He's all I have to offer, really.'

He began to ease himself forward, ready to stand, and paused to gather himself. 'Listen, Ned. If there is anything – if you came for something special – let me know. If you want me to donate my stuff to The Spirit of America – anything really – tell me. I betrayed Davie with Kate. Perhaps there might be something that would make it less of a betrayal. I don't know.'

He pushed on the arms of the chair and was halfway up when Ned put out a hand and managed to choke, 'Please don't go. Not yet.'

Victor collapsed instantly, then laughed. 'That's easy. Easier than going.' He turned sideways. 'There is something. Tell me. I know McKinnon is a good man really. I don't care where my work goes. Kate and your father were Trustees. It's only right—'

Ned said fiercely, 'I don't care about that either. Your stuff is never going to die wherever it goes. I want something else. I want something . . . *something* . . . to get my family back.' Tears were pouring down his face. He thumped his chest painfully. 'I want something here. Inside me. A knowledge.'

'Perhaps we should sleep on it. Tomorrow is another day and all that?'

'Mum said that. Did you get that from Mum?'

'Probably. I got so much from her.'

'That might be too late. You might die in the night.'

Victor sat back, roaring with sudden laughter. Ned realized what he had said and tried hard to pull himself together and then deliberately went on, 'It's true. We're here at rock bottom, somehow. Impetus. All that stuff. You have to go on talking. Something . . . something might come. Like an anchor . . . just to stop the boat from drifting. We're drifting, you see.'

Victor was silent. Ned took out one of Mark's handkerchiefs and blew his nose fiercely.

Victor said at last, 'Where shall I start? Will it hurt you if I talk about Davie?'

'I don't know.' Ned stared at the handkerchief. It had a wildly embroidered M and B in one corner, probably executed by Jannie several years ago. It was stained with paint. He stuffed it into his pocket. 'Start where you can.'

'I have to start with Davie. If it hadn't been for Davie your mother would never have come into our lives. Your mother was a nurse, Ned. Of course you know that. She took on private nursing. Twenty-four-hour nursing. She told me she wanted to concentrate on one person, all the time.' He looked down at the dog. 'She did that. She was like my mother, who used to talk of wrapping me in cotton wool when I was ill as a small boy. Kate did the same sort of thing. She wrapped Davie in her love, they became two parts of a whole. I heard her say once, "Give the pain to me, Davie, let me carry it for you," and Davie believed that she did just that. On good days Kate would lay a special afternoon tea on the trolley – one of those cake stands, with two chocolate eclairs and the bone-china cups that had belonged to my grandmother. After Davie died she kept it up and made me eat an eclair and drink tea from the cups and – and – oh God – make

204

conversation.' He tried to smile. 'She said she would stay until I was on my feet and she timetabled my day, hour by hour, so that I wouldn't fall into the hole.'

He held up his hand as Ned opened his mouth to speak. 'No, I'm all right. I need to say these things and you need to hear them. Kate's goodness was . . . wonderful. Totally practical. We went for walks and she would ask questions about the city and the cathedral and Bishop Hooper. She probably knew more about the history of Gloucester than I knew myself but she never corrected what I told her and often I made it up so that we could go back to the house and eat pikelets and stare into the fire.' He paused. 'You can guess what happened. I never slept and I was probably half mad by the time spring came. I went to her room.' He heard Ned's protesting cry and said quickly, 'Sorry. Sorry, old man. Let that go. Suffice it to say we got married as quickly as possible and you were born six months later.'

They were both silent. Frank stood up and put his head on Victor's knees. Ned knew that meant the old man was distressed. He gritted his teeth and tried to whip up some of his old anger.

'So then you felt guilty and you tried living with other artists and it didn't work so you dumped us. After all my mother – your wife – had done for you, you left us. She had to work at the cottage hospital and I drifted around on the beach after school.' As he said the words Ned recalled uneasily that there had been an 'arrangement' with someone who would look after him for that hour before his mother came home but he had skipped off to the beach and asked Jem if he could help with the donkeys. And then there had been Gussie.

Victor was startled out of his other world. He turned in his chair, jolting the dog away as he did so. 'We talked about it – Kate and Dennis and me. She knew – she understood. There was a weekly allowance – the little cottage – you remember the little cottage. And then we divorced and halved everything.' He swallowed audibly. 'Ned, you have to believe me. I was not a fit husband or father. All right, I came here for my own sake, but also for yours. I could have dragged you down with me.' Frank put a sandy paw on Victor's swivelled knees and gave a tiny whine.

Ned shifted in his chair, stretched his legs against threatening cramp, took in the poorly lit room again. His father had lived in this solitary place for over twenty years, a lot of that time on his own. He closed his eyes, heard the old man settle back, say something soothing to the dog.

'She never spoke about it. She was like that. I did not realize how much she disliked the studio cottage until we moved into Zion Cottage. When Dad's stumps were hurting him she never asked him about it, but I knew she was worried.' He sat forward and rubbed his legs. 'Sometimes . . . well, I suppose I got the wrong messages. And I filled in big gaps with my own versions.' He tried to laugh. Then he levered himself up. 'But I know she missed you. That was probably why she worked at the hospital.'

Victor moved too. 'I missed both of you. I nearly came back. Lots of times. But I had no right.'

Ned said, 'I have to walk around a bit. Please don't go. You haven't really told me about your first wife.' He looked at Victor's face. 'You said you had over twenty years together and they were happy years.'

For a moment he thought Victor was going to clam up. Frank almost held him to the chair with his paw and Victor made to move it, and then left it where it was and settled back again. But all he said was, 'I have a life here, you know, Ned. Conrad and me . . . we check the shore, we make notes about the weather every day. I have done what your mother did. I have blocked out certain memories – the ones that are negative.'

'You still work?' Ned had spotted a bottle and some glasses on a side table. He poured a small measure of whiskey into a glass.

'Every day.' Victor accepted the glass and indicated that Ned should join him. 'Those abstracts McKinnon wants – they are actually scapes of one kind or another. I drowned myself in sand, sea and sky when Dennis left. They represented the universe to me. I told McKinnon he could have them. He wanted some of the others, too. I said no.'

Ned sipped the neat whiskey and was reminded of Rory. He sat down again and put the glass on the floor. He was shocked. Mack had become an ally, a friend. And all the time he was angling for something else.

'I had no idea,' he said. 'I promise you that is not why I came to see you.'

Victor held up a hand. 'I know. I know. He told me I must not involve you in any kind of argument. And I am not going to do that, Ned. But some time while you are with me, you must come into the shed – I refuse to call it a studio – and look at the stuff he wants. We won't talk about it. We will just look. Will you do that?'

Ned said, 'Of course.' And then, 'With great pleasure.' He was relieved; obviously Mack was . . . all right.

Victor took an enormous breath and let it go. 'There are many paintings of Davie.'

Ned waited, gnawing his lip, tasting the unfamiliar whiskey.

Victor said, 'Did you know she was my cousin?'

'I know nothing about her.' But the words electrified him.

'Her name was Davina Daker. Her mother and my mother were sisters, very close. I held Davie in my arms when she was born. We had always known each other. She was quite a bit younger than me and it made a difference for years. In fact, I was in love with her mother for a very long time. And Davie was in love with another cousin. It was all a bit incestuous. That's another of those over-used words these days.' He did not smile. 'Gloucester was small then. My grandfather was a tailor with a large clientele. Davie's parents ran a clothing business. My mother was a hairdresser and knew everything about everyone!' He managed a small laugh. Ned gave him a quick, curious glance. The close-knit family picture that was appearing was miles from the hermit-like existence of this elderly man.

Victor went on, 'I was three years in a POW camp during the war, and when I came home she had changed. She was beautiful, talented – a singer, you know. But she had built a protective wall around herself. The love affair that had been a large part of her life since early teens – it was over. And she wasn't going to let it happen again. Ever.' He laughed again, a different laugh, almost a chuckle. 'And then this crock of a cousin – another cousin – returned from Germany and couldn't seem to talk or paint or shave or sleep . . .' He shook his head. 'She had a job to do. And she did it very well.'

He sighed and finished his whiskey, then put the glass next to Frank, who sniffed it, shook his head violently and sneezed. They both laughed then.

Victor said, 'That's it really. Davie achieved fame. She was soloist with a great many orchestras. I went on painting. After the war pictures, I did landscapes. We were surrounded by the Cotswolds. And then came the industrial scapes. I painted Gloucester while it was still a working port. We were sublimely happy. No children. It was my fault. I was glad it wasn't anything to do with Davie. But . . . it was my fault.'

Ned frowned and almost asked a question; but then did not.

'The first we knew of the illness was when she lost her voice.' Victor drew an enormous breath. 'And the rest is history, of course.'

He began to get up. 'Time, gentleman, I think. Don't you?'

'Right.' Ned leaped to his feet and held out an arm. 'Grab this, if it helps.'

It did not help but Victor grabbed the arm anyway and they staggered past Frank.

'I'll switch everything off, old man. You take the dog and go.' Victor stopped by one of the lamps. 'Did it help? In any way?'

Ned hesitated by the door. 'Yes. It helped. I'm not sure yet how or why, but I know it did. Just one thing.'

'Yes?'

'You said that it was your fault there were no children from your marriage. But then . . . there's me.'

'Quite.' Victor looked across the room. 'It's taken a long time to believe in you, Ned. Thank you for coming to see me.'

He flicked a switch and said, 'Go on, Frank. Stay with Ned.'

Ned held on to the doorjamb; he could feel tears on his face. He said, 'I'm all right, Victor. Let Frank be with you tonight.'

He crossed the hallway into his bedroom. Conrad had switched on the bedside lamp and turned down the bed. Ned fell on to it, face down. He clutched the pillow and wept. These were new tears. These were tears for Victor and Davie Gould.

Sixteen

Contrary to her careful plans, Jannie went home at Easter.

She almost wept when she told Robert Hanniford.

'I know I'm leaving you in the lurch, Robert, but now that Kai's family are taking him off on this adventure holiday, there will be only the three boys. And you always cope anyway.'

'My dear girl,' she always hated it when he called her that, 'just relax, for goodness' sake. Geoff and Elizabeth would normally be on their own, district nurses at the ready as usual, of course. I'm staying so that I can use the workshop. You know all this, Jan. Stop beating yourself up. I understand. In fact, I'm envious. My parents have both embarked on second marriages and certainly don't want an adult son turning up. Not for a while, anyway.'

He laughed but Jannie chose to think of him as rejected. She tightened her mouth against a flow of sympathy and that drew down her snub nose and made Robert laugh more.

'What?' she asked.

'You look exactly like Kai looked when he was pestering his parents to take him on this holiday. And that's another thing, Jan. He is the one who fusses and makes problems. With him out of the way, the other three are almost independent.'

'And I'm like him, am I?' But she knew what he meant, and she smiled and relaxed. He was right, of course; he always was. She said, 'It's just that I don't want to leave you for three whole weeks.'

He nodded. 'I know. But, Jan, we have to slow down. We need to make a bedrock. We've known each other such a short time. You were twenty-one two months ago, I'm twenty-six. I work as a handy man at a residential school in the back end of Devon and you're still a student.'

'I know. But you're a genius and I'm so good with geniuses! My dad was one and my mum was another in a different way. In fact, you and me, we're just like them, Robert. No, honestly. And this isn't a resurrection wish – have you not heard of that? It's the absolute opposite to a death wish. Yes, all right, I made it up. But, oh my God, Robert, I know in my bones and my soul that we're meant to be a pair. I can slow down if you like, but we both know that, don't we?'

He looked at her and sighed. 'Yes, Brisket. We both know that.'

She loved it when he called her *that*. Nobody ever had before. It was his special, special name for her. She loved it and she loved him.

But she could not let Gussie be all alone at Easter. And Ned was staying in California indefinitely, it seemed. When she thought of the three of them so far apart it frightened her. Gussie had had that awful time in France with that dreadful woman who was her mother, then all the uproar when she got back home because the woman had accidentally pushed someone into a river and then dived in and rescued him. Luckily Gussie had been at Aunt Ro's. But then she had insisted on going home and had already had over a month of her own company. And now Ned had announced he still couldn't leave his father.

Jannie had protested vigorously into the phone. 'You've already stayed weeks longer than planned. I don't get it.' The connection was brilliant; he could have been standing right next to her.

'You haven't got all the loose ends to tie up like I have, Jan. Just believe me, I need him at the moment and he needs me. He really does. He's doing this painting. He started it right after Nine Eleven, when Mack visited him. It's of Mum and Davie and Dad. It – it's *wonderful*. It's for the Trust. He keeps asking me things about Dad. He's got photographs but he says he needs to know his inside as well as his outside. He wanted to know Dad's favourite joke. And all the little details of how he managed his tin legs. I played him the recording of our message. Then I had to describe the legs and he painted them, stacked against the wheelchair like they so often were. And they are absolutely spot-on! And Mum – Mum is so beautiful. It's as if I'm seeing her for the first time. I've told him about the gates of glory and the kissing gates along the cliff path. He closes his eyes and puts his fingertips on the canvas as if he can feel their faces like a blind man . . .'

Jannie couldn't hear him so well then because her sinuses were blocked with tears. She wanted to ask who the heck Davie was; later she was glad she could not talk through the tears because she remembered Ned telling her about Davina. The stepmother he never knew.

At last she managed to whisper, 'I feel so guilty because you and Gussie have to go through all this and here I am . . . falling in love. I must be so shallow, Ned!'

'Bollocks!' he said robustly, sounding like Awful Uncle Rory. 'You're the normal one. And I always thought you were just a spoiled brat!' Then he said quietly, 'Are you really fall-ing in love, Jan?'

That was the second time he had called her Jan. She must be growing up at last. Gussie was now Gus and Jannie was Jan.

She whispered back, 'I am.'

'Can't you take him to meet Gussie?'

'No. We have to slow down.'

'Oh dear. Now I know it's serious. When – *ever* – has Jannie Briscoe been able to slow down?'

'Anyway, Gussie and me, we need time together. She was so quiet and withdrawn when she popped in on her way home. Did you know that the chap Zannah Scaife pushed into the river—'

'I thought he fell in all by himself!'

'That's the official version. The real story is that he was engaged to Gussie for about five minutes yonks ago and he was after her. So Zannah tried to kill him and then had second thoughts and rescued him. I think it's all a bit much for Gussie. It's not *her*, is it?'

'No. It's not her. Did you make it all up, Jan?'

'Of course not. Well, some of it. I sort of joined it up so that it made sense. I remember Gussie being engaged and then not being engaged and I always wondered about it. And if he broke her heart, then it would be natural for her mother to try to kill him, wouldn't it?'

There was a long pause, which was very wasteful as this was a transatlantic call so Jannie started to fill it with a de-scription of Robert Hanniford.

Ned interrupted her. 'Did he succeed? Did he break her heart?'

Jannie stopped talking and frowned, thinking back. 'I

don't think so. But it put her off men for good. Something awful must have happened. I'll ask Aunt Ro about it. And listen, if you're not back home for the summer, we're officially not speaking. OK?'

Ned said easily, 'OK.'

So Jannie arrived on the main-line platform at St Erth the week of Good Friday and hurried over the bridge to the branch line where the local train to St Ives was already waiting. She was hunched over with the weight of her backpack and made for the first open door, where she dropped some of the bags she was carrying and had to scrabble around frantically.

'May I help you, madam?'

It was Gussie, first of all holding the door open and then gathering three plastic bags at once with her long arms. Someone with a green flag bundled them on to the train. They were laughing, trying to hug.

Jannie collapsed on to a seat. 'Oh my God! I'm home! Gussie, you shouldn't have come to meet me. I was going to have a taxi and arrive on the harbour in real style and now you'll insist we walk.'

'I will indeed.' Gussie sat in the opposite seat and put the sundry bags around their feet. 'I've got the trolley at the station and we can stroll down Tregenna Hill and look in the shops.'

'With the infamous trolley?' Jannie groaned. 'I know I thought it was great when Ned made it because I could ride on it. But now . . . we'll have to use the road and the cars very much resent it. I think we should skid down Skidden Hill and do the shops later.'

'All right,' Gussie said placidly. 'In that case, you can have a ride on it. As a special treat.'

But in the event the two of them were needed to hold the trolley back, and by the time they reached the harbour and met a taxi coming up, even Gussie had to admit the trolley had had its day.

'Perhaps Ned could narrow it down a bit,' she panted as they shoved it along Lambeth Walk, avoiding the prams and dogs and people with difficulty.

Jannie cocked a sarcastic eyebrow. 'Perhaps.'

'Or you could bring less luggage,' Gussie came back.

'Not possible.' They both panted with laughter.

The big cellar kitchen looked just as it had at New Year. Jannie dropped her stuff at the foot of the stairs and walked around feeling the edge of the table, touching the mugs on the open shelves, inhaling the unmistakable smell of mackerel in the oven. Gussie fetched bread from the crock and began cutting and buttering it.

She said, 'I thought, an early supper. It will help to orientate you. I found food did that for me – in France and when I came back last month. Then we can sit by the range and chat or even have a walk. It won't be dark till sevenish. What d'you think?'

'Lovely. We can do both. Talk and walk. And we can start on the project.'

'Project? What do you mean?'

'I'm into projects. They have them all the time at Hartley. Motivation, that sort of thing. We might need motivating again. So we're going to find all the kissing gates we can. I'm going to list them and mark them on the map. And when I bring Robert down in the summer, we're going to use them. For kissing.'

Gussie laughed but raised her brows as she brought hot plates from the side oven. 'A statement of intent? A way of

gently introducing the fact that you have "found someone"?'
She rolled her eyes dramatically. 'There's just a hint of
defiance in your voice.'

'Gussie, stop right there. You have known about Robert
since I first met him, so don't pretend it's a shock way of putting you in the picture.'

'Oh, darling, I'm teasing. You've always been upfront. I
love it and Ned loves it. We know exactly where we are with
our baby sister. And I like the idea of the project very much.'
She took a roasting tin of sizzling mackerel from the main
oven, pushed it on to the table and looked quizzically at
Jannie. 'The gates of glory, yes?'

'Yes, Gussie. They're going to crop up in all kinds of ways.
But we can start with the kissing gates. Ordinary. *So* Mum
and Dad.'

'Yes. I've been playing the tape every day. And its ordi-
nariness is what makes it so extraordinary.'

'Oh, Gussie.' Jannie's eyes flooded in the old way and she
squashed the tears away angrily with her flattened hands.
'I know just what you mean. But . . . was it really awful in
France?'

'No. At first it was so odd and strange I couldn't believe
I was there. And then, subtly, it changed.' She pushed the
bread-and-butter plate to her sister. 'Jannie, I learned to
love my mother again.' She gave a wry smile. 'When she left
us, all I could see were her faults. And I saw them again,
immediately I arrived. And then . . . oh, I don't know . . . I
had to find a way to take them on board – love her the way she
was.' She started to laugh. 'When she did that final furious
mother thing, protecting me from Andrew, it was just comic.
I mean, I'd actually looked into his eyes and seen that he was
scared stiff of me. I knew about him. I could have ruined his

image – he was all image, no reality – so I was free already. But she didn't know that. She revenged me.' She started to laugh. 'It was so typical, Jannie. I'll tell you more bit by bit, but you still won't really understand it because I don't myself. But it happened. I told Rosemary all about it and she seemed to get it. Not sure. Our Aunt Ro is so – so complicated. After all that has happened I think she still loves Rory. By the way, Rory has gone over to stay with Zannah for a while. I might spend time with her this summer.' She paused then said, 'She's got a brain tumour.'

Jannie, halfway through her mackerel already, stopped eating and stared. 'Oh my God.'

'Quite. Will you want that slice of bread and butter?'

'Yes. And another. I'll get some. This is delicious.' She got up and fetched the bread. 'I don't know what to say, Gus, I really don't. All this was happening and I was falling in love. And Ned is sitting with his father waiting for him to die. Are we going our separate ways?'

'Not sure. I don't think so. But perhaps.'

Jannie, used to instant reassurance from her older sister, stopped buttering bread and said again, 'Oh my God.'

'Sit down and finish your supper,' Gussie said. 'I'll do the same. Then I think we'll go for that walk.'

They strolled the length of the harbour and took the footpath that ran alongside the railway line to Carbis Bay. They found a kissing gate leading up to one of the big hotels.

'That can't be even associated with a glory gate,' Jannie said, wrinkling her nose. 'It's much too – too civilized. We'll have to get out on the moors somewhere.'

'It would have to be somewhere Dad could manage,' Gussie reminded her. 'And he could certainly manage this one. They've surfaced the path and there are street lights even!'

'Hmm. There weren't many places Dad couldn't manage. But I get your point. I see it in my head as right out on the moors somewhere. Above Zennor perhaps. Or further down, towards Pendeen and Botallack.'

'And not obvious,' Gussie agreed, nodding slowly. 'Somewhere they found.' She stopped and looked at her sister. 'Darling, are we kidding ourselves?'

'No!' Jannie was emphatic. 'I can remember them so well. Mum going down on her haunches to reach Dad. They would laugh a lot and then suddenly stop laughing. Oh my God, Gussie, is that how they felt when they jumped?'

They hung on to the gate and then each other. It was Jannie who recovered first. She held her breath on a sob and ran her hand down Gussie's single plait.

'Come on, big Sis. Let's go home. We'll phone Ned, clear up the mackerel plates and go to bed.'

Gussie took the tissue Jannie was pressing on her and drew back.

'It was a good idea, but if we're going to end up like this every time—'

'It *is* a good idea! And if we end up having a good cry, then so be it. Perhaps we haven't cried enough so far.'

Gussie put a hand on the blond hair so unlike her own. She smiled wryly. 'Are you going to end up the wise old woman of the family?'

'I always have been, and the rest of you just didn't see it. That's why I had to keep yelling all the time!'

They turned and walked back the way they had come. They held hands as they did so often.

They did not go on with the 'project' until the Saturday. The sun shone brilliantly on the Thursday and Old Mrs Beck, still doubled up with her winter arthritis, wanted to sit on the Friendship bench below Zion Court and talk to anyone who felt similarly. She wore her coal-scuttle hat and a black shawl over a high-neck blouse. The girls helped to settle her and took down cups of tea at regular intervals. When there was room they sat with her and she would tell them the news.

'And I en't making it up like you always do, our Gussie!' she said, poking Gussie's arm quite painfully with her gnarled fingers. 'Just had a lady from America telling me her granddaddy was a tin miner and emigrated when Wheal Alice closed down. She was mighty proud of being what she called a third-generation American. But she hadn't seen our Ned. Makes you wonder whether she were making it all up like you did, young lady!' She cawed a laugh, echoed joyously by Jannie.

When she was tired and wanted to go back to Old Beck and the warmth of their cottage, she had to be almost carried up the steps. She stood at the top getting her breath. 'I do remember your parents pulling me up here many a time. Your dad would have me on one arm and his stick on the other. Marvellous, he were. You'd never know there was anything wrong with him. Unless you did know, o' course!' She cackled again and then added soberly, 'Poor little Rosemary Briscoe. Couldn't be blamed really. She was only four. Just showing her baby brother the view. That's all it was.' She started to plod forward again. 'Never the same since.' The girls exchanged startled glances over her head.

Old Beck was sitting dourly by the radio and looked up as they came in.

'Well, my maid . . .' he waited till they settled his wife into her chair, 'I reckon 'tis time for us to go.' Jannie stifled a giggle and was glad she did when he spoke with very real grief in his voice. 'The old queen be dead. The wireless is full of it.' He nodded at the ancient radio sitting on the dresser.

'Well . . .' Old Mrs Beck nodded. 'She were twenty-one when I were born so she's done well. And she's back with her Bertie.' She looked up at the two concerned faces above her. 'She had to wait a long time to see him again – just you remember that.'

'I wouldn't have minded waiting for you, my maid,' Old Beck maundered. 'Like you waited for me when I was fishing up north.'

'You sound like you been drinking more than just tea!' his wife snapped back unsentimentally. 'Just push that kettle over on to the range and fetch the bread and that pot of jam the vicar's wife brought us. Don't just sit there!'

The girls beat a hasty retreat. They had been spring cleaning most of the day and planned a late swim before their meal. Now they wanted to switch on the television and hear about the Queen Mother. Questions about Aunt Rosemary were forgotten.

On Easter Sunday they went to church. Father Martin was so delighted to see them that they were embarrassed. They had managed two services at Christmas and had tried to describe for him what he called 'the New York experience'. Gussie had mentioned the coincidence of both services referring to the gates of glory. He'd nodded and replied, 'Well, of course, there are certain phrases that are repeated. For some people this makes the liturgy less important; for others it offers great significance.'

They had walked back home alongside Thaddeus Stevens and his dog, and Ned had muttered dismissively, 'Idiot. He could wet blanket a wet blanket!'

Thaddeus had suddenly piped up, "'E do mean well, my 'andsome. Lissen 'ard to 'is words. 'E do mean well.'

On Easter Sunday the girls found themselves with Thaddeus again. The weather had deteriorated since the previous day when Old Bessie Beck had sat on the Friendship bench in the sunshine.

'Not quite so nice, today,' Gussie said, smiling at him. 'Your dog decided to stay indoors?'

Thaddeus cleared his throat. 'Naw. 'E died yesty. Went off with the Queen Mother, I reckon.' He stopped to let a push-chair go by. The girls stopped too, shocked. 'I thought of going to that-there dog rescue place, Helston way. Still got Jock's feeding bowl. All his stuff really. Pity to waste it.'

Jannie said, 'We'll drive you. They might be closed to-morrow – bank holiday and everything. Shall we go on Tuesday?'

The old man looked astonished. "'Tis mightily kind of you. But, no, I can't make up my mind ahead of itself. I 'ave to wake up and think this is the day for taking on another dog. The consequences have to settle themselves inside me. I en't a live wire like you, January Briscoe. I 'as to think and I 'as to feel.' He started moving on. 'I 'ope you understand and won't take me unkindly. And I thank you greatly for your offer.'

They watched him go and they turned left and took the Academy Steps towards Barnoon. As they tugged themselves up by the handrail, Gussie called over her shoulder, 'D'you remember at Christmas he told Ned to listen to Father Martin's words? My goodness, Jan, I listened to what Thaddeus was saying and I heard so much. Did you?'

Jannie was busy holding back tears for Thaddeus and his dog. She stopped climbing and held on to the rail with both hands, panting loudly. She forced herself to say sturdily, 'Yes, but if he lives life as he said, then what on earth is he going to have for his Easter dinner?'

Gussie stopped too and turned to look down on her young sister. She smiled lovingly. 'Oh, Jannie Briscoe, I hear what *you* are saying! You know very well he goes to his son's every Sunday!'

Jannie said, 'Clever clogs. Get going. If we're going to pay homage at the Clodgy kissing gate and get back before the chicken is burned to a cinder, we need to put a move on!'

So the girls strode out along the cliff path and found the gate that led away from the sea towards the road to Zennor, Gurnard's Head and eventually Cape Cornwall, Sennen Cove and Land's End.

The gate and its pathway were thick with shoulder-high ferns. This was a way rarely used by walkers. The ferns blocked the glorious coastal views and the path emerged very prosaically at a bus stop. Jannie took her notebook from her bag and carefully noted this second gate.

'Another one that is much too obvious and well kept,' she commented. 'Dad would have wanted a view. He loved feeling himself part of the landscape. That's where you get it from, Gus.'

'Get what?'

'Your peculiar staring. Dad did that all the time.' Then in case that sounded too slushy she said, 'Shall we wait for the next bus? My feet are killing me.'

'OK.' Gussie was balancing on a milestone, gazing over the ferns. 'I didn't realize you could see Seal Island from here.'

She stepped down and Jannie took her place. 'Oh, yes. And before that, there's that cove where we used to jump into the sea at high tide and float up into the cave – d'you remember?' She laughed. 'Let's do that tomorrow. We want to go that way for the next gate. Let's take our costumes and leap again like frogs. Go on, Gussie – please!' She leaped from the milestone and did an imitation of herself at ten years old, hands together in supplication.

Gussie did not reply. She bent down and untied then re-tied her sensible walking shoes.

Jannie reverted to the infant school playground, put her thumbs in her ears and waggled her fingers as she mimicked. 'Oh, all right, I get the message. Only the beginning of April . . . risk of hypothermia. "Ne'er cast a clout till May is out . . ."'

Gussie whipped off her long scarf, doubled it and advanced menacingly. Jannie began to run. Gussie chased her until they were at the next bus stop and far away from any sea views.

'Here's the bus.' Jannie dodged into the shelter and turned, holding up hands in surrender this time, laughing and then doubling up. 'Sorry, Sis. Sorry. You know Mum wouldn't mind me using her words – no, OK, that was not as she sounded. Actually, it was meant to be you!'

The bus drew in and Gussie panted, 'You never used to be quite so cheeky as this! Where's the respect for your older sister? Ten years older, I would remind you!'

'Not till August!'

They paid for single tickets to Royal Square and the driver said, 'No need for 'ee to run like that, m' dears. I'd've waited.'

They settled into one of the double seats like birds into a nest and the driver called out, 'Next stop, the Stennack.'

Someone negotiated for a stop before that. 'Got to see Granny Perkins. Staying with her sister, Barnoon way.'

'Cemetery corner, then?'

'Do very nicely, m'dear.'

Gussie said, 'It was just like this on the country buses in

France, except there was probably a crate of hens some-where!'

Jannie smiled contentedly. 'Devon too. I like to think of people on buses and trains and planes, sharing space and time together. Not for long. Just a touch of hands in passing.'

They were walking back home along Fore Street when Gussie said out of the blue, 'Yes, let's do that. Wait for Ned to come home. We need a calm sea and the tide to be just right.'

Jannie had paused at the display of Leach pottery in one of the windows.

She said, 'I loved making pottery when I was a kid. That thumb pot on the windowledge – that was my first attempt.' She frowned and added in the next breath, 'Are you talking about Bamaluz Point? Jumping in? Ned would never do that.'

'Probably not.'

Jannie's frown deepened. 'Well, we could do it anyway. I was only half serious, Gus. It's not important. Is it?'

'To me. Yes.'

'Can you tell me?'

'No. I can only show you. That's why Ned should do it too.'

'Is it before my time?'

'Don't try to make it into a guessing game, Jannie. Please.'

Jannie was silent and they resumed walking. She guided herself close to her sister; Gussie reached out; they held hands. Jannie said, 'What shall we have for supper? Shall I do pasta like I used to?'

Gussie's face split into a grin. 'You did it once and once only!'

'I've improved since then. Students live on spag bol – you must remember that!'

'I loved it, actually. So . . . yes, please.'

'Then shall we ring Ned?'

'What time will it be on the West Coast?'

'No idea.'

'We'll find out.'

Jannie hugged her sister's arm. 'We're still in the same boat, aren't we, Gussie?'

'I think so.'

They reached the steps to the cobbled court of Mount Zion. A long black car was parked next to the Friendship bench. It was a hearse.

Seventeen

Old Beck had died. He had gone to the Fishermen's Lodge for his usual five-minute yarn, which had lasted from three to four o'clock. Then he had spent another ten minutes talking to a visitor about the Tate Gallery before going in to sit by the range till his missis came home after Bright Hour at chapel. When his Queen Victoria mug was full of tea and she had almost finished recounting the events of her afternoon, he announced he was going to close his eyes. Just for five minutes. His wife drank his tea.

She looked smaller than usual, as if her Old Beck had taken something of her with himself. She could not stop talking.

'I did know 'e was going. Nuthin' to be done about it. Sat by him and felt his body empty of 'imself. Put out my 'and to stop him. No good. 'E were gone.' She looked up at Jannie who was trying to cradle the stiff old body into her own young shoulder. 'They took 'im off a bit quick. I went round to your place to use the phone and by the time I got back to 'im, they was 'ere. With the doctor – they couldn't take 'im without a sustificate. Mr Salem always used to say we coulda been brother and sister, 'im an' me. 'Is daddy were engaged to my mother. Then my mother fell off the end o' Smeaton's and Arthur Kennett did pull 'er into 'is boat. And that was

227

that. What the sea do give you is yours. But old Mr Salem, 'e did marry the undertaker's daughter and did very well for 'imself.' She paused and added, 'I shan't 'aff miss Old Beck. 'E were the best friend I ever 'ad.' She peered up at the two girls. 'When we was together like, private, 'e did used to call me Bessie.'

Jannie thought of Robert and felt her heart fill with tenderness; she must remember to tell him that. Gussie paused in her tea-making and thought of Mark and Kate . . . so many different kinds of love.

She said gently, 'He wouldn't have wanted you to spend the night keeping watch.' She poured tea and laced it with rum from Old Beck's naval days. 'That was why Mr Salem took him to the chapel of rest. You come round to us and sleep in the double room.' No one had slept in Mark and Kate's room since they left for America, and Old Mrs Beck knew this was an honour.

She said grudgingly, 'Wouldna 'urt to spend one last night sitting by the fire together. But then . . . 'e'd gone. It woulda been no more than sitting by his clo'es. And they was smelly enough, 'eaven alone knows.'

Jannie avoided Gussie's eyes in case they both laughed. And Bessie Beck wouldn't understand laughter at such a moment. Old Beck and his missis had been good friends to the Briscoes ever since they could remember. She had kept an eye on them before Jannie, in the days when Zannah came and went. And after that Old Beck had taken Ned out in his boat to bring in the lobster pots. It was another ending, another forced beginning.

The Bamaluz Point project was dropped for the rest of Easter, as was the search for the special gate of glory. They went with

Old Mrs Beck to register her husband's death and then to arrange his funeral. They cut sandwiches, made scones and cakes and borrowed trestle tables from the restaurant on the wharf to set up on the cobbles of Mount Zion itself. Luckily the weather, though grey, was still and dry. People came and went until every scrap of food was gone. Then the women stayed and helped to clear away.

Jannie hardly knew how she felt about going back to Exeter. The end of the Easter holiday seemed to be upon her suddenly; only two days left before the new term started at Hartley. It would be wonderful to see Robert again, but somehow there seemed a lot of unfinished business right here.

'We were going to ask Aunt Rosemary about Rory,' Jannie said mournfully. 'And didn't we say we'd go to Trewyn House and see what was happening there?'

Gussie looked away. 'That was you. I don't want to see it again. When I went for the clothes it was creepy. Besides, it belongs to some big consortium now. We'd probably get ourselves arrested for trespass.'

'There you go, excuses again. I hope you're not becoming a wimp in your old age!' Jannie came behind her sister's chair and put her arms around her shoulders, her face against the dark hair. 'I'm going to miss you.'

'I thought you'd be thrilled to get back to Robert.'

'I am. Of course. But . . . I'd be happier still if I thought you were happy.'

'Jannie, that's not fair. We've had a lovely time. You can see I've been happy!'

'Oh, I know you're pleased about getting on so well with Zannah. But – but you still can't see a future. I know there's something else.' She straightened, impatient with herself.

'It's Robert's fault. He's made me supersensitive and it's not really me!'

Gussie relaxed at last, turned in her chair and butted her sister's arm. 'Oh, yes, it is. You don't know you like I know you!'

Though their last two days were full of laughter, Jannie still rang Ned from her room at Exeter and told him to 'hurry up and come home and do something about Gussie'.

His reply was completely irrelevant.

'Do you know whether Gussie gave this address to United Chemicals?'

'What? Oh . . . your firm. No, I've no idea. But she would have said if there had been an enquiry.'

'When did you leave?'

'Yesterday. I came to Exeter first. I need to see my education tutor.'

'So they could have contacted Gussie today? No, that's stupid. They need to have written two or three days ago. They did not know I was here. I resigned before Christmas and they wrote back then, accepting my resignation with much regret. Now, today, I receive a letter saying they cannot after all accept my resignation. What's that all about? And how the hell did they know I was over here?' He paused. 'It's from my director, too. I don't get it, Jan.'

'I don't either. But does it matter?'

'I don't like mysteries. My mother should have told me about my father. And now Gussie . . . all this business about her long-lost fiancé. She should have told us about that. And why on earth her crazy mother decided to push him into a river – what's all that about?' He sounded strangely angry.

Jannie said, 'Hey, my dissertation has got me a First. I'm

telling you now, before I've phoned Gussie. OK? No mystery there.'

There was a pause, then an explosion in her ear as he laughed. 'Oh, Jan, sorry – and well done! How marvellous. You deserve it. Congratulations.'

'It was rather a nice surprise,' she said. 'He phoned me – Howard Summer – isn't it a lovely name? I never thought so before. He always seemed such an old stick-in-the-mud. He wanted to see me to discuss my future. I was going to get the bus out to Hartley yesterday but Robert and I chatted it over and it seemed more sensible to get the interview over first, then leave here. The kids will be back by then and settled in. I'm going to stay there for the whole of the summer term. Make myself absolutely indispensable so that Geoff has to offer me a job.'

'If that's what you really want.'

'I do, honestly. I can tell you and Gussie think it's only because Robert is there but I am pretty certain that if Robert had not been there, I would still have adored to teach those children. They are so . . . worthwhile.'

'Oh, Jan, you've hit the nail on the head. That's what we all need – to be doing something worthwhile! Conrad looking after Victor, and Victor painting people who matter! And now you getting your honours degree and knowing just what to do about it – good for you!'

For a moment Jannie was overwhelmed by her brother's praise. Then she said robustly, 'Don't forget all your work with United Chemicals. And Gussie's wonderful gardens.' She thought of her sister, alone, marking time and went on quickly, 'And I think you're wrong about Gussie and her mystery. I think she was dumped by this Andrew Bellamy. She was very hurt in all kinds of ways. And she did not want all of us worrying about her. She's private but she's not secretive, not in the way you are imagining at present.'

He said hesitantly, 'All right . . . How was she?'

'Up for it. She met me at the station three weeks ago with your awful old trolley. We've put it back in Grampy's studio but I suggest you chop it up.'

'Go on.'

'What with? Oh, Gussie. I'd worked out a project for us to do – keep us occupied and not broody. You know.'

'Yes, I do.'

'It's called the glory gates project. We're looking – mapping – all the kissing gates Mum and Dad could have used. There might be a special one somewhere. We might plant a cross or something. Don't know. We haven't found it yet. Oh, and we've decided we will jump off the cliff at Bamaluz Point, like we used to.'

'I did it only once. Never again. Count me out.'

'Gussie is waiting for you to join us before we do it.'

'Wait on, Macduff.' He laughed. 'Listen up, Junior. When you talk to Gussie tomorrow ask her whether she knows anything about United Chemicals.'

'Ask her yourself. She always has to phone you. It's not fair.'

'I'm going to New York tomorrow with the paintings. Victor wants me to hang them – or advise on the hanging. It will have to wait till I get back.'

She heard him take a deep breath; it sounded like a force-nine gale.

He said, 'It's time I came home.'

She was shocked at his tone. 'Don't you want to?' she asked sharply.

'More than anything.'

'Well, then.'

'You won't be there. Old Beck won't be there. Mum and Dad—'

'Shut up, Ned! Gussie is there. She needs you.'

'I'm a coward, Jannie.'

'What utter rubbish!'

'I've got a place here. A role. With my father. I've got to start again if I come home.'

Jannic almost shouted down the phone, 'You've always had a place. Your mother is my mother, my father is Gussie's father. I thought you understood this better than I did. I thought you always knew it and I didn't really get it till after they were gone and we were left!'

There was a shocked silence. She calmed down and said quietly, 'Just come home, Ned. If you're going to New York tomorrow, say your goodbyes and get a flight home from there. It sounds as if you've done what you went to do.'

Still he did not speak.

At last she said sharply, 'Hello? Are you still there?'

He said, 'Yes . . . to all that. Thank you, Jannie. Speak again soon. Congratulations.' He pressed a button and was gone.

Robert met her at Hartley's post office. The bus drew in and there was no sign of him or his van. The driver lifted her suitcase on to the wide pavement and looked up and down the road.

'He's late, miss. And I reckon it's going to tip down with rain any minute now.'

She said with complete confidence, 'He's on his way. I phoned him at Otterdown and he was already crossing the river.'

Then the post office door pinged as it opened and there he was, blessedly and wonderfully familiar in jeans and oiled wool sweater, one of his silly pseudo-naval hats pulled well forward over floppy ginger fringe, thin face halved by an enormous grin and green eyes alight. She went to meet him, dragging her case, shouldering her backpack. She felt the usual tenderness filling her physical body. It had happened the first time they had set eyes on each other. She knew it would always be there.

She said, 'I haven't been lovesick. I promise. Have you?'

'No. But that doesn't mean I haven't missed you every minute of every day.'

She swallowed. 'Likewise.' She looked away from the clever face, down to the big, capable hands. She said, 'I couldn't tell her – I couldn't tell Gussie. I'm sorry, my darling.'

He said, 'You didn't phone so I knew you hadn't. Will it matter to her?'

'No. But there is something between us at the moment. She has a secret.'

He lifted his hands and took hers and pulled her down. 'So have you, my darling.'

She crouched and held on to the wheelchair, and he cupped her face in those wonderful hands and kissed her. She closed her eyes; it was a butterfly kiss. She savoured it. She whispered, 'I could not have borne it if she had been . . . cautious.'

'Why would she be? Her father was a wheelchair user.' He kissed her again, this time on the tip of her nose.

'That might have been a reason for caution. She is different. She used to be my older sister. And Ned's too. Now . . . she needs someone, something.'

'In other words, she needed you, and you were scared that if you said your new boyfriend had ME she would feel you were moving away?'

She opened her eyes abruptly and stared into his. She saw they were full of laughter but still said angrily, 'You are not – a hundred times not – my new boyfriend! And Gussie is not "needy" like that – not one bit!'

'OK. What am I then?'

'You are my love.' She held his gaze. 'You are the light of my life. You and I were put on this earth to be together.'

They stared, not wanting to pull away, recognizing one of their moments of what Robert the practical called 'interlocking connection'.

At last he said, 'You deserve that honours degree, Jan. You've got a brain and you're not afraid to use it.'

The van was parked behind the post office with its ramp open on to the door of the storeroom. Mr Perks, the postmaster, was loading two crates of tinned food into the interior next to a rack of tools. Robert manoeuvred his chair carefully past other groceries and ran it into the driver's well. He grinned as he passed Mr Perks.

'I know you were running a book on whether she would come back – well, she's here. How does that suit you?'

'Very well, Mr Hanniford.' Mr Perks pushed Jannie's case beneath a bench and winked at Jannie. 'He bet me a trillion pounds you'd come back. I nearly rang you up and told you to stay in St Ives and we'd split the money between us but as I knew he'd only got his teacher's pay, it didn't seem worth it, really.' He took her backpack and shoved it after the case. 'Welcome back, Miss Briscoe.'

'Thank you, Mr Perks,' she came back demurely as she settled herself beside Robert. 'See you soon, I expect.'

Robert used his remote to close the ramp, and they drove through the village and turned in at the school gates.

He stopped the van and she got out and shut the gates, breathing in the air appreciatively. It had been a long and bumpy ride from Exeter and the bus had smelled of its occupants. The drive that led to Hartley School was hemmed in by rhododendrons already showing buds; its smell was completely different.

She hopped back into the van. 'I have a cat's sense of smell. When you come home with me this summer, I want you to think about smells. The difference between seaweed and rhododendrons.'

'Is this one of your projects?' He did not wait for an answer but added, 'You'll have to tell them before I appear.'

'Yes. And yes again. You're absolutely right, they are quite used to having a man around in a wheelchair. It's no big deal, honestly.'

'Yet you did not tell your sister.'

'Like I said, there was something different about Gussie. I'm still not sure why I didn't. Afraid it might make the chair into a problem – just not wanting it to be a big deal, I guess.'

'I told my mother about us. When I said I wouldn't visit for a while – give her and Jonathan time to settle in together – she came here. Just for the day. Two hundred and fifty miles. Just for the day.'

Jannie looked at him. 'So . . . she wanted to see you. Fairly urgently.'

'She said things about children from broken homes.' He grinned sideways at her. 'She doesn't quite believe in the ME. Lots of people don't. She thinks I was subconsciously traumatized by knowing about Dad and his girlfriends. It's her way of thinking that tomorrow or the next day – maybe the one after – I'm going to leap out of the chair and go for a run.'

She reached over and put a hand on his arm. 'She doesn't quite trust me to stick around. Did you tell her about my dad?'

'I told her about his wheelchair. And, of course, the Twin Towers.' They were silent while he rounded a thicket of rhododendrons. 'She just said that we all had to take the opportunity of happiness where and when we could.'

Jannie drew in a quick breath. 'That's wonderful, Robert! So lovely.' And he nodded.

He slowed right down as the house came into view. It was Georgian and had a wide porticoed frontage. Every pillar was decorated with balloons. They floated in the breeze.

Jannie held his arm. 'Stop. Let me look.'

He stopped, pulled on the handbrake and said, 'I reminded her I had not lived at home – not properly – since I was eighteen.'

She still held on to his arm. 'She was anxious about you. You were wrong about her forgetting all about you. She must have been anxious. It was a long drive.' She rubbed her forehead against his shoulder. 'You told her about us. You told everybody about us. Didn't you?'

'It was a bit difficult not to. When I started to do the balloons yesterday, Cathy Johnson offered to help.'

'You mean she snatched a balloon from you and popped it!'

'No, I don't mean that. She said, "I want some of that." She spoke, Jan. She actually spoke. She came here last September, an elected mute. And she has now elected to speak. She has blown up eighteen balloons and tied them herself.'

Jannie felt her eyes fill. She tried to tell him how wonderful that was, but he was still talking.

'You see, Jan, I had to tell someone. About us. About how it feels to be half of someone else. About the joy but also about the – the – responsibility. You for me. Me for you.' He sighed. 'She doesn't speak. But you know that somehow she understands. So I kept on with the balloons, but I told her. And she understood. And then she spoke.'

'She meant she wanted some love.'

'And she understood that the balloons were a symbol. They all wanted to blow balloons after that. Elizabeth said it was good for their lungs. So Geoff got the steps out and tied the higher ones.'

Jannie whispered, 'Oh, Robert, do you realize you have made our own very special glory gates?' She twisted in her seat, held his face in her hands and kissed him.

None of them, not even the suddenly loquacious Cathy Johnson, had become angels. For the younger girls the balloons meant a future wedding with a new teacher taking on some of the English students. It would be OK to turn discussions of *The Tempest* into possibilities of sex from a wheelchair. Cathy Johnson decided that, on the strength of her blond hair and intensely blue eyes, Jan Briscoe was Swedish. Her parents, ecstatic that she was now talking, were staying in Hartley and as the voice became louder and louder each day, eventually agreed to take her into Exeter and have her hair professionally bleached. They had been going to cancel a much-needed holiday abroad but Geoff persuaded them not to do this. In spite of having no speech for the last eighteen months, Cathy was doing extremely well academically and should continue with her school routine. She would spend time with Miss Briscoe, who was an excellent role model, each day.

Jannie, hearing of this later, passed it on to Ned and Gussie without delay.

It was a week later, when she was waiting for Robert to join her for their usual evening walk that she had what she dubbed a V.I.S.T. with Gussie – 'a very important sister talk'. She knew that she had to work up to it carefully in case Gussie simply put down the receiver at her end. So she started off with some anecdotes from that day's timetable. Gussie laughed.

Jannie went on, encouraged, 'Seriously, darling, I want you to come to the next event. We can get another bed into my room so that you will be part of the school. It's on the side of a sort of dell – trees all around and a gorgeous view of the countryside in front. You'd just love it. In fact, Geoff's wife, Elizabeth, wants to ask your advice about growing grapes. Lots of space and calm but such excitement too. Robert is still working on the electronic hand and he's got three of the sixth-form boys and two of the girls really involved. There's a chap called Derek Newman, who has no arms – about six inches – who tests the hand now and then. He's actually an artist, would you believe. And the art department – wow! That's all I can say. Wow.'

She went on to say a lot more, however, and when she paused Gussie said slowly, 'D'you know, Jannie, that's the first time you've actually mentioned any of the children having impairments. Isn't that absolutely marvellous?'

Jannie smiled. 'Yes. It is. Especially as a lot of them spend time with the therapist most days. But you've got it, Gus. Geoff – all of us – concentrate on providing experiences that include impairments. For instance, Marcus, the deaf chap, is teaching us BSL – that's British Sign Language.' Her smile turned to a grin. 'Most of us have now got at least one remark we can make across a crowded room.'

'Well? What is it?'

Jannie started to laugh, but Gussie heard her very clearly. 'What a plonker!'

Gussie spluttered, 'Oh, Jan! You make it sound great. But then of course that's because of Robert.'

'No. It is great because somehow Geoff and Elizabeth have made it so. We have all found a place for ourselves here. I am in the right place, Gus. And so is Robert.' She was suddenly serious. 'Gus, I thought being in love was a sort of constant ecstasy – adoration. It's so much more than that. It's being in the right place with the right person.' She stopped talking for a whole two seconds and then blurted, 'Have you told Ned your secret yet?'

There was a shocked silence from the phone. Then Gussie said, 'How do you know? You've spoken to Zannah? How could she? I can't believe she would do such a thing!'

Jannie said quickly, 'Of course I haven't been in touch with Zannah. *I* don't know your secret – how could I? But I know it's there because I know you. And whatever it is, Gus, you have to tell Ned. That's important. When he comes home, you have to tell him.'

'He is the last person on this earth . . . I couldn't bear him to know.' Gus was obviously crying. Jannie gripped the receiver in both hands, fighting against her own sudden rush of tears.

And then, quite suddenly, Gussie's voice was calm again. She said, 'Darling, don't cry. I'll tell you myself one day. Soon. But Ned . . . no. You will understand, I promise.' Her tone changed again, became brisk. 'Listen. Something odd's going on about Ned's work. I've had a visit from one of his colleagues at United Chemicals – Head of Research

– about the special project he was working on pre Nine Eleven.'

Jannie was successfully diverted. 'Really? That's strange because – I meant to tell you – he was wittering on when he phoned me at Exeter. Apparently he sent in his resignation just after – or before – Christmas. Can't remember which now. They accepted it then, but now he's had a letter to say they've changed their minds. I think he asked me to contact you about it. Oh dear, I'm sorry, Gus. I completely forgot everything once I arrived.'

'Well, it's about his resignation. This woman, Margaret Scott – Dr Margaret Scott – wanted to see him to persuade him to stay on. She was evasive; obviously didn't want to discuss him with me. But it seems as though some extra money is being injected into the project. It has suddenly become the most important piece of research in the organization. I told her that Ned was one of a team and the research would proceed as it always has done. Anyway, she seemed so keen to talk to him that in the end I gave her that cellphone contact. And then yesterday Ned phoned me to say he was arriving home in a week or so.'

Jannie said, 'Is it to do with this business? Because actually he was going to New York to oversee the delivery of his father's work to Mack. And I sort of suggested that he should come home from there. And he seemed to agree.'

'Really? I assumed Margaret Scott had telephoned him and he was coming back because of that. But . . . was he coming anyway?'

'Yes, I'm sure of it. He knew that once his father had finished this special stuff he was painting, that would be it.'

'Oh. I'm glad.' Gussie sounded lighter somehow. 'I really

thought he had – how did you put it? – found a place out there. He seemed so settled. Happy.'

'Perhaps it's to do with finding a place within himself? He needed to know where he came from, Gus. After all, you always knew all about your background. He never did.'

'True. You're turning out to be the wise Briscoe, Jannie!'

'I am. I probably always was. But my family never realized it.'

'Shut up.' Jannie did and Gussie added anxiously, 'I didn't mean it. Speak to me!'

'I jolly well am, only you can't see me. I'm saying over and over again – what a plonker!'

She clicked off the phone, put it on her pillow and ran to meet Robert, who was bowling his chair along the terrace.

'I made a mess of it! She thought I knew her secret. Oh, Rob, it must be awful. D'you suppose she murdered someone? And that awful Andrew Bellamy was blackmailing her so Zannah tried to kill him?'

Robert looked up at her and said nothing.

'I know. I'm going off on one. But the sooner Ned gets home the better!'

Robert said, 'Let's go to your room. I want to kiss you and I can feel the eyes of several of your group boring into my back.'

Jannie looked up at the long row of sash windows above them. Sure enough the evening sun highlighted the newly bleached hair of Cathy Johnson and Rita Meares. In unison they performed the well-learned sign. Jannie and Robert pretended they had not seen anything. Slowly and with great dignity, they moved back to the staff wing.

Once in her room they clasped each other and laughed helplessly.

Eighteen

Jannie told Robert that the first few days of that summer term were to be spent in 'cementing' their relationship. Robert took it literally and explained in detail that the old stonemasons needed no mortar. Their building blocks, large and small, were perfectly matched. He cited cathedrals and castles and named a few names. Jannie listened because she loved the sound of his voice when he was expounding something, she loved the breadth of his knowledge, his curiosity and the way his eyes became greener as he got into his subject.

He paused, then concluded, 'We fit together, Jan. We knew it the moment we set eyes on each other in the workshop. That's what they must mean when they talk about a good match. I never thought of that before.'

'But you convinced your mother.' She kissed him. 'Of course. That's why I didn't bother to tell Gussie about the wheelchair. Because you'll do it for me.'

She sat back smiling and then looked very serious. 'Darling, I know it's not really my role to bring this up but I think we should get married before the autumn term begins. Some time during the summer break. What do you think?'

He stared at her, eyes wider than she had ever seen them.

She thought it was one of his jokes, pretending to be shocked at her brazen suggestion.

But then he breathed, 'Jan. Darling. Are you pregnant?'

She was shocked too. Not so much by his question as his tone. He was almost breathless with sheer anticipation. They had made love twice; it must have been on his mind ever since, yet it had barely occurred to her. Well, it wouldn't, of course, because her period had come on time as she arrived in St Ives. She looked at his face and felt her own heart leap at the thought of them making a baby.

She smiled, kissed him, held his face in her hands. 'That is still to come, my darling. This is much more mundane.' She studied him and he tried to adjust his expression. 'It's about living quarters. And you and me being teachers. Like Geoff and Elizabeth. But if I have to be pregnant before you'll marry me, then we'd better get on with it!'

He pulled down one of her hands and held it hard. 'Sorry, Jannie. It would have been so bloody marvellous. But I'll settle for a non-shotgun wedding.'

'That's a relief. We don't have many shotguns in St Ives. She laughed and so did he. She flipped open her diary. 'How about the fourteenth of August – that's a Wednesday? We'll have been in St Ives a few weeks. People will know you and you'll know them. Bessie will have put it about that you're lovely—'

'Bessie?'

'Our neighbour. I've always called her Old Mrs Beck but since Old Beck died we really do need to call her by her given name. She's a sort of public relations officer for a number of people, including us.'

'Does it have to be so public, Jan? I thought a registry office somewhere.'

'Darling, Father Martin will be so upset if we don't seal the knot in church. I promise it won't be public. It will be a weekday. Just your mum and dad and their partners. Ned and Gussie. Aunt Rosemary won't set foot in St Ives and Uncle Rory won't even know about it. Tell you what – I won't breathe a word to Bessie. That way she will deny any rumours that might start elsewhere. How would that be?'

She put her head on one side as if she were encouraging him to take a spoonful of medicine. He reached out and grabbed her and she pretended to fight him off. But not for long. And as they kissed and kissed and purposefully let their feelings build, Jannie wondered whether she should have delayed this particular moment until they had talked more about making babies. Then she simply crossed her fingers and put it out of her head. Gussie would be delighted.

During the next two days she decided to tell Gussie about the ME. The wheelchair would not be an issue, she was certain of that. Ned might jib at the wheelchair. He could remember a time in his life when it was not omnipresent and having reconnected with a father who, at over eighty years of age, did not require one, might well colour his feelings. Gussie – like Jannie herself – had never known a father who was not dependent on a wheelchair. So, in a way, she had not considered it a secret when she had spent those three weeks with Gussie at Easter. It had been like trying to describe Robert's deftness as a welder or as a carpenter. So many, many characteristics added up to the sum total of Robert Hanniford.

But to cover all angles she must somehow let Gussie know that a baby was an imminent part of the plan. Any objections would be swept away by that. Gussie was now thirty-one years old and seemed uninterested in men, let alone babies. The mystery of her engagement to Andrew Bellamy could well have put her off marriage and babies for ever. A nephew or niece was the obvious answer. Jannie chewed her lip as she considered this. What on earth could have happened? Just what was the mystery about? And if Jannie told her about their plans, Gussie might feel obliged to do likewise and explain her feelings?

She offered to do the shopping trip into Hartley that Saturday. Robert was working with Derek Newman, the sixth-form boy who had no arms. They were testing the electronic hand. It always happened on a Saturday out of the timetable and this time the physiotherapist was there. Jannie sensed that Robert was being supervised in some way, especially when he asked her to do the shopping trip without him.

She drove the van to the post office and parked next to the storeroom. Between them she and Mr Perks loaded the next week's supplies into the vehicle and then she made her phone call from the kiosk next to the pillar box.

She counted ten rings because that was how long it took to get from kitchen to hallway, but when it went on to fifteen and then twenty she thought Gussie must be next door with Bessie Beck or fetching weekend shopping from Fore Street. Then the ringing stopped and Gussie's voice said breathlessly, 'Have you broken down? Where are you?'

'Gussie – it's me. Jannie.'

'Oh, darling . . . hello. I was expecting Ned really early. He was staying with Aunt Ro in Bristol overnight and expected to be here for breakfast. But no message and he hasn't turned up.'

There was fear behind the breathlessness. Jannie said,

'Try Aunt Rosemary again. He could have been delayed, for some reason.'

'He could. Thanks, Jan. The voice of reason. I'll do that now.' And she put the receiver down at her end.

Jannie stared through the window at the post office and the van, and beyond that, the little River Otter and a field of cows. Gussie thought she was phoning from Hartley so she would ring back there. Jannie was filled with the kind of childish frustration she remembered so well from her childhood. For two pins she could have cried as she would have done then. Then she said aloud, 'Perhaps it wasn't meant to be. Trying to do a deal with secrets!'

She went back to the van, intent on returning to Hartley and the telephone as soon as possible, only to be stopped by Mr Perks as he emerged from the storeroom.

'Glad you haven't gone yet, Miss Briscoe. Your brother's out front. I said as how you might not have left. Come on through the shop.' He led the way as if she didn't know it, then pointed past the counter. 'The Ford Consul. See it?'

As if she could miss their family car. She shot past him and gathered Ned to her. She hadn't realized how much she had missed him. She felt the old familiar tears in her throat and swallowed them fiercely.

'Just phoned Gussie – very worried about you – you should've phoned her yourself.'

He was grinning as he extricated himself and drew her into the car.

'You don't change. Still moaning about something!' He pulled a tissue from the box Gussie always made sure was with the maps. Jannie snatched it from him and bunched it into her hand.

'She's there on her own. You'd left Bristol—'

247

'I intended dropping in here anyway. Meet your young man.' He minced the words comically. 'Give him the once-over properly – intentions and so forth,' she punched his arm – 'and ring Gus from your room. Stop it, Jannie. That hurts.'

She calmed down suddenly. 'Sorry. Actually, so glad to see you and I can't think why when you've kept delaying coming home. We thought you'd be with us at Easter.'

'I know. Sorry, Jan. There was a place for me there. It wasn't simply getting in touch with Victor Gould and my past, it was being there while he painted his last picture. I've taken photographs, of course, but I can't wait for you and Gus to see it *in situ*. And then – you were right – once I'd seen that into its place there was nothing to stop me coming home. And here I am.' He looked at her smilingly. 'And to such a welcome! Oh, Jan, I can see you're in your own place. Lucky girl. Is it going to work?'

'Yes. It's going to work. But you're not going to meet him this morning, Ned. *He's* working.'

Ned made a face, then said, 'Perhaps it's as well. I wouldn't have got away before mid-afternoon, which would mean a late arrival home. I can tell you my news and be off again in an hour. Anywhere we can go for a coffee?'

They walked across the green to the tearooms run by Mr Perks' cousin. She was delighted to see them. 'Dead as a dodo until the school holidays.' Jannie was not surprised; the small white-painted room was bitterly cold.

She asked for two coffees in disposable mugs. 'My brother is on his way to St Ives, Doris.' She made it sound urgent. It was urgent. She did not want Ned to change his mind and stay until the afternoon.

Ned was impressed. 'You sounded so – I don't know – firm. You sounded like a teacher, for goodness' sake!' He laughed delightedly. 'Who would have thought our baby sister would turn out to be a natural-born teacher!'

They settled themselves back in the car and Jannie directed him to one of her favourite spots by the river. 'You can see otters here if you're lucky,' she told him. Then added, 'You sound very pleased with yourself. I'm really glad your trip was so successful, Ned. And in the end you went along with what Mack wanted in the first place! You were a sort of ambassador for the Trust.'

Ned reversed the car a few yards so that they had a view of the willow-lined river. He wound down his window. 'This is more like it.' He took his cup from Jannie and prised off the lid. 'Considering it is now the merry month of May, that little café must have been refrigerated.' He sipped and looked at her through the steam. 'Good to see you, Little Sis. How is Gussie?'

'Not quite the same – perhaps we never will be the same again. She was fine in one way – coped with Bessie Beck when Old Beck died – couple of swims, long walks. But, there is something. Something to do with that Andrew Bellamy. She laughs it off; says that particular fear is dead and buried. Of course, I didn't realize there was any fear connected with him.' Jannie sighed sharply. 'She makes it sound so funny – Zannah acting like a tigress protecting her young. But I don't think it could have been funny. Not really.' She looked at him. 'Can you stay until school breaks up for the summer?'

'Most definitely yes. And then will you be with us?'

'Yes.' She hesitated looking into her cup. 'Ned . . . don't be shocked. I am bringing Robert with me. His parents are divorced and have new partners and it's . . . difficult. He could stay at school and work on this electronic hand, but I think he needs to see . . . us. Be with us for a while.'

'I think that's wonderful,' he said. 'I'm not shocked in the least.' Then he sighed. 'We'll miss Old Beck. Things keep changing.'

Jannie cleared her throat. 'I know. But listen, Ned, we plan to get married. Probably mid-August time. I would like him to be around for the first anniversary.' She looked up; her eyes were very bright. 'I would like him to be the fourth person in our boat, Ned.'

He was silent, staring at her. He reached for a tissue and she felt in the sleeve of her cardigan. 'Still got the last one you gave me.' She held it for a moment then replaced it carefully.

He said, 'OK. It is a bit of a shock. I have to admit. But . . . OK.'

She did cry then. 'Oh, Ned. Thank you. You'll like him, you'll really like him. I know we're too young and all that rubbish but, you see, it might be like Mum and Dad. We might not have too long. We have to do this while we can. You do understand, don't you?'

'Oh my God.' He skewed awkwardly to take her in his arms. 'I do. I really do.' He scrubbed at her back with his knuckles. 'Perhaps that was why I stayed with Victor longer than intended.'

She sniffed mightily. 'And Gussie got on with Zannah.'

Ned held her away and said, 'Robert . . . he isn't terminally ill or anything, is he?'

'No.' She met his anxious eyes. 'He's got ME. And his parents are both on second marriages.'

'Sounds enough to be going on with.'

He used his tissue and mopped gently at her eyes just as Gussie used to. And, she noticed, dismissed the ME as so many people did. Which meant, of course, that he didn't 'get' Robert one bit.

'Come on, Jan. Cheer up. I really should be getting on down to Cornwall and I have to tell you my news.'

She drew back against the passenger door and stared at him anew. 'You've met someone!' She was horrified and tried to hide it.

But he laughed. 'It was practically a hermitage over there – no one for miles! Besides . . . No, I haven't "met anyone", as you put it. But I'm late getting down here because I went into United Chemicals on my way. I needed to see Margaret Scott.' He saw Jannie's bewilderment and added, 'She was the director who went to see Gussie. And she wrote the letter telling me UC would not accept my resignation after all.'

Jannie nodded. 'I remember. It was all a bit odd.' She was enormously relieved and did not know why that should be.

'You can say that again!' He grinned. 'I was mad at first – talked to Victor and Con about it. I said I felt used. They both laughed at that. But I felt the same way as when we were in New York together and Mack seemed to be angling for me to see Victor and persuade him to donate his work to The Spirit of America. D'you remember how huffy I got?'

'Of course I do. And in the end, that is exactly what happened.' She was interested now, hoisting her leg up so that she could twist properly and give him her full attention. He wasn't going to come back to Hartley and be introduced to Robert. And he hadn't 'met anyone'. She smiled. 'Are you being seduced back to work? You know it's the right thing to do.'

He was surprised. 'Is that how you see it, Jannie? I was fed up with the whole thing – never intended to go back into research again. Quite seriously.'

'I know. Just as Gussie was never going to do any land-scape design ever again.' She paused, thinking back. Some time during their explorations at Easter, Gussie had said something, done something, that had been . . . significant. Jannie could not remember what it was and finished lamely, 'She's still saying no to work – trying to be, just *be*.'

'You're worried about her.'

'A bit, yes. I thought she would be the first to – to – find an anchor.' She sighed sharply. 'Anyway, go on. Don't tell me you're going back to work next week. Please.'

'No. Well, yes. I suppose I am. But from home. I'm writing a paper for the BMA. How's that for erudition?'

Jannie stared at him and then rummaged up her sleeve for the tissue. Ned said, 'Oh, Jan, please don't. It's no enormous breakthrough. Just another step along the way, that's all.'

She choked, 'Dad would be so pleased. Oh, dammit, Dad *is* pleased!'

He put a hand on hers and looked away and then said, 'Oh look, Jan, it's a kingfisher! Can you see? Where the willow branch is dipping – he's there!'

She couldn't focus but she said hoarsely, 'Yes, yes, I can see. Oh, Ned!'

They watched and Ned said, 'Nothing to do with science. But everything to do with life.' His voice dropped. 'I wish Gus was here.'

'You'll see her later,' Jannie said quickly. 'You can tell her.'

'Of course.' He turned almost briskly. 'I'll be there all summer, Jan. All the computer stuff has to be collated and shown in every possible way – text, graphs, photographic images.'

'Oh Lord . . .'

'I can't wait, actually. Just to make sense of all that endless testing.' He released her hand, swigged the dregs of his coffee and squashed the cup flat. 'The thing was – is – the

252

Swedes are working along the same lines as we are. It so often happens that way and becomes a race for results. But this is an opportunity for collaboration and we have both been offered a joint prize to develop our work together. A man called Svensson is in charge of the Stockholm organization and, apparently, I am in charge of the Bristol one. The prize is called the Svensson-Briscoe Award.' He laughed at her expression. 'What it could mean, Jannie, is that there could be severe complications if I was no longer heading the British team. Like, no Briscoe, no cash!' He shook his head. 'As Con said, "You'll have to go back. They've got you over a barrel." And Victor said, "Give in gracefully." So I decided to do that.'

Jannie continued to stare incredulously at her brother for what seemed like ages. Then she said tritely, 'This is the best thing since sliced bread. And if it leads to something wonderful . . . Oh, Ned.'

He nodded. She could tell he was near tears himself. He said, 'Sven and I have talked on the phone often. We get on well. When the BMA wanted this paper he was all for it. Reckoned it would be like an archive and help the two of us to make plans.' He paused then said, 'I'm really excited, Jan. Does it make any kind of sense for you?'

'Of course. Especially the excitement. I feel like that about Robert's electronic hand. And the end-of-term production of *The Tempest*.'

'I'd better come with you and see the hand. It's important stuff. I can phone Gus from the school. Don't want to get too wrapped up in this award thing – tunnel vision and all that sort of thing.'

'No.' Jannie used what she supposed was her teacher's voice. 'Let's say goodbye now. You go on down to Gus.

Please. And I'll drive back to Hartley with the groceries.' She grinned. 'When we did the funeral feast for Bessie, we got very emotional and Gussie said, "Cheer up, there's always some washing-up somewhere to be done!" In this case, for washing-up read delivering groceries!' She leaned forward and kissed the tip of his nose. 'So long as you're all right to be at my wedding, I can live with the Svensson-Briscoe Award and just get on with delivering groceries!'

He hugged her to him. 'Jan, I love you. When you arrived we were a proper family. You linked us all. Do you realize that?'

She held on to him as if she were drowning. 'Thank you, Big Brud,' was all she could manage.

Jannie spoke to Gussie after she and Elizabeth had stored the following week's supplies. Gussie had telephoned Aunt Rosemary, who had alleviated her fears about Ned's delayed arrival; Jannie was able to add her own reassurances.

'I can't tell you his news, darling. That would be stealing his thunder. But it's terrific in all ways. And he's so much stronger. Spending the last few weeks with his father must have been the right thing to do.'

'Few weeks? I suppose that's all it was. I haven't seen him since I left here in January – nearly four months.'

Jannie frowned; Gussie was surely not sounding . . . dreary?

'Well, I think you'll recognize him. He still can't control his hair. How did Mum used to describe it?'

'A là flop.'

Jannie thought she could have been smiling.

'And I think he'll need to catch up on all the local news. So you'd better start thinking up something exciting. Any more pink cauliflowers this year?'

Gussie's laugh came over the wires; Jannie grinned, pleased.

Gussie said, 'How is Robert?'

Jannie took a deep breath. 'I'm bringing him home for most of the summer holidays, Gus. We're going to have a very quiet wedding. I want him to know us. I want you to be able to . . . accept him. I want him to be one of us.'

Gussie said instantly, 'It sounds great. But, darling, I hate to say this – you're both so young and you've hardly—'

Jannie finished for her, ' – got to know each other.' She took a breath. 'We know each other. As if we'd lived together all our lives.' She took another breath. 'Gussie, I'm going to say something and then put the phone down so that you don't have to think of a reply. Robert has ME. He uses a wheelchair.'

She replaced the receiver and left her hand on it, closing her eyes. At least she had given up on any so-called deals. Whatever secret Gussie may or may not be holding, it was still hers. She turned to leave her room and find Robert.

The phone rang.

'Darling? It's me again.' Gussie's precious warmth and understanding filled Jannie's head. 'I do understand. Sorry to be an idiot. Would you like me to mention a wedding to Father Martin?'

Jannie said, 'Oh, Gussie. I love you. Listen to Ned. We'll see you in six weeks' time.' She paused. 'Dad would like him. I promise.'

Gussie laughed. It sounded like music and Jannie held the receiver high so that it would fill her room.

Gussie's laughter sustained her for some time to come. Robert was cast down because, after all the electrodes from the hand had been carefully aligned with nerve endings in Derek's right-arm stump, he had been unable to move it. That would not have worried him too much because he needed a neurosurgeon to work on that side of things. What had 'rattled his cage', as he put it to Jannie, was that Derek had broken down completely.

'I had no conception – none at all, idiot that I am – that this meant so much to him. He has always been a willing helper. That is how I have seen him. Perhaps he had no idea himself how much it might mean to him. It was awful, Jan. Awful. Poor kid. And it's my fault.'

'Rubbish!' What else could she say? 'He'll bounce back. Wait till supper tonight, he'll be the one who will want to try again after the next adjustments.'

But Derek did not appear for supper, and Elizabeth took him sandwiches and cocoa to his room and stayed for some time.

It was the night the storms began. The rain and wind hit at the same time and within an hour there was news of flooding on the north coast of Cornwall. Jannie slept through it all and felt guilty when she found Robert glued to his television set as the breakfast news brought pictures of devastation up and down the coast. She telephoned Zion Cottage immediately and was thankful to hear that St Ives had escaped the worst of the storms.

Even so, there was a constant roar from the other end of the phone and Ned shouted against it. 'Gussie and I went to the Sloop before the weather arrived – just to say hello to everyone and get some chips for supper. A Russian ship had made it into the bay and decanted half the crew on to West Pier. They couldn't get back on board, of course, so the churches and chapels are full of them.' He still sounded like the old Ned: buoyant, excited. He bellowed, 'What about you? We can't get a picture on the television and the radio is full of static.'

'We're all right. No damage. The garden furniture is all over the place. We're sheltered here. The Georgians knew what they were doing when they built Hartley House.' She lowered her voice. 'Robert didn't have good results from his test drive.'

'Tell him about me. The years of sheer drudgery. And more to come. Tell him to bring all his paperwork when he comes to us. We'll go through it together. I'm no engineer but another eye might make all the difference.'

She could have wept. 'Ned, I just love you,' she said.

She told Robert and was surprised at his lack of enthusiasm.

'Darling, Ned is not a genius,' she said. 'He's like you – he's a worker. That's why they are making this funding into a prize – to honour all of you who spend hours isolating problems, examining them, starting again. He'll do that with you. It's not competitive, Robert. He wants you to take him where you are going. If you are interested he will take you to where he hopes to go. I'll ask him to let you read his thesis.' She could feel herself being carried away.

He said, 'Take it easy, Jannie. Let's get to know each other first. You are setting such store on us becoming instant colleagues. We're working in completely different fields.'

'Not really – not when it boils down to the essence. Research is research is research—'

'Darling. Shut up.' He pulled her down to his level and kissed her, and she looked into his green eyes and said, 'That's the first smile for twenty-four hours. Thank you, Robert.'

'Will you promise me something?'

'You know I will.'

'Will you just let it happen. Don't force anything. Anything at all.'

She considered crossing her fingers, but decided against it.

'What if something goes a bit wrong and you take against each other?'

'Then let it happen. It will sort itself out. Or it won't.'

'All right,' she agreed reluctantly. 'You might have to remind me. And it might be something that needs . . . debate.'

He ignored that and said they should go to the dining room for breakfast.

'We could have it here,' she said. 'I can do toast and coffee in your kitchen.'

'I have to show my face. Everyone will know about Derek by now. Come on. Smile, please!'

He led the way, bowling along the open corridor so that she had to trot to keep up. It was worth it. Derek was already there, coping as usual with the short stumps that were all the arms he had and avidly watching the two deaf girls who were signing frantically at each other.

He greeted Robert and Jannie with a big if rueful grin. 'I might not be able to sign but I can still understand what they are saying. It's a jumble. They've got friends on the south coast badly affected by the storms. And they think I'm a big prick because I said last night I wasn't going to bother about prosthetics any more.' He scooped up a slice of toast and bit into it. 'Everyone thinks I blamed you, sir. The boot was on the other foot. I let you down. And I thought that was that. But Elizabeth says she's going to have a word with the surgeon at Exeter, see if anything can be done to stimulate the nerve endings in my stumps.'

Robert brought his wheelchair alongside Derek's chair and waited until the toast was gone.

'I intended to apologize to you. And I will. I am sorry the hand didn't work for you, Derek. It came so near. The linear mark on the paper recorded a blip – did you feel that?'

Derek stopped chewing and thought. 'No,' he said reluctantly.

'It was not a movement. It was a pause, that was all. Were you conscious of stopping your efforts at any point?'

'No.' Derek swallowed the last of his toast. 'I'm really sorry, sir. But Elizabeth says I have to be honest otherwise there is no point . . . and sometimes a negative is as useful as a positive.'

'She's right, of course. We both hoped desperately that this time there would be a positive.' Robert smiled. 'We have to settle for an automatic pause – not instigated by you.'

'Is that good, Robert?'

'I don't know. It's up to me to make sense of it.'

'And me.'

Robert's smile went from ear to ear. He took the toast Jannie had buttered for him and reached for the marmalade. 'Let's battle up to the ridge and see what we can see this morning. Clear our heads.'

The two of them did that while Jannie took her English students into the library and talked about *The Tempest*.

She knew a moment of intense happiness when Cathy Johnson said thoughtfully, 'I reckon old Shakespeare was bringing up our probs in this one, miss. Don't you?'

'Go on, Cathy,' Jannie encouraged.

'Well. Look at Caliban. It was his bloody island, after all. And on they come, calling him names, excluding him. That's what they call it, don't they – exclusion? We know about that. Just like he did. Poor little bugger.'

The others laughed. Jannie automatically reached into her sleeve for a tissue and then stopped herself.

'Shakespeare could well have been before his time. My God, he was faced with enough examples of segregation to write a hundred plays about it. Let's look at the whole thing from Caliban's angle. OK?'

'OK!'

Cathy Johnson, newly blonde and – so importantly – newly vocal, grinned at her, very well pleased. And Jannie knew yet again that she was indeed in the right place.

Nineteen

The trouble was, everyone wanted to be Caliban. They solved that by having everyone appear on the stage at the end, taking their bow and saying in various ways, 'I am Caliban.'

Representing all of them was Kai. His stunted, twisted body was also supple; he began to see it as his greatest asset and as he writhed around the outdoor stage he seemed to be able to communicate with the audience in the strangest of ways. Hanging from one of the remaining elm trees, he declared his love for Miranda and fixed his gaze on a small girl in the front row. 'What can I do?' he asked her. She held out her arms to him, tears in her eyes.

Robert reported back to Jannie during the interval.

'Your brother and sister are absolutely in there!' He moved his chair away from Cathy who, as Miranda, was teasing her blond hair into a halo around her head. 'Who is the vicar – surely he hasn't come to talk to us in his official capacity?'

'It's our rector. He did two memorial services for Mum and Dad last year. I wanted Ned and Gus to bring him. So glad he could come.' She spoke absently, her mind already on the next piece. 'Ferdinand, go for the laughs. We want a lighter mood now. Miranda, flirt as much as you like. Don't forget, when Ferdinand promises no sex before marriage, turn to the audience and make that ghastly face.'

Cathy and Derek exchanged looks. This was probably the sixth time Miss Briscoe had given this particular stage direction.

Robert said, 'I'd better go.' He tried to give Jannie a reassuring smile but he was as nervous as she. Then he added, 'Your family are great.'

And she smiled back, nerves forgotten just for a moment.

Some of the children went home with their parents that evening. Others stayed until the end of the term, helping to wash and fold the costumes from the play, enjoy poetry readings in the woods, give extra time to exercise classes. Derek haunted Robert's workshop and Cathy haunted Derek. She had fallen in love and brought Jannie a poem she had written. It was blunt and very much to the point.

'I want to sleep with him,' she said. 'No flowery language for that, is there?'

'Have a think about Derek himself. As a person. As the person who blamed himself for not being able to use Robert's electronic hand. And then read some of these poems. John Keats died very young. But he found the time to look around him and see what a wonderful world we live in.' She looked at Cathy's jutting lower lip. 'Just do it, Cathy. You can't bludgeon Derek into anything – not like you bludgeoned your parents into letting you bleach your hair. Keats will help you to understand yourself.' She made shooing movements. 'Go on. Take this book, walk to the sea – alone – and then read the poems.'

'It's over a mile to the sea! What about my leg?'

'Remember how you chose not to speak for two years? Are

you choosing to have these pains in your leg? Robert tells me you have requested a wheelchair.'

'Changed my mind.' Cathy's expression went from stubborn to defiant.

'I should think so. Derek is a member of the North Devon Harriers. You could train for that, you know. Ask Fizz for some help.' Fizz was their live-in physiotherapist. 'You don't have to shock all of us into submission either, Cathy. You are beautiful and talented. But keep that poem you've written. Show it to him when you're married with a family.'

Cathy's face opened wide and she reverted to being an adoring schoolgirl. 'Oh, Miss,' she breathed. She took the book of poems from Jannie and pumped her legs energetically on the spot. 'See, now that I am talking again, there's no reason for me being at this school. And I was expelled from two others before coming here.'

Jannie started to laugh. 'Can you really see that happening here? You've got two more years before your A levels. Derek has got a provisional place at Birmingham. You should bear that in mind when it comes to choosing courses for next year.'

Cathy stopped pumping. 'I was thinking I'd only got another two weeks of seeing him.' She frowned. 'I'd never make university, Miss. Would I?'

'Why on earth not?'

'All the students sleep around then, don't they?'

'No. That's what is called their public image.'

'But I'd see him. Most days prob'ly. Oh, Miss . . .' She held Keats close to her chest and departed.

Ned settled back into Zion Cottage like – as he put it – a hand into a glove. He spent a few days adapting his big attic room to take the extra books and the computer on which he had entered test results. He had a telephone installed on the deep window embrasure, which was also his desk. Charts hung from the sloping ceilings and he bought a Swedish dictionary from a bookshop in Penzance.

Gussie was full of admiration.

'I remember seeing the lab when you first went to work at United Chemicals. It was all a bit iffy because of funding and I thought they'd gone overboard with spending it on so much equipment. But it's brought forth enough results to last a lifetime, surely?'

'It doesn't really signify how many results we get, nor how much equipment. Unless we can see a pattern, make something of the results . . . it's a bit like not seeing the wood for the trees. Obviously the people who have made this award know we're close. That in itself is encouraging.'

'Who exactly is donating this money, Ned?' Gus eyed the printer, which was sited on Ned's old chest of drawers. It was chattering away and spewing out paper unstoppably. She had used a computer herself graphically. Somehow this constant churning out of facts was not the same. Not a bit the same. It made her nervous. She saw Ned in a new light. It distanced him from her.

He said, 'It's a trust – yes, another trust. But it's got a connection with the Nobel Trust, which gives it a certain . . .'

'Cachet?' she suggested.

'Yes, but more than that. Stability. Gravitas.' He grinned. 'Definitely cachet.'

The printer stopped chattering and he lifted out a big wodge of paper and slid it into a file. 'Copies of stuff I've emailed to Sven. You'll like Sven. He's your sort. Visionary.'

'Visionary?' She laughed. 'I'm no visionary, Ned. In fact,

I'm nothing much. I want to be another Kate. But it doesn't seem to be happening.'

'I meant that you could visualize stuff. In this job, for instance, you could look ahead and forecast results before they materialized.' He waved his hands helplessly. 'You sort of think. Oh God, I don't know. When you meet Sven you'll see what I mean. And see that you are the same sort of person.'

It had struck him quite suddenly that Sven and Gus were very similar in some ways. They would get on. Really well.

'Not that he's planning to come over here. I'm going there as soon as we get sorted.'

'You're going away again?' Gussie looked dismayed.

'Not for ages,' he reassured her, and hugged her to his shoulder. Then he released her and walked across the room to the dormer window and looked out across the harbour. The sun was settling into the sea at Porthmeor beach and there were flowing streaks of it sweeping around into the harbour. Behind him Gussie was still standing by the computer window, looking out, silently absorbing all that beauty. He thought of Victor and Connor; of Kate and Mark. He thought of Victor's beautiful Davina and Mark's eccentric Zannah. He and Gussie were the results of those people. Was it possible they might make a pattern?

He said huskily, 'Gus, don't try to be Kate. Or Zannah. Not even Mark. You are yourself and that is at it should be.'

He moved slightly so that her back was reflected in the dormer window. She stayed very still but said nothing.

He blundered on, 'Kate was my mother and Mark was my father. Jannie is our sister. You . . .' She was wearing a conventional summer frock, patterned with daisies on a dark blue ground. He wondered whether it was one of the bundle that Uncle Rory had brought round. It was short on Gus, but would have been the right length for Aunt Rosemary. 'You are . . .' He wondered how to tell her that all his feelings of joy, sadness, wonder, every damned emotion in the world was because of her. She had taught him how to feel. He could have summed it all up by saying, 'You are my own true love.' But that might wreck everything for ever.

He saw her turn; she was smiling; she was about to try to rescue him from one of his notorious word blocks when he so often put his foot right into it.

She said, 'I am your best friend, I hope. You certainly are mine.' She sat in his office chair and whirled herself around. 'Do you remember our first meeting on Porthmeor beach when you were helping Jem with the donkeys?'

He turned and watched her properly, and made a sound in his throat.

'I knew then we would always be best friends. Didn't you?' She stopped the revolving seat and looked up at him humorously. He made another sound in his throat.

She grinned. 'I'll tell you something now, young Ned. When Dad told me he was going to marry Kate, I didn't approve. And then he explained that Ned would live with us and be my brother. And that made it all right!'

Ned dragged another chair forward and sat on it. He said, 'Likewise. I mean . . . what I meant is . . . I felt the same.'

She put her hands behind her head and leaned back on them. Her dress rode up her legs. She had the most marvellous legs. She and Jannie usually wore jeans and shirts but they both had beautiful legs. She leaned forward suddenly and put her elbows on her bare knees.

'We had such fun, didn't we? We mustn't forget the fun we had when we were kids.'

He knew her so well, so intimately. She was older than

he was but he had been the one who picked her up when she fell down – she was always falling over those long legs – bandaged her up with his handkerchief, wheeled her up to the Out Patients at the Cottage Hospital on the luggage trolley he had made in the old Scaife studio. And he had done her maths homework for ages . . .

She said, 'I taught you to swim properly. D'you remember sitting on the sea bed and watching the waves roll over our heads? And when we were intrepid mountaineers and climbed all over Clodgy?'

He recalled something Jannie had said. 'Well, do you remember jumping off the cliff at Bamaluz Point? I wouldn't want to do that again!'

There was a long pause. She dropped her head and took a breath. Then she said fervently, 'Neither would I!'

Jannie was right. There was something haunting Gus. Something underneath the horror of Kate and Mark.

Ned forced a grin. 'Where on earth did you get that dress? Makes you look like a schoolgirl – an old-fashioned schoolgirl.'

She laughed. 'You're an expert with the back-handed compliments! I think it was one of Rosemary's. I must have kept it back. And it's been too hot for jeans. Listen, I haven't got a thing for supper and now the car is back, shall we go out somewhere for a meal? That pub near Constantine – or Mousehole – what do you think?'

'I most definitely think. Either.'

'I'll go and change.'

'Oh, in that case I'm not coming. I planned to wear my shorts and pretend you are still twelve and I am ten.'

Gussie pretended reluctance. 'Oh, all right then. But why ten and twelve? We've got most of our lives to choose from.'

He couldn't remind her and just shrugged. But he had been ten when he had watched Gussie cuddling little January and known he had wanted to marry her.

In July, when they went to see *The Tempest* at Hartley School, Jannie had suggested that Father Martin might like to come with them. He was delighted by the invitation. They'd asked Bessie to come too but she was shocked.

'Like what they do on the Island on midsummer night? My mother wouldn't have nothing to do with that sorta thing. You be careful, Gussie Briscoe. That's when you meets your man and it dun't matter whether he's good, bad or indiffrent – you got 'im for life!'

'Oh dear.' Gussie gave her a look and she managed a little smile.

'I wun't come, m'dear. Don't want to be far from 'ome these days. Just in case Old Beck do drop by for me.'

'Oh, Bessie . . .'

'I know. But that's 'ow it is.'

'All right. I'll tell Jannie you are otherwise engaged.''

'That's it zackly!' They both laughed.

At the end of July, Robert and Jannie arrived.

The ice had been broken during the school supper after *The Tempest*, but it had been a fragmented introduction to Hartley as much as to each other, and already Robert could not remember what Ned had looked like. He remembered Gussie because of her single plait of hair, and even during their brief conversation – held behind Jannie's back as she leaned forward to pass Ned yet another pasty – he had registered the fact that she did not 'see' the wheelchair yet she was absorbing him and revealing bits of herself in return.

He remembered Ned had red hair – that was a start.

The interior of Robert's van, usually filled with groceries for the school, was packed with everything Jannie had accumulated over the past three years in student accommodation, plus Robert's tools, which ranged from a coal hammer to the sort of screwdrivers used by watch repairers. The hand itself, aluminium, unbelievably delicate, had its own carton protected by his sleeping bag.

They parked in the Scaife studio. Ned was there to meet them and had somehow managed to open the big double doors, closed since the last of Gerald Scaife's enormous seascapes had been taken out. Robert drove inside cautiously; there was even space enough for the ramp to be lowered and for him to manoeuvre his wheelchair to the concrete floor.

He shook Ned's hand and they moved away so that Jannie, now in the driver's seat, could operate the ramp. As it raised itself and clicked into place, Robert gazed up and around, amazed.

'It's like a cathedral,' he said, forgetting that he had been nervous about this moment.

Ned laughed. 'Of all comparisons! Gerald Scaife was, well, profane. No other word for it. When you meet our uncle Rory you will understand what I mean. Cornwall produces such characters now and then. They should be pirates. It's hard to take them on dry land.'

Jannie emerged from the driver's seat.

'I told him to park as close to the left as he could. It will give us room to use the ramp for unloading. But we'll do that tomorrow and just take our overnight cases for now. It's been a long day.'

Ned could see she was nervous and was surprised. He and Robert had got on well when they had first met at the

performance of *The Tempest*. He had expected to feel . . .
something else. A resentment? This man – boy, really –
breaking up their precious threesome? Surely he wasn't that
petty? But whatever he had expected did not happen. Robert
had accepted Ned and Gussie, and they had accepted him.
On the way home Father Martin had gone so far as to say,
'Well, that Robert Hanniford seems well suited to your sister.
You will make a good quartet.'

Ned hugged Jannie now. 'Good to see you made it. The
traffic is always ghastly in July. Let's show Robert the easy
way home. Give me those bags, Jan. Robert, you all right
under that suitcase?'

'Think so. Steps?'

Ned was used to this sort of shorthand. 'No. Not the back
way. But cobbles. Dad reckoned they kept your insides good
and healthy.'

Robert laughed at that but said, 'He had a point, I think.
Especially in my case. The longer I don't use my legs, the
bigger the risk of losing them.' He shifted the suitcase and
grinned up at Ned. 'Bring on the cobbles!'

They lurched down the backstreets towards Zion Cottage.
Ned felt Jannie relax by his side. He liked Robert even more.

Gussie met them at the gate. She was wearing a pinafore the
Becks had given her last Christmas, pristine new, displaying
a leaping dolphin. Above it her face was bright red and her
plait was fraying damply. It had been a hot day and she knew
now – too late, of course – that she should have got mackerel
and soused them in vinegar and put them on Kate's enormous
meat server surrounded by a green salad. As it was, she
had sweated with a recipe for John Dory braised with baby
shallots, lots of Cornish potatoes not much bigger than peas

and an enormous cauliflower. She had put cochineal in the cauliflower hoping it would turn pale pink, but it was now blood red.

She leaned over and kissed Robert.

'Welcome, future brother-in-law. Bit of a disaster in the kitchen department but everything else awaits you.' She raised her head and grinned. 'You might as well sample the worst of my cooking immediately, I suppose.'

He smiled up at her overheated face and noticed a bead of sweat travelling down the length of her nose. He agreed with Jannie: she really was beautiful.

'It's so good to be here. As we turned off at Hayle, the air was fresher. The views so wonderful—'

'And we got away from some of the traffic!' Jannie was laughing now, happy that it was all going well, blissfully unaware of the cauliflower. 'I know it's a Saturday in July, Gus, but we were two hours driving from Launceston to Jamaica Inn. So hot – ghastly!'

Gussie made suitable noises of sympathy and led the way inside, where a jug of iced water was duly appreciated. Then Jannie explained the workings of the stair lift, which involved a platform for a wheelchair and a safety chain. She followed Robert's chair, explaining things as they rose to the hall.

'Uncle Rory can remember when the Nollas – they lived here and left the house and their boat to Dad – dried their washing down the hall. Every Monday you had to fight your way through flannel combinations and blouses with very high necks!'

Robert laughed, not at the story but because the enormous Scandinavian-blue eyes, on a level with his, were so full of life and happiness.

They went up another level and turned left into one of the two big bedrooms.

'Mum and Dad's room,' Jannie said briefly. She opened a door on the opposite wall and revealed a shower room.

'Couldn't be better,' Robert said just as briefly, then added, 'Heart sank a bit when I saw how tall the cottage was.'

'Dad had it changed when he inherited it. But the main bathroom is still on ground level.' She grinned. 'Ned is at the top, and in the middle of the night he can do the round trip in five minutes. Gussie and I have timed him!'

'Why on earth doesn't he use this bathroom?'

She grinned. 'I think he might have done. Just once.'

He grinned back as he edged himself on to the bed and lifted each leg in turn. He stretched luxuriously. 'And which set of genes is prevalent in their youngest child?' he said, using a voice supposed to be that of their psychologist.

Jannie flopped by his side, then lifted herself on one elbow and looked down at him for at least ten seconds.

'I've got large helpings from both sides,' she whispered. And she kissed him.

Two floors below, Ned said, 'If you fiddle with that John Dory much longer he'll bite off your hand! Sit down for five minutes and cool off. You're looking like a boiled lobster yourself!'

Gussie put the dish back in the oven and sat down in the open doorway.

'Why on earth didn't I do something cold? I don't like the way the sauce has gone sort of grey.'

'Dearest Gus, everyone will enjoy every mouthful, and that cauliflower is worth putting in the flower show next week.'

But she couldn't see the funny side of it. Plus there was the fact that – very unexpectedly – the familiarity of the wheel-chair inside the cottage but with someone else in it, was a shock.

She lowered her voice to a whisper. 'He was so nice, so unassuming when we met him at the school play. But here, don't you feel odd about it?'

'No. Actually, Gus, no. He seems a bit more mature here than he did at Hartley. They both seem more mature to-gether. And, of course, the wheelchair is like a passport to us, isn't it?'

She dropped her voice lower still, and he could only catch the one word. 'Interloper'. He was almost shocked.

'Darling, that doesn't sound like you. You've overdone it and the heat is suddenly too much of a good thing.' He stood up and came behind her. 'Let me have a go at your neck.' He put her plait gently over her shoulder and began to roll his knuckles gently from the outside of her shoulders into the nape of her neck. She became still and then, tremblingly, he felt her relaxing.

He said cheerfully, 'D'you remember how I did this just before you took your A level examinations? You didn't want me to, and then I reminded you – furiously, I expect – how I'd always been the one to pick you up when you fell over those big feet of yours!'

He laughed and after a moment she joined him. 'I had forgotten. Thank you for reminding me.'

It sounded such a formal acknowledgement he was sur-prised. He had felt a kind of embarrassment several times since he'd come back home and it had gone unnoticed. In fact, she had dealt with it as she always had; as his older sister always had. This was the first time she had shown any awkwardness.

He used the tips of his fingers and moved behind her ears and on to her scalp. Her hair was thick with salt. He said quietly, 'Shall I undo your plait and have a real good go? I could give you a shampoo, if you like.'

'No. It's good of you, Ned, but they'll be down any minute now and I want to get the meal over and done with.'

He went back to her shoulders and finished off. She was no longer relaxed and he knew he would not get rid of her tension now.

'I'll wash up after we've eaten. You take a plate of food round to Bessie's and stay for an hour while they settle in. OK?'

'Thank you.' She stood up and went to the oven to look at the fish yet again. 'I think they must be settling in now, don't you?' She tried to sound roguish and failed.

'They're young and they're getting married on the fourteenth of August. We'll have to get used to it, Gus.'

'You mean, I'll have to get used to it.' She straightened and looked at him with a familiar wry smile. 'You're doing splendidly and you've got a lot in common with him.' Her smile died and she said suddenly, 'Oh, Ned, I feel I am losing Jannie.'

'Ah.' He came to her and held her against his shoulder. 'Mum didn't envisage this, Gus. When she sort of handed Jan over to you, it wasn't for life. You knew that.'

'I did.' She clung to him. 'I did, of course. She knew I needed a bond. She was a wonderful woman, Ned.' She looked into his face. 'Ned, I miss her so much I sometimes think – I think . . .'

'What do you think?' He did not want her to move away; he prayed she would stay hanging on to him, whatever the reason.

'I think I must be like Zannah. Whirling around and getting nowhere.'

'Except that Zannah sounds completely off her trolley at times. And you are the most sensible, centred, wonderful woman I know.'

Her look turned into a stare and then she burst out laughing and dropped her hands.

'What on earth are we talking about, Ned? As if we could lose each other. That's the real legacy Mum and Dad left us – each other.' She patted his cheek as if he were still six years old. 'Come on, brother-of-mine. Let's dish up this ghastly supper and get started! If they're asleep who cares? We can stick theirs in the slow oven. It couldn't look any worse than it does now!'

They had just finished putting the pink cauliflower in pride of place when they heard the whine of the stair lift and the wheels of Robert's chair appeared. Jannie leaned over his head. She looked wonderful.

'Did you think we'd gone to sleep? We're showered and in our pyjamas so that we can collapse immediately afterward! My God, what on earth is that?'

Robert said, 'How wonderful. It's the pink cauliflower, isn't it? What could be a better welcome! Thank you so much. Oh, and John Dory, my out-and-out favourite!'

Ned liked him. Gussie was laughing and looking natural with her plait hanging down her back and her damp hair in tendrils around her face. He felt a strange sensation in his chest and could not put a name to it.

He was washing up much later; Robert and Jannie had gone to bed, Gussie was still round at Bessie's. He hung the tea towel over the guard rail and shook the cloth outside.

Yearning. That was the word that fitted his chest pain. He

275

was yearning. For his sister. All those weeks in America when he had come to believe that the terrible deaths of Mark and Kate had bound the three of them for ever, were only a part of a solution. Everyone who had suffered such an enormous bereavement was bound together in a universal grief. It was a support. It helped enormously. But there were personal sadnesses too.

He no longer saw Gussie as a much-loved sister. He yearned for her. And she did not yearn for him.

He took the stairs two at a time. The attic was stifling and he opened both windows and stood in the dormer, staring down at the apron of cobbles and the granite steps leading to the wharf. After a while Gussie emerged from Bessie's yard, walked slowly across to the steps, walked down them and sat on the Friendship bench below. He could see the white of her scalp where her dark hair parted and swooped around her head and into its plait.

He withdrew his head and crossed the room to the other window. He switched on the computer, pulled up the swivel chair and logged on to the email. There were two messages from Sven. He tried to imagine the small island within sight of Stockholm where Sven Svensson had a summer cottage. He wondered whether there was an inhabitable island within the Scillies archipelago where he could isolate himself.

He sighed sharply and clicked on to the first message.

Twenty

It took a week for the four of them to shake themselves into some kind of pattern. During that week, Jannie and Robert visited Father Martin twice and found him, as Jannie put it, 'lacking on the advice front but very helpful about the privacy bit'. He thought he could arrange the ceremony in the little church on the Island where the first of the memorial services had happened after the disaster last September. 'I'll have a word with the bishop. It will be much easier to ensure a private wedding there – obviously. Also, a very significant church in your circumstances, my dear.' He turned to Robert. 'Will your parents be present, Robert?'

'Both sets are abroad but they are delighted.' Robert grinned. 'It helps them with the guilt thing. I'm a bit of a liability.'

The clergyman glanced at Jannie and hurried on. 'So Mrs Beck and Thaddeus Stevens will be present? Your brother will give you away and your sister is your only attendant.'

Jannie said, 'Don't sound doleful, Father. Don't you see how special it makes it?'

For once, the rector smiled. 'I am not in the slightest bit doleful, January. I always sound like this.'

She was surprised. 'Yes, you do. How sad.' She leaned

towards him. 'I know I shouldn't ask this, but why didn't you get married?'

His smile died. 'I did. She left me. I thought everyone in the parish knew that.'

For once Jannie was speechless. Robert took her hand and looked across the big old-fashioned desk. 'Probably not. We are so sorry, Father. It must be hard for you to officiate at so many weddings.'

'Not one bit. The state of matrimony is instituted for the best possible reasons and if some of its participants fall along the wayside that is no reason to think less of it.' He nodded at Jannie. 'Don't look stricken, January. Your marriage is going to be for life. I can usually tell. And that must be because of my own sad failure – something useful to come out of it after all.'

She swallowed and tried to thank him. Then said, 'You think you know people and then find you don't.'

'Quite.' He looked at his notes. 'So it is at ten o'clock on the fourteenth of August.' He looked up. 'And at Zennor for lunch afterwards. Thank you for your invitation and I am delighted to accept it.'

They waited a few seconds for the 'advice bit', then realized that in the circumstances it might well sound hollow. Robert released the brake on his chair and Jannie stood up. They both smiled and nodded as the rector voiced his good wishes for their future happiness, then they emerged into the sunshine and wandered through the Warren and along the path bordering Porthminster beach. It was a very hot day and the coastline disappeared in a silver haze beyond Hayle Towans. Jannie picked a seat well shaded by a giant rhubarb plant; Robert backed his chair in beside her. They held hands and watched some children digging a miniature

Suez between the oncoming tide and their sandcastle. They chatted in a desultory way; old friends already.

'If this weather holds we could cancel the meal at Zennor and go for a picnic further down the coast.'

'We could. But in case it doesn't hold, Plan A is probably the best bet.'

'Mmm, yes. By that time we'll be Mr and Mrs Hanniford. That's what it's all about.' She giggled. 'Jannie Hanniford. I like it.'

'Me too.' He squeezed her hand. 'Jan, do you mind about my parents?'

'No, of course not. But I am surprised your mother didn't want to come.'

'She wants to make her new marriage work. She blames herself for Dad's . . . defection.'

'And you don't?'

'Dad had an affair with his secretary when I was fourteen. It went on from there. I knew when he had another model because he always bought a new shirt for their first date. Nothing lasted until Marcia. She ran her own company very efficiently and she got tired of her unofficial status with Dad. It wasn't Mum's fault.'

'Oh, Robert, how awful for you.'

'It was awful. Mum was totally demoralized. I told you she didn't really believe it – still doesn't – but still manages to blame herself.'

Jannie knew this part. Geoff and Elizabeth had been visiting the orthopaedic hospital with one of their students and had been introduced to Robert, who was adjusting a wheelchair. Whatever Geoff had said that afternoon had led to Robert finishing his engineering course and starting his internship at Hartley School.

'I didn't know for ages that Mum had listened to an interview Geoff gave to a programme on Radio West and had written to him!' He shook his head. 'She wouldn't take credit for that either!'

Jannie squeezed his hand and he looked at her and started to laugh. 'Thank God for Jonathan.' She opened her eyes wide at him and he nodded. 'I know. I'm pretty dismissive about the whole thing. Couldn't stand him at first, I admit it!' He made a face. 'Meeting you and falling in love . . . it changes everything, Jan. Everything.' He pulled on her hand and she leaned forward and kissed him. Then they whispered what Robert called 'sweet nothings' and – eventually – drew apart, smiling idiotically.

Jannie said, 'Every time these moments happen, we are plighting our troth – did you know that?'

'Of course. And when I heard that phrase first I thought it was "plaiting". I rather like the idea of plaiting our troth . . . intertwining it.'

She smiled, felt tears behind her eyes and blinked hard. 'I wish I had known you sooner.'

'Yes. But perhaps no. We might have been such good friends that we could not become such wonderful lovers. Like your brother and sister.'

She drew back and stared at him, astonished. 'My God! How did you know that? I've hardly dared think it, let alone put it into words! It's all so delicate and fragile—'

'And obvious.'

'Is it? Is it really? Does Bessie know, and Father Martin and – and Aunt Rosemary and Uncle Rory?'

'I haven't got the faintest. Perhaps you need to arrive on the scene when it has become obvious, like I have . . . if you get me.'

'Yes. I think so.' She stared at the sky above his head. 'What can we *do*?'

'Nothing. Until we can.'

She switched her stare to him again.

He spread his hands. 'It's not like one of your projects, Jan. There might come an opportunity. But until that happens—'

'Seize the moment, you mean?'

'I think that's what I mean.'

'Oh my God. Suppose we miss the moment?'

'I don't know. They might make their own moment and we won't know it's happened. That's how it must have been for Jonathan and my Mum . . .'

'Go on. Tell me,' she commanded as he hesitated.

'Well . . . I was interning at Hartley at the time, went home for Christmas and there he was! I wanted to talk about special education and he wanted to talk about knitting!'

She raised her brows. 'Knitting?'

'I told you they met at an evening class. Traditional Arts and Crafts. He'd gone to talk to them about whittling. Balsa wood and a Stanley knife – you know the sort of thing. Evolved from your farm labourer with the kitchen knife and alder wood sitting outside his cottage whittling – carving – a doll for his youngest daughter . . .' He was laughing wholeheartedly now, but she had long-ago memories of Mark whittling Joanie dolls.

'You told me only that your mother had remarried and he was a lecturer.'

'Well, I gilded the lily slightly, I suppose. But the best of it is, Mum's traditional craft is knitting, especially the old traditional Fair Isle patterns. And now that's his speciality as well! They sit in their armchairs and knit for England!'

She laughed, but reluctantly. 'Actually, it sounds marvellous!

Like you helping me with *The Tempest*. Oh, I wish so much they could come to our wedding. I just know I'm going to love them.' She put her face close to his and said emphatically, 'Both of them!' And then kissed him, drew back and said, 'My God. You haven't even told them, have you?'

He stopped laughing and looked rueful. 'No. They'd already planned this delayed honeymoon and I knew she would cancel it. It wasn't a terrible thing to do, was it?'

Jannie thought about it, then said slowly, 'I'm not sure. Perhaps you should write to them and explain. Then you could tell them about the tiny church on the Island and how the service was held there the day after Nine Eleven had happened. Make it . . . real. I'll write too. Would you mind? They will be my family now, darling, not just yours.'

'I wouldn't mind. It's just that . . . I was trying to uncomplicate things, Jan. You've got a lot to deal with, the three of you.'

'And that reminds me – ' she darted a kiss to his nose – 'we're going out tonight. You and me. Late . . . just before midnight, I think it is.'

'Not another search for the special glory gates, is it?' They had made two forays into the narrow, fern-edged paths across the moors to kissing gates that had proved unusable for a wheelchair. The heat, the ferns, the flies had been – as Robert put it – 'a bit much'.

'Not yet. I want you to keep thinking about that, however. This is something completely different.'

Jannie and Robert cooked the supper that night. Afterwards, the four of them sat in the yard and watched the constant promenade of visitors gradually dissipate. Ned brought down some notes and discussed them with Robert.

The girls went next door to check on Bessie.

Ned closed his folder and cleared his throat. Robert looked across to the next yard and wondered aloud whether Bessie was all right.

'They'll be another half an hour, that's the usual.' Ned glanced at his watch; the girls had been gone less than five minutes. He cleared his throat again. 'D'you realize you'll have been here a week on Saturday?'

'Well . . . yes.'

'What d'you think of St Ives?'

'We used to come for the day when I was a kid. Before this lot.' He indicated his legs. 'I loved it then.' He paused, heard his own words and said quickly, 'And of course now – Jannie's spiritual home, as it were.'

'Not built for a wheelchair, of course, but you're managing well.'

'Jannie has shown me all the routes through the old town. To avoid the steps.'

'You can cope with the hills then?'

'So far. I've got a small power pack thing in the van. I can fit it so that it works off one of the wheels. Not terribly efficient but if we walk to Carbis Bay – she wants to do that some time – I would use it up Skidden Hill. Possibly. Well, probably.'

'Can't think how you managed to get up to the coast road looking for the glory gates. Breakneck Hill is named for a reason!'

Robert nodded. 'One of our less successful trips. That was when I decided to unearth the power pack.'

'She'll spring something on you sometimes. When you'd rather have a bit of a warning. Know what I mean? She is very impulsive.'

Robert remembered that they had a 'date' for that evening and felt a twinge of alarm. 'You think I should fit the pack now, perhaps?'

'No. Not this time, anyway.' Ned cleared his throat for the third time and Robert wondered whether it was sore.

There was a short and awkward silence. Then Ned said, 'It's supposed to be a surprise, not a shock, of course. I expect she's told you lots about our parents and the antics they got up to. It's just that she's sort of hoping to keep some of those kind of things . . . er . . . going.'

Robert said, 'Oh, yes. They sound so wonderfully matched. I realize Jannie hopes so much that we can be as happy in every way as they were.' He laughed uncomfortably. 'At first I wondered whether my disability was part of the attraction, but now—'

Ned interrupted quickly; he wanted no confidences about how they managed to overcome the wheelchair difficulties.

'Dad used to do it all the time, of course. I mean, he came to St Ives every year with Rosemary and Gran and Granddad, and then when Philip Nolla died and left him the cottage and the boat, he lived here. I think his wife, Zannah, forced him to do it – she was crazier then than she is now. Poor old Dad. Fancy having to put up with that. Not that Jannie is like Zannah, of course – I didn't mean that. Neither is Gussie, thank God. But Jannie thinks it would be a good idea if you followed in Dad's footsteps, as it were.' He stopped speaking and Robert wondered what on earth he had been trying to say. Over the wall they could hear Jannie's laugh as the girls emerged from Bessie's cottage. He finished hurriedly, 'It's just meant for a surprise, that's all I wanted to say. Good intentions and so forth.' He stood up and went to open the gate. 'Good luck!' he hissed over his shoulder.

Robert sat very still and stared as Gussie appeared, smiling, calm, her plait fraying as he noticed it did at the end of the day. He decided he liked Gussie's plait; it reminded him of plaiting his troth. He smiled as Jannie came after and immediately kissed him. He told himself he didn't care what surprise or shock she had in store for him. He – quite simply – loved her.

They left the house as the other two went up to bed. Gussie obviously had no inkling of any surprises in store; she was arguing with Ned about something to do with the infamous Uncle Rory. He was still staying with Jannie's stepmother in the South of France somewhere. Gussie thought he was 'pushing his luck'. Robert could hear her on the stairs saying something about a brain tumour and though Ned's reply was not clear his tone was scoffing. Robert wondered what it might be like to belong to this family. The Briscoes seemed to him, the only child of disparate parents, to have more than their fair share of genius . . . or craziness. He grinned up at Jannie as she helped him out of the cobbled yard; she had a good mix of the Briscoe genes and above all else she was gentle and kind. He said quietly into the soft dark air, 'I love you, January Briscoe. Do you think I'll ever become one of your family?'

'You've only known them for a week and you're having doubts already?'

She was dismayed, and he grabbed her hand and put it against his face. 'My doubts are in case I don't qualify for membership.'

She snorted. 'It's whether they can make it with you! Anyway, after tonight they'll just love you. I promise.'

'How do you mean – what do you mean – is this some

kind of test? I thought I was in for a bit of passion on a dark beach.'

'Absolutely right.' They had arrived at the top of the slipway behind Smeaton's Pier. The old ruined pier was above them, full of anglers and sunbathers in the daytime, now deserted and casting a deep shadow over the sea as the tide moved heavily, indecisively up the slope of the slipway, black and dangerous.

Robert said, 'I can smell sulphur – rain behind it. We're in for a storm.'

'Right.' Jannie stopped and snapped on the chair's brakes, completely ignoring his comment. 'D'you need help with un-dressing?' She whipped her T-shirt over her head at the same time as wriggling out of her jeans. She stood before him, her skin lit whitely by a sudden emergence of the moon. Her pants were negligible and she wore no bra. She scuffed off her sandals and grinned at his astonished expression. 'Well? Wasn't this what you had in mind?'

He spluttered, 'Shameless woman!' He lifted his arms straight up as if in surrender and she pulled his shirt off with one swoop, then leaned down and removed his trainers. He eased himself up with his elbows and she tugged at his jeans until they too lay on the enormous granite slabs of the ramp.

'Be gentle with me,' he begged. She laughed, throwing back her head and showing her white throat to the sky. Then she snapped off the brake, took the handles and charged down the slope and straight into the sea. He flew from the chair and entered the enormous blackness on all fours.

He gave a shout as the water engulfed him; the air was still warm from a day of intense sunshine and the sea felt like ice. He turned and floated and looked back at Jannie, who was pulling the chair back to the top of the ramp and locking it with its brake.

'I'm going to drown you. Come here, you hussy – I thought you were gentle and now I discover—' He took a mouthful of water and spluttered incomprehensibly. She was running back to him, diving off the side of the slipway, disappearing and then grabbing his legs and pulling him down beneath the water.

They emerged, both spluttering, helpless with laughter. She held him close, glorying in the sheer length of his body held closely to her own. They were panting for breath. She put up a hand and wiped water from his face and then kissed him. He kissed her back, suddenly serious. He found he could paddle his legs, and he kept them both upright.

He whispered, 'What was all that about?'

'Mum and Dad used to do this,' she said. 'Ned wanted me to tell you about it first. But then it wouldn't have been an adventure. It might have been a therapy. And that would have made it sort of condescending.'

'What did Gus say about it?'

'Didn't tell her. She would have worried and she's worried enough anyway. Every little thing worries her lately. She taught Mum to swim so that Mum could go in with Dad like Zannah had.' She grinned at him wetly. 'Gets complicated. Just enjoy it. The best bit is yet to come.'

They found the edge of the granite ramp and he swam in until his knees scraped on its hard surface. They made love in the shallows, completely carried away because he was suddenly so mobile. Afterwards they lay on their backs and stared up at the stars.

'I don't remember those stars being there . . . before,' he whispered.

'Nor me.' She sat up, waist-deep in water. 'I wonder if it was the same for Mum and Dad?' She looked down at him and was suddenly weeping profusely. 'Oh, Robert, I was just about to say I would ask him because I could ask him any-thing – anything at all – any time.' She put her hands over her face. 'But not any more. Not now.' She gave an enormous sob. 'I'll never know whether the stars came out for them after they had swum in the moonlight.'

He sat up slowly and took her in his arms. 'Of course they did. It's a gift they've passed on, my darling. It comes from them.'

That made her cry more but differently. She held on to him as if she could never let him go, and the tide swept up to their necks and then over their heads, and they had to scrabble further up. She stood up and he continued to pull himself along with his arms while she grabbed the wheelchair and took it back down for him. She dried him with her T-shirt and let him do the same for her. Her tears left tracks in the salt on her face and neck, but she was smiling and then laughing as he dried beneath her arms and the laughter died as he kissed her body and whispered what he called his sweet nothings.

Later, when she sat on the old pier dangling her legs, her head on his knees, she said, 'I've known you a fraction of my present life span, Robert, and I know I could not live with-out you.' She tilted her head and stared into his green eyes. 'Mum and Dad were lucky after all, weren't they?'

'In that way? Yes. I suppose they were.' He smoothed her salt-wet hair. 'I wish I'd known them, Jan.'

'That was part of tonight, darling. You know them because you are living in the cottage, you manoeuvre your chair like Dad did, and now we have swum together like they did.'

They were silent until he felt her shiver against his shin.

'Time for bed. I'll make us some of our special cocoa while you get a hot shower. OK?'

'Definitely OK.' She jumped up and they started back along the wharf.

The next day Jannie announced at breakfast that she had baptized Robert the night before. Gussie was aghast.

'It's all very well, darling, but did you know if Robert could swim?'

'I've seen him in the hydrotherapy pool often enough. He plays water polo for Devon, too.' Jannie knew she sounded defiant and grinned. 'Sorry, Gus, it's not that exciting. Now, if I'd insisted he should jump off Bamaluz Point—' She stopped speaking as Gussie put a hand to her throat.

Ned said easily, 'Don't worry, Gus. As soon as they left I rigged up Dad's old telescope in the dormer and kept them in my sights.'

Jannie was aghast. 'You what? That's terrible, Ned! What sort of stuff did you get up to in America? You'd never have done anything like that before!'

'I've always had to keep an eye on you, missie!' He intended to sound like a television hillbilly and failed miserably. They all laughed except Jannie; her face was very red indeed. Gus looked relieved, however, and shook her head resignedly.

'Sorry, Robert. I don't know what else she might have in mind for you. Was it some kind of test you devised, Jannie?'

'Not at all! It was the most romantic event of my whole life! And – and that rotten Ned has ruined it!'

Ned held up a hand. 'Stop there before you give anything away! It was just before the storm – very dark – not a star in the sky. And anyway, Smeaton's Pier blocked anything that might have been going on behind it.'

Jannie seemed to be holding her breath. She looked across at Robert, who was staring at her.

'Sure it was that dark, Ned?' he said.

Ned raised his brows. 'It was about an hour before the thunderstorm, wasn't it? Those thunderheads blocked out the moon and the stars – come on, you were there!'

Gussie poured herself more tea. 'You timed it exactly right. Thank goodness you weren't caught in that storm.' She held the teapot in Ned's direction and he shook his head. 'I looked out towards Hayle – just gone two o'clock it was – and the whole place was illuminated by the summer lightning.'

Jannie switched her gaze from Robert and held out her cup. 'We were fast asleep by then,' she said comfortably.

Ned said, 'If you haven't got anything planned for today, how about Robert and I looking through some of my stuff?' He turned in his chair to face Robert. 'It's tedious, in a way, but I'd like you to start on the ground floor, as it were, when it comes to methodology. You're going to have to go through that sort of grind yourself while you're testing the electronics in the hand you've made. By the way, I'd like to take photographs of it – the hand, I mean – for my father in California. It's beautiful in its own right.' He looked round at Jannie. 'How about it, Sis? The foliage up on the moors is going to be sopping wet; Robert will get soaked if you plan to look around Bamaluz Point for the glory gates today.'

Jannie nodded. 'If the car is free, will you come with me to Zennor, Gus? Get some menus and decide how we're going to do the table?'

Gussie nodded. 'I'd love that. Shall we take Bessie?'

'If you like.' Jannie had hoped for a tête-à-tête.

'Not if you don't like.'

'No, honestly, it's OK by me.'

Ned said, 'Let's go, Robert. They're multiskilled – can wash up and have these fascinating debates at the same time.'

Robert smiled at Jannie. 'Is that all right, Brisket?'

It was his very private name for her and she blushed slightly and avoided Ned's suddenly alert gaze.

'Perfectly all right,' she said. They had far bigger secrets than that. She thought of those stars and was filled with a huge, engulfing content. She beamed at Gussie. 'Let's take Bessie. She'll love seeing Mabel Finch, who does the washing-up at the pub now. She was at school with Mabel's mother and they got up to all sorts of things.'

They cleared the table and listened to Ned already explaining his 'system' as they went slowly up the stairs to the accompaniment of the faint hum from the stair lift. The attic door closed.

'Poor Robert,' Jannie sighed.

Gussie was swilling water around the teapot and turned, surprised. 'What do you mean? Ned is a really good teacher. Even I can understand what he's talking about – well, most of the time.'

'I know. But Robert is still so low about the last test he did.'

Gussie said acutely, 'He shouldn't be testing people he knows and cares about so much. It should be totally objective.'

'Yes. But they've been in on it from the beginning. They're . . . *there*. Actually, almost queuing up for their turn. They want good results for Robert as well as for themselves.'

'If it's such a joint project, then disappointments must be shared as well as successes.'

'Oh, darling, you're such a comfort. Can you say those sort of things to Robert?'

'Not yet. Robert and I need time.'

Jannie paused in drying a plate; she looked stricken. 'What d'you mean? Don't you like him? Oh my God, I thought Ned might disapprove – he can be so stuffy at times – but never you! You've got to like him, Gus! You've got to do more than that – you've got to care about him and take him under your wing like you do with me and Ned and everyone. He hasn't had what we've had – all that love and yet complete freedom – he needs you, Gus!'

She put down the tea towel and the plate none too gently and tried to clasp Gussie around the waist. Gussie held her dripping hands high and turned, laughing but shocked.

'Darling, what on earth brought that on? I like him immensely.' She put her wet hands on the back of Jannie's T-shirt and held her close. 'It's wonderful to see the two of you together. There's a line of communication between you all the time.' She rocked gently. 'Yet you never exclude us. I can see he's good and true, and everything you told us. We all need time . . . of course we do. He needs it to accept us – we're not a run-of-the-mill family, after all – and we need to make room in our boat for him!' She tried a laugh and held Jannie away so that she could see her face. 'What was that about, for goodness' sake? Are you just doing your drama-queen stuff or have you had a row with Robert?'

'Don't know.' Jannie forced a grin. 'Yes, I do.' She picked up the plate and towel and scrubbed vigorously as a sign that everything was back to normal. 'Don't know whether I should tell you or not. I can tell you but I can't . . . explain anything.'

Gussie emptied the washing-up bowl, rinsed her hands and dried them.

'Say nothing,' she advised. 'It's always the best way.'

'No – no, it's not!' Jannie was vehement again. 'However . . . absurd it sounds, we should share things.' She busied herself with the other plates in the rack. 'It's just that something so special happened last night. It was fun, of course. I knew it would be. It was so hot – the calm before the storm, I suppose. Except I was actually asleep before the storm came.' She glanced at her sister; Gussie was deliberately putting away the dishes, pretending that this was one of their usual inconsequential chats. Jannie cleared her throat. 'It's nothing really, just that it was so dark. Like Ned was saying, the clouds were building up. There was a bit of moonlight but no stars. But afterwards, when we were dressed, before we started back home, there were stars. Masses of them, right across the sky.'

Gussie straightened from a low cupboard, went to the table and sat down. Jannie joined her. They were conscious of the usual morning sounds outside; the gulls screeching and a cricket match getting under way on the harbour beach.

Jannie said, 'What are you thinking?'

'The same as you. That Mum and Dad are still around.'

Jannie whispered, 'Oh my God.' And then, 'Thank you, Gus.'

She waited for Gussie to stand up and go on with the chores. Nothing happened for as long as ten seconds. Then Gussie took a deep breath.

'All right. You shared with me. So I will share with you.' She let the breath go and sat back in her chair. 'You're curious about Bamaluz Point, aren't you? And it seems to be cropping up a lot lately so perhaps it's time to . . . face it. It was there – looking out to sea – that I told Andrew Bellamy I was pregnant, and when I refused to agree to an abortion he pushed me into the sea.' She ignored Jannie's gasp and kept going. 'You and I both know that's not such an awful thing to do, but he didn't know that and when I didn't appear – because I was swimming into the cave – he thought he had killed me and he ran away. I miscarried in the cave, then when the tide went back out I came home. No one was here at the time – that was why I brought him to St Ives.'

She stopped speaking and looked at Jannie's face, then said quickly, 'Now you understand why Zannah tried to kill him as she did – by pushing him over the edge of a ravine and into the river below.'

Still Jannie was turned to stone.

Gussie said, as if answering a question, 'Yes, then she saved him. She saved him because she saw what a poor creature he really was. Just as I had done when I saw him again that morning in Nice. He wasn't worth another thought. I mean that, darling. He simply did not matter any more.'

Jannie swallowed visibly, then opened her arms wide. Gussie suddenly began to weep. She dropped to her knees and put her head in her baby sister's lap and cried freely. Jannie said nothing.

The tears did not last; Gussie sat back on her heels and tried a watery smile.

'It really does not matter any more, darling. It bonded Zannah and me in a strange way. It was just . . . the baby.' She shrugged. 'I won't have children now, of course, and I would have rather enjoyed being a mother. Kate taught me so much . . . it's rather a waste.'

Jannie's face worked uncontrollably and Gussie said warningly, 'Don't you dare cry over me, January Briscoe!'

Jannie said, 'I'm not. I promise.' She swallowed. 'Have you told Ned?'

Gussie shook her head violently. 'He must never know, darling. Think about it. It would completely spoil our threesome. His anger – his disgust – would be . . . terrible.'

'Of course it wouldn't.'

'Jannie! Listen to me! You have to promise me you will never breathe a word of this to Ned! Do you understand?'

Jannie's silence was mutinous for just a moment, then she crumpled.

'Yes. Of course I understand. He can be such a stuffed shirt at times.'

'Never mind all that. I do not want him to know.'

'I promise, Sis. I really do.'

Gussie took another of her deep breaths and stood up.

'Come on then. Let's go and collect the car and drive up to Zennor. We can have lunch there and go and see the Mermaid and walk to the headland – pick some blackberries. Yes?'

'Yes.'

Jannie called up the stairs and then followed Gus up to the Scaife studio. She felt a dragging pain in her chest. She had wanted to know Gussie's secret and now she did.

Twenty-one

August the fourteenth sounded doubtful on the long-range weather forecast.

The week before was grey and humid; the threat of thunder welcomed but never delivered. Jannie, determined to be optimistic, remarked on the profuse and brilliant patches of gorse encrusting the Island. She thought she would go into Penzance and try to find a suitably bright yellow summer dress. She became typically carried away by the idea: she would take the secateurs and cut a bouquet of gorse – wrap it in foil or something else protective – and be the first bride in the world to have a thorny bouquet. Gussie, reluctant to be any kind of wet blanket, tried to tell her that yellow wasn't really her colour but it was Ned who decided her against a trip to Penzance in search of the dress. Without any apparent irony, he said, 'Well, you want it to be different. This is just splendid. Poached egg on toast. No one can say humour is dead, Jan! Well done!'

Later that day she went across the landing to Gussie's room.

'Gus, I didn't throw away anything of Aunt Ro's clothes – you know, the ones Rory brought round that day. Look, this is her wedding dress, isn't it? It's so sixties! Like a long satin vest – totally plain. And gloves to go with it, and this little cap. If I wear it d'you think she might come? Shall I ring her?'

Gussie said, 'You can try. I rather think the resurrection of her dress will make the occasion more unacceptable than before!' She held the dress up and looked at it. 'Try it on, Jannie. If it fits it will look stunning.'

Jannie wriggled her way into the slippery tube and smoothed the satin over her hips. 'What do you think?'

Gus nodded. 'It's a perfect fit and it looks special. Different. There's a sort of fishtail at the back. If only you had long hair you'd become the Mermaid of Zennor!'

'Oh my God, that's just right. Meant. Intended. You know what I mean.' Jannie twisted around, trying to see the fish-tail. 'Let's get the boys up here and see what they think.'

'They've gone round to the studio. In any case, Robert mustn't see you if there's a chance this is to be your wedding dress!'

'Oh, damn! That's so silly. Rather like saying that Aunt Ro's marriage went wrong because she wore this dress!' She looked at herself in Gussie's long mirror. 'I am definitely wearing it. It's great.' She fitted on the pearl-encrusted cap. 'What are they doing at the studio again? They're always disappearing round there. I wanted them to get to know each other, but this is a bit much.'

Gussie grinned. 'I think they're actually doing some en-gineering on Robert's electronic hand. He's had enough of Ned's methodology, perhaps. It will do Ned good to help with practical stuff.'

Jannie pulled a face, then turned and looked at her sister.

'Darling, are you going to be all right after the wedding? We don't have to go away – it's not as if it's an actual *honey*moon

– just meeting Robert's mother at the airport and spending a couple of days in Bristol getting to know her, and taking Aunt Ro out for a meal. Well, you know all that. It's not important stuff.'

'It's very important stuff, Jannie, and you know it. It's bringing the family together, making sure no one feels left out.' She adjusted the cap slightly and passed Jannie one of the gloves. 'And of course I'll be all right. I'll miss you, of course. You wouldn't want it any other way, would you?'

'No. I suppose not.' Jannie wrestled with the left glove. 'What about Ned?'

'What about Ned? We've always got on well – long before you were born, I would remind you.'

Jannie stretched the left glove and shook it hard. Talcum powder flew everywhere. They both coughed and Jannie said hoarsely, 'You know what I mean. You should tell him, Gus. It's coming between you. He thinks you're growing away from him because of Nine Eleven.'

Gussie said in a low voice, 'You promised, Jannie.'

'I know, I know, I know. And of course I'll never tell him. But it's there. You don't even realize it. You should have told Mum. And Ned should take over from Mum.'

'Ned is the very last person . . . the very *last* person . . .' She coughed to a stop and they both took big clear breaths. Gussie's face settled. 'Anyway, I don't actually see much of him. Really. He's busy upstairs and phoning this Sven chap. It's so right for him, Jannie. He's coming into his own.' Gussie took over the glove and began to ease a thumb into position. She went on in the same reasonable tone. 'These are real kid, I hope you know. Before we all realized what we were doing when we wore the skins of animals.'

'Are you trying to put me off? These are antiques. I'm

going to donate the whole outfit to the museum after the wedding!'

Gussie worked in two fingers and sat back, grinning. 'You thought of that just in time to quieten your conscience, didn't you?'

'Yes, but it's a good idea, isn't it? There are plenty of people in St Ives who remember that wedding – and all the fuss in the years afterwards. They'll enjoy seeing the dress again.'

'True. Very true. But you must ask Rosemary's permission first.'

'I will. She knows I've got the dress and stuff. In fact, she actually suggested I should try it on.'

'She will absolutely love the idea of you wearing it next week. But whether she will be so thrilled about exhibiting it – I'm not so sure about that. It will remind people of her marriage to the local pirate chief.'

'Mmm . . . yes. All right. I'll save that bit until Robert and I take her out for a meal. Now can you peel me out of the gloves? We must give ourselves plenty of time to get ready next week, Gus. Dress and cap – fine. Gloves, time-consuming.'

'Yes. All right.' Gussie stood and began to pull gently at each finger. 'Plenty of talc – that's the secret.' Her eyes met Jannie's as she spoke that word. Secret. She suddenly enfolded her baby sister to her. 'Dear, dear Jannie. You are so beautiful and so like your mother. Kind. So many ripples and waves on the top – deep and calm underneath – like the sea. Don't you realize that telling you about that awful time has put it into its place? The past. Done and dusted, Jan. Honestly.'

Jannie buried her face into the long neck and concentrated on not crying. But before she let Gussie release her she whispered, 'Ned should know, Gus. Ned should know.'

Gussie rolled the gloves carefully in their tissue. She smiled. 'So that he can go and avenge his big sister – finish Andrew Bellamy for good and all?'

Jannie shrugged. 'You say you're all right. And I'm certainly not concerned with Andrew bloody Bellamy. But Ned, Ned himself, needs to know.'

Gussie's smile disappeared. She unzipped the sheath of a dress and let it drop to the floor. 'No, he does not,' she said quietly.

They hung up the dress behind Gussie's door. Jannie knew the conversation had most definitely ended.

That night she clung to Robert harder than ever.

He whispered directly into her ear. 'I've never seen you cry like this, Jan. What's happened? Have you changed your mind? I don't care if we live in sin for the rest of our lives, if that's what you want!'

'I cry all the time. I'm known for being a whingeing idiot. And if you try to get out of marrying me I'll sue you.'

'Then that's all right. But you don't actually cry all the time, you know. You hardly ever cry. And your tears are very wet indeed.' He used a corner of the bed sheet and dried her face. 'Going to tell me?'

She pillowed her cheek against his shoulder. She almost told him. Then she said, 'Nothing to tell. Except that it's not going to happen – Ned and Gussie. It's Gussie's fault, really. She looks at Ned and sees her young brother. And he must see himself that way, too, because otherwise he'd burst through all the reserves and – and – pure silliness – and just grab her and – and – fall in love!'

'Just like that?'

'Exactly like that. All this living together and taking

care of each other . . . He offered to cut her split ends the other day, for the wedding. And when she said no he was aggrieved; said he always had done and what was different now! He knows what is different now. And she must know subconsciously otherwise she would have let him get on with it!'

'Split ends?'

'Hair. Pay attention, Hanniford! She can't just let the plait grow and grow. The ends of the hair split and have to be cut off and it's not as easy as it sounds, and Ned started doing it when he was thirteen. Oh God!' She rolled her face over and wept again, and Robert kissed her pale hair and was grateful that it was short.

The weather improved and they spent a day in the sand dunes at Porthkidney. For the first time since they had left Hartley, Robert took two sticks and with some difficulty stumbled slowly over the soft sand to where Ned had opened a special folding chair, higher than most. With exaggerated aplomb Robert hooked the sticks over the back of the chair, held the arms and lowered himself into the seat. They all cheered and more tears gathered in Jannie's eyes.

'I've been practising in the studio,' he said. 'Ned found the sticks and I told him about the therapy I do at Hartley, and he said, go on then and I did!'

Ned said disgustedly, 'You even sound like Jannie these days!'

Everyone laughed again.

Later, they swam into the surf and rode the waves back, then there was lunch and a sleep. When they woke the tide was too close for comfort so they decamped and drove over the moors, looking at the ancient stone maidens, the quoits, the burial chambers. They continued down to Zennor and Robert used his sticks again to climb the steps and look at the wooden mermaid carved in a pew end.

'Can't imagine what anyone saw in her,' was his comment.

But when they parked on the homeward stretch and looked across the patchwork of fields dotted with unidentified stones, he was more interested. He fished his binoculars from the map pocket. 'I see what you mean about the glory gates.' He fiddled with the adjustor. 'There's a sheepway across these fields and the stones follow its line . . . four of them . . .' He panned his binoculars across the enormous scape of sea and land. 'Now . . . if there were two pillars, one each side of the track, wide enough for a wheelchair . . . you're sure they had a special place – a special kissing gate?'

'We're not sure of anything. It's one of the bees your future wife gets into her bonnet.'

'It's not a scientific investigation, Ned!' Gus protested.

And Jannie said, 'They always made a fuss about kissing gates – wouldn't go through them without obeying the rules—'

Gussie interrupted again. 'More than that too, Jannie. There was always plenty of kissing with those two. This was something else . . . something they saw – a view – a view that was special to them.'

Ned said reluctantly, 'Yes, they were always framing views, weren't they? Dad did it so that he could really inspect everything.'

Jannie said, 'And Mum said it was like making pieces of jigsaw and putting them together. Oh my God.'

'What?'

She looked round at all of them. 'Supposing, just supposing that the gates of glory – the ones Father Martin and Mr

Selway were talking about – supposing they *are* the – the – completed jigsaw.'

Robert grinned, all ready to laugh with the others, then let his grin die on his face. Nobody spoke.

Gussie said at last, 'Was that why they jumped like they did – as if they were jumping into the sea?'

Ned said, 'It's rubbish, of course, but that last bit makes sense. And it was quite a private thing. Dad didn't want to be seen getting into the water. Mum had to shove him off the chair usually. But we know they jumped off Clodgy at high tide. Often.'

Jannie wanted to tell them all that she knew and where to look for that precious viewpoint, that special glory gate. She held her breath.

Gussie said quietly, 'That is how it was. I know it.' She looked at Jannie and smiled. 'Breathe, darling. You've been right all along. We might never find it but we know it's there. Somewhere.'

Jannie let her breath go and still said nothing.

Ned looked at Robert. 'Sorry, old man. All that wet fern and all those flies – all for nothing.'

Robert said, 'Surely that's what the process of elimination is all about?' He grinned. 'Your words, Ned!' He swept the skyline with his binoculars again. 'The words "view" and "point" rule out the idea of stone gateposts. The sort of gate we are looking for might be a small hole in a stone.'

Jannie found her voice. 'A quoit. Like Lanyon Quoit. They could still kiss through it. That's important.'

'Why?' Robert lowered the binoculars for a second. 'Does it give us another clue?'

Jannie shook her head. 'Tell you later. But it *might* give us another clue. If Dad was in his chair – and he usually was on these sort of jaunts – then it won't be buried in stones or grass and nettles. There would be room for them to be one on each side of the stone and still lean forward to kiss through it.'

He reached for her hand. 'When we get back we'll find it. We need to find it.'

'Yes. I know.'

Gussie cleared her throat. 'Ned, I think it's time to get home, don't you?'

She expected him to crack a joke or just grin at her. He did neither; just got back into the car and clicked on his belt. She felt suddenly cut off from him. It was a sensation that was becoming familiar.

The weather forecasts had been much too cautious. At seven o'clock in the morning, the fourteenth sported a mother-of-pearl sky, a lazy sea gradually retreating from the moored boats in the harbour and a kind of promise in the crisp air. Jannie, creeping past the stair chair, thought of a word. Steadfast. And then another. Exciting. She must remember them for Cathy, who had, at the very least, two years to wait for Derek. She was glad she had not met Robert when they were sixteen; as it was, there was an urgency about their courtship. Urgency. That was another word; she would not pass that on to Cathy. Perhaps it was a word that had a personal application only because of what had happened to Kate and Mark.

She went into the big basement kitchen and plugged in the kettle, and then unplugged it and took it to the sink and filled it from the tap and plugged it in again. 'Typical, Jannie,' she murmured aloud. 'You're making a cup of tea for your soon-to-be husband and you almost boiled a dry kettle. Well done.' She smiled slightly as she felt her heartbeat slow down. She remembered her mother finding her crying among her favourite shell collection spilled over the floor and saying calmly, 'Just tell yourself what you've done and what you have to do to put it right. You dropped the shells, now you pick them up.' She had crouched by the small girl. 'I don't know where you get this heavy drama stuff from, but you might as well make use of it. Right now you are an expert shell collector. Probably you would pick up each shell separately and examine it – tell your invisible audience what it looks like and where it came from. Nothing to cry about.' And Jannie had looked up, face streaked with tears, and said, 'I'm looking at them and seeing a lot of empty houses, Mummy.' And Kate had stared for a moment then laughed and gathered her up and hugged her and said, 'Jannie Briscoe, I love you!'

Jannie ignored her tears and made the tea, fetched mugs and milk and poured it carefully, then made for the stairs again. At hall level she suddenly paused, then put the mugs next to the phone, picked up the receiver and by squeezing her eyes tightly she saw Sheila Smith's number in her head, dialled it and waited.

She counted twelve rings before Sheila picked up at her end and said nervously, 'Hello, who is it, please?'

Jannie said, 'Oh my God. Sheila, I had forgotten it was so early. I'm so sorry. But I had to tell you that I am getting married and this is my wedding day and I – I suppose I hoped it would make it a bit special for you too if you knew about it.'

She waited and could hear Sheila telling May that it wasn't an emergency, it was good news. Then she spoke into the receiver.

'It is Jannie, isn't it? I'm not having one of my dreams? It is? And you are getting married? Today? This morning? Oh, how wonderful! The weather is perfect and you are getting married! Oh, Jannie, I am so pleased . . . yes, May, we are so pleased. Both of us. Is it in church? Is he nice? What are you wearing? Oh, Jannie, I can't say it but you know what I am thinking.'

'They're going to be there – both of them – Mum and Dad.' She answered their questions, then said she had better go and, still murmuring goodbyes, she put down the phone.

Robert was sitting up in bed expectantly.

'I knew you'd gone to make tea. You've been ages. You'll probably get better at it as the years roll by.'

'This is a one-off!' she warned him, then told him about the phone call. She put the mugs on to the tables either side of the bed and clambered in beside him, still talking until he stopped her with a kiss.

'You're nervous! Bridal nerves! For goodness' sake, the whole idea has been to make it stress-free. Look at me – cool as a cucumber.' He raised his cup, then brought it slowly to his mouth and sipped, and immediately his face changed. 'It's cold! You must have been ages on the phone!'

She wasn't even contrite. She was intent on telling him that she wasn't in the least bit nervous, but so very conscious of all those people still grieving and lonely, and wishing that they could be happy and relaxed and stress-free for just one day. He stopped her eventually by removing both mugs of tea and holding her tightly to him. And it was then she knew what she could do; not much but it was all she was allowed.

She put a hand up to Robert's face and pressed her mouth close to his ear.

'Gussie and I – we saw it from the bus stop. At Easter. I

should have known then that there was something special about that view because Gus clammed up like a – a . . .'

Robert murmured, 'Clam?' and she nodded.

'Just like a clam.'

Robert waited, then said, 'So . . . ?'

'So all Ned has to do is follow the footpath from the bus stop and keep an eye out for . . . something.'

There was another pause. Robert said, 'That's it?'

'No. Not really. But perhaps – just perhaps – if Gussie realizes that that drop – that jump – is the one Mum and Dad took . . . it might help.' She leaned back and looked at Robert. 'It's all I can do,' she finished pitifully.

'Darling, this – this – jumping business. It matters to all of you, I can sort of understand. When we get back from seeing Mum and Jonathan, and your aunt, and Geoff and Elizabeth . . . do you want us to do it?'

She was startled. 'I hadn't thought . . . it's quite a jump, though it looks worse than it really is. I don't know.'

He grinned at her. 'Hey, I'm one step ahead for once! Shall we make it our post-wedding project?'

'You – you think it's wise?'

It was his turn to be startled. 'Who are you exactly? I went to bed with Jannie Briscoe. I never heard her say the word "wise" so you can't be her.'

She pounced on him. The discussion was fragmented after that.

Ned and Robert took their suits into Bessie's and used Old Beck's front parlour to change. Bessie, resplendent in a navy-blue dress bought from Truro, and sporting an unlikely sailor collar, had been ready for two hours and was impatient to 'get going'.

'At this rate, Thaddeus Stevens will have opened up and done the necessary and be thinking we ain't a-coming,' she complained, retreating down the stairs to her kitchen.

'You haven't told anyone, have you, Bessie?' Robert asked, following her closely.

'Course I 'aven't! I want to be the only one there, don't I?'

She slammed the door with unnecessary force and Robert looked apprehensive again. 'Jannie says everyone will be at work. But your parents were well known, Ned. Surely every-one will want to know about their daughter getting married.'

Ned made a face. 'Bessie's got a guilty conscience. She wants to get into church long before Jannie comes out of the house. But this whole privacy thing is ridiculous – one of Jannie's dramas. The banns were published the minute you arrived here, so what's the big secret?'

'Jannie says nobody goes to church because they're all chapel.' It sounded lame. He looked at Ned and grinned. 'Is it a big con? Not for my sake, surely?'

Ned shrugged. 'Who knows? Come on. Let's get ready. We've got our own surprise to spring. Are you up for it, Robert m'lad?'

Robert hesitated for a moment then nodded once.

They had arranged between them that Ned would be Robert's best man, and Gussie would give away her sister. Jannie had wanted her to wear the very short spotted summer dress from Aunt Rosemary's pile, but when they decided on their roles, Gussie chose a pale green linen suit, and just the night before Ned had made a buttonhole from some gorse blossoms. The girls helped each other to dress, Jannie pale and suddenly intense, easing on the gloves with great care.

'I should have ordered a taxi, Gus. I'm going to feel a

stupid show-off walking up to the Island like this. What on earth would we have done if it had been raining?'

'Ordered a taxi, of course. I can do that – d'you want me to do that?'

'No.' She made a wry face as she pushed the glove over her fingers. 'I'm a stupid show-off, Gus.'

'No. You wanted a private wedding because of what has happened to us, darling. And you have ensured that, because the chapel on the hill holds twelve people at the most. But you're happy to walk through the town in your wedding dress – to share the public bits of the wedding. There will be people waiting to see you – you know that, don't you?'

'I suppose so. Perhaps I'm ashamed at being happy so soon after last September . . . I don't understand myself.'

Gussie took the other glove and rolled back the cuff.

'Don't even think of being ashamed, darling. There might be only the four of us in the church, but we have the whole town outside.' She wriggled successfully and Jannie flexed her fingers. Gussie said, 'Did you know Thomas Martin is an expert photographer?'

'Thomas who? Is that Father Martin? Since when have you been on first-name terms?'

'Since he asked whether you would mind him taking some photographs. And then displaying them in church.' Gussie was suddenly grinning from ear to ear. 'I took it upon myself to agree, of course. I have to have something to show Zannah. She'll be so frustrated at missing such an occasion!'

Jannie grabbed a pillow from the bed and aimed it at Gussie's head and then stopped. She said, 'Poor Zannah. She and Daddy must have painted the town slightly pink at one time.'

'Yes. I think so. But . . . she wanted to keep going at that pace and Daddy didn't – couldn't. And I wasn't up to it either.' She sighed, looked into the mirror and added, 'She loved him. She still loves him.'

'I thought . . . got the impression . . . that Rory and she might – well – be having a bit of a fling.'

Gussie laughed and replaced the pillow back on the bed.

She said, 'I'd be surprised if they weren't. That would make no difference to Zannah. She is amoral.' She leaned over the bed and pecked her sister affectionately. 'Come on. Let's get going. We mustn't keep Robert waiting.'

They walked along the wharf, already cluttered with deck chairs, skirted the head of Smeaton's Pier and down the steps at Bamaluz. One or two people began to follow them, and by the time they had walked the half-hoop of Porthgwidden beach they had a small following. The hump of the Island, crowned with the tiny church, seemed to be a natural stopping place, and the crowd waited at the base, settling themselves on the seats along the pathway or on the flat-topped rocks among the ferns. Gulls rode the thermals, circling above; where there were people there was food. This time they were wrong.

Halfway up the last steep incline, Jannie stopped and took some deep breaths. 'It's harder in a long skirt,' she panted. 'No wonder it was only the men who used to come up here on a Sunday!' She kept her eyes front. 'Many people behind us, Gussie?'

'Quite a few. Nothing to do with Bessie. Just visitors who enjoy weddings.'

'I should have opened it up – like we did for Old Beck's funeral. A big picnic for whoever was passing.'

'I think you've done the right thing. We can't shrug off last year as if it never happened.'

'I do regret not telling Robert's mother about it. I must explain.'

'She will understand. She sounds so completely understanding. And when she sees how much Robert is improving, she will love you whatever you do or say!'

'Do you really think he's improving?'

'Yes. I do.' Gussie started to laugh. She stopped again and looked up. Jannie, hanging on to her arm, perforce did the same. Above them in the doorway of the church, Ned appeared, looked down and waved. Then he stood aside and a man joined him. Tall and straight. He looked down too. Then he lifted both arms in a gesture of both triumph and surrender. The people below cheered.

Jannie said, 'Oh my God. It's Robert.' An enormous sob caught in her throat and was somehow subdued. She tried to run and almost fell over.

Gussie said, 'Steady, the Buffs!' just as her father had so often said before her. Jannie steadied herself, then lifted both arms to the densely blue sky; the ribbons from her bouquet fluttered slightly in a breath of wind from the south-west and became pennants. The past and the present were here; the future stood in the doorway of St Nicholas's Chapel. They walked slowly towards it.

Thaddeus Stevens had a new dog who was not yet trained in church procedure. Thaddeus had brought a small boy with him, who walked Ethel around the church on a lead and could be seen passing the open door at intervals throughout the service. Father Martin, who so rarely smiled, only just managed to suppress a broad grin every time the dog went by. Bessie obviously disapproved of dogs attending weddings, even at a distance, but Thaddeus had been a good friend of Old Beck's so she too managed a smile in between sightings.

The service was strictly conventional, the hymns too. As their voices floated thinly down the hill, unaccompanied yet confident, the congregation, which by now had overflowed into the car park, identified 'Love Divine, all loves excelling', and joined in strongly.

Afterwards the seven of them stayed inside the tiny space with its narrow windows looking across the Atlantic towards America. It was obvious the walk back down to where a mini-bus waited to take them to Zennor was going to turn into a procession, and there were some things to be said. Robert propped his back against the massive bench-like table that was the altar and shook Father Martin's hand repeatedly while Jannie hugged him unrestrainedly. He understood that both of them, their voices inextricably linked, were thanking him.

Thaddeus called in the small boy and the dog. ''E got to get used to it. Might as well start training 'im now. Come on then, Ethel, lie down, there's a good dog.'

'Why Ethel?' Ned asked.

''E were called Ethelred on account of 'im never knowing when or where to cock 'is leg. Ethelred the Unready, see. We've sorted that out and 'e do use the garden just like my ole boy used to. Now we got to sort out the church.'

Ned and Gussie exchanged glances. Gussie realized that they had not done so since Ned returned from America. She felt light with happiness. Ned cleared his throat. 'You must have a special way of training dogs.'

Thaddeus looked surprised. 'I just speaks to 'em. You got to keep going. Over and over again. But they usually gets it. Eventually.' He rolled the last word around his mouth, looking at Ethel, who was cocking his leg just inside the door. Bessie made a fuss of flattening her sailor collar.

'Never did like dogs,' she said as Thaddeus took the lead from the boy and led the dog on to the grass. 'We always 'ad cats in my day. St Ives was full of cats. Before the cars came and mowed 'em down.'

Gussie hugged her. 'Dear Bessie, you have such a turn of phrase. Did you enjoy our mini-wedding?'

'I did. I did. I just wish Old Beck'd come for me now. Right now. Sweep me away, like.' She looked at them looking at each other and sighed. ''Tis 'ard to think of now, but 'e were that romantic when 'e were young. Used to pick me up as if I were a feather and swing me around . . . 'E didn't 'ave many words, see. So it 'ad to be action!'

Ned said, 'Action. Well, they say it speaks louder than words, don't they?' He did not take his eyes off Gussie.

Jannie launched herself at him. 'Darling Ned! Robert has been telling me about the physio stuff in the studio – you are a lovely brother – thank you.' She turned him towards the altar. 'Robert's got this thing about carrying me over the threshold and that will have to be the mini-bus. Yes? So if I settle myself on to his lap, like so . . .' She matched action to word and Robert gathered her to him. She beamed up at everyone. 'Could two of you make sure that we get down the hill without falling by the wayside?'

Ned nodded. 'We've worked it out. Gussie and me at the helm. Father Martin in front of us. Bessie and Thaddeus bringing up the rear. Will that do?'

'You planned it – of course you did. How marvellous!'

Father Martin snuffed out the candles. 'Shall we go? Mr Stevens, you will lock the door.'

'I will indeed, Reverend.'

The small boy now had the camera. He darted around the rocks snapping as if he had done it all his life. Thaddeus gave Ethel's lead to Bessie, whose expression turned from soulful to disgusted as she waited for the very modern padlock to be fastened. And then, slowly, they took each step and walked down to the car park.

People clapped, others cheered, some threw rice. 'I suppose the gulls will clear it up,' Father Martin remarked, only too aware of local criticism.

'Swell in their stomachs and likely explode them!' Bessie said with sudden enjoyment.

So it was that their dignity left them and they eventually entered the minibus laughing hysterically.

The meal was excellent; the stroll to the headland afterwards was something they had often done. Jannie insisted on the wheelchair for Robert. Gussie and Bessie picked black-berries, Thaddeus lumbered after Ethel – "E's enjoying every minute, but 'e's still very unready' – Father Martin had taken over the camera work from his senior choirboy back at the Island, and now moved about like someone half his age, walking backwards in front of them, clambering up banks, thoroughly enjoying the whole occasion.

Ned walked with Jannie and recounted past adventures along this route for Robert's benefit. 'Mind you, I doubt whether anyone has done this walk in a bridal outfit before. You'll have to watch out, old man. Now that she's tipped you off the slipway, she'll want to tip you over the edge at Bamaluz Point. That'll be the next project.'

Jannie held her breath but Gussie was ahead of them, harvesting a particularly good crop high on the bank.

Jannie looked round at Ned. He must know. It could not be a coincidence.

But Ned and Robert were laughing and Robert was capping that story with another from Jannie's now famous production of *The Tempest*. It was good to see them together. Robert needed a brother. And so did Ned.

She joined in. 'Listen, Ned, I think I know how to find the Briscoe kissing gate. I worked it out. A bus as far as Cripplesease. Stand on the milestone immediately opposite the bus stop. Look out to sea. That's the view. All you have to do is climb over that stile and follow the path until you get to the view-finder. It will be a quoit – we're pretty sure of that. And it should still be fairly clear of nettles and stuff. But it won't be immediately obvious otherwise other people would know about it. I can't help more than that, Ned. But – stop being silly, please – this is serious – when you see what is framed in the circle of stone, you will begin to understand.'

Ned intoned, 'Jannie has spoken.'

Robert twisted himself like a corkscrew to look up at his wife. 'Is this what it was all about this morning?' he asked.

'I can't remember this morning.' She forced lightness into her voice. Gussie was clambering down the bank waving a polythene bag full of blackberries. 'Too much has happened in between!'

'Poor old thing.' Couldn't Ned ever be serious? Jannie kicked sideways and found his ankle.

They gathered at the stile far above the Atlantic. Father Martin took some more formal shots. Ned flung his arms wide and quoted, '"O the opal and the sapphire of that wandering western sea" . . . how does it go, Gus? The Hardy poem. You taught it to me when I was a baby and we had to act it out with me on a rock and you galloping in the shallows.'

She smiled. 'It was you who wanted to act it out. You were eighteen – your romantic period!'

He linked his arm into the crook of her elbow, suddenly the brother she had always loved. 'Listen, Gus, Jan's just been giving me instructions about the glory gates project. Apparently we need to solve it before she and Robert return to the fold. Let's do it tomorrow. We need not even get the car out – bus to Cripplesease, stand on the milestone and follow the path down the cliff. What say you?'

Gussie glanced at Jannie, who was shading her eyes and staring out at a lone boat below them.

'Why not?' She bent down to fiddle with her shoe and rid herself of his arm. 'We'll probably feel a bit flat when they've gone.'

He looked down at her, suddenly uncertain. 'Not if you've had enough of looking.'

'Let's see how we feel.' She straightened again. 'Meanwhile, shall we have a cup of tea before going back?'

Jannie said gladly, 'I thought you'd never suggest it! Come on, Robert, back to the pub! Pronto!'

Twenty-two

It was a strange time. People called as they had called the previous autumn, but this time it was quite different. They all 'understood' why the wedding had been exclusive. One of the artists summed it up very concisely. 'If you couldn't have Mark and Kate there, you didn't want many others'. Then spoiled it completely by adding, 'But we had to turn up to throw some rice . . . see the four of you. It's great that you've got another wheelchair in the cottage, isn't it?'

Ned said heartily, 'Oh, just great!' and avoided glancing at Gussie. And Gussie, in one of her sentient moments, saw her father's face, his smile, his total acceptance of his disability and behind it all something protective. What was behind it . . . another secret? Thank God for Robert's openness. He was even now introducing Jannie to his mother and stepfather. It was sad that he was the reason for 'another wheelchair in the cottage' but it was not the end of the world.

Ned took to working all hours. Gussie spent time with Bessie and went to the beach on her own most afternoons. There was plenty of clearing up to do in the cottage and she found herself annoyed with Ned for disappearing so often. She missed his strong arm when it came to moving furniture; she missed Jannie's energy.

Later, during that post-wedding week, Ned came upon her in the parlour. She was sitting in her father's chair opposite the window that looked down on the cobbled courtyard; her elbows were on the table and her head in her hands.

The old Ned would have flipped her plait against her neck; held her close, perhaps, if it was something serious. The new Ned said brusquely, 'What on earth's the matter now?'

'Nothing. I'm tired, that's all.'

'You've been on the beach all afternoon.'

It sounded like an accusation and she snapped at him from beneath her hands, 'How do you know? You've been in the attic all day. Didn't even come downstairs for lunch!'

'Saw you go along the wharf with the beach bag.'

'If you'd looked out again an hour ago you would have seen me come back, and since then I've shoved out that bloody heavy sideboard and removed a ton of woodlice and two enormous spiders.'

'That's a lie. I would have heard you screaming.'

She heard the humour but was quite unable to respond to it.

'I learned not to scream when you were in America and Jannie was working at Hartley School!'

He squatted on his haunches so that he could look up into her face. His voice was unbearably tender. 'Dearest Gus. We have – all of us – been alone quite a lot this past year, but we always come back to base. The three of us. Same boat. Remember?' He tried a small laugh. 'Therein lies our strength.'

She looked down into the dear familiar face; she saw again the five-year-old boy. Honest, straight, wanting to be with her always. He had put her on a pedestal then and she had been on it ever since. She imagined, just for a split second, what would happen if he found out about her dead baby.

She said, 'Sorry. Obviously I am more tired than I realized. It was the thought of Christmas.' She sat up with an enormous sigh and looked at the window. 'I'll have to start on the angels soon. And somehow it just doesn't seem worth it any more.'

He hoisted himself into a chair and started to laugh. 'Gus. It's August – your birthday month, remember?'

'Yes. But in September Jannie and Robert will be gone and the nights will come early and you'll go to Sweden to see your Sven—'

'Come with me. I expect it'll be all snow and troikas.'

'That's Russia, and anyway, I don't know anything about anything.'

'As far as I'm concerned you know everything about everything.'

'Don't be silly. It's a business trip. Your business trip.'

'Like Mum and Dad going to New York together? Is that what you mean?'

She did not look at him; she felt a tear track down the side of her nose. Unexpectedly it all rose up and threatened to engulf her and she said, 'I don't think I can bear it.'

He was still, appalled by her words and the way she said them. The silence stretched. And then, like a fire alarm, the telephone rang. He leaped to his feet, stood for another moment looking at her downbent head, then turned towards the hall.

'I – I'd better see to that . . . don't go away. Please.'

She nodded. Her limbs felt weak. She should go down to the kitchen and start their evening meal. He hadn't

319

eaten since breakfast and neither had she. In an effort to be 'normal' she had bought an ice cream from the kiosk and had to throw it away because it made her feel sick. She doubted whether she could get downstairs. Or upstairs. Tears were dropping on her clasped hands. If it was Jannie on the phone she would have to go to speak to her. She squeezed her eyes as if she was wringing out a mop, cleared her face with the heels of both hands and sat up very straight. On the other side of the door, Ned was dealing with the call in his most monosyllabic way. Nevertheless, it was going on and on. It wasn't Jannie; Gussie would have recognized her high-pitched cadences. Supposing it was Aunt Rosemary . . . reporting an accident?

'Of course . . . of course.' A very long pause. 'Yes. We're fine. Go ahead.' There was another pause during which Ned walked the length of the telephone cable towards the open front door. And then there was nothing. Gussie strained her ears. The silence was suddenly overwhelmed by yells from outside as two children chased a runaway football down the court and the steps on to the wharf. When they had gone, it was still there. Heavy. Pregnant.

Then, at last, Ned's voice said sharply, 'Of course I'm here and of course I've got the message. Is that it?' Gussie breathed in and out three times. He said, 'Right. Well, thank you. I'll see to it this end and be in touch again.' His voice was coming back down the hall. She breathed normally; he wouldn't be sounding businesslike if anything had happened to Jannie or Robert. He replaced the receiver without even saying goodbye to whoever was on the other end, and came back into the parlour.

He made a face. 'You gathered it was not good news? It never is when Rory rings, is it?'

'Oh.' She puffed a sigh of sheer relief. 'He wants to come here, does he?'

'Oh, Gus . . . oh, dear Gus . . . no, it isn't that. He was ringing from France. He's been with Zannah all summer. Darling . . . there's no easy way to tell you. Zannah died just half an hour ago. I'm so sorry, Gus.'

He kneeled down by her chair and put his arms around her waist, his head into her shoulder. She held him to her with one arm and with the other hand she stroked his hair. She felt a little surprised at his grief and then realized it was for her, and she held him closer still. He responded with a grip of iron.

She said soothingly, 'It's all right, Ned. I've known – ever since I left her – that time was running out. We spoke. Often. Much to my surprise she loved having Rory there. Honestly. They were two of a kind in a way. I haven't worried about her. She told me he was a wonderful nurse.' She felt Ned's arms tighten still more and smiled wryly above his head. 'I know. The mind boggles, doesn't it?' She patted his shoulder. 'The important thing is that we had that time together. Just the two of us. She still loved Dad. In her strange way. Perhaps she left us because she knew she was no good for us . . . perhaps not. She will always be an enigma. But she was my mother and I am glad that finally I could be proud of her . . . We danced, you know. It turned me right off at the time because I knew she was pretending I was Dad. But now . . . I think it's one of the treasures that brings comfort.'

He sobbed then, a single body-racking sob. She tried to look into his face but his forehead was butted into her waist. She made more soothing sounds. Gradually he relaxed and she sensed him controlling his breathing.

She ruffled his hair. 'Let's go down and have an early

supper. We're both in need of sustenance, and there's mackerel in vinegar and a bag full of baby tomatoes and a new loaf. How does that sound?'

He got up with difficulty, his voice was strangulated. 'This is crazy. I was standing out there listening to that old reprobate going on and on, and wondering how I was going to comfort you, and here you are – comforting me!'

She stood up and led the way downstairs to the wonderful familiarity of the kitchen; her limbs were no longer weak. She thought of Zannah and smiled.

'She was wild and wonderful,' she said.

'Sounds like a good epitaph.' Ned went to the fridge and took out a bowl of tomatoes. 'Rory wants me to organize the funeral. I'll go and see Salem and Sons tomorrow. She wants to be buried above the beach and her stone is to include the names of Mark and Kate.' He fetched butter and bread, and began to hack slices indiscriminately. 'We hadn't thought of a memorial stone for them, had we? How do you feel about including them on Zannah's stone?'

Gussie placed plates and cutlery, and put the pickled mackerel in the middle of the table. She stared down at it, thinking.

'It's lovely,' she said. 'We'll work something out. We'll have to mention the – the – circumstances.'

'Yes. Dates and names. But for the epitaph we can't do better than our two reverend gentlemen. How about, "Let the gates of glory open wide"?'

'Oh, Ned. Oh, that's marvellous. Jannie will love that.' She smiled at him; her old loving smile that held nothing back.

They ate slowly, appreciatively. She said, 'Would you like banana and ice cream for pudding, like I used to do for you years ago?'

'I'd like it more than anything in the world.' He looked at her and she saw the tears in his eyes.

'Ned, this sounds incredibly sentimental,' she said, 'but Zannah has left me something very special. I am at peace. I know I have been difficult since you came back from America. I'm sorry. But now, I am totally at peace.'

He nodded. She thought he was reassured. He said, 'I'll get the ice cream.'

'Right, we'll probably have to chisel it out. I turned the freezer right up when this hot spell got under way.' She reached for the fruit bowl and picked out two bananas. He watched her. Her plait lay over her shoulder. She raised her brows at him. She was beautiful.

He said hoarsely, 'Gussie. Just now, before that phone call, you said you couldn't go on—'

'That was why I told you about Zannah's legacy to me – this peace.'

'Not total peace – not yet. Is it? Is it, Gussie?'

She was suddenly wide-eyed, staring at him across the table.

He said, 'There is this thing between us, Gussie. And I am like you. I cannot go on. I cannot go on like this.' He watched all that carefully nurtured 'normality' drain from her. He hated what he was doing. He said, 'I know. I *know*. Rory told me on the phone. In detail. Explicitly. Zannah told him just before she died.'

She dropped the bananas and put her hands to her throat.

'Zannah. Oh my God, she promised – she promised me.'

'If I'd known – if you'd told me . . . I had him, there in the Scaife studio – he was after all the art work he could get on the cheap. He'd already arranged with Rory to auction Trewyn House – I could have killed him then and there.'

'That's one of the reasons I couldn't tell you.'

'I thought you trusted me in the same way I trusted you.'

'That's why I didn't tell you.' Her voice went up the scale, her hands went from her throat to cover her face. 'I was so ashamed. It was so awful. And I brought it on myself.' She lowered her head to her knees and her voice went with it. 'Nothing will be the same now. You will never trust me again!'

Somehow he was on his knees in front of her, trying to lift her head to his shoulder. She pulled away frantically, twisting herself in the chair, arms now on the table. 'I can't look at you, Ned! I can't! I wanted to feel easy with him, like I did with you, so I made him cut my hair . . . he said I was a tease and that I had seduced him. I thought the baby would make it all right – I thought he'd be pleased – that's something I didn't tell Zannah.'

She started to wail through her fingers and he gathered her up somehow and rocked her. 'Don't say any more. You are not a tease, not in the sense he meant. He had you under his control, didn't he – the typical bully – you should have told Kate. You should have reported him to the police. Why didn't you report him? For God's sake, he had tried to murder you.'

'Because you would have known about it. I didn't want you to know. I didn't want you to be ashamed of me too.'

'Gussie. I couldn't be ashamed of you, my dearest love. You are my mainstay. My reason for being on this earth. This – this swine – Bellamy or whatever his name is – don't you see, he was deliberately taking away your confidence? Even then he must have been after some of Gerald Scaife's work, and in the end you might have given him something . . . free, gratis and for nothing! My God, what a slime-ball!'

Gussie became very still. She seemed to be holding her

breath. Then she whispered, 'I think I knew this when, in the jewellery boutique in Nice, I saw him hugging Zannah. I stopped being frightened of him then. Because when he realized that it was me standing there, *he* was so frightened – really frightened. He thought I might tell someone. If he'd known I'd already told Zannah and she was – well – Zannah, he might have guessed that the damage was already done.' She shifted slightly on his shoulder. 'I thought it was over then. But . . . it wasn't. The shame was still there. The horror was still there.'

'If only she'd left him in that bloody ravine!'

Gussie puffed a sound into his T-shirt. 'Ah, Ned. Had you known her . . . She never could have done that. Everything is a game with her. And, underneath it all, she is kind.' She gave a dry sob and lifted her head. '*Was*. She was kind.'

'He's not fit to live!'

'Ned. Don't. This is another reason for not telling you. Hatred is not a good emotion.'

'Yes it is. It's better than being so bloody unhappy all the time because I'm your brother and you're my sister and you'll never see it any other way. Maybe if it hadn't been for Bellamy you would eventually have seen me in a different way. You could have understood that it is possible for us to fall in love and marry and have a family and live here, in this cottage, just as Mark and Kate did. But he came along and took you over – took you away—'

He stopped speaking because she straightened enough to put her hand, very gently, over his mouth. She said quietly, 'I never stopped loving you, Ned. Not for a moment. But you were out of bounds, and I had to get on with it.' Her hand slid to his ear; she tugged it with a kind of heartbreaking familiarity.

She said, 'Nothing has changed, my darling. Has it?'

He looked at her, letting her fill his head. 'So much has changed, Gussie,' he said. 'So much. Mum and Dad have gone. Jannie is married. And you – you are free. I am free. We are not related except by our love for each other.'

He stood up creakingly, pulled her up too. The evening sun, setting into the sea at Porthmeor, found a crack in the huddle of cottages and beamed into the old fish cellar. Ned's hair was an orange aureole around his head and to her he looked like the little boy she had met on the beach over twenty years before.

She said nothing, looking at him as he was looking at her, with total absorption. The sun shifted and highlighted the crock of mackerel and the bread, rough-cut by Ned half an hour before. It shone on the two discarded bananas and then the fruit bowl with its pale grapes from the vineyard started by Gussie, its bright red apples from an orchard near King Harry Ferry. It shone on the nets still drying as they had dried in the time of Philip Nolla.

They kissed. Slowly and tentatively they kissed as if tasting wine.

His hands moved from her shoulders and cupped her face. He whispered, 'My darling girl, I love you so much.'

'I love you too.'

'Is it going to be all right?'

'How can we know that?'

He smiled and his colourless eyes glinted in the last of the sun. 'Shall we risk it?'

Through her exhaustion she felt a strange sensation and recognized it as excitement. She said, 'Like the time we sat on the sea bed and let that enormous wave go over our heads?'

'We could have drowned.'

'We would have been together.'

Her words dropped into the room one by one, assuming huge significance.

She reached up past his hands and drew his head to hers. She said, 'Yes. Let's risk it, Ned.' And she kissed him without shame.

Much later she made tea and they drank it, and looked at the bananas and laughed together. They were both filled with wonder and could not stop touching each other as they moved around the kitchen clearing up for the night. Every small action was new and special. Gussie felt physically light.

She said, 'I won't bother with the angels just yet.'

And he said, 'OK. I agree to that. We need to get used to this before Jannie and Robert come home. Then perhaps the angels . . .'

'All right.' It was as if they had solved an enormous problem. They kissed and she outlined his face with her new feather fingers. Then, with great care, he undid her plait and spread her hair over his hands again and again.

Before they slept he murmured, 'Tomorrow we have to do something special, something really important.'

She smiled, eyes closed. 'Of course.'

He said, 'Yes, but what I meant was . . .' he kissed her ear, nose and then mouth, drew a breath and said, '. . . we have to find those glory gates.'

'Thank goodness. I thought you were going to say something else.'

'That too.'

She opened her eyes. 'You don't like heights,' she reminded him.

'Neither do you now.'

'No.'

She felt a familiar tremor of fear. 'Is this part of the risk we are taking?'

'Probably.'

'We'll talk about it in the morning.'

'OK.'

She kissed him and thought he was asleep. Then discovered he was not.

Twenty-three

Ned woke at two o'clock. For a split second he was shocked by Gussie's presence and then, with a rush, he remembered everything. He lay on his side, head resting on elbow, gazing at her face with sheer wonder. For so long they had been 'out of bounds' for each other, as Gussie had so succinctly put it. And now, they were not. It was so simple yet so complicated and amazing. If that word – amazing – meant going through a maze then it was the only word for them.

He looked at her dark lashes, crescents above her cheekbones. A long strand of dark hair lay across her mouth and as she exhaled it moved and she twitched. Tenderly he moved the strand and could not resist kissing her lightly. She seemed to smile. And as he looked, he was filled with a terrible grief. During that wonderful evening, they had barely mentioned what she called 'the incident' at Bamaluz Point. The realization of what they had now had pushed everything else away.

Now, as she lay there next to him, his love for her seemed to intensify the horror of what had happened. He stared down at her. She was unique, wonderful, he should have protected her and he hadn't. This was what he couldn't bear. That she had been abused and he had done nothing. He had to do something. He could not just lie here and do nothing. He had to get up and do something.

Downstairs it was as if all colour had been leached out of the kitchen; the moon was doing its best but it was grey rather than silver. He opened the top half of the door and leaned out, sniffing the air. Same door, same air, but completely different. He thought of Gussie asleep upstairs. Unbidden came thoughts of Bellamy . . . Before he pushed her off the cliff had they slept in Gussie's bed . . . or, worse still, in his parents' room? The hatred and the guilt grew, side by side. He tried to shut out images of the man. Pushing the woman. There was an overhang of rock on the edge of Bamaluz Point. She must have been standing there; if she had been anywhere else her fall would have taken her into the cliff itself; she would have been killed. He dropped his head on to his arms and squeezed his eyes shut, trying to eliminate the picture of Gussie crashing from rock to rock. The image refused to go.

He shoved open the bottom half of the door and took the steps to the wharf in one leap. He jumped down on to the harbour beach and went into the water, wading out to where the first of the boats bobbed gently. He held the mooring rope to steady himself; the water was up to his waist and, in spite of the spell of hot weather, was bitterly cold. He stood there, gasping, Bellamy forgotten.

And, suddenly and unexpectedly, Zannah came into his head. Zannah Scaife, Gussie's mother, who had left home when Gussie was eight years old, yet left no hatred behind her . . . Why was that? Until a very few months ago, Ned had hated Victor for leaving his wife and son. Victor had wanted – had chosen – to become an outcast. And in a strange way so had Zannah. And now, Zannah was dead.

The sea rose up his chest and lapped into his mouth and he shook his head impatiently.

Rory had been distraught when he phoned. Of course he had: Zannah had died just half an hour before he made the call. He said that her death had released him from his promise. And then, because Ned had been unable to speak, he had hammered the stark words yet again down the phone. 'Don't you get it, boy? Gus was pregnant and she wouldn't get rid of the baby so he shoved her off the cliff at Bamaluz Point and thought he'd killed them both, and that's why Zannah did the same to him. She isn't the crazy, heartless mother you thought she was, is she? Is she, boy? For God's sake – are you still there?'

Ned made a sound somewhere between another gasp and a scream, then he pushed himself under the water, the keel of the boat knocked his shoulder and he fell sideways and floundered helplessly for a moment before finding his feet again. Spluttering, he stood up and began to wade back to the shore. He was shivering. That was good because he could no longer hear Rory's voice in his head. He stripped off his sodden shorts and top in the yard and flung them over the clothesline next to Gussie's towel and swimsuit. His heart ached at the thought of her swimming from Porthmeor beach this afternoon. On her own. He grabbed the towel and wrapped himself into it and went back into the warmth and security of the kitchen.

Gussie had been right about hatred: it was insidious, poisonous. He could feel it in his veins. He made tea and drank half a cup. On the shelf above the nets something caught his eye and he ran his hand along and brought down two old half-crown coins, some mackerel spinners, and Mark's ancient and worn kitchen knife, which he had always used for whittling.

There was another voice talking to him now. It was his mother. It was Kate saying gently, 'Why don't you do a Joanie doll, darling? Come on, sit by the fire and I'll find you some wood. You know it always calms you down.'

There was no fire and no wood, but he had the knife. He lit the gas stove and left the door open, hunted around and could come up with only the wooden wedge they used as a doorstop. He sat at the table. After a few moments, he began to whittle.

Gussie woke at six and had forgotten nothing. She too propped her head and gazed down at the dear familiar face that was somehow quite different, almost new to her. She began to kiss it, little butterfly kisses that grew in intensity until he stirred and flung his arms up to the bedhead.

She whispered, 'Wake up. It's the most beautiful morning. We could have a swim before breakfast. Nobody will be about. We'll have the harbour to ourselves.' He made a sound and wrapped her around with his arms. Her mouth was next to his ear. 'Then we can come back to bed, if you like. Swim first?'

'Already had swim.' She could barely discern the words. 'Need sleep.'

The arms were heavy and she lifted them gently away from the back of her neck and held them while she kissed him again. 'I'll get the paper and bring the local news. Sleep on, my darling. Sweet dreams.' She kissed him again and slid out of bed, crossing his arms on his chest. She nodded; he even looked like a saint.

Downstairs a damp towel was hung over the door of the gas oven, a pile of wood chippings lay on the table and next to the two bananas was a Joanie doll. She stared at it. It was nothing like the traditional dolls. It was so fragile that she did not touch it.

She unbolted the two doors and went outside. His T-shirt and shorts were still dripping on the clothesline, and her towel had disappeared. It must be the one on the oven door. She grinned. He had gone through a stage in his teens when he had delighted in midnight swims. He had brought school-friends home with him and they had gone in together, waving their trunks above their heads, imagining themselves to be very daring indeed. She pictured Ned, waking at the stroke of twelve, fizzing with excitement after their lovemaking, plunging into the sea fully clothed, stripping off with some difficulty and trying to wave his soggy shorts and shirt like twin banners of triumph and joy.

She gathered up the clothes, went back inside and through to the laundry room – literally dug out of the cliff – and hurled them into the washing machine, then added her towel from the oven door. She was still smiling as she went along the harbour to get bread, milk and newspapers.

Ned appeared when she was on her second cup of tea. He looked dishevelled.

He said, 'I'm wrecked. If this is going to happen every night I'll have to go and live in Sweden with Sven.'

Gussie poured tea for him and produced toast from the toaster like a conjuror.

'If you will go for midnight swims in the buff, you must expect to feel wrecked.' She met his eyes and spread her hands. 'Nothing to do with me. Here I am, as fresh as a daisy, having managed to do without a swim or a session with Dad's knife and our doorstop!' She grinned. 'I think you need a few lessons about Joanie dolls, my love. They're meant to be handled – handled by children – quite roughly. That poor little creature hiding behind the fruit bowl wouldn't last five minutes with a normal two-year-old!'

He sipped his tea gratefully and grinned back at her. 'Couldn't sleep so got up and had a dip – absolutely freezing, it was – and sat by the oven doing some whittling to calm me down, and all I get is criticism!'

'Sorry, darling.' She went to the hob and removed a saucepan. 'There are two eggs in here, probably a little hard-boiled but sustaining if we're on the trail of the glory gates.'

He watched her decapitate the eggs and remembered Conrad's enormous breakfasts. And the dog.

'D'you fancy having a dog?'

She put the egg cups in the middle of two plates and placed them carefully on the table. 'Not really. But if it's one of those things you've always wanted, then let's go for it.'

'Not enough room, probably.'

'Probably not.' She looked at him. 'Is anything wrong, Ned?'

'Not now.' He reached across for her hand. 'What makes you ask?'

'Well, the Joanie doll and the swim . . .' She squeezed his fingers. 'I slept so splendidly, my love. Was it because I gave all my worries to you?'

He pulled her nearer, leaned over and kissed her. 'No.' He kissed her again. 'As a matter of fact, what you said about hatred was true. I got rid of it, came back to bed and slept like a top.'

She relapsed into her chair again. 'Oh, Ned, I'm sorry. I wish there was something we could do to wipe it all clean.'

'I've done it, love.' He picked up the carving from last night and placed it between them. 'And if we find that special kissing gate, that will be the icing on the cake!'

They started on their eggs. Gussie touched the wooden sculpture gently, then picked it up. 'It's much stronger than it looks. And . . .' she glanced up at him, '. . . it's a baby! It's a proper baby, curled up like a kitten!'

'A baby still in the womb. In the foetal position.' He grinned. 'It's for Jannie, of course.'

'Jannie?' Gussie put her spoon down with a clatter and stared at him, astonished. 'Jannie would have told me! If she'd had the slightest suspicion she was pregnant she couldn't have kept it to herself!'

'I doubt whether Jannie knows. Bessie told me.' Gussie looked at him with an open mouth. He said defensively, 'You know very well that Bessie Beck can forecast a pregnancy with amazing accuracy! She told me when we walked down towards the headland at Zennor on the day of their wedding.'

'What did you just say about old wives' tales?'

'Darling, it's different when you know the old wife personally, like we know Bessie. D'you think Jannie will like it?'

'I'm not sure. I think she'd rather be the one to tell us, don't you?'

'Perhaps.' He looked so crestfallen she had to stand up and lean over to kiss him again.

'Listen. Let's keep the baby up on that shelf by Dad's knife until she tells us. Then you can produce it and tell her you knew it would happen.' She sat back down with a bump and picked up the tiny carving. 'Oh, Ned, it's sweet. Now that I know it's Jannie's baby it seems to look like her. Tiny but strong. Oh, Ned.'

'Are we going to have children, Gus? It doesn't worry me one way or the other but I thought I ought to get into doing more carving if – you know . . '

She pulled the cushion from behind her back and threw

it at him. Then she sat on his lap and they discussed their future family. When they got as far as names – 'I'm not keen on Victor really but—' 'Victoria would be marvellous for a girl' – Ned remembered something and started to laugh.

'What?'

'I keep hearing things, Gus! Now I can hear Dad saying how much he disliked hypothetical conversations – p'raps this and p'raps that – d'you remember?'

She too laughed and nodded, then told him that she had something definite to say. 'News from the Fishermen's Lodge noticeboard. No more pink cauliflowers, just the bus time-table. There's a bus leaving for Polgarrick at eleven fifteen, returning at three fifteen. That will give us time to go into Salem's when we get back and talk about Zannah's funeral. Or should we do that first?'

'Let's go for the eleven fifteen bus. It's our day. Our special day, Gussie!'

There were four slices of toast in the rack and Ned slapped them together with cheese between and put them in a plastic box with a jar of pickled onions. Gussie found some apples. He put the lot in his backpack and stood before her, saluting. And then, very tentatively, he leaned forward and kissed the end of her nose. It was a particular kiss. The kind of kiss he had given her so often in the past.

She laughed helplessly. 'Ned, are you testing the water? What is the result – am I your sister, or your lover?'

He smiled at her and thought of something else Rory had said just last evening on the telephone: 'It's bloody obvious that you and Gus are made for each other – marry her, for God's sake!'

He said, 'Yes . . . I think I was testing the water. And the end result is . . . we are everything to each other. Love is . . . well, love. That's what has come from this past year, Gus.'

'Love conquers all?' She was still gently mocking him.

'Yes. Truisms are called truisms because they are true!'

He pulled her to him and held her tightly. 'We are so lucky, Gus – extra lucky. Because we know that. In our bones we know it. It's so easy for us to be everything to each other – that's how we've lived our lives. It's as if Mum and Dad knew, right from the beginning, that we would always be together.'

Gussie held on to him and closed her eyes. She knew that this moment was precious for Ned and she must never forget it. She consciously registered the smell of the sea in summer, the squawking of the gulls. She sensed that Ned was coming out of a dark place and taking her with him. She opened her eyes and made a note of the tiny Joanie doll, and the bananas; nothing special. And then, just for an instant, she had the strangest optical illusion. Something swung past the window that looked out into the yard with its crisscross of washing lines . . . It looked as if the yard was full of paper angels.

It was midday when they got off the bus high on the moors above Zennor. The driver called after them warningly, 'Three fifteen from Penzance, my 'andsomes. After that the route goes along the Lizard and you gotta change at Truro – take you best part of two hours!'

'Three fifteen from Penzance it is!' Ned called back. He crossed the road after Gussie and immediately clambered on to the milestone, balancing his backpack on one shoulder. He shielded his eyes and saw the usual patchwork of fields, thrusting rocks, thistle heads floating upwards, a mine shaft fenced off, and to the left of it the broken engine house of Wheal Tregowan. He saw instantly what was interesting about this view. Three or four miles down the sloping fields, where the sea chopped off the land and eventually melted into the horizon, the small headland known as Bamaluz Point pointed like a finger back towards St Ives.

Ned pretended to be searching for anything that could be described as glory gates. He shaded his eyes with a hand and turned his head slowly, ninety degrees one way and ninety degrees the other.

Gussie shaded her eyes too and looked up at him. 'Any spare quoits littering the countryside?' she said.

'There might be something down there. A tump of land . . . some trees . . . D'you want a turn?'

'Not really. I remember it from before.' She was already scrambling over the stile and breasting a thicket of fern before reaching the first of the fields. He followed, caught her up, held her elbow. He manoeuvred her to the north and they came to the fenced-in shaft and peered over into its depths.

He said, 'Of course, this is why we used to be able to climb up from the sea! Good Lord, Gussie, that cave below Bamaluz Point acts as an adit to this shaft.'

She said nothing and he thought she might find an excuse for turning back; when she ploughed on, skirting the strange menhirs and making for the trees, he knew that she felt as he felt; it was something they must do.

They came to another Cornish hedge: the traditional dry-stone wall sprouting with growth. There was no stile.

Gussie stood where she was, frowning. 'This can't be right. Dad would never have managed the track we've come along. And why on earth does it stop here where there's no way to get through?'

Ned skirted the wall for a few yards and shouted back at her. The gate he had found had actually been a kissing gate; the curved walkway was still obvious. But it was broken and the gate itself opened wide enough for a wheelchair to get through. What was more, running at right angles to their path was another one, cleared and gritted, and obviously used by a tractor on a regular basis.

They went through and followed the tractor-way down the sloping field. Below them a plume of smoke from an invisible chimney brought cooking smells with it. To the right was a footpath, grassed and overgrown but leading upwards to the tump with its crown of trees.

'Quoit or no quoit, for God's sake let's eat our picnic when we get to the top!' Ned panted, bending double to support the backpack.

'It's the smell from that cooking range. But, yes. Let's.'

They walked through the small plantation of trees. The wind sang in the branches. It was overgrown. Ned worked out that Mark and Kate had not been here for two, maybe three, years. He unloaded their picnic where the sun filtered through the foliage and then went on through the trees, thrashing at the nettles with a stick. Gussie undid the pack and took out the box of toast sandwiches. Ned appeared before her. He said quietly, 'Come and see this, Sis. It's the right place and it's the right quoit. I know it in my bones.'

She scrambled to her feet and followed him. At the edge of the sea-facing wood was a traditional granite quoit. It was facing due west. Nettles choked the empty circle, bindweed bound it like a bandage, alder saplings sprouted all around it. Ned had pulled away a space so that the front of the quoit was clear. They stared. They could imagine it so well. Kate one side, Mark the other. Gussie reached for Ned's arm and he caught her hand in his and held it tightly.

One of them said, 'These are the glory gates.'

The other replied, 'For them and for us.'

It was almost too much. They turned and went back to their picnic and gnawed their way through hard toast and sweating cheese, looking at each other with a kind of awe.

Ned said, 'We'll get rid of the growth and we'll have a look through. Never mind the three fifteen bus from Penzance, we can walk back along the coast path!'

'This is so wonderful, Ned. I can't believe it. Jannie was right – this is important. One of those moments. And we're seizing it!'

Ned stared at her, then nodded.

They packed up the bag and went back to the quoit, both armed with sticks. It took twenty hot sweaty minutes to clear the quoit sufficiently to kneel in front of it and look through. And there, as if framed for a camera shot, was Bamaluz Point.

'It must be a mile away and it looks just a few yards.'

'Too far for us to walk now. It's already two thirty. To go down there and back would mean missing the bus definitely.'

Ned took her hand again. 'We don't need the bus. We really can walk home along the coastal path. What is it – three miles? It will take about an hour.'

Her hand held on to his. She said, 'I'm not that keen, Ned.'

He said immediately, 'All right.'

She was silent, gnawing her lower lip, looking past him into the trees. She took a breath and blurted, 'You don't want to do it either, do you? It will stir it up again.'

'I'm not sure.'

'It might – I suppose it might – help to – to – sort of – put it in perspective?'

'You sound like the bloody educational psychologist I used to see!'

She was surprised, diverted. 'I didn't know. Why?'

He shrugged. 'You were at Cirencester. I got into a fight with a chap. They thought I was going to kill him – dragged me off. Then they tried to tie it in with my father leaving Mum and me. The psycho bloke wanted me to invite Dad over – facing my particular demon, he called it. Needless to say, I didn't send any invitations. He wouldn't have responded, I know that now.' He sighed sharply. 'Anyway, eventually I took the advice given me all those years ago and faced him – as you know. And he wasn't a demon at all. Is that what you've got in mind? Looking over that cliff edge again and remembering being shoved off it?'

She wanted to ask him more about his fight. She looked at him, held his face in a way that was already familiar. She kissed him.

'Dear Ned,' she whispered. 'Why didn't you tell me when I came home from Cirencester?' She saw something in his clear eyes. 'Ah. The boy said something about me?' He still said nothing and she kissed him again. 'Thank you, darling.'

She leaned away from him and smiled. 'I think we'd better jump off the cliff together. Don't you?'

He looked at her. 'We've seen it, darling. No demons. That will be enough.'

She kept smiling. 'I've got a feeling about today. Your psychologist had something, Ned. Demons. We don't need them. Let's be honest, darling. You didn't have a joyous midnight swim last night, did you? You didn't sit calmly carving Jannie's lovely gift. You were fighting demons all the time.'

'We can't do it, Gussie. What about the backpack – our clothes—'

'They stay on the edge, waiting for us.' She was already pulling him up. 'Come on, the tide's just right. You said yourself we can easily walk back.' She aimed a 'sisterly' kiss at his nose. 'This is our day, Ned, this is our moment! Let's go for it!'

He went with her because unexpectedly he saw there were no other options.

It was very hot when they emerged from the trees in their underclothes. They both searched the footpath that ran from the Point round to Zennor and Gurnard's Head. 'If anyone is in sight, it's off,' Ned announced. 'They'd call out the coastguards and they would alert the rescue helicopter and the whole thing would be a complete fiasco.'

'OK. If there's anyone about we'll cancel.'

He said, 'I didn't mean cancel, for Pete's sake! I meant we'd have to wait a while. Until the place is deserted.'

'Did you? Did you really? Oh Ned, it could be fun; it could actually be *fun!*'

He stopped scanning the countryside and looked at her. He grinned.

They ran to the overhang and stood there hand in hand. He turned suddenly and said, 'Never mind the demons, Gus – they don't matter. This is for Mum and Dad.'

'Oh, yes! *Yes!*' She lifted her free arm high and shouted into the cove, 'For Mark and Kate, who made this possible!'

They jumped.

It was three weeks later, and Jannie and Robert had gone back to Hartley. During their visit to his mother and new stepfather, Jannie had felt suddenly sick and had taken an early pregnancy test. She was physically incapable of keeping their news to themselves, and she phoned home. Gussie was cleaning Bessie's cottage in her absence and Ned picked up the receiver.

'Ned – darling – you're not going to believe this! I have got the most stupendous news. You'll never guess!'

Ned spoke as laconically as he could. 'You're pregnant,' he said.

She was a hundred miles away but he could see her face go blank with astonishment.

'How did you flipping well know that? Oh, it's a joke. Well, sucks to you, Brud, because it's true. Robert and I are having a baby!'

He grinned wickedly. 'Bessie told me. Gussie didn't believe her, said it was a tale put about by an old wife. But Bessie's never been wrong yet.' He could hear Jannie practically snorting frustration and laughed. 'Dearest Jannie, many, many congratulations. You're going to be marvellous parents. By the way, it's great that you're getting on so well with your new mother-in-law, but don't hang on too long. We want you at the wedding.'

'Who's getting married?'

'Gussie and me, of course.' He replaced the telephone and scooted next door to tell Gussie he was popping in to the Sloop for an hour and Jannie wanted a word.

Zannah was laid to rest in the cliffside cemetery above the Atlantic. Jannie read aloud the epitaph on the temporary marker. '"Wild and wonderful." I feel I know her from that. Will you miss her, Gus?'

'Yes, but it's not like missing Mum and Dad.'

'No, nothing is quite like that. It's great that you're going to have their names on Zannah's stone. I love "The gates of glory opening wide".' Jannie looked sad. 'It would have been perfect if they'd been here for this baby. Thank goodness he's got you and Ned. A proper family.'

'He'll have the whole of Hartley School as family too. Remember that. And why are we calling him "he"?'

'Just a feeling.'

The wedding took place three weeks later at Penzance Registry Office. Bessie was there again, so were Rosemary and Rory. Jannie had already acquired a habit of holding a protective hand over her perfectly flat abdomen. Thaddeus was not well but he had offered Ethel, and Gussie had accepted the dog's presence very happily.

Rory took Ned aside at the lunch in a hotel. 'Should be saying something, lad. Standing in for one of your fathers. Speech. Or similar. After all, it wouldn't have happened without me. Though why you hadn't thought it through for yourself I'll never know.'

'Incest, Nunc. It hadn't worked for you – marrying your aunt's daughter was a bit of a mistake. We didn't want the same thing to happen.'

Rory loved that and guffawed with laughter. 'Cousins, that's all we are, old chap. And you and August are not related at all.'

Ned pursed his mouth consideringly. 'You've heard of the latest theories – that environment has a great influence on relationships? Gussie and I were brought up as brother and sister—'

'Codswallop! You've always known. You sound like Rosemary. D'you know, that woman refused to have children because we were cousins? Thought they would be damaged in some way.'

'Take after you? Yes, I see her point.'

Rory frowned, assimilating this, then said, 'You're sharper than I thought, boy. Zannah said Gussie wouldn't fall for anyone who was dim.'

'Zannah?' Ned frowned. 'Gussie spoke about me to Zannah?'

'Can you see that happening? Neither of you seem to realize that it's been obvious since you were children that this day would come. Bit late, I agree, but better late than never.'

Ned put on a solemn face and nodded wisely. 'I see it as a natural progression in our relationship.'

Rory turned away with a doubtful 'hmm'. Later Ned heard him say to Bessie, 'Dull as ditch water – she could do better.'

Bessie was holding Ethel, who was eager to explore all possibilities of the hotel. She dumped him unceremoniously on to Rory. 'Hold him for a bit while I go about my business, there's a dear. Can't think why our Gussie wanted 'im here in the first place.'

Rory sat down with a flump and let the dog help himself to the contents of his glass. He looked around for Rosemary and saw her talking to the chap in the wheelchair, Robert . . . Roger. He probably reminded her of Mark. He felt his eyes mist over. Mark Briscoe and his bloody wheelchair; Zannah Scaife had loved him, Kate Gould had loved him and Rosemary Bridges had loved him, treasured him, blamed herself for him . . .

Rory started to cry and Rosemary came over, put the dog on the ancient carpet where he proceeded to clear up every crumb that had been dropped, and led Rory on to the balcony, telling him that if he insisted on raking up the past every time he had a drink it might be better if he gave up alcohol completely. He told her about Bessie Beck, who was waiting for Old Beck to drop by and pick her up. She said comfortingly, 'I expect Zannah will come for you in due course.'

'I want it to be you, Rosie. You are the one – the one and only.'

'And you want me to die soon, then? Shall I jump over this rail or will you push me?'

'More your sort of thing, surely?' He was suddenly back on form. 'Do you still wake up every night screaming about it?'

Jannie appeared. 'Come on, you two, they're leaving. And then we're going too. Room in the van for an extra two.'

Gussie and Ned spent three weeks in Sweden. Gussie loved the islands, and agreed with Ned that Sven had the ideal holiday retreat.

They came home to an empty house. September was nearly over. Jannie had left notes everywhere. 'Don't forget we will start the paper angels at half term.' 'Bessie has moved in with Thaddeus since his operation', and what must have been earlier news, 'Bessie looking after Ethel. Thaddeus still not well.'

Ned had separate notes from Robert. 'The formula for wrist action same as page 42 of your diss.' 'Walking round furniture OK.' 'Practising on stairs.'

Gussie said, 'I understand those two: Robert is exercising regularly.'

'We started off in the Scaife studio when he wanted to stand on his legs for his wedding.'

'But you let Robert read your dissertation?'

'I know. What has molecular structure got to do with electronic prosthetics? But the methodology can run parallel.

Sometimes. And it seems that perhaps – maybe – I must look at page forty-two.'

Gussie found another note from Jannie and went to the freezer to find her little sister had provided a complete meal for this homecoming. And another note in a thick plastic bag sealed with clothes pegs. She took out the covered container and carried it to the kitchen table with the plastic bag on top. She took off the clothes pegs and shook out a note. It said starkly, 'Just in case.' She shook the bag again and out fell a pregnancy testing kit.

She could not stop laughing and Ned called down to ask what all the merriment was about.

'Tell you in a minute.'

She went into the shower room, switched on the light, which meant the fan came on. She sat on the lavatory seat and read the instructions and then carried them out very carefully. She waited the prescribed time, staring at the ceiling, making a little rhythm from the hum of the extractor fan. She looked at the display, washed her hands and left.

She stood by the table, looking around the kitchen. She hoped heaven was like this. She absorbed the fact that she was home. She could hear Ned taking the luggage into the house via the front door, there was a bump and he swore, and then went on to the stair lift. She could smell the familiar scents of the house, the sounds from outside. It was almost a year since she and Ned had returned Jannie to Exeter and come back home as brother and sister. The tourist season was over; the tides were still turning.

She took a deep breath. She could almost feel everything settling into place around her. A surge of pure content went through her body. She had never felt it quite like that before; everything was new, unknown, frightening, wonderful.

Ned came into the kitchen, smiling. 'Good to be home.'

'Yes.'

'We'll unpack later, yes? There's no rush.'

It was what her father had so often said as he eased him-self around the furniture on his legs.

Gussie stayed very still and he looked at her, brows raised. She indicated the plastic display in front of her. He looked at it, looked at her, looked at it again.

He said, 'Not really? Oh, Gus – my God . . .'

She crossed the room and wrapped her arms around her husband. He wrapped his arms around his wife. They stayed very still, holding on to each other, eyes closed. They looked for all the world like two Joanie dolls carved from one piece of wood.

Epilogue

Twins were born to Robert and January Hanniford on 12 May 2003 at Hartley School. They were christened Mark and Katherine. One of the godmothers was Cathy Johnson.

Edward Briscoe delivered his daughter on 21 June 2003 on Porthgwidden beach just before midnight. August Briscoe had walked down with him for his midnight swim and within an hour gave birth to Victoria Zannah Rose.

Bessie and Thaddeus made a 'convenience match' and were married just before Christmas of 2002. Bessie anticipated the will she and Old Beck had written and gifted her cottage to Edward Briscoe. He changed it very little. Robert and Jannie used it at Easter and brought the twins down for the whole of the summer holidays. After his daughter was born Ned invited his father and Conrad to visit them and they pronounced the cottage to be a 'home from home'. They arrived in the early summer of 2004 and stayed for three months.

Vicky fell for them both; held up her arms to be picked up by Conrad so that she could look her grandfather in the eye. He said she was the image of Davie.

Rory and Rosemary continued to enjoy occasional sparring matches.

Father Martin became godfather to all three children and seemed to thrive on it.

The tide came in, smoothed the sand into a firm floor ideal for making sand pies. And then it went out.